RIS

Also by Ritchie Smith

Fortune
Winning

RISK

Ritchie Smith

HEADLINE

Copyright © 1992 Ritchie Smith

The right of Ritchie Smith to be identified as the Author of the Work has been asserted by him in accordance with the Copyright, Designs and Patents Act 1988.

First published in 1992
by HEADLINE BOOK PUBLISHING PLC

10 9 8 7 6 5 4 3 2 1

All rights reserved. No part of this publication may be reproduced, stored in a retrieval system, or transmitted, in any form or by any means without the prior written permission of the publisher, nor be otherwise circulated in any form of binding or cover other than that in which it is published and without a similar condition being imposed on the subsequent purchaser.

All characters in this publication are fictitious and any resemblance to real persons, living or dead, is purely coincidental.

British Library Cataloguing in Publication Data
Smith, Ritchie
Risk
I. Title
823.914 [F]

ISBN 0-7472-0548-5

Typeset by Falcon Typographic Art Ltd, Fife, Scotland

Printed and bound in Great Britain by
Richard Clay Ltd, Bungay, Suffolk

HEADLINE BOOK PUBLISHING PLC
Headline House
79 Great Titchfield Street
London W1P 7FN

This book is dedicated to all those who have had dreams. Without dreams and risks, sweat and blood and tears, there is no achievement.

This book is for Lisa S, with love.

Chapter One

High noon, north of Osaka. The mountains of Japan stood above this high valley, with snow on the peaks and green further down. Industry had not come here yet.

Alex Stanton cupped his hands together. 'Now's your chance! You can shoot me, Maggie!'

An ominous weight began grinding towards him: a T-55 tank, shaking and belching blue-grey diesel smoke – an ugly, clanking monster the colour of khaki. It was fifteen yards away . . . then ten . . .

Alex did not step back, not even when the sloped turret jerked through a few degrees so the 100-millimetre gun was turned on him. He stared out the killing machine. Its motor revved as the Soviet T-55 came forward a few slow, additional paces. There was a gear-grinding sound. The tank, supplied to Egypt and captured by the Israelis in the Negev desert during the '73 war, finally stopped.

Without firing.

'All right?' He came forward, then kicked the sagging metal tracks which had left long gouges on the earth. How many thousands or tens of thousands of these tanks had the Soviet armies? For once, Alex's memory failed him. He circled the huge machine cautiously; fumes wafted around, and he felt the heat from the engine. He was fit-looking and tanned, though he walked with a limp.

After a moment the top hatch clanged open; he saw a waving arm, then Maggie Langton's head. Her red hair was impossible to mistake. Her dress was tight and revealed firm femininity. She was struggling out of the steel turret using both elbows. A butterfly, from an armoured chrysalis.

Alex waved towards the city. 'Say "hi" to the future rulers of our world, Maggie. That's why we're here in Japan.'

'What if I have different ideas about the future?'

He laughed. 'It might be safer to stay at home.'

'I think it might have been. My bag is caught, Alex! Oh!'

Seeing her slide down the turret he stepped forward quickly and caught her as she tumbled forward off the chassis. Her arms tightened around his shoulders and he could feel her breasts flatten against him. 'An armful of trouble. But quite delightful.'

'You should be so lucky, Alex!'

He laughed. 'I have been that lucky. Remember?'

She struggled, red, pine-scented hair swirling. 'Forget it.'
He gave a bold grin. 'Impossible.'
'And put me down!'
'Your wish is my command.' He lowered her on to the soft earth of the training ground.
'Occasionally.' Maggie squatted down, rubbed at one ankle and winced. Then she flicked up part of her skirt to look at a dimpled knee. 'Laddered my nylons.'
'Don't worry about it. You still look great to me.' He gave her his hand and hauled her up without effort. He was tall and very trim and a little past thirty, with blond hair swept back, and lively, intelligent eyes.
'Thanks, Alex,' she said, a little breathlessly. She still carried white shoes in the same hand as her shoulder-bag. Summer was enfolding them both in humid heat.
He waved to one of his men and said something into the walkie-talkie he carried before he turned to her again. His face seemed kindly and commanding at the same time. 'Liked manning my tank, did you?'
'No,' she told him. Blue mascara had dried below her eyes, and she tried to beat off the grime on her skirt with her free hand before she slipped on her shoes. Her once immaculate make-up was smudged. 'Even for twenty minutes that was a *nightmare* – hot and cramped, stinking of oil and sweat. A tiny space you have to hunch up in, you can't see out, and there's so much deafening noise you can't think – what it must be like in a war I can't begin to imagine.'
'It's terrible in combat, Maggie,' he told her quietly. They were standing quite close together, and she did not step back or look away. Neither did he. 'I saw the aftermath of the tank battles during the last round of the Arab-Israeli troubles.'
'The Sinai and the Golan Heights?'
His eyes clouded over. 'I saw tanks burned out, Maggie, tanks like these burned to the bare brown metal; you never forget that – or the burnt stink of plastics and rubber and human flesh. Our Stanton tanks were on both sides.' He spread his hands. 'But the war wasn't my fault.'
'I suppose not.' She looked around her: a field with tanks and trucks and two parked fuel tankers, with Alex's mechanics and demonstration staff everywhere. The other two tanks were positioned in front of the bulldozer-raised ridge of earth off to the left. Here, large wooden bullseyes had been erected, but were now eaten away with shell-holes like Gruyère cheese.
The T-55 began reversing away to join the others, the commander's head poked out of the turret now. 'Noisy bastards, aren't they?'
'Too bloody noisy!'
He waved at the retreating tank. 'Well, that is thirty-nine litres of V12 water-cooled diesel inside. That's the power you need to move thirty-five tons of metal.'

'And it's so *ugly*. Like your own Mark VIII.'

'Tanks are meant to look brutal. Killing machines should inspire fear, and tanks are still the best close-quarters shock weapons ever devised.' He had continued to stare at her, his male appreciation obvious. 'As they like to tell me over in Israel, there's a passage in the Bible about this. Judges i, 19. "And the Lord was with Judah, and he drove out the inhabitants of the mountains; but he could not drive out the inhabitants of the valleys, because they had chariots of iron."'

His voice had sounded commanding, even to her. 'And they have plenty of iron chariots in Israel, don't they? Thanks to you and men like you.'

'You always criticize the profession of arms, but I'm not ashamed of what I do.'

'No, you're not, are you?' She stroked at her long red hair.

'In '73 the Israelis were saved by courage and energy as well as by their armaments. But I'm proud of my own small part in that.'

'In such a terrible business!'

He frowned, leaning on a silver-headed cane. 'Suppose I did close down the Armaments Division? Throw in the subcontractors who depend on us, and that might be thirty thousand jobs. Your father's union members. Your friends from childhood, and mine.'

She gazed at him. She had known him since Oxford: a decade, now. 'You now seem – larger, somehow. More certain of yourself . . . no, that's not quite right. More of an impersonal force.'

He said firmly, 'I see things through, and I always finish what I start. Everywhere.'

'I hate what you do now and I always have.'

'Yes.' He sighed, then his eyes showed a blue flicker of amusement. 'Anyway, you didn't shoot me.'

'No.'

'Was it a temptation?'

'Of course it was!' she said, ignoring a faint embarrassment. 'But I'm not like you – not aggressive.'

'No, you're meek and mild!' He laughed openly, though it was exuberant and good-natured.

She scowled, pulled away from him. 'And you always go too far.'

'Me?' He stood there smiling, trim at the waist and broad at the shoulders, wearing a dark Savile Row three-piece instead of the pale Italian suits he normally favoured. Japan was a very formal country, and of course this was a very formal occasion. 'Well, I came here, Maggie – and this might qualify as "too far". But you came too.'

'Yes.' She sighed, looked down. A single drop of sweat went down one cheek like a tear. 'To Osaka.'

'*Osaka*.' He gave the word the harsh Japanese stresses. 'So, what did you think of my Mark VIII-C battlewagon?'

She stooped over to ease her shoes. 'Good technology. The optical sights are fantastic – that shack they targeted half a mile away looked as if it was right in front of us – and you've got a baby computer on board, haven't you?'

'Right. Optics and calculating devices courtesy of the Hideki Corporation, by the way. And you'd hit that shack, every time. Or a Russian T-72, one of the big new machines. And we back up the tank's gun with laser ranging and five different kinds of ammunition.'

She looked at him, sad-faced. 'What a waste, Alex.'

He turned away abruptly, stick digging into the soil. 'Follow me to the viewing stand. They'll be here soon – some of the most powerful people in Japan.' He moved away with the old bouncing self-confident stride, lamed only slightly by the terrorist bombing they never talked about.

'Aren't you still arguing with Japan over trade?'

He stopped, tossed the familiar dazzling smile at her: she had never found him more attractive.

'Arguing? It would be impolite to say so openly – here in Japan, at least.'

'But what about the takeover bid for your company? It's an open secret that most of the money came from Japan.'

'It's not so easy to take Stanton Industries away from the family,' Alex said softly. He showed her a momentary, harder expression: the arms dealer who met with Adnan Khashoggi and the Pentagon, Saudi princes and the Shah of Iran. 'Is this really relevant to an article on the company's latest activities in Asia?'

She flashed her green eyes, then flicked open a spiral-backed notebook and proceeded to read in a careful voice: '*The rescue of the biggest defence contractors outside America has made headlines everywhere. For the second time in his life, Alex Stanton's face has been splashed across page one; he is a celebrity, he has a £250 million chequebook, and who would deny that he deserves it all?*'

He was standing overlooking the testing ground, listening thoughtfully. 'Very touching. Flattery?'

'That £250 million in gold bullion must have been the biggest publicity stunt ever!'

'It was money from the Iranian central bank; the loan I hoped would save the Stantons' power inside Stanton Industries. I just hope it has worked, Maggie.'

'Of course it will work.' Maggie Langton was still hoping to make her interviewee relax enough to be vulnerable. 'And your rescue bid for Stanton Industries, did it *really* cost you £250 million?'

He laughed. 'Wait till the emergency general meeting of the shareholders; all will be revealed then. That's the law, Maggie.'

'Exactly how many shareholders have backed you?'

He sighed. 'What does that matter, as a detail? Even one additional share is enough, if it gives you that magical fifty percent plus one which means control of the Board of Directors when it comes to a showdown.'

'You're claiming victory. I see.' She brushed back her red hair, smiling sweetly. 'But, then, you would say that.'

'I do say that – and it's the truth. If the proxies show that cousin Hugh and I control a clear majority of the shares, unimpeded mastery of Stanton Industries should pass back to us and to the family trust funds we control. The emergency general meeting of the company's shareholders should confirm that.'

'Should?'

He chuckled. 'Now don't play the innocent, Maggie. There's many a slip, as we both know. In life as well as business.'

She dropped her gaze to the open notebook and produced a pencil. 'So. How do you feel about doing business here in Japan?'

'I like a challenge.' He took a breath. 'And now I'm ready to go into action. A Tokyo office, a sales staff, all the technical back-up I need. And, as you can see, the tanks are right here in Japan. Flown in from Britain, a pre-production Mark VIII-C with the new armour. From the Golan Heights, a Soviet T-64 as recently used by the Syrian Army. From the Sinai, when the Egyptians were at the Mitla Pass, a T-55. Both supplied courtesy of my old friend Colonel David Saphir in Tel Aviv.'

'From the Yom Kippur War, you mean?'

He nodded, eyes seeking out everything that was happening here on the testing ground. A squad of mechanics swarmed over the Mark VIII again.

'Were they badly shot up? If so, your technicians must have done a great job in the repair shops.'

'Essentially undamaged, both T-types. Simply ran out of fuel. Supply problems can cripple any kind of effort.' He glanced at her. She was asking too many questions, even for an investigative journalist. He decided to change the subject. 'It's good of you to take such a personal interest.'

'My father asked me.'

'Did he now?' Alex thought that over, walking quickly. Maggie's father was a union leader. So he, very sensibly, wanted this order. 'Changed your opinion of me?'

'No,' she said to his turned back, starting to run to catch up. 'We both think you're a bastard, Alex Stanton.'

He gave her a tight humourless grin. 'I've spent years cultivating that reputation – because it's the reputation I need.'

She scowled at him, suddenly looking young and earnest. 'Why?'

'Because I want to be a name in the world, Maggie. I need that like air to breathe and room to move, because I have things I must do. Any risk there is I'll take, if that's what it takes to succeed. I intend to be the one man who'll stop at nothing to win – because there's nobody else to do it.' Then he said the unforgivable. 'And I bet your ambition is just the same.'

Her high-cheekboned face flushed. She opened her red lips and her eyes flashed.

'But you can't go on, Alex! Nor can Stanton Industries go on selling arms to everybody. That's proliferation to the point of insanity! And what happens after every Third World nation has gorged itself sick on your conventional arms? If they have enough tanks will they automatically want poison gas, and then the atomic bomb?'

'Exactly like your father,' Alex said toughly, 'I have to live in the real world and do business there. I *don't* have to like it, or approve of it. I've come to Japan to sell arms, and I mean to get involved here, because by the end of the millennium this economy will be the most powerful on the face of God's earth. But if we win back control of the Board at home I intend to set up a civil projects division, full-scale. Quote me on that! Maybe I'm not just the warmonger you think I am.'

Finally, she looked away. 'I suppose Stanton Industries still needs a bastard pulling the strings.'

'Come on,' he said over his shoulder. 'Let's get ready for this delegation.'

'Which delegation? The politicians? Or the great Saigo Hideki himself?'

'The men with the chequebooks. Whom I *must* impress.'

Chapter Two

Stanton Industries is an empire in industry.

It has international subsidiaries and trading outposts which cover the world. It operates shipyards and factories on the great rivers of England, and an aircraft division based in the south-west. Most of all, it has a company history second to none.

The Stanton family had made cannon before 1588 to fight the Spanish Armada. Stanton dreadnoughts fought at Jutland – and Stanton tanks against Rommel. In the Middle East, more countries used Stanton Industries weapons systems than any other company's: the latest artillery, tanks and missiles. The firm made ships and steel, and it mined the earth for ores. Now it was operating among the North Sea oilfields – for Britain's great new hope was oil money. If Alex Stanton issued orders to his own Armaments Division, thirteen thousand people listened. The business overall was worth six hundred million dollars. It was a prize worth fighting for – and it had been fought for.

And, as Alex Stanton reminded himself, it was still being fought for today.

Even by late afternoon the Japanese sun was still bright and hot. Alex and his staff stayed in the shade of the awnings erected over the reviewing stand, till the three luxury cars drew up in line.

This was it.

With his chief aide McCourt by his side Alex went down the wooden steps to welcome his guests. He was excited. 'They're all here, Ken. Industry, politicians, the military. Hideki and his team. And I'm sure they'll be impressed.'

'I'm sure they will be,' replied the dry Ulster voice. 'But will Hideki really get you on the inside here?'

Alex's eyes narrowed, though they could not be overheard. 'There's money in this for him, and he thinks a lot of Stanton Industries – he's proved that by trying to buy us, right? I mean, £200 million plus says a lot. And he has influence with the Tokyo government.'

'But I do not know, Mr Stanton, if he will exert that power for you,' Fujiko lisped from his other side.

In the first dark limousine sat the military men: two generals with different titles in the Japanese Self-Defence Forces. A Ground SDF colonel called Itoshi accompanied them. Alex bowed and murmured memorized pleasantries. Fujiko, the pretty and selfless Japanese who ran the administration of the Stanton office in Tokyo, escorted them up to the stand. Next came three high-ranking bureaucrats: two from the JDA – the Japanese Defence Agency – and one from the Ministry of International Trade and Industry. McCourt accompanied them.

From the last car stepped first the politician: a squat heavy-featured man called Akira Hakagawa. Alex shook his hand. Saigo Hideki himself emerged last of all. He was a small, tight-lipped man in a black suit. He greeted Alex formally, shifting a rolled-up umbrella to his other hand, and bowing. Then a young associate quickly opened the umbrella for him and held it over his head to shield him from the sun. Thus protected, Hideki marched up the stairs, gazing around. When he spoke in English, the wheezing accent was thick. 'I am please be here, Alex Stanton.'

'Likewise, Mr Hideki. *Konnichi-wa?*'

Hideki gave a thin smile at Alex's Japanese. His eyes were eerily bright and alert, despite his age. Alex was well aware of Japan's Confucian respect for age and status and achievement, rather than for mere celebrity. 'This is Paul Takahashi.' Hideki gestured towards his young associate. 'First assistant in private office.'

'I remember very well.' Alex nodded, his gaze leaving Hideki only for a moment.

'Both, please. Shake hands, in front me,' Hideki said.

Though Takahashi was now smiling, the coldness in his dark eyes did not alter. He did not move.

The old man turned first to his aide and then back to Alex. 'I have no sons now,' he said, with sad dignity. 'I ask you, both. Be friends!'

Though not a celebrity abroad, Hideki was the great man here that he deserved to be. Alex could not but feel respectful in his presence. 'The Emperor of Japan, Inc.' was Hideki's nickname in the Western world's press, though he rarely featured in personal publicity. He had always struck Alex as a Victorian figure – tough, ruthless, hardworking and moral in his own prickly and authoritarian way. Here in his own country his power and wealth meant his prestige was huge.

So Alex finally shook Takahashi's hand.

On the platform Hideki chose to stand between Alex and the burly Diet member and Defence-Forces Minister Hakagawa. The Japanese delegation stood shoulder to shoulder, smiling, for the formal reply to their welcome. Then Hakagawa began the discussion with something which Takahashi translated as, 'I represent Otsu in Shiga Prefecture, next door to Osaka. I am greatly interested in self-defence for a powerful Japan.'

'I can give you that powerful defence,' Alex replied urgently. 'Anything you need. There are no limits.' He took a breath, glancing at Hideki. 'A 1975 analysis from your own JDA revealed that in battle against your likely enemy, the Soviet Union, the Air SDF might last just an hour, the Maritime SDF could perhaps resist for a few days, and the Ground SDF would be lucky to stand up against invasion for as much as a week. Naturally you will wish to improve that – perhaps starting here.'

As he spoke, the three tanks rolled slowly towards the concrete stand. Their guns were pointed directly at the platform party; but only the Stanton 120mm was fully stabilized, so it could be accurately fired while in motion. They stopped, a ragged row.

'Let's take a walk,' Alex continued as the engines drummed, 'and you can check the machines at close quarters. Remember, my tank is in production and war-proved and immediately available. Unlike the American-German proposals for the Leopard and Abrams tanks, with the Mark VIII there have been, and will be, no political problems.'

Everyone followed him in solemn, sweating procession. Later the tanks would be examined in great detail by Japanese experts and full technical reports had already been passed on. But that was the easy part; this was the crux – the sale.

Alex stood looking around as the visitors banged their fists on metal armour, hunkered down to look at the metal tracks, or, frowning, stared into the long gun barrels. Engines growled quietly, but only the Stanton tank was powered by Rolls-Royce. Maggie Langton kept well away from the commotion, watching everything without expression.

Finally, everyone climbed the steps again to see the special display, and Alex spoke into his walkie-talkie. 'Start.'

With a roar the three tanks accelerated away from the platform, in reverse. The Stanton Mark VIII soon drew ahead, and by the time the other tanks had reached some white lines painted on the earth, it had already begun the next series of manoeuvres.

The tanks continually altered course, reversed, turned about through 360 degrees in front of the reviewing stand, rapidly, endlessly. The tactical patterns changed frequently. The British tank was faster, but could also both brake and accelerate more quickly. As McCourt pointed out in rapid-fire Japanese, it was also the most heavily armoured, with the biggest gun, its Rolls-Royce engine was the most reliable and powerful, and it could carry more ammunition than the two Soviet tanks.

Binoculars had been produced, and Alex could tell that the Japanese officers were impressed. But he was also aware of Maggie scribbling in her notebook, frowning.

Alex said over the engine noise, 'The T-55 over there is still the Warsaw Pact's standard battle tank, along with the T-54 – though they're both being replaced by the other, the T-64, and there's a newer model coming in also, which is codenamed the T-72. That'll be a potent weapon, built because of recent battle experience in the Middle East, but our Mark VIII has better specifications all round.'

Hideki listened to Hakagawa make a comment, then turned to Alex, 'He say the tanks do not seem well-made – except perhaps for Stanton tank.'

Hakagawa's eyes glinted merrily.

Alex explained, 'You will find our Mark VIII is state of the art. Full NBC protection and, as I said, better than the new T-72, and much better than the T-62, let alone the T-55 – which only mounts a 100-millimetre gun.' One of the uniformed officers here asked for accurate statistics about the tanks' fighting power, which Alex provided. All the while the tanks moved about, engines growling. 'The Soviets still concentrate on sheer weight of numbers – shock attacks, they call them. The Red Army has three and a half million men under arms, over one hundred and sixty first-line divisions. A single Combined Arms Army has two or three motor rifle divisions and a tank division; each Tank Army has three or four divisions of tanks.'

That should put the fear of something up them, he thought with satisfaction. McCourt added in fluent Japanese, 'That seems an overwhelming weight of armour. But our tank is the best, whether for defence against all that, or in counter-offensive, or in the attack.'

Alex put this into perspective for the élite of Japan. 'Such large forces have not been used here in the Far East, as yet. The Sino-Soviet conflict has consisted only of smaller-scale skirmishing along the Ussuri River – so far.'

Hideki frowned, then said something to Takahashi which he translated. 'My master wonders how the Russians can afford this gigantic military machine.'

'By ruthless measures against their own population.'

'We can imagine that,' Takahashi said, hiding a smile. Then, after a moment, 'You know we're at war, us and the Russians?'

'I beg your pardon?' Alex said.

'World War II continues for us. Didn't you know?' The expression seemed guileless, at first. 'Last month of the war, 1945, Stalin's Russians attacked us – without warning – and they occupied some of our land. They still do. There's never been a peace treaty, therefore we're still at war.'

'Is that so?' Alex said slowly. Was this really how Takahashi saw the world?

But Hideki had interrupted, and after listening to him respectfully Takahashi translated. 'Of course, that's only a legal technicality. Except for certain outstanding issues like our islands . . . But there are the North Koreans, also. Ancient enemies of ours, and now of course Communist, with Kim Il Sung protected by the Russians. Did you know he has extensive nuclear research and production facilities?'

'Facilities for atomic weapons?' Alex was shocked.

'At their atomic research plant in Yongbyon – or so it is said,' Takahashi murmured. 'The Koreans do arms import-export through Macau; the rumour is that they want anything helpful to making atomic bombs. And, of course, North Korea has refused to sign the nuclear nonproliferation treaty.'

'With Russian or Chinese encouragement, you think?' Alex said quietly. Could that be true? But the Third World's dictators were no longer entirely answerable to their masters, neither Eastern or Western. The Middle East confirmed that, beyond doubt. 'Even with the current trouble between China and the Soviet Union, and between the two Koreas, besides the war in Vietnam, I didn't realize *you* saw Asia as so unstable and threatening.'

Hakagawa had been listening carefully. He growled something that Takahashi translated as, 'There is trouble everywhere, except in Japan. Arms will liberate us from worry. It's that simple. We wish to be strong enough to say "no" to anybody.'

'To be a Japan able to say "no"? I see.' Alex added thoughtfully, 'If you ever moved against the Russians –'

'No,' Hideki said sharply, before turning to his aide once more.

'Mr Hideki wishes to say that in Japan we are interested in self-defence forces only, and are not at war with the Soviet Union and never will be, as all we desire is peaceful coexistence and prosperity for everyone. That war is all over.'

Alex saw Hakagawa's face change, just for a moment. Disgust? Rage? It was a shock to sense the power of this man's personality. He understands a little English, therefore. Alex made a mental note to investigate him further, and asked, through McCourt, where Hakagawa's family was from.

The man gave Alex a bleak smile and said with heavy emphasis, '*Hokkaido – kita.*'

North Hokkaido, or north of Hokkaido? Alex's interest quickened. He wondered what Hakagawa meant exactly, and he filed away the question for future consideration.

The army man Itoshi then interposed: 'Your Mark VIII is in mass production, yes? Though not with the new composite armour?'

'*Hai*,' Alex said. 'Sold to Egypt, Israel and Jordan. Also to Britain, Holland, Canada, Argentina, to India and Pakistan, and some other countries. And proved in war; most especially the October War in the Middle East. It is, as tanks go, *ichi-ban*.'

'What of your Mark IX?'

'Hardly more than some notions on the drawing-board,' Alex said quickly. The Mark IX was still top secret.

'Stanton production . . . What about strikes?' somebody else inquired, the trade and industry bureaucrat in a dark suit.

Things were warming up now, Alex realized. 'Britain's image as "the sick man of Europe"? I hope Stanton Industies will make you change your minds about that.'

Then one of the bureaucrats said something which McCourt translated. 'Is it true that in the Soviet Army atomic weapons are in the hands of local commands?'

Alex glanced down the rank of men. 'Yes,' he said. 'It's true. Even the smallest units have access to their own nuclear arms. And unit commanders, on their own initiative, can decide to use them.'

It was as if some reserve in the Japanese character had now been breached, and suddenly their questions came thick and fast. 'Stanton Industries people were involved with the American A-bomb?'

'That's only a story,' Alex said quickly. 'Anyway, it all happened in the past, in my grandfather's time.'

Itoshi, a small but active man with fiercely questioning eyes, was persistent. 'But your Stanton submarines are nuclear-powered?'

'Yes. Our shipbuilding division maintains a specialist yard at Barrow-in-Furness in Cumbria, in the far north-west of England near the Scottish border. Our aircraft division is based in southern England, whereas the armaments and shipbuilding divisions are mainly in the north-east. We have links to many other companies, including Mr Hideki's corporation here, and we have subsidiaries such as Stanton Industries (Australia), which produces iron ore and uranium ore among other things. Think of Stanton Industries as Europe's Mitsubishi. Extensive experience in heavy industry, second to none.'

The exhibition continued till the sun began to sink and a tinge of redness entered the sky. Refreshments were then served; bitter green tea for the Japanese, and Earl Grey for the British contingent.

Alex wore a fixed smile, though he was perspiring. He had hoped for something more positive from Hideki by now. Christ, he thought, maybe he intends to try and see Beauford's takeover through, fight us in the courts afterwards if he loses the bid . . . The rest of the contingent were perhaps taking their cue from Hideki; they too were extremely polite but noncommittal. Alex spoke quietly to McCourt. 'I wonder how we're doing, Ken. We're selling the tank well, but are they buying?'

'All the statistics point in our direction,' McCourt said.

'Not enough,' Alex told him. 'The psychology of selling is different from the psychology of science.'

Hideki was sitting bolt upright on a camp chair, sipping his tea. His face was expressionless.

Alex turned back to McCourt. 'Plan B, I think.' His chief assistant went over to the radio and spoke quietly into a microphone. The tanks suddenly took prearranged positions, then stopped. Men climbed quickly out of the Russian tank. The Mark VIII faced the T-55. Each tank's gun was levelled at the other.

Alex addressed his audience. 'The gun mounted in our Mark VIII is reckoned to be the most powerful and accurate tank gun in the world. Please observe.'

The Stanton 120mm gun thundered. A flash showed a clean hit on the T-55 turret: the armour-piercing solid round blasted straight through the Russian armour at supersonic speed. A terrible ringing clang faded over the field. Then a second round of high explosive blew the turret clean off the Russian chassis, metal fragments flying.

Utter destruction, in two shots. Alex turned around, knowing he had impressed the men he had to impress. 'Well, gentlemen?'

Then Takahashi spoke up in a loud voice, 'The Stantons have invented something called Cumberland armour, is that right? Used here on your Mark VIII-C?'

McCourt reminded them swiftly: 'It's a metal and ceramic combination, unique to us, and secret. Usually an armour that resists, say, high explosive, is vulnerable to high-velocity solid shot. But we believe that our special armour is the best all-round protection for armoured fighting vehicles, and the best armour in the world.'

'Then let us see it.'

'Of course,' Alex said. 'Test our tank to destruction. Test it any way you want. We'll even let your technicians take it apart – under supervision.'

'No, that is not what we mean,' Takahashi said impatiently. 'Let us see how powerful your own armour is, here and now. This is what you call a "live-fire exercise", isn't it?'

Alex heard the dare in his voice. So did Maggie; so did some of the others. 'Very well,' he said crisply. He looked round slowly as he spoke, his voice deep and resonant. 'Just to show you, all of you, how much I trust my product, I'll drive the Mark VIII myself, and I'll let one of the Russian tanks take a shot at me.'

There was rapid-fire Japanese as this was explained. Hideki turned his head, approval clear on his face. 'You have much confidence in your Stanton products.'

'I do,' Alex said quietly.

He gave his orders quickly. He saw the T-64 pull away, drive east. The Mark VIII stopped in front of the stand. Alex put the walkie-talkie back on his belt and waited, arms folded, till his four-man crew left the Stanton tank.

'All right,' he said to McCourt, his voice grim and quiet. 'I'll head towards the T-64, slowly. At two hundred metres range open fire: one shot.'

'Alex' – McCourt's voice was low with unexpressed anxiety – 'are you sure this is right?'

No, Alex said to himself. Aloud, he said only, 'You have my orders. One live round only, high explosive, okay?'

Alex moved to the front of the reviewing stand, went down the wooden stairs, then paused. The tank loomed up in front of him like a symbol of death. In the still, warm air its aerials stood up like insect antennae.

He clambered on to the hull, perched on the rim of the hatch on the turret. Up on the platform the visitors leaned over to watch. He waved, then slid downwards into the driver's seat. Equipment surrounded him in hot oil-smelling air. He clanged the hatch cover closed, dogged it shut. With the sunlight shut out, the inside of the turrent now seemed dark and eerie in its cathode-ray glow. Impossibly crammed with equipment, there was no space here; claustrophobia closed in.

Alex moved quickly to open the radio channel and reverse the turret. Then he tried to make himself comfortable in the driver's position, checking the periscope view and testing the well-remembered controls.

There was a burst of static. Then, harassed and high, Maggie's voice was heard over the radio, 'There's no need for this. Alex, that's a *big* gun. This is *dangerous!*'

He said nothing as he operated the heel-and-toe gear-change. There was a low growl from the engine. In second, he drove the tank forward very slowly. He hunched down, sweating, expecting the blast any moment. The Stanton Cumberland armour was a composite of steel, ceramic and hard plastic; it absorbed shocks and blows better than any alternative, but it was certainly not invulnerable – and this was a preproduction VIII-C. Any unsuspected weakness in weld or casting and the whole tank might disintegrate, catch fire, or blow up.

He sank down further, hoping the expected round would hit the chassis rather than the turret. He was sweating. But I have to risk it, he thought. I can't send men into battle inside Stanton armour, and duck the challenge myself.

Then the world exploded.

His head banged into the periscope and for a moment his vision blurred. The noise was deafening.

But the Stanton tank still moved forward regardless, its powerful Rolls-Royce engine purring.

'I'm all right,' he said quickly, exultantly, into the radio, thinking: I got away with it! Part of the left side of the turret had caved in, but the equipment there seemed unbroken. Metal creaked. 'Any external damage?' he asked.

There was a pause, then McCourt answered. 'A bloody big dent in the turret, but no penetration – is that right? Nothing I can see through these binoculars, anyway.'

Alex looked around, still feeling the relief that had flooded through him. 'No penetration,' he confirmed.

After driving back to the reviewing stand, he climbed out of the top turret to a burst of applause from his relieved crews. Looking down, he saw that part of the turret had been smashed inwards, but still held. He held down the shock he still felt, and smiled.

Hideki was standing nearby. 'A man of belief,' he said firmly, gazing up at Alex with approval.

'Belief in Stanton Industries,' Alex answered, then jumped off the chassis.

Once back on the reviewing stand again, Alex called for the finale of the display. First there were fireworks; and then recorded music thundered over the proving ground – Holst's *Mars, the Bringer of War*. The tanks opened fire on the platform party. Everyone except Hideki and Alex ducked. Only Itoshi smiled afterwards.

'Blank rounds,' Alex explained politely.

The Japanese then crowded round to congratulate him. Only Maggie, he noted, hung back.

Suddenly, it was all over. Alex turned to the key man. 'Mr Hideki?'

Hideki bowed. 'I will attend you in London.'

No sale? He said, 'I was hoping for something more positive. I was led to believe . . .' He stopped short, eyed his competitor and ally and godfather inside Japan. No sale. Not yet, anyhow. He bowed in return, face politely impassive. 'In London, then. Or before, perhaps. Mr McCourt will escort you to your cars.'

Maggie moved up to him, wearing fresh clothes and shoes, her heels clicking. She stood silently beside Alex as the Japanese formally, one by one, took their leave. Their expressions were now either stern or emptily friendly. Alex bowed and shook each hand extended to him. He watched as McCourt led them back to their waiting limousines and then car doors began to slam.

Finally, she stood alone with him, the warm breeze swirling her red hair. She glanced at her spiral-backed notebook, looked up at Alex, then closed it. '"No comment", I guess?'

His expression was thoughtful and sober. 'Nothing I'd want attributed.'

She seemed very serious. 'They're the real thing, aren't they – like you? The ones who mean to win.'

'Yes,' he said quietly, thinking it over. 'They are the ones who mean to win.' Suddenly he felt a lot less confident about the proxy battle and the emergency general meeting of the company's shareholders. He turned to her, genuinely curious. 'What's *your* opinion of Hideki?'

'A man in a hurry, despite his age. A fierce man underneath it all.'

'My business partner,' he said grimly. 'And?'

'Very, *very* rich. And dangerous.'

'Dangerous for us? You may be right – but I hope you're wrong. For his rivals and enemies he is certainly dangerous.'

'I think he wants to leave his mark on his country one last time,' she told him with certainty.

His eyes were keen. 'You've heard something?'

She shrugged, not denying she had inside information. 'He's in the history books for what he did before the war as well as after it, whether he wants to be or not. I'm just wondering why you thought you could trade with him here today.'

'Well, Stanton Industries and the Hideki Corporation have been doing serious business since 1971. We've even discussed merging some of our subsidiaries. Hideki wants access to the Middle East and America; and we want Japan and the rest of emergent Asia. After he funded Lord Beauford's takeover bid he led us to believe the market here could be opened up for us – if we operated through him.'

'Will you sell your Mark VIII tanks here?'

He gave her a sour smile. 'I'll sell them something.'

She wrinkled her nose. 'I bet you it won't be Mark VIII tanks. Not on this occasion. And I can't say I'm sorry.'

He was looking at her, but he was thinking of Hakagawa: *Hokkaido – kita*. 'Why did you really come here, Maggie?'

'Maybe I want to see you fail.'

'Do you? I was hoping you might help me.'

Her face flamed. 'I would never help you – or anybody else – get blood money out of weapons.'

'I see.'

'But do you understand?' she asked fiercely.

'Now who's angry?' He frowned at the empty arena. 'I don't understand what they want, Maggie. I only understand they want so much.'

'Like the world?'

'I'm prepared to do business about that. Or I would be, if –' His face changed. 'Hideki and Hakagawa are in something together. I can tell.'

'Such as?' she asked him, seemingly innocent.

He considered her carefully. Investigative journalism – and Maggie was right here in Japan. He put it to her. 'Why don't *you* find out? Ask around, Maggie. Saigo Hideki, representing heavy industry. Akira Hakagawa, representing politics, who is a big wheel in their defence set-up and likely to get bigger. And *Hokkaido – kita.*'

'Isn't Hokkaido the last big northern island in Japan? The one closest to the Soviet Union?'

'I believe so.'

'And *kita* means – ?'

'North.' He shook his head. 'No, I can't solve the mystery. Except, I know this about what we've seen here today. It's the Japanese system. Industry and politics, arm in arm. And here they both mean money.'

'They do everywhere,' she said cynically.

He gave a short laugh. 'True. But not so much as they do here.'

'You know that much about Japan, do you?'

He showed her a wry smile and threw off his depression. 'Why don't you run one of your famous investigations here? Into *them*. Into Hideki, his man Hakagawa, the things they really stand for. I'd subsidize it.'

'Most of what I know I learned from Kiko, who – is somebody who doesn't want to go on the record.'

His voice was a caress. 'Can't you find out what's really happening here in Japan, Maggie? I'm genuinely interested.'

She laughed, then looked pained. 'Investigative journalism in *Japan?*'

'Well, why not? It's a democracy, isn't it? Of sorts.'

'For once, you haven't done your research, Alex. The press here is monolithic. Three big papers, *Yomiuri Shimbun*, *Asahi Shimbun*, *Mainichi Shimbun*. One has a circulation of over eight million, and they dominate almost completely. If you check the last edition of the day you'll find, or so I'm told, that three-quarters of the front page stories will be virtually identical from paper to paper, sometimes even with the same headline, and *always* with the same non-controversial slant. Editorial teams even have meetings to decide what to keep out of the papers.'

He nodded, beginning to follow. 'Everything that might upset the power-holders, you mean?'

'Exactly. Industrial accidents, the imperial family, party infighting, nearly all of what *we* call "politics" – everything like that is strictly off-limits. I'd hate to live here. *Everything* in Japan is managed and regulated – including the so-called "free" institutions. Journalists, to work at all, have to join press clubs run by the institutions they're supposed to be reporting on – and that means the police, the government ministries, the famous Japanese business houses.

'So you do what you're told. If not, if you report anything unfavourably, true or not, then the word will be passed, pressure will be applied . . . and you're no longer able to function as a journalist – or you're no longer a journalist at all.'

For a moment he brooded over the advantages and disadvantages of such a system, finally deciding that the drawbacks were worse. 'It sounds quite English.'

'Doesn't it just,' she said. 'They even drive on the left.' She looked at him. 'So, what happens now?'

He gave a bitter smile. 'They go off somewhere, and they'll be Japanese together. Then a consensus will emerge.'

'And then you'll be told?'

'Exactly. Then they'll tell me.'

She shook her head, a little pleased that he had been humbled. 'Do you still think you can compete with them?'

'I must,' he said calmly. 'We must. Whatever the risk, whatever it costs.'

'Is that really what you think? Business before everything?'

He tore his attention from where the limousines had vanished and stared at her. She was very lovely to him still, her legs long in sheer nylon, clutching her glossy leather case. And he remembered her, sailing with him through the isles of Greece – and what she had made of her life subsequently. 'This is what I believe. There is no alternative, Maggie. No alternative to industrial success. No alternative except degeneration and poverty. And in our heart of hearts we all know that is the truth.'

She said nothing, still looking at him wide-eyed. Then, 'How are things otherwise? You don't sound very happy, somehow.'

He smiled. 'My wife, you mean? I married Caroline, so I suppose I have to live with that. Just as you have to live with Terry Katz.'

'I don't *have* to do that,' she told him sharply. 'We stay together out of love, or need, or something. We didn't stand up in a church and make all those promises in front of our families and friends – in front of God, if you believe in Him.'

He shook his head. 'If you only knew how little I've found to believe in, Maggie. You think that because I inherited some money and a great responsibility it's been easy? Not so. To live up to that responsibility I've had to risk everything – much more than money – and discard almost all of the comfortable, complacent certainties I was born to. That's been terribly painful. At least *you* can comfort yourself with your family, and your political ideals. And even though I believe your politics have failed, I can tell that your faith still comforts you – and your father. At the moment.'

'My father's politics haven't made his life easy,' she said scornfully.

'I think you underrate the quality of his devotion – and the satisfaction he gets from it, from those old simple loyalties. I admire him, Maggie. Even now he's having to discard much of what he inherited, just like me, so that we can make the industries of our country survive.'

'And so you'll deal with Hideki?'

'If I must.'

'But you're doing something else with the Japanese, aren't you? Something you don't like to talk about – that Arigata thing?'

'I'm doing what I have to do, for the sake of my family and my company and, yes, my country. Is that so difficult to understand?'

'Yes,' she said at last. 'Having no principles is very difficult for me to understand, and I'm beginning to think you're unprincipled! But it's not so hard to turn my back on all the things you are. Like this, Alex!'

The dust of Osaka whirled around her, and he watched her go, till she had vanished in the lengthening shadows, and he became aware that a hot wind had risen. He wondered how long it would be before they met as friends again. He looked towards Osaka city, the pollution haze red above it. Then he looked back for Maggie, wondering if it was over for them forever – or if it might somehow start again.

But she had vanished.

Chapter Three

In Tokyo, the next afternoon, representatives of the two corporate giants assembled to try and finalize the deal Saigo Hideki wanted: a partial merger between Stanton Industries and the Hideki Corporation.

Stanton Industries had flown in its other two division heads, and a small team of in-house legal and financial advisers. Alex was in charge of negotiations. On the table was new money, provided by the Hideki Bank of Nagasaki: 225 million dollars, for a supposedly subordinate stake in the British-based Stanton company. If both Boards of Directors could be persuaded to recommend it, the first part of the merger would happen within a month.

For the beginning of the talks, sitting with MacKenzie of Shipbuilding and the Financial Director, Victor Sainsbury, Alex had dressed immaculately in a silk shirt and pearl-grey Italian suit. He folded his hands together and looked around the oval table. He remembered Maggie's strong moral doubts about the Hideki enterprise, and he even had doubts of his own. Yet, because of the ongoing takeover bid back home, which he believed Hideki had financed, he knew he couldn't afford to antagonize this big Tokyo conglomerate, and he had made that clear to his colleagues.

He began simply. 'Mr Takahashi, it seems the takeover bid you set up in England may well fail. We are here today, therefore, to see if we can negotiate something satisfactory to *both* parties.'

His own people nodded. Takahashi answered quickly, warm and polite on the surface. 'I'm sure we will find satisfaction.' He was quite tall for a Japanese, supple and muscular and vaguely threatening: his face was flat and a little arrogant and a thin black moustache traced the flat arc of his upper lip. 'Now, our main interests are these: first, the Stanton involvement in the North Sea oil boom, both exploration and servicing, and, equally important, the armaments division.'

'Aircraft is out of the deal for the moment?' Alex asked.

'Yes, though we are happy to continue licensing your products – such as the avionics systems we are to assemble and sell to the civil market here.'

'Good,' Sainsbury said.

McCourt added, in his slow Ulster brogue, 'With your assistance we've already bought Tyne-Wear Engineering, allowing us to be involved in the Arigata fast breeder reactor. Armaments . . . is still under negotiation, we trust. We are prepared to listen with great interest to any further proposals.'

'Then we can all be optimistic,' Takahashi said, stroking his pencil-thin moustache.

Alex thought, As you always are, you cheap hustling bastard. Yet his smile looked blandly pleasant, disguising his thoughts. I remember you here in Tokyo, last time around. You are a thug, Mr Takahashi, underneath the Harvard accent and the old-time politeness.

Takahashi sat back from the table. 'Mr Stanton has already agreed, in person as well as Head of Division, to help us with Arigata.'

'Yes.' Then Alex put it unambiguously on the record, pleased that Hugh had been persuaded to protect himself by staying away, 'It's my responsibility, Arigata and the rest of our business in Japan. Solely my responsibility.' He stared into Takahashi's eyes.

'We want to be on the side of Stanton Industries, and we want the company to be on our side,' his opponent replied. 'Let's talk about how we can do it.'

'Very happy,' Alex said tersely, wondering if he could really spin the negotiations out until the emergency general meeting of the Stanton shareholders, which would settle the destiny of the company for years to come.

I'd better be able to, he thought.

'Unfortunate that your cousin Hugh is not also here,' one of Hideki's people said softly.

Alex assured them, hoping and intending there would not be another stage, 'I'm the only Stanton you need to deal with at the moment.'

From these cool and air-conditioned rooms on the twenty-fourth floor, which were rich with cherrywood panelling and the latest electronic equipment, you could see on a clear day both Tokyo Bay and sacred Mount Fuji.

On the Hideki side, as these gruelling negotiations began in earnest, only the man who had given his name to the giant company was absent.

Saigo Hideki was at that moment inside a steel-grey Mercedes limousine, being driven through an upmarket shopping street in the Ginza district. There were bright lights everywhere, behind and above the crowds. The long grey car stopped in front of an art gallery bearing signs in French and English as well as Japanese. HIDEKI GALLERY, the English letters proclaimed. He could not help showing his distaste at this internationalism.

Hideki entered by himself, spry and upright in spite of his age. There were canvases hung everywhere among the luxury and comfort. Alien canvases, in the main. Little notices showed French, German and American names, and brief biographical details.

Two neat girls dressed in white bowed respectfully, then approached, but he waved them away, till a young Italian-American male came to escort him to the back office.

Here the proprietor bowed deeply, also. A French business suit she wore with style, and her lovely face could almost pass for a teenager's.

Without waiting for an invitation, Hideki slumped on a Swedish designer sofa and lit a cigarette. His expression was still surly.

The lovely woman ordered green tea, then sat down beside the old man. 'It has been some time,' she said hesitantly. Her skin was an exquisite gold, her features perfect.

'Since we last spoke, granddaughter, or since you were last living here where you belong?' Looking at her, he saw his son's wife all over again. How many years ago was it since she had died? All of thirty, he realized suddenly.

'I prefer Paris to any city of ours,' Akiko Hideki told him coolly.

'I warned you! If you go abroad, live as a foreigner, who will marry you then? Apart from –' He made a chopping gesture with both hands. He was upset and he was old, and terribly alone. His chest heaved and for a moment he had to choke back a sob. 'How can you turn your back on your own soil, your own traditions – your own *family*?'

She lowered her eyes demurely, but he knew that her spirit was as fierce and intractable as his own. She was wringing her own hands now and he was glad that she could not face him, her ancestor and her conscience, undisturbed. He sighed in a pretence of calm. 'My dear, what is wrong with our country? This Land of the Gods has become great again.'

She stared at him, dark eyes flashing. 'You know as well as I do what the old ways have cost this country, and me! As for today, what of it? More useless wealth, that never reaches the poor! More conquest – this time with money instead of guns!'

He said curtly, 'A great nation like ours advances with self-confidence and self-belief, not with self-criticism.'

'Then it is no advance,' she retorted. '*We* began the Great Pacific War, and we paid for it. But now I see the way things are developing again, and I am full of fear.'

'I tell you, you are wrong! This land is great. It will become even greater when it is true to itself again. Love this land!' He glanced around her office, displeased. Works of art, cool abstracts from New York and London and Berlin, and framed propaganda posters about ecology.

'I will tell you how things are developing. In 1971 your friend Nakasone had the peace dove removed from the Self-Defence Forces' coat of arms. Our army and navy and air force is growing stronger every month, every year. Now all the leaders thrown up by this corrupt one-party system, leaders which men like yourself buy and sell, go to the great Yasukuni Shrine to revere the war dead – including Class A war criminals like Tojo himself!'

Hideki's face was thunderous. 'How dare you! Am I so unworthy of respect! Who else but *you* would dare to defy me like this!'

She did not look away, but her eyes filled with tears. 'Nobody else, grandfather. For I am of your blood, and I have inherited your courage, and I am so deeply, deeply sorry that we can agree on so little.' She squeezed tears away and wiped them with one free hand. 'I apologize for offending you. I know you are sincere . . . But I am sincere also.'

He reached out to her, and for several seconds his hand was poised above hers. Then it began to tremble. She did not move, or acknowledge him in any way. Finally, he withdrew his hand, without a touch from his only living descendant. Suddenly he was in a pit of loneliness and depression only her youth and brightness could have saved him from.

He had lost her. Lost his only son's only child. Lost her, and perhaps the soul of Japan.

He dropped the teacup and moaned. The flash of memory was vivid and painful, like the atomic flash, stunning in its brilliance. For a while he had thought the gods had blinded him.

And once he had entered his home town, he wished they had . . . It came back to him. Akiko his granddaughter, in the burnt wreckage of Hiroshima, in the time just after 6 August, 1945.

In the Mercedes afterwards, driving to his estate, he began to think of that day again. Hiroshima, his home. *Hiro-shima-jo*, the castle of the broad island; historic port upon rivers, 2nd Army headquarters. His home. He had been returning from a visit to the navy in Kure, driving in an old Ford sedan from before the war.

It had been early in the morning, he remembered. A clear and warm day, with sunshine everywhere. The road almost empty, with the city only a few miles away.

A single B-29 bomber, droning high above, then two others. He frowned, never sure since if he really remembered those planes, or if it was something time and imagination had added to memories gone over a thousand, ten thousand, times . . .

First an overwhelmingly bright light: as if the doors of heaven had opened for a bare moment.

Or the doors of hell.

He had been dazzled but had been looking at the road, so he was not blinded for long. His driver pulled over immediately, on the crest of a small hill, and as the sound thundered by them, they saw it. He could never forget. The fire, boiling up red inside of the black cloud; and the cloud swirling up vertically, black like oil, evil, dark. Hiroshima was set among rivers and canals, in a bowl of hills, and it was burning.

An hour later Hideki entered the city, crossing the Ota Canal.

His granddaughter was not to be found inside the shattered family mansion. Try the little school, they told him. So, with some of the servants, he went in search of Kiko and her mother.

He went into hell. He saw, first, damaged houses, shops, factories, the destruction getting worse as he proceeded into the burned heart of the city. Streets full of rubble. He saw screaming, maddened people he could not help, blinded women, people burnt black all over because their clothes had burned on to them with the firestorm heat of the explosion. Skin hung off them in strips. Hair was charred black. He saw huge blisters had formed on bare, bleeding flesh. It was all he could do to fight back his nausea. Everywhere was weeping and moaning. But he had to find his family. In a dream, he went on, hardly recognizing the streets, avoiding distorted red faces so swollen they looked like red balloons, without human features.

He went on into death.

Screaming children, orphaned in an instant. Sobbing, wailing mothers, made childless in the same instant.

It was hot in Hiroshima and getting hotter. There were fires everywhere, and the sky had turned black. In front of one school he saw the bodies of young boys laid out in rows. Then he saw the remains of Aioi Bridge, and realized he was now in the heart of the city, the heart of death. He looked around, stunned by the devastation the American bombing had left behind. Part of him prayed for vengeance, but that was for the future. Here and now, there were blackened and blasted bodies everywhere. The bomb had played obscene tricks, too. He saw a dead woman standing upright, a statue of burned-black flesh, still clutching a child to her breast. Was the child feebly wriggling? He thought of his beloved Kiko, but passed on anyway. Streetcars here were still full, but only with the dead. The river had continued to run, but it seemed only corpses were flowing between its banks.

He wanted to scream out his rage and his pain, but he dared not. He thought that if he let his emotions loose, even for a moment, his mind and spirit would shatter.

Fires continued burning all that day. He did not find his family, though he saw dead friends lying here and there. He looked around as night fell, realizing that he was alone, and he saw that Hiroshima Castle had been utterly destroyed, and so he knew that the old ways were broken for good.

He slept in a half-ruined house. It was not till late afternoon the next day that he at last found Kiko in what passed for a hospital. A hospital almost without doctors or nurses, or drugs or bandages: but filled with casualties dying slow, agonizing deaths.

She had cried a lot, he remembered, though her burns had already been dressed.

'Where can we go? Where can we go, grandfather, to be safe?'

Probably he had not been thinking. So he thought then. Where could he take her, to be safe? Tokyo was a burned mass of ruin. To the country, then? But what about the invasion the Americans planned? To the branch of the firm in Nagasaki, perhaps?

She howled again, 'Grandfather, where will we be safe?'

He wanted to hold her, but she was burned too badly. Finally, miserably, he admitted to her, 'I don't know. I don't know where it would be safe.'

After the war he had rebuilt his great wealth, till his power was even greater than before, but sometimes it was ashes to him.

As he settled back in the leather upholstery of the Mercedes, face entirely without expression, he realized now – had in truth always known, since the surrender in '45 – that his land had been robbed of its soul, just as he had been robbed of his family.

For even Kiko had been taken. Akiko Hideki, his own granddaughter, was now both stranger and enemy.

What else could he seek now, except revenge?

In Tokyo, the negotiations lasted another two days.

'So,' Alex said, going through a sheaf of papers one last time, 'you're saying an arms deal is possible, a deal *much* bigger than a few regiments of Mark VIII tanks, but only if there is a large-scale merger of interests between us?'

Takahashi was beginning to wilt from lack of sleep. The others, on both sides, had been mostly dismissed by now. 'Exactly,' he croaked. 'Stanton Industries has arms production inside NATO, and raw materials and North Sea oil through its subsidiaries.'

Alex still seemed fresh and relaxed. 'And you're offering?'

'All the money you can imagine, Alex Stanton. All the money you would need in order to expand – and on far, far better terms than any bank in America or England could offer!'

Alex nodded. He sat forward in the chair and made a steeple of his fingers. 'But first you want three seats on Stanton Industries' Board of Directors, with Saigo Hideki as deputy chairman, with heavy influence over our policies.'

'I'm asking for that, not because of all the shares we own, but as a favour, right?' He grabbed Alex's wrist and squeezed hard. 'From you to me, one coming man to another.'

'Mr Hideki is still in overall charge, surely?' Alex said quietly, taking his hand away.

Their eyes locked, brown fixed on blue, and equally hard, but Alex did not look away.

'Just do it for me, Alex Stanton.'

'For you, or for Saigo Hideki?'

'Just do it! And I'll open all those doors for you!'

'We will consider everything you have said, overnight,' Alex told him. 'I'll sleep on it, then consult Mr MacKenzie and Mr Sainsbury before they catch their plane home.'

'Then?'

This was obviously of great importance to Takahashi's career.

'Then we will put whatever is agreed here to my cousin Hugh. He will soon be the chairman of the company again.'

'Put whatever . . . But you can *tell* him what to do!'

Alex lounged back. 'I promise he'll consider carefully everything – everything – I tell him.'

Takahashi, very foolishly, relaxed.

Next morning, the advisers began to disperse. As Alex had intended, the two companies could not quite come to a final agreement in Tokyo.

It was all going to plan – Alex's plan. But he had to fight a subtle delaying action till the next board meeting and perhaps beyond. In spite of the optimism about the deal Alex had carefully encouraged, Takahashi wanted a firmer commitment. So Alex allowed Takahashi to accompany him on his flight home, still trying to firm up a deal as they headed for Europe together in a Stanton Industries shuttle 727.

Neither slept. It was a point of honour to maintain constant effort rather than rest.

Also on the plane with with them were civil engineers and power engineers from a Stanton subsidsiary company called Tyne Wear Engineering. TWE was effectively Stanton Industries' civil projects division, helping build Arigata in Japan.

Alex glanced around at them, as the plane started its descent over the Scottish highlands. Some were playing cards. Some were sleeping. He turned back to Takahashi, giving him a dazzling smile: he was enjoying this game. 'Let's see what my cousin has to say. He is to be company chairman, after all.'

The great house was built of a mottled stone that was now streaked yellow-green with summer ivy. This was Craigburn at its best, in a simmering August. The Stanton family's huge private estate was situated up in Northumberland, and Craigburn was one of England's finest houses.

A red sports car skirted the broad and glittering man-made lake which had been first dammed for hydroelectric power in the reign of Victoria. It was approaching the house itself as a black Rolls-Royce Silver Shadow came down the gravel drive. The Rolls stopped quickly, so that a tall blond man could step out and flag down the speeding Jaguar.

Alex smiled at the driver who peered up out of the E-type's leather-lined cockpit. 'As you can see, cousin Hugh, I'm back from Japan. With a "friend".'

Fingers tapped the sports car's steering-wheel. Hugh's cold and disdainful gaze turned from Takahashi's shuffling impatience back to Alex's grin. He said without real interest. 'And I can tell from your manner that you think we all need to talk.'

'We do indeed.'

'Right now, I'd prefer,' Takahashi said, red-eyed and overtired. He grimaced a smile. 'Good to meet you again, Mr Hugh Stanton.'

Alex's gaze swept over the low-slung car; he rubbed his hand over the gleaming bonnet. This was his very own pillar-box red E-type Jaguar Hugh was driving, a modified Series I which he intended one day to put into the famous collection of classic cars the two cousins sometimes worked on as a hobby. 'A problem?'

'Touch of brake fade, I think,' Hugh said. He was frowning deliberately at Alex, carrying on a charade to make Takahashi assume the two cousins were rivals and enemies – and therefore divided and vulnerable.

Alex opened the driver's door, glancing back at Takahashi. 'Let me give it a spin, and you a second opinion, Hugh.'

'And a third opinion!' Takahashi broke in. 'I know sports cars, Ferrari, Jaguar, Porsche, whatever.'

'Of course you do,' said Alex, his voice coolly patronizing. 'Try this one with me.'

'When the brakes need servicing? You're in a daredevil mood,' Hugh said grumpily. He climbed out, tall and stooped, then rounded the long, low bonnet to open the door on the passenger's side. He took his cue from Alex and ignored Takahashi as he stepped in self-importantly and yanked the seatbelt tight. 'I take it Japan didn't quite please you.'

'Not as much as this.' Alex took the three-spoke wheel, glanced at the dashboard: speedo, tachometer, clock. Clutch down, he tapped on the accelerator and heard the big 4.2 litre engine begin to boom.

Then they exploded forward, spraying gravel behind. Alex moved quickly through the gears. He swept left, then right, checking the dials and listening to the lion's roar from the exhaust pipes. He held the wheel firmly as the speed climbed higher, touching the brakes only occasionally, judging the moment superbly as he went hurtling on to the tarmac road that hugged the big lake on the Craigburn estate. Then the first real bend approached.

Orthodox opinion says a driver should take a line as he approaches a corner, lose power, change down, get through the apex of the bend, then accelerate out of it.

But Alex had his own way of doing things: a light but incredibly alert touch on the throttle and the brakes, keeping the car in balance and the power up as he swept through the corner with the minimum of slowing. The wheel was vibrating in his hands and the slipstream was tearing through his swept-back hair and bringing tears to his eyes.

There was not quite enough straight road ahead to use the full 140 miles per hour speed, but Alex whipped the suntopped coupé round corners and used the brakes first lightly, then to the full. 'The brakes *do* need doing,' Alex yelled, accelerating even more.

'You're going *faster*?'

'To test the brakes and steering.' Alex weaved about, violently, so that Takahashi gripped the dashboard and pushed himself back from it, gulping.

Takahashi stayed braced inside the Jaguar's cockpit on the bucket seat. His expression became a frozen rictus. They climbed up a steep section of track, high, higher, the lake a silver glow to their right, then Alex braked violently, the car slewing.

Takahashi called out something in Japanese and threw a hand over his eyes as Alex stopped the car inches from the sheer slope.

The deer had stayed on the road in front of them, big-eyed.

Alex laughed, sounded the horn. 'Sometimes happens,' he said to Takahashi. 'Think I'll get back to the lake road.'

There Alex left the road a moment, so that saplings slashed at the red flanks of the car and at their heads.

Takahashi jerked back further. 'Any problems?' he quavered.

'Still drinking oil! But that's the nature of the beast,' Alex yelled, exulting to drive this most responsive and powerful vehicle with its triple carburettors, twin overhead cams and stainless-steel exhaust. The E-type was the greatest sports car so far made. He went sailing through yet another corner, again tapping the brakes. Limited problems so far, but overheated disc-brakes naturally tended to fade . . .

Takahashi made himself smile as Alex hit the brakes hard and began a terrifying handbrake turn. They were both rattled about inside the cockpit, and the tyres screamed on the tarmac. Then Alex accelerated again, hitting a straight section of track at over a hundred.

Then, a bend.

He loved this, all of it. He did not want to hand this over to Hideki and his heirs.

On the third circuit, when he felt for the brakes again, he knew they were becoming steadily less responsive. 'Hugh was right about the disc brakes.'

'You can't brake this thing!'

'I like to push things to their limit.' The hundred-mile-an-hour gale pulled Alex's laughter away from his mouth. 'Think it's time we stripped the brakes down again.'

'We can stop now?' Takahashi was looking a little sick.

'If you like.' Alex took another bend fiercely, engine howling and the wheel and gearstick quivering in his hands. Braking pushed him and his passenger towards the dashboard: then four-litre acceleration yanked them backwards. 'You want to bring Hugh in immediately on our discussions.'

'Maybe I'll . . .' Out of the corner of his eye Alex saw his opponent swallow again. 'Maybe I'll take a shower and rest up first.'

'Of course. Exactly as you wish.' He slowed decisively.

Hugh was waiting for them under the grand portico of Craigburn, the smooth green lawn stretching out in front of him, interrupted only by the curving gravel drive and a few clumps of colourful shrubs. A man was hosing down the flight of stone steps.

The passenger climbed out quickly. His legs did not seem very steady.

'I suppose,' Hugh asked innocently, 'that Mr Takahashi might like to lie down for a while?'

'I guess so.' Takahashi seemed to find it difficult to walk in a straight line, let alone make it up the stone steps unassisted.

'I took the liberty of having your bags sent up,' Hugh said. 'And my man here will show you to your room.'

The two cousins waited till Takahashi had gone inside the house. Hugh grinned, rubbing his hands together. 'Works every time.'

Now the cousins were entirely serious and businesslike and friendly.

'It certainly does. Once or twice I thought he was going to be sick.'

'What about the car?'

'You were quite right, Hugh. Therefore, no delaying over the brakes,' Alex said. 'Let's get busy soon as they've cooled down enough to handle.'

'As you wish. And you might even tell me why you're keeping Takahashi at arm's length?'

Alex's hands tightened on the wheel. 'Let's go inside to the house for a drink and then we can start to discuss Japan. It's a complicated situation.'

'If you're just back,' Hugh said politely, 'you'll want to ring your wife, anyway.'

Hugh himself took the car to the workshop. Meanwhile, phoning from the little lobby, Alex had to leave a message for Caroline, as she was out. He frowned as he put the phone down. Caro had too many temporary enthusiasms for his taste, and her lack of consistent, disciplined effort in anything was beginning to annoy him, but he had to choke this down. This marriage had been a family arrangement, anyway. Relations between the two of them varied between pleasant insincerity and a curt briskness as their separate lives met or collided. Only the sex was good, and he could remember many combats in that battleground of sweat and passion which they could both win. He even missed her, sometimes.

Alex left the main house by way of the kitchen door. It was still hot outside, even in the shade at the rear of Craigburn. He walked over to a long low red-brick building at the rear of the house, which ran parallel to the stables.

Inside, a man looked up from polishing brightwork with a rag. 'Mr Hugh's behind, sir, in the workshop.'

Alex waved in acknowledgement, glanced at the car finishing restoration. It was English, a gleaming Riley Sprite from 1937, just prewar, though not unusual enough to become a permanent exhibit. 'How did it go?'

'Not too bad, Mr Alex. Bodywork was good; we were able to use nearly all the original panels in the restoration. Engine's in fine fettle, now.'

'Excellent.'

'And what about your trip to Florida, sir?'

'To check out the '32 Cadillac Fleetwood? Went well. I think we may bid when it comes up for auction.'

'Was it really Al Capone's car?'

'Certainly was.' Alex laughed. 'One of them.'

Whistling, Alex strolled on between the cars exhibited in the Stantons' private museum, looking up once at the narrow skylights, which were too narrow for burglars to slip through. A state of the art security system blinked its red lights at him.

It was strange to think that the early products of a car-designing genius such as Enzo Ferrari were now as valuable as some of the famous English paintings in the great house itself, though Alex preferred a fast car to a Gainsborough or Stubbs any day. For his business contacts in America, Germany and Japan, coming to the Stantons' Craigburn was an occasion. Hispano-Suiza, Mercedes, Ferrari; they were great names. The two dozen cars, all drivable, were set on low platforms, and gleamed in the fluorescent light. These classics were guaranteed to impress most Stanton clients; indeed, they even impressed the cousins themselves.

Hugh, now wearing Stanton Industries overalls, walked out of the workshop, automatically reaching out to touch one golden-yellow car: a 1926 Silver Ghost with immaculate Pall Mall coachwork. 'Beautiful, this Rolls-Royce,' he said. 'Now, let's get to it. You can tell me all about Mr Hideki while we work.'

Once in the workshop, Alex changed into company overalls and collected some tools. Hugh had the Jaguar up on blocks already. Now, they began the complicated process of dismantling the brakes. They needed to say little about the task they shared. As always, it was soothing to work on such fine machinery.

Alex began to speak. 'I didn't get the reception I was hoping for in Osaka, Hugh.'

Hugh, flat on his back, turned his head in surprise. 'They weren't impressed by your Mark VIII?'

'Yes, they were. But it all cuts much deeper than that.' Alex tapped a long wrench into the palm of one hand.

'You look concerned.'

'I want those contracts, and Hideki knows it.'

'So there'll be a particular price, you think?' Hugh coughed. 'How far did those discussions go?'

Alex thought for a moment. 'I think Hideki really does want close relations with our company, Hugh.'

'If he *is* behind Beauford's takeover bid, £200 million proves it.'

'I agree. So, he wants us: for North Sea oil and NATO armaments – and I suspect because of Arigata . . .'

'But you're inclined not to be engulfed by his bear hug?'

'Exactly.' Alex stood up, and began to walk about, pulling at the open collar of his shirt. It was hot here in the workshop, but it had been sweltering in Japan. 'Let me make it explicit. I want to finish Arigata, as we've agreed, and I want to sell our armaments to Tokyo. But I don't want to see the active presence of the Hideki Corporation on our board, Hugh.'

There was a continued clinking noise under the car, and it was a minute before Hugh spoke. 'That seems hard to avoid, given his large shareholding and the imminence of the general meeting of the shareholders.'

'It does, doesn't it . . .' Alex turned around restlessly. 'I'd perhaps allow Hideki himself on the Board. We could even present that to the old man as a special honour.'

'He's too old to attend regularly, anyway. Is that what you mean?'

'That's about the size of it.'

'I think I'll change this oil,' Hugh said after a pause. Hugh, gaunt and stooped over, worked slowly and thoughtfully and with great precision.

'So I'd like you to try and work something out with Lord Beauford.'

Hugh's head jerked back. 'Alex, I think he hates you.'

'No doubt. But you're not me. Try anything. Threats, bribery, whatever. Officially, remember, he's the owner of record of the great bunch of shares Hideki's money allowed him to buy.'

'Keep Beauford on the Board of Directors, even?' Hugh frowned. 'Not as chairman, I hope.'

'No, but keep him on rather than have the active participation by Hideki – the lesser of two evils, Hugh. Takahashi suggested *three* Hideki appointees to the Board.'

'Including himself, I suppose?'

'What do *you* think?'

Hugh sighed. 'I'll try. It won't be easy, but I'll try.' There was another silence, as Hugh poured in more oil. 'Anything else?'

'I met Dr Sidqi again,' Alex said harshly. 'I stopped over in Jordan on my way to Japan. He seems to have heard about Arigata.'

'Ah,' murmured Hugh, lifting a micrometer off the long work bench. He sighted along it. 'Dr Sidqi. Now I wonder if I need to know about that officially – or even unofficially.'

'It's no problem,' Alex said. He had a long screwdriver in his right hand, weighing it thoughtfully. 'Obviously I was polite, but I'm not going to supply the Ba'athists in Iraq. Not with what *they* want, anyway.' He took a breath; one hand flashed in a blur of motion. The screwdriver, thrown like a knife, now vibrated in the middle of a tipped-up wooden workbench. 'Which from us means prospecting experts and expertise from our mining subsidiaries, because there's uranium ore in Iraq – and then equipment and technicians to help refine it. And, eventually, reactors.'

'I thank God those people will never have the bomb.'

'You think not?' Alex said sharply, knowing that al-Bakr was on the way out and Saddam Hussein was set to become life president in Iraq. 'Don't say that in Paris.'

'The French – ?'

'Are going to provide an Osiris research reactor – with full government approval, naturally. The Osiris gives a much higher thermal output than its equivalents, apparently, and my technical staff advise me it produces something else, too.'

Hugh's eyebrows asked: '?'

'Weapons-grade plutonium, Hugh.'

At the other end of England, on this hot but grey afternoon in the late summer of 1974, similar topics were under discussion in an office made colourful by fresh flowers and framed photographs and magazine covers. Mick Jagger hurled a microphone in Paris. Mikhail Baryshnikov posed on one toe-tip. Nixon's face looked tragic after his resignation.

'No. Maggie, I'd much rather not be taped.'

Maggie Langton heard something stronger than reluctance, as the elegant hand moved between her own hand and her Sony tape-recorder's 'on' switch. She stared at Akiko – Kiko, in casual form. 'Look, I contacted you as soon as I got back from Osaka.'

The pert face said, 'Yes.'

'Then you flew to London almost immediately.'

'Yes.'

'So I thought you wanted to tell me the whole story – or as much of it as you know!'

'But not on the record.'

'Not even on a tape, just for me?'

Kiko's tone was light, her English precise. 'Tapes aren't private, Maggie. They can be copied, or lost, or stolen. And then somebody might recognize my voice.'

'You're *that* frightened – of your own grandfather?'

'I am.' A pause. 'You met him, Maggie. A dangerous man. I'd like to keep this secret, therefore.'

'All right.' Maggie stood up and stretched. Light was pouring in through the tall windows of the photographic studio high in a converted warehouse on the south bank of the Thames; dust motes flickered. She saw herself reflected, tall and red-haired, in the mirror wall. 'You're inclined to be cautious. That's fine. But . . .'

A small smile. 'Maybe I am over-cautious, you mean? Especially if I cannot say my story is guaranteed to be true.'

Maggie sat down, shrugged. 'Japan is your country, not mine. *You* have to find out what's happening there and decide what's true and what isn't.'

'But my grandfather is building Arigata. That is a known fact.'

The green eyes blinked. 'So you told me. But how does that connect with me?'

'Arigata is being built with help from your friends, Maggie. Stanton Industries and that man from the Armaments Division, Alex Stanton.'

Her pulse accelerated. 'Alex. I'd heard that.'

'It is true; provably true. Arigata is a nuclear reactor complex. When it opens it will be a fast breeder of nuclear poisons – and of plutonium and uranium 235.'

'Terrible.'

'And without Stanton Industries, it will not be finished!' Kiko stared at her, small fists clenched. Fury blazed in those dark eyes. 'And I am convinced my grandfather, who will one day have a source of pure fissionable material from Arigata, intends to rearm Japan. With, eventually, atomic weapons.'

'What?' Maggie gasped. 'Are you certain?'

'Almost certain.'

'That would be one of the biggest stories of all time – and one of the worst scandals.'

Kiko's eyes lit up. 'You think so?'

'If we could prove it.'

The delicate face fell: sorrow and determination welled in Kiko's dark eyes. 'You must prove it, and have it stopped.'

Maggie now spoke from sad experience: it had taken years to stop the American effort in Vietnam. 'Even if we could prove that, and I put it on the front pages of all the newspapers in the world, I still don't know that we could stop it. And as of now, we can't prove a thing.'

'There must be something we can do.'

'I don't know what.' Maggie started walking around, restlessly. What had Alex said, back in Osaka? North Hokkaido, or north of Hokkaido . . . 'We can't do much without hard evidence.'

There was a knock on the door and one of Maggie's junior researchers entered, with a burst of radio music following her inside. She was a nineteen-year-old with hair tied up in lots of little blonde plaits. She handed Maggie some papers. 'The Castro interview. Havana Foreign Ministry says yes, as long as you can get your crew there in the next three, four weeks.'

Maggie jumped up, aware that Kiko had deliberately turned her face away from this intruder. 'Confirm immediately, settle a date, then start ringing round people on the media crew A list.'

'And David Bryant's Rockefeller article.'

'Proof-read it and have it on my desk back in Notting Hill by lunch.'

'Can do,' Sally said jauntily, hitching up her tight jeans.

Even after the door had closed again, Kiko Hideki hesitated. 'My grandfather. There are other things, I have heard – in the Hideki factories.'

Maggie was listening hard. 'Go on.'

'Plans for – I would rather not say everything. But tanks, and artillery, all planned to be the best in the world. And Stanton Industries is to be used as the supplier of ideas and hardware for all this. I am sure I can find evidence enough for that.'

Maggie remembered the proving ground, north of Osaka: the tanks, and how all the men there had approved. 'But what does all that add up to, Kiko?'

'Enough, to me,' Kiko said, suddenly shivering with rage, 'because Article IX of our Constitution forbids those things forever.' Her brow furrowed. 'Yet I can't even prove that they are *his* plans, or made with his approval. I only suspect it.'

'If you could get me documents, pictures, a signed statement or two –'

'Or a tape, Maggie?' Kiko asked innocently.

'Maybe I could do something then. Exporting armaments is still pretty controversial. And, remembering Pearl Harbor, I don't suppose the Americans would much like a nuclear-armed Japan. Still less the Russians, since any armaments would presumably be aimed at them initially.'

'How could I acquire such proofs?'

'Find a source inside your grandfather's company.'

Kiko spoke in a tortured voice, 'I must put someone else at risk – to find this proof?'

Maggie felt sympathy, and respect for Akiko Hideki's scruples. 'You really want to investigate? Then you must take on both Stanton Industries and the Hideki Corporation.'

Kiko's eyes closed for a moment. 'Yes. Because what I suspect . . .' The delicate Japanese face was averted now. 'But I still beg you. Help me.'

Maggie went up to the window. On the opposite bank of the Thames, she could see St Paul's Cathedral, its skullcap of stone pale under the summer light. If you followed the river west from here, she mused, if you passed under four or five London bridges, you would find the coffin-plan Stanton Industries headquarters . . .

'I'll try,' Maggie said, at last.

'And your friend, Terry Katz? Could you interest him in this?'

'He's in Cambodia taking photographs.' Maggie grimaced. 'And I find it difficult to interest him in anything these days – except maybe screwing some Hollywood starlet.' Then her journalistic instincts spoke up. 'There is one thing I heard in Osaka that might be relevant. Something that concerns your grandfather and his political allies and the Japanese military. Something about north Hokkaido, or north of Hokkaido. Does that mean anything?'

'No.' Kiko looked puzzled. Then she snapped her fingers. 'There is one thing. An old Imperial-era map my grandfather owns. He showed me it once, when I was a little girl. North of Hokkaido . . .'

'Is what?'

'Four main islands. Kunashir, Shikotan, Habomai and Etoforu. Part of the Kurile chain, and Japanese from ancient times. But they were occupied by the Soviets in 1945 after the bombings, and still remain so.'

'God,' Maggie said, 'and your grandfather and his cronies want them back!'

Now there was fear. 'But the Russians *will not* give them back, Maggie. Because they guard the entrance to the Sea of Okhotsk. And there, in Vladivostok, is where the Soviet Pacific Fleet is based.'

Maggie shook her head. 'This is real war mongering, isn't it?'

'That's what I'm scared of.'

'Why did you really come to me, Kiko?'

The small hands kneaded a clutch purse of soft black leather. 'I know you – and you know me. I just felt you were the right person. You believe in freedom, in ecology, in creating one whole green world. And you have your magazine, and your television programmes, and all that famous journalism behind you. And . . .'

Maggie had sat back, and pulled both knees together. There was more coming.

'And you once told me that you and this powerful man inside Stanton Industries –'

'I went to Japan to help publicize his business there. That's all.'

'To help sell his tanks?' Kiko said with evident distaste.

'Look, my father is a trade union leader,' Maggie answered, 'representing the men who make those tanks. It isn't just a matter of business profit to them. It's their work; their *lives*.'

'But there's another link, isn't there, between the Stantons and you? You said you and the younger one were once lovers.'

'That was a long time ago,' Maggie said steadily, though the memories remained a colourful flood, 'me and Alex Stanton. It doesn't mean very much now.'

She wondered if she was telling a lie – and if so, about whom.

Chapter Four

'David, how are you?'

Alex's friend since Oxford, and Maggie Langton's from a shared Tyneside childhood, was David Bryant, Labour Member of Parliament. Having picked up the telephone in the hall, he needed to swallow a piece of toast before mumbling a reply. 'Fine, Alex.' He coughed up crumbs. 'How's Caro?'

'Off sailing somewhere,' Alex replied crisply. Then, 'Did you see Maggie's latest issue?'

David carried the phone to the table by the cottage's front door. Here the mail sent to his Fishguard home was piled up neatly. He pulled out one large item addressed to him. 'Let's see. A familiar-looking envelope. London W11 postmark. It looks like that wonderful magazine of listings and investigative journalism whose owner and managing editor is—'

'Our friend Maggie Langton. Anyway, read it carefully. You might be amused. It describes my attempt to conquer Japan; the Osaka tank trials and everything.'

'I could do with some light relief.'

'Of course you could! But you'll be back in London when?'

David sighed and lowered his voice. 'Monday. In the House. Later I should be available in my office.'

'I'll try to get hold of you there, or at your flat later on. Two things. First, the shareholders' meeting is next Thursday. I still want to persuade you to take up that directorship.'

'I don't think that's politically possible,' David said with regret, 'the Labour Party being what it is. But thanks for the offer. What's the other thing?'

'I'm still involved in a battle to control Stanton Industries.'

'I thought you'd won that. I heard you and Hugh had £250 million from Iran and could buy up enough additional shares to give you a controlling interest.'

'It isn't that simple. Lord Beauford still sits on the Stanton Board of Directors as chairman and he, in essence, represents Saigo Hideki's corporation. Their bid has been conducted well: they will have a good chunk of our equity. And the firm's regulations say that a holding of thirty percent of the shares guarantees representation on the Board. So Hugh and I will come under pressure to allow Hideki to be directly represented on the Board.'

'I see,' David said dolefully. 'And you don't want that?'

Alex took a breath. 'Not such close links, David. Bad enough Lord Beauford, but three directors answering directly to Tokyo would be intolerable. I have reason to be suspicious of how the Hideki Corporation conducts its business. But with us, the company will be supported and grow strong again.'

'I see. So what is it you want *me* to do?'

'I'd like you to raise the matter in the House of Commons. I suggest you play the patriotic card against Beauford: that he's an asset-stripper selling off our industry to foreign businesses. There's a good reason to keep Hideki and his people – and that includes Lord Beauford – at arm's length.'

'What reason?'

The voice became very quiet. 'Our friends in Japan are thorough right-wingers, and it's been hinted to me that, just possibly, they might be conspiring to do a whole lot more than merely update the Japanese armed forces.'

David brooded a moment. A possible political conspiracy in Japan? If there was a chance of that, Alex's request was reasonable. 'Very well. I'll ask a question in the House myself, and I'll arrange for a couple of other members to raise the issue also. I'm no admirer of Beauford and his methods. Frankly, I consider Lord Beauford to be a traitor.'

'And so do I, David. Thank you. Enjoy Maggie's article.'

David picked up the copy of *Capital Life* Maggie had mailed him and went back into the kitchen, where his family were still having breakfast.

As the children spooned up their cereal David acted out the tank battle, from Maggie's article. The girls enjoyed it, unlike their mother.

'And Alex lived, I suppose?' his wife inquired. 'Even after inviting Maggie to shoot him?'

The windows were open, it was warm, and he could see a bright silver-blue gleam; the harbour water of Lower Fishguard. 'He certainly did, Megan.'

'The devil looks after his own.'

Alex was an amazing character, David thought as he read Maggie's words. The article made it seem likely that the Japanese self-defence forces would eventually buy Stanton Mark VIII tanks. A superb coup for Alex, if it happened. And a success like that would help make 1974 end on a better note for David Bryant also. He admired Alex's buccaneering energy, though often disagreeing with Alex's politics, and so had actively helped to promote Stanton Industries' interests. He knew that the national economy had to come right, and since Stanton Industries was so important to that process almost anything had to be considered acceptable to protect all the Stanton jobs and its wealth-generating industry.

David patted his magazine flat and looked across the kitchen at his wife. Megan was pretty and dark-haired, and flushed pink as she scraped a blob of marmalade off the kitchen tablecloth and gave a look of mild reproof to their younger daughter. It was warm and homely in their cottage kitchen in Fishguard, amid the odour of baking bread.

'What else does it say in the magazine, David? More election speculation? I know what Maggie's interests are there!'

'Well, there has to be another general election soon. Things can't go on like this. Every time we lay a piece of legislation before the House it gets thrown back at us. A minority government spends all its time just horse-trading bills with the other parties.'

'If there is an election, will you be a minister, Daddy?' Naomi asked.

David gave his daughter a doubting glance. 'How long have you been taking an interest in politics, young lady?'

She shrugged, her bright, brown eyes losing interest as she put another piece of buttered toast in her mouth. 'Suzanne at school asked me about you nearly being a minister. Her dad's a minister too,' she explained, with the slight lisp he found so charming. 'So, will there be an election, Daddy?'

David was more than a little surprised by this coincidence. Another minister here in Fishguard? He regarded his youngster with indulgent seriousness. She was heartbreakingly beautiful, with her winning, innocent smile.

'Well, since you ask, I'd say there will be one. Now, why do you want to know?'

'Because,' she sighed, 'I hope you win and become a minister and get a church.'

'A church?'

'Suzanne's daddy's already got one.'

He had to laugh.

'Frankly, we'd like you to resign.'

Lord Beauford stretched out his legs. 'So you and Alex have agreed, Hugh? And then you get back the chairmanship of Stanton Industries yourself?'

'Unless you have some objection.' Hugh reached out for his drink, then left it on the table. He felt very uncomfortable.

'Or does the despicable Alex become the master in the company?'

'That's a family matter,' Hugh said. 'I really see this private meeting with you as preparation for the emergency general meeting, and that mainly a matter of – decorum.'

The bar was panelled with wood and decorated with prints and paintings. Lord Beauford looked around and sniffed. Mark Birley's nightclub, Annabel's, was an accustomed and comfortable haunt for him: you could occasionally see major business celebrities here, as well as a few kings and other, more louche connections with the Establishment. He turned back to Hugh Stanton, big eyes wounded. 'I'm prepared to go along with you, Hugh. In fact, I wash my hands of the whole business. Hideki gave me certain assurances; but he let me down. Now the damned man's underlings get on the phone and try to give me orders – yes, bloody orders!'

'You took Hideki's money,' Hugh reminded him.

Beauford shrugged. 'I'm a merchant banker. Taking money is my business. Of course, no one could predict that Alex would ask the Shah of Iran for help – nor that the Shah's assistance would amount to £250 million. I'm stunned at the fuss there's been over this takeover bid – shrieks in the press, and in parliament, too! I was merely acting for a client, Hugh – Mr Hideki – in the usual fashion.'

His arrogance is truly pristine, Hugh thought. 'You can't blame Alex for resenting what happened. We were almost usurped, Monty, he and I. Suppose someone tried to take Beauford Cleves, your own bank, away from you?'

The peer swept a hand away. 'Entirely different, Hugh. Mine is a bank founded by a charter from Queen Anne herself. Finance, the City. It's entirely different to the Stanton outfit, for God's sake. That's industry.'

'So this time you'll be on our side?'

The peer shrugged, not answering directly. 'Not much else I can do. I suppose. Tell Alex that.'

Hugh regarded him. 'I must be able to assure Alex that you won't stand in our way.'

'Or else?'

'Draw your own conclusions,' Hugh said coldly. 'You know my cousin's reputation.'

'So,' Alex greeted his cousin Hugh next morning. 'Come in.'

In the Stanton headquarters in London, Alex's private office provided a stupendous view of the Thames. As Head of Division for armaments, it was his due.

'I've seen Lord Beauford, Alex. In my opinion he won't stand in our way. Time to take stock, therefore.' Hugh Stanton was very tall and thin, and he had to almost fold himself up to sit down in the leather armchair.

Alex saw him glance around this room. 'You don't approve of my mix-and-match decor?' Alex was standing in front of a framed blueprint for the family's supersonic STA-C. On the cream walls were framed photographs: a Czar and two Presidents, posing with earlier Stantons.

Hugh sighed. 'I like the view of the river, of course, though I don't find the Vauxhall side particularly attractive.'

'And these things?' Alex tapped the polished rosewood of his desk, an antique from seventeenth-century France, supposedly once Cardinal Richelieu's. Yet a long modern table running at right angles to the tall windows supported state-of-the-art IBM computer equipment.

'Not a permissible combination, in my view.'

Alex chuckled as he unloosened his silk Hermès tie. Hugh was a very conservative figure in his blue pinstripes.

'Any more news from Japan, Alex?'

'Nothing yet, about tank sales. Hideki will certainly hang on till our shareholders' meeting, or even afterwards, before committing his company to buy.' He grimaced. 'The more distrusting part of my soul wonders if they really want our tanks.'

'I see.'

'Still, at least the family concern is ours again.'

'Are we quite certain of that?'

'I thought you'd sorted everything out with Beauford,' Alex said sharply. 'If so, we should clean-sweep the Board of Directors – as sure as the sun rises in the east. The firm is a great thing to be entrusted with, Hugh.'

'A great responsibility, you mean,' his cousin replied tartly. 'That's what Stanton Industries is. I am conscious of that now as never before.'

Alex reached out to spin his nineteenth-century globe of the world. When he stopped it, his right hand was spread out west of the Pacific. 'Eastern Siberia to Japan,' he mused.

'Has that significance?'

'It might for some. For Saigo Hideki, for instance, who once was a power in Manchuria. And for the Russians, of course. Currently, Stanton Industries does business with every major power bloc in the world, with two exceptions: Japan, and the Soviet Union. We are an industrial empire second to none. And within that empire you and I will soon be again, as the Japanese say, *ichi-ban*: number one.'

'Except,' Hugh said dourly, 'that Saigo Hideki now controls something like one third of our shares, perhaps more, and if he forces the issue and Beauford concurs will *have* to be represented on the Board of Directors. I think you will find him a very significant number two.'

Alex showed his white teeth. 'Let's just see what happens at the shareholders' meeting. Look, what did Beauford say, exactly? There's been a bit of a splash in the press and in parliament against him representing the Japanese so actively.'

'Yes. He is annoyed about that, Alex.'

Alex spread his hands, looking innocent. He had already decided what he wanted to happen during the emergency general meeting of the shareholders. First the chairmanship, a formal office, would be taken from Lord Beauford and returned to cousin Hugh. Though Alex would continue as Head of Division for armaments, he planned to give himself an additional title: Executive Deputy Chairman. Then he and Hugh would bring new blood to the Board. But Alex intended to keep armaments as his personal domain, though his own man McCourt would run things in the division day to day. That way, if anything controversial happened over Arigata, the responsibility would be his alone. 'But he'll back us – or at least back off?'

This time Hugh frowned. 'I sincerely hope so.'

'Good. Then there'll be new civil engineering projects, too. Rapid-transit systems, new oilfields in the North Sea and elsewhere. But I think Arigata will remain the key issue, as well as our largest single

contract. The most up-to-date fast-breeder reactor in the world . . .'
Alex slung his jacket over the back of a swivel chair. He unbuttoned gold cufflinks and began to roll up the sleeves of his shirt. His arms were heavy with muscle. 'I'd like my friends David Bryant and Ray Hacker on the new Board of Directors. Would you agree? I think they'd both be very distinguished, Hugh. And formal links with America and the present party of government here are important.'

'It always makes me uneasy when I see you roll your sleeves up.'

Alex laughed, brushed back his blond hair. 'I'm not going to assault you, Hugh. I have other targets in mind.' He saw Hugh's expression. 'Most of them perfectly legitimate. So, when can we restructure our Board of Directors officially?'

'At the emergency general meeting of our shareholders. Not before. And I'm happy about Hacker and Bryant, though I don't think Bryant will be able to accept.'

Alex was satisfied. 'Maybe not. But as soon as we get through the meeting and win, we can get our shares graded high again. Then we'll be invulnerable to short term stock market pressures.' Alex looked at his watch, sighed. This was not a confrontation he was looking forward to. 'That bastard Takahashi followed me here to London, too. I think he's trying to set himself up as the old man's heir.'

'Is that a good thing for us?'

'No! I'd trust him about as far as I could throw him. Less than that, in fact.'

'Do you think Hideki at all disapproves of his employee?' Alex shrugged. Hugh added cautiously, 'If so, why doesn't he jerk his leash a little?'

'I don't know how involved the old man is in the day-to-day running of his company any more.'

'You mean he stands aloof? Out of place in the modern era? Rather like my father?'

'Not necessarily.' Alex came up on his toes. 'It might be the Pontius Pilate touch; everything is conveyed through intermediaries, so the main man keeps his own hands clean . . . Anyway, it is time we made a start. Suppose we can keep both Beauford and Hideki powerless in the company? That would be wonderful. Look, I'll get Patricia to invite Hideki here for the EGM.'

'What kind of deal with Hideki did you have in mind?' Hugh asked cagily.

'A seat on our board for him alone.' Alex raised a hand. 'I know that must surprise you. But I think he'll be flattered and that he might accept. Arigata is important to him; so is the rearming of Japan. And we hold the keys to both. Anyway, Hideki is a Victorian. He was born in the 1890s,' Alex reminded Hugh. 'He's *old*. So whatever he has in the way of wealth, gravitas and intelligence, there are still those two facts: he is eighty and he is Japanese and lives there. He wouldn't attend very many meetings of our board, I bet you. So let's lay on the flattery and offer him a meaningless honour. But – nothing else. No Takahashi. No strong representation on our board for the Hideki Corporation. Never. I'd rather keep Beauford on.'

'You think Saigo Hideki will come to us under those circumstances and he'll go along with what we want?'

'We give him the treatment: nods and smiles, anything at all – *except power over us*. We hope he can open doors for us in Japan. But for him, Stanton Industries can help open the door to the entire world.'

So Hideki came, three days before the general meeting of the shareholders, and the Stanton cousins lavished attention on him. He visited the tourist sights of London, was taken to museums and parliament and gentlemen's clubs, and spent one night at Craigburn among all that fine art and English history. He was given presents and flattery, and gave back the same.

Now it was the day of the crucial meeting. Alex was still determined that Hideki would not get active representation on the Board of Directors, and should not merge any part of Stanton Industries into his own company. Alex had to hope that Hugh had managed to square things properly with Lord Beauford. Now Alex also had to somehow make sure Hideki did not realize what was happening until too late.

He had a little surprise planned, to make sure 'too late' arrived early . . .

In the main corridor outside Alex's office Hideki suddenly stopped and pointed, surprised, at a photograph. 'Flying Japanese flag, this battleship?'

'Indeed it is,' Hugh said. 'An earlier example of Anglo-Japanese cooperation. That is the *Mikasa*, built by our own firm on the Tyne, which was the Japanese flagship when you sunk the Russian Baltic fleet in 1905.'

'I see. Against Russians, your ancestors help Nippon. As you do today.'

Alex pressed the call button for the lift. 'You know, you make this merger seem so sensible, Mr Hideki. As long as our new bankers offer support, and the board . . .' He let that trail away, one vaguely positive sentiment out of many.

On the ground floor, where a fortune in gold bars had once been displayed, he led the others from the executive elevator and through an anonymous door. Reid, his burly driver and bodyguard, made a discreet sign as they approached, to indicate that this rear lobby was empty.

'We are going straight to City?' Saigo Hideki asked. Hideki was a small man, with cropped grey hair and hard dark eyes. Words in English came awkwardly from him.

'First to the bank, and then to the meeting of our shareholders,' Hugh explained politely.

Alex could not help wondering why Hideki had agreed to accompany the two Stantons today without the usual entourage. Was he hoping to seem unthreatening?

Hideki came closer. 'You have commission deal in Japan, *neh*? Me satisfied today over board, you satisfied tomorrow.'

Alex nodded, without meeting the other man's eyes. So you become a power on our Board of Directors, Saigo Hideki, and I sell my tanks and make a whole lot of private money . . . maybe. A crock of gold, or a crock of something else.

Reid was first outside, glancing alertly up and down the side-street. Alex followed the others through the revolving door and headed for the company Rolls, a black Silver Dawn from 1954.

'Hello, Alex.'

He turned around instantly, on guard. 'You!'

'Yes.' Maggie Langton stood there, good-looking and self-confident in a quilted red anorak. She held a small microphone in her hand and a tape recorder was slung at her hip like a weapon. 'And that is Mr Saigo Hideki of the Hideki Corporation of Japan, isn't it?'

He saw that Hugh and the Emperor of Japan, Inc. had already vanished into the black limousine. Reid started the engine, and the Rolls rumbled comfortably. By the time Alex turned back to her he was overpoweringly angry. 'I never discuss the firm's business out on the street.'

'It *is* him,' she said crisply. 'And what would you like to say about your involvement in this controversial Arigata project?'

'Two words,' he snapped. 'Which you couldn't print!'

She smiled suddenly – as if a big light had been switched on. 'Care to give us an alternative quote?'

He hesitated, remembering that she was only doing her job. 'I'd better be polite. So let those two words be these: No comment.'

'What about this afternoon's extraordinary general meeting of the Stanton shareholders? Have you already come to an arrangement with Mr Hideki, without consulting your fellow directors?'

He gave her his familiar dazzling smile. 'No comment, again. But *you* won't be allowed in.'

'Anything else?' she persisted.

'How about goodbye?'

It was not a long drive to the City, EC1. The others conversed quietly, but Alex was worried. He stretched out his legs and stared at his highly-polished shoes. Arigata was supposed to be confidential. Who or what had pushed Maggie into investigating it? And, more importantly, was there anything concrete she could find out?

'We would be happy to give you, personally, a place on our board,' Hugh pressed Hideki, 'as long as you are prepared to support the other members; the members *we* intend to choose, that is.'

Hideki grunted and turned his head away. 'We must see.'

As the Rolls-Royce passed city streets full of offices, Hideki commented on one name, Old Jewry. Hugh explained that it had not been a ghetto since medieval times. Then their car drew up by the kerb and stopped. Ahead stood the fortress-like Bank of England. Clerks and messengers hurried by.

Hideki emerged from the Rolls, blinking up at the massive office building to their left. 'So, this is new bank you recommend, for us and you?'

Alex answered indirectly. 'I'm afraid I'd find it difficult to work closely with Lord Beauford again. I hope you appreciate that. I consider his actions during the takeover battle to have been unethical. And I have a Japanese attitude towards disloyalty.'

Hideki gave him a gap-toothed smile, but did not reply.

Hugh Stanton led them through the ornate entrance and into the vast, high-ceilinged lobby full of counters and clerks, and dominated by a huge clock. The bank's headquarters was built on the heroic imperial scale. They were escorted into a lift, then into the bank chairman's anteroom.

'So,' the banker said after some routine small talk, his hands folded comfortably over his paunch, 'the Stantons and Stanton Industries no longer feel entirely happy about the service they receive from Lord Beauford's bank.'

'A most discreet way of putting it,' said Hugh Stanton, in his blue pinstripes. 'And as our Japanese associate here will explain, we have some very extensive and expensive ambitions. Mergers and acquisitions, you know.'

The banker glanced from Hugh to the Japanese. 'Mergers – or acquisitions?' he asked blandly.

Hugh refused to commit himself. 'International ambitions.'

'I see.' The well-fed face glowed. This would mean huge fees.

They entered the private dining room, and talked pleasant generalities about travel and politics as the meal was served. The banker himself offered them wine, one of the *crus classés* clarets, a Léoville-Barton. Then Hugh was persuaded to sample a rich Sauternes, but Alex drank mainly mineral water, Hideki only tea.

In honour of their foreign visitor, the cuisine was English. The first course was leek and potato soup with herbs or Tweed salmon mousse. Alex spooned his soup with pleasure. The main course was a choice of spiced, delicious lamb cutlets or grilled mixed fish, with steamed vegetables and saffron rice.

After dessert, they moved into the bank's historic boardroom to begin the serious business, sitting together at the long antique table.

Alex glanced around at the famous tapestries hanging under the high windows. They were dark and wonderful, and designed, he recalled, by Lutyens, the architect of New Delhi in the imperial age. But although the bank had famous links with pre-revolutionary Shanghai and Hong

Kong he saw no sign whatsoever of Far Eastern colour and vitality on the gloomily English walls.

'We hold Stanton Industries' emergency general meeting later this afternoon,' Hugh began. 'By the time it is over I should have recovered the chairmanship, and our Board of Directors will be extensively restructured.'

The bank chairman glanced at the Japanese industrialist. 'You will support the Stantons with your own shareholding, Mr Hideki?'

The old man folded his hands together. 'I think prefer the word "co-operate".'

Alex interposed. 'At Mr Hideki's invitation I have already been to Japan, where I demonstrated a range of our latest ground armaments, including the new Mark VIII-C tank with composite armour. Naturally, buying weapons is a government decision, but with Mr Hideki's good offices there we hope for a positive outcome. If successful, we might expect contracts for between one and two hundred million dollars initially.'

'And if Mark VIII becomes accepted as standard Japanese battle-tank, much more than that,' Hideki added. 'Market is large, and increasing. Same for artillery and small-arms. And even planes, and missiles like your famous Paragon system. All for Japanese self-defence forces.'

'A series of such large contracts would greatly increase the value of your own holding in Stanton Industries,' the bank chairman observed.

'Such a fortunate coincidence,' Hideki said blandly.

Hugh said, 'As you may know, we intend to expand our links with the Kintyre Ross merchant bank. However, we now operate on such a scale that the involvement of one of the main clearing banks is also necessary – preferably one with the excellent international links of your own.'

'We are honoured,' the chairman said, smiling. He began pouring each man a small glass of whisky.

'Health,' Alex said formally, and took a sip. 'So, may we have your agreement in principal? We must leave for the EGM shortly, and we would like to announce your involvement there.'

'In principal,' the chairman said cautiously, 'I will say yes.'

As they headed back towards Westminster in the company Rolls, Alex felt well pleased. But when Hideki was again offered a seat on the Board for himself, he was merely graciously noncommital in reply, and did not indicate whether or not he would accept the position.

Alex was still determined there would be no executive influence from Tokyo on the company.

When the car stopped in a street leading to the green expanse of Vincent Square, it was raining gently: the bitter, grey rain of London approaching autumn. Alex stepped out quickly, and Reid raised a large black umbrella and opened the door for Hideki and Hugh.

'I hope this door isn't closed,' Hugh murmured as they approached the rear entrance. 'We are a little late, you know.'

'There are no closed doors in my world,' Alex said roughly, 'and this is our damn meeting.'

They had almost reached the entrance when a huddle of damp clothing under a red umbrella revealed itself as two people: a woman in scarlet, and a smooth-faced black youth.

'Hey!' Maggie was wearing the same quilted anorak. The young man with her – obviously staff from her magazine *Capital Life* – produced a large and expensive Pentax camera with flash attachments. 'Are you going to allow us in with you, Alex?'

Alex answered sharply, 'This is a meeting solely for shareholders of Stanton Industries, to be addressed by the company directors. I don't see there's any place for you.'

'Oh, there is,' she said, flourishing a piece of paper. 'One way or another.'

He steadied her wrist to read the slip of paper, then cocked an eyebrow. 'One whole share, Maggie?'

She pulled the hood back on to her shoulders, tossing her red hair about. 'Right. And that means my presence here is perfectly legitimate, doesn't it – behind the podium or in front of it! So, which way do you want it?'

'Alex . . .' Hugh began, warningly.

Sudden inspiration came to Alex, and he decided to follow his instinct. He headed for the doorway, which was blocked by two uniformed guards from the Stanton security office, both ex-military. One had a walkie-talkie dangling from his belt which emitted occasional bursts of distorted conversation. Alex waved a hand. 'They're all with me.'

'As you say, Mr Alex.'

They proceeded along a darkened passageway.

Maggie's photographer began snapping flash picturers as they walked. First Hideki with Hugh and Alex, then others. Alex found Hideki's irritation over this strangely entertaining. He knew Hideki usually shunned publicity. A door was opened.

Hugh muttered, 'I think we're losing it, Alex. We must persuade Hideki to come to terms.'

'I know,' Alex whispered. 'The stake he has in our shares is a crucial one – and we *can't* afford more trouble at board level! See if you can work on him some more. Get him to agree with our nominations to the Board. We'll do that first. Then . . .'

As Hugh nodded and guided the party forward Alex slipped away to follow the booming sound of amplified voices. He opened a side door leading on to the stage. Looking up, he saw the big screen. Here giant tanks engaged each other in distorted, cinematic combat. A shell exploded, fountaining earth. A loud voice-over spoke about the Yom Kippur War of '73 and Stanton Industries' vital part in it.

Alex glanced down at the shadowy mass that comprised the audience. Their shareholders, but fewer ordinary people than before, he knew, and that vaguely saddened him.

Several office staff were waiting for him now, and they escorted him back to the large reception room where existing board directors stared uneasily at the would-be candidates for their positions.

Maggie was probing Hideki sweetly. 'And I'm so interested in this great enterprise. Arigata.'

'Arigata?' A blank face.

'Arigata, the fast-breeder reactor. When will it be finished, do you think?'

Hideki glanced at Alex. '*Eh? Nan dess ka? Wakari masen.*'

Alex was there immediately, taking Maggie by the elbow and leading her away. 'Behave yourself. Remember, you're my guest.'

She glanced back at Kiko's grandfather and the look of repulsion on her face shocked Alex. 'This time I am. But there'll be other times.'

He could not help wondering exactly what she knew about the reactor project and how she had learned it. He took her to one of the firm's PR staff.

Hugh came over. He spoke in a quiet, angry voice. 'Why did you bring her here?'

'So that Hideki knows he'll do nothing to this firm – without paying a high price in publicity. And, believe me, he won't want to pay that price.'

Hugh considered. 'I just hope we don't pay, either.'

'I hope—' Then Alex stopped speaking, seeing another familiar face.

Lord Beauford was sitting by himself, his hands folded neatly in front of him. He looked more grey-jowelled, elephantine and unhealthy than ever.

'Ah,' said Alex, a bright, violent light in his eye now, 'come to the block for public execution, eh?'

The peer's gaze did not waver. 'It may seem that way.'

Alex glared at him until Beauford was forced to look away. Then, glancing at his watch, he turned to one of the company secretary's staff. 'When do we start?'

'There's already been a half hour's delay,' the man said worriedly. 'The PR film ends in about ten minutes. I wouldn't leave it much past that.'

'Very well.' Alex moved energetically among the crowd, shaking hands, sharing the odd joke, patting a few shoulders. He had considerable presence and he chose to exercise it now. Then he saw Maggie closing in on him. He got his retaliation in first. 'Where's your man, Maggie?'

Her face froze for a bare moment. 'On photographic assignment. Cambodia, this time. The siege of Phnom Penh.'

He found himself apologizing. 'Sorry about freezing you out from Hideki.'

She looked at him. 'What are you doing with him?'

'Business,' Alex said. He raised both hands, palms out. 'And please don't interfere. This is a very delicate situation – for Hugh, the company, and for me.'

'I was going to ask a question, on the record, about your business in Japan.'

'I'd prefer not.'

'But what,' she said toughly, 'if you're getting into something you shouldn't be, with Arigata?'

His gaze commanded her. 'I would not let this firm, nor myself, be involved in anything despicable. I would resign and take action to stop it, first.'

'Truly?'

'Have some faith!'

She sighed, then, watching as her photographer surreptitiously snapped Hideki and Lord Beauford together. 'Hideki must be one of the most powerful men in Japan. Look at those two together. Money talks, eh?'

'Sometimes it whispers, and other times it shouts.' Then Alex saw Hugh escort Hideki away from Beauford's orbit, obviously still trying to charm that stern, shrunken figure into compliance. Alex excused himself and quickly crossed the floor to give his cousin backing.

'It would be a real honour for us,' Hugh was repeating. 'Join our board: we would be most happy to have Japanese representation.'

'Then I agree,' Hideki said as Alex joined them.

Hugh's jaw dropped. 'You'll be a director?'

Hideki shook his head. 'Japanese representation, this I want,' he told them cheerfully. 'I could not possibly be present here every week. Not every month even. Therefore I must nominate someone else who can.'

Alex was already frowning. 'And that is?'

Hideki gave his gap-toothed smile. 'My assistant. Takahashi. Remember him?'

'I remember him perfectly well,' Alex said flatly. He saw how it would be. The Stanton business investigated thoroughly, its secrets learned, its markets seized forever. 'My response is this: no.'

'Alex, you're overruled!' Hugh interposed quickly. 'My cousin means we would have to consider that suggestion carefully. Although we would indeed be honoured to have you *personally* on our board –'

Hideki gazed at them, his expression innocent. 'What is problem?'

A bell rang, and the other members of the Board stood up.

Alex knew suddenly that they were losing control and that there was worse to come. Through the open doorway he heard the rising murmur of the crowd.

'But I know rules of company,' Hideki said with obvious humour. 'I must regretfully insist. Takahashi, two others and myself if you wish.'

It was too late to say more. A procession had formed, and the Stanton Board of Directors began to troop out on to the public stage.

Chapter Five

Alex looked round. This was all as public as could be. Most of the British press were here, and television cameras also. How could he turn this to his advantage? How could Hideki be controlled?

First he needed to find out what Hideki planned. Alex turned to the Company Secretary's assistant. 'You have a list of the shareholders present, and their holdings? Give me a copy. Quickly!'

He then followed the others out on to the platform and sat down behind the long folding table that had been set up in front of the cinema screen. Sitting on Hugh's left, he pored over the list, quickly finding the name TAKAHASHI, M. Takahashi was officially listed as representing some of the large shareholding Hideki had admitted to owning. Hideki's man would have the power to vote on any resolutions now put to the shareholders, with Beauford's massive weight of shares to back his decisions.

Alex cursed silently. Outwardly, he seemed calm and entirely relaxed, blinking under the bright lights towards the audience as Lord Beauford, who was still the acting chairman, gave a short introductory speech.

'As we all know,' Beauford was saying, 'there has lately been a decent, fair and entirely open contest for control of Stanton Industries.' He added some even more smoothly outrageous lies, 'This has been conducted in a frank and public-spirited way – a lesson for the City, in my belief.'

He smiled at that point, and gazed around the hall. 'It has been agreed that the final result of the takeover battle should be given here and now. The bid sponsored and managed by myself has, of course, been conducted by my own firm, Beauford Cleves, though partly powered by certain Japanese investors.

'My friends the Stanton family have been advised and supported by an excellent firm best known for its friendly rivalry with a larger and more historic financial institution – that is, my own bank. But Kintyre Ross is represented today by its senior partner Lord Ross as well as by Lord Kintyre of Mackinnon.

'Detailed figures appear in the document which the stewards are now distributing to you, but the result of the ballot in percentage terms is as follows.

'Acceptances received by Beauford Cleves, forty-four percent.'

There was a gasp. That was not far from a controlling interest.

Beauford adjusted his half-moon glasses and glanced around the hall.

'Acceptances received by Kintyre Ross, forty-nine percent.' of Stanton Industries.

'Shares remaining in other investors' hands, seven percent.'

There was a confused murmur throughout the big hall. Alex gritted his teeth, though it was not quite news to him. He and his cousin had control of the firm again, though only on sufferance. There were enough shares still unaccounted for to tip the balance one day – and both Lord Beauford and Hideki knew that.

Alex glanced down at the agenda printed on heavy watermarked paper. There were only three items.

1. To have reported the result of the shareholders' ballot.

2. To receive the Directors' Report and Current Accounts.

3. To declare that, unless there are nominations forthcoming from the meeting, the following will be elected as Directors . . .

Alex's own name was there, of course. He glanced towards the front row left, where sat the press and their photographers, all representing major newspapers and news agencies. Flashbulbs occasionally popped, and he remembered to maintain a dignified smile. The Stanton Industries story would run on a while yet, it seemed.

Beauford went on to give a quick update on the financial state of the company, but disquiet continued. Neither party battling for the firm had quite achieved fifty percent or above.

Over to the right were powerful institutional shareholders: middle-aged, sober-looking men from the City in dark suits. Alex saw his father-in-law Lord Ross sitting grim-faced with Kintyre, Alex's friend from the Borders and from Oxford. A single youthful Japanese face was behind them.

Takahashi. Hideki's man.

Alex felt furious all over again. Nevertheless, he had something secret in reserve. He stared at Beauford and wondered how much influence Hugh had over the peer.

Lord Beauford finally removed his half-moon spectacles and gazed about him wolfishly. 'Now that we have accepted, by vote, the Directors' Report and the Current Accounts as a fair and true expression of the financial state of our business, we must begin to restructure the Board. I am myself retiring as Chairman of the Board and would like to propose to the meeting that the following be accepted as directors of this company.' He turned to glance first at Alex, then at Hugh. It seemed an innocuous gaze, bland and pleasant. But as the pause lengthened, Alex became conscious of his own powerful heartbeat and of stirrings among the audience beyond the stage lights.

His collar felt tight. Now was the moment of truth. Then Beauford announced that he would read out a complete list of proposed directors in alphabetical order.

Alex leaned over and whispered urgently to Hugh, 'Look, are you sure Beauford will go along with our plans?'

Hugh was obviously struggling to put up a confident front. 'I bloody hope so.'

Alex said through clenched teeth, 'What if he puts up names of Hideki's choosing?'

Hugh closed his eyes for a moment. 'Then Takahashi and two other people are on our Board of Directors, perhaps for good!'

Then Alex turned to him, furious. 'Did you hear that? He must want to stay on the bloody board instead of gracefully backing away from the firm!'

Lord Beauford of Mancham had put his own name first on the list. But the only other candidates were the ones the two Stanton cousins had proposed. Beauford glanced across at Hideki and then said, 'I suggest after full discussion we take a vote on these names.'

Alex bit his lip, and decided that the lesser of two evils would have to be accepted – for the moment. Beauford, instead of the Tokyo contingent.

The Stantons had intended to retain only five of the former directors, and would dismiss the others, summarily and without compensation, because they were too closely identified with the old régime of Lord Beauford and fulfilled no practical function. But today Alex and Hugh needed to establish a working majority in the Board of Directors.

Somehow that seemed to be eluding them.

Alex quickly interrupted Beauford. 'I would like to propose Hugh Stanton as new chairman of Stanton Industries.'

Beauford said calmly. 'I must overrule you. Under the company rules the chairman is elected by the Board, not by the shareholders.' He smiled, clearly enjoying himself.

Alex stood up and moved over to Saigo Hideki, who sat looking totally calm. 'You will still support our push into Japan?' Alex asked crisply, coming straight to the point.

'A favour for a favour,' replied the Japanese industrialist. He was as solid as history as he said, 'You continue to help my corporation, most especially over the Arigata project, and all things will be possible for you in Japan.'

'Then you must agree,' Alex said, 'to support the Board of Directors as presently constituted.'

'You demand much. I own nearly half firm. My plans huge.'

'Damn it,' Alex said quietly, 'I've already agreed to help you! But in return, you must stand back from this firm. Leave its control to Hugh and me. If necessary, you have Beauford to look after your interests.'

Hideki said nothing.

It came in a rush. Alex felt that he was battling to save the firm: Hideki wanted to take it over, for unknown purposes. Alex remembered both that Maggie had been hinting about Arigata and his own suspicions of Hideki. 'Whatever happens today, you must hold still for it. Otherwise, I'll personally give your Arigata project the biggest jolt of publicity this world has ever seen – and I'll do it in Japan, too.'

'Arigata?' The old face showed nothing. 'Arigata is your company's biggest single contract. You yourself have signed to *personally guarantee* completion.'

'I know, but if I'm forced to I *will* tell the world what Arigata is to you.' Now, the old eyes blazed, shockingly forceful. Alex took a breath and knew he had found out something. 'So, it's agreed: you won't push things today?'

A moment. 'I agree. Today.'

Alex went back to Hugh, keeping a very straight face. 'It's all in the bag. For a while, anyway.'

'You're up to something, aren't you?' Hugh said fiercely. 'Listen, we can't stop Hideki from getting representation on our board; we *can't*, under our own rules!'

'Just trust me, Hugh,' Alex said out of the side of his mouth. 'It's important to keep the Japanese at arm's length. I'll explain why later. All we have to do for now is put up with Lord Beauford for a while longer.'

'Very well,' Hugh said, as the vote was taken. 'Unless Hideki chooses to back Beauford – which he may – we can eventually dispose of him. We are certain to command a working majority among the directors.'

'But we still have to make sure,' Alex said carefully, 'that Arigata is a big success. We need that contract, Hugh.'

Hugh, as pro tem chairman, was handed a piece of paper. It was the result of the voting for a renewed board, and he read out the names exultantly: the Stantons had control again. Except for the retention of Lord Beauford, it was a clean sweep.

Then a couple of people stood up, several rows back in the middle of the audience. 'Warmongers!' one of them yelled. 'Blood on the Stanton hands! Blood on the Stanton hands!'

It was some kind of demonstration – or worse, terrorism.

Two smoking objects were hurled at the Stantons from out of the audience. Hugh turned to Alex with shock and horror on his face, as one hit a nearby chair and rolled under the long table. 'Grenades!'

Alex grabbed for the main microphone, but already women were screaming and men were on their feet, expecting bombs and blood. 'For reasons of safety,' Alex thundered, 'I must declare this meeting closed! Please leave by the emergency exits, in orderly fashion! Stewards! Please, no panic!'

There was a loud hissing as choking white smoke billowed up from under the table.

Hideki made no move. He simply sat and stared at Alex, and Alex wondered if he realized .. . .

But it was too late to affect the course of the meeting. Hideki remained unrepresented on the Board of Directors, and the Stantons were back in charge.

The hall was full of screaming, drunken men, for this was the last bout of this eighth day of the *basho*.

The two sumo warriors stood outside the clay ring, arching their legs and flexing their huge muscles, pointedly ignoring each other. The spectators continued to cheer.

Takahashi was sitting cross-legged as he leaned over to Alan Hoyle. 'See how they do it.' The big men were very big indeed. One was Hawaiian; the other, only a little smaller, was native Japanese. 'You see how they try to dominate through sheer force of personality and will to win.'

Hoyle scratched at one tanned cheek. His hard eyes were thoughtful. 'And, as they're both Japanese, the competition is thoroughly ritualistic and rule-bound – and safe.'

'A good point,' Takahashi replied in his Harvard Business School English. 'Whereas American sports like football and boxing are all about smashing the opposition and making victory very physical and obvious – kind of self-destructive, even, from an outsider's perspective.'

In the eyes of Alan Hoyle this sumo was more ritual than combat, but fascinating in its own right. He watched each man-mountain enter the canopied *dohyo*, the clay arena sanctified by a Shinto priest. Now, the contest began in earnest, with the big drum beating. The Hawaiian stamped on the clay and for a moment outstared his opponent. They both moved up to the mark with style, flinging purifying salt about in handfuls, and their gazes locked again.

This was the moment. Hoyle watched very carefully. 'A hundred dollars on the Hawaiian,' he said instantly. 'Somebody just blinked.'

'Make it a thousand?'

'Five hundred – done?'

'Done!'

Takahashi shook a fist. More salt was thrown, then both huge fighters stepped back from close confrontation, and broad backs were turned. The referee waved his fan, crouching, and the Hawaiian seemed to swell up as he inhaled three times before turning round.

'The Little Mountain specializes in *yotsu-sumo* – the pulling-holds. He is very quick and accomplished. The Hawaiian – there they go!'

It was almost too fast to follow, and the sheer speed of it impressed Hoyle. The giant Hawaiian's features distorted with anger as he began slapping at the other man's face – the clear staccato of hard flesh on softer flesh. The Little Mountain tried to grapple, then sidestepped, off balance. The surprisingly nimble Hawaiian pushed him out of the ring.

'*Yori-kiri*,' Takahashi said. 'Forced out of contention by superior skill.'

'And superior aggression. So,' Hoyle added brightly, 'you lose your bet.'

'Luck.' Takahashi looked at his Swiss watch, looked at Hoyle. He did not like to lose, especially to a man who scared him and knew it. 'If we go now, we can beat the rush.'

They did not speak again till they were in the seventh-floor hotel room provided for Alan Hoyle. Takahashi pulled out a black instrument with an electric lead, and swept the room for electronic bugs. Even though he found none, he turned on the television and kept the sound high.

On the screen appeared aerial shots of Northern Ireland's Maze Prison, burning. Then they silently watched rioters taking to the streets in the cities, and troops on foot and in armoured cars moving into position.

Takahashi lowered the volume, though it was still high enough to drown their voices. He made no pretence of sympathy. 'Unthinkable in Nippon. Your country must be about to disintegrate.'

Hoyle sipped his whisky, shrugged. 'So it seems. A tiny-majority government, increasingly under the influence of the hard Left, things disintegrating in Ireland, Wales, Scotland – oh yes, push a little harder, more strikes and disruption, and we could see the beginning of the end.'

The Japanese stroked his thin moustache. 'We may need you again.'

'Of course,' Hoyle said languidly. He was a tall man, with a deceptively lazy way of moving; but if you ever saw him move when he wanted to be fast, you would not forget it. He had eyes of a chilling shade of grey, though his smile was ready and warm. 'That's why I'm here.'

'How is your organization in Britain, this Forward?'

Hoyle scowled for a moment. 'I let others get on with it, now. Let's say I've lost some faith in Marx and politics. Forward still provides me with recruits, though, and a trained cadre of personnel in the UK. That means espionage, surveillance of people on our enemies' list – and work for foreign governments willing to pay. And some of the students we recruit will be in high places one day, committed to our organization because of their past misdeeds.'

'Yet you live much in the Middle East? Iraq, mostly?'

Hoyle shrugged, showing his teeth. His eyes had a strange flat quality, something not quite human. 'I told you, I prefer direct action. And people who pay me for it.'

'But you will take our money, too?'

'I sell fear.' Hoyle picked at his teeth. 'Also, I spoke to Dr Sidqi. I'll be your intermediary.'

'Good. We have Arigata, but that is not the same thing as weapons.'

'And you can't do much research in Japan, can you?'

Takahashi answered honestly. 'Not yet, Alan Hoyle. Not until the government changes.'

'So do some nuclear research in Iraq.'

'Exactly.' Takahashi pursed his lips. 'But it's *vital* to us to keep that connection secret.'

Hoyle's eyes glittered. 'Now I understand. I heard you couldn't get the Stantons to knuckle under . . . so, tell me. Do you want to give me another chance to take a hit at Stanton Industries?'

'Nothing direct.' Takahashi paused. Hideki had given express orders: though he disagreed, he had to obey. For the moment. 'This is the position. The takeover bid meant we could apply pressure, and we did. We are powerful! So Alex Stanton has personally committed himself to seeing the Arigata deal through, and to providing Nippon with arms – should we choose to buy. Good for us, right? So my boss says to keep him safe.'

Hoyle raised his glass, considered it. 'Pity.'

'But maybe one day I'll be calling all the shots. If so, I'll put Alex Stanton on the list.'

'Find me, that day.' Hoyle sat back. 'Soon after, Alex Stanton will be a dead man.'

'I will shed no tears. *If* that day comes.'

Hoyle's eyes narrowed. 'Then what's the problem at the moment?'

'Inquiries about my master and his company and his past.'

'Who? The Bloom woman? Surely not!' Hoyle had arranged the killing of her husband, and the Tower of London bombing with its toll of American, British and Italian casualties should have been warning enough.

'There are always more enemies,' Takahashi said fatalistically. 'No, it seems another person you know has been making some inquiries about the Hideki Corporation. That is Magdalen Langton, the investigative journalist – your friend.'

He scowled. 'A hit on a friend? I don't know about that. I really don't.'

'No, no, that would court bad publicity! But to wipe out her sources, if she is successful in cultivating any. It occurred to me you could put one of your Forward people into her magazine office, or into her film and TV business, with a specific brief to report to you on anything she's involved with linked to Japan.'

He thought a moment, then nodded. 'Makes sense to me. But I'll monitor what she does myself. It'll cost you, though.'

Takahashi grinned. 'Money is no problem, friend Alan. The Hideki Corporation is a giant conglomerate, already strong in California and about to open on the East Coast, in Saigon and in Hong Kong, cash rich and generous to its friends. As long as we buy your loyalty for all time, and your violence whenever we judge it necessary. Sold?'

'Sold,' Alan Hoyle said.

He waited till Takahashi had left, then he went into the bathroom with the cheque in his hand. It was made out for forty thousand American dollars, drawn on a Hong Kong bank. He stuck it in a corner of the mirror, and began to strip off. He showered in painfully hot water, then came out, grabbed a towel. Naked, he grinned at himself in the mirror, flexing his big shoulder muscles. 'Who loves ya, baby?'

At the first meeting of the new board the additional Stanton directors were elected.

Alex was overjoyed at the selection. All had either notable business acumen or distinguished international contacts; and most had both. The new directors included Alex's close friend from Texas, Ray Hacker. Under the articles of the company, Lord Beauford himself could not be removed without changing the rules at another general meeting, since he still nominally represented more than a third of Stanton's shares – Hideki's shares. Hugh and Alex had to accept his continued presence stoically, and for his part Beauford restricted himself to bland sarcasms, not even bothering to attend every meeting. Otherwise, if there were hard but necessary decisions, the cousins would not shirk them. But with a united and positive-minded Board created to back them, the Stanton cousins had finished their first shared task.

It greatly pleased Alex that his colleagues seemed prepared to take his sincerity and determination at face value. He had already explained to them his plans for expansion inside Japan. The new Mark VIII-C tank was available, and the Arigata project was ahead of its speeded-up schedule. Things were going well, and Maggie's criticisms he put out of his mind.

But he did not forget Hideki: that face so expressive of supreme self-control, certainty and willpower. A winner's face, Alex knew. This combat was not over yet.

There were still problems for Stanton Industries, but Hugh risked a small rights issue to gain £55 million of new capital, which would be used to reduce the heavy burden of the family firm's interest payments, and then begin some of Alex's modernization schemes.

The actual reorganization of the company turned out to be more complicated and expensive than the cousins had imagined. However, Alex was determined that Stanton Industries had to become competitive, and its managers had to learn that they were personally responsible for the successes and failures of their sections of the firm.

Yet there were successes even in the gloom of the oil shock, though oil prices had recently quadrupled and economic despondency was general. MacKenzie, for instance, had revitalized his shipbuilding division under very difficult conditions; besides a high-tech British frigate, the first two Stanton-built oil drilling platforms were under construction, destined for the North Sea. And there was more to come – as long as the money came from Japan to support these initiatives.

David Bryant was pleased by the Stantons' success, but he already knew his own position might well be difficult.

The summer had brought rumours that the Secretary of State for Industry wanted massive extensions of state ownership. His wing of the party had demanded nationalization of private firms right across the board – and partly because of direct pressure from Forward, Stanton Industries was said to be high on the list of targets, though it was efficient and profitable. David Bryant, and the electorate, had no illusions about what that would mean – rule by trade union militants and government yes-men. People were afraid – afraid that the Labour Party and its trade union sponsors wanted political control of British industry and finance. In other words, David reflected sardonically, political control of everything – with Alan Hoyle and his sort starting to pull the strings.

The shortest parliament of the twentieth century came abruptly to an end when the Prime Minister announced that the second election of 1974 would be held on October 10th.

David campaigned hard, and this time he was almost a national figure – even profiled in *The Times*, and favourably. In his own constituency a carefully-oiled local machine swung into action. With Megan behind him he had no need to worry about his own base in Fishguard, so he was able to address meetings and appear on local television and radio all across the country.

When the results came in, almost exactly one million votes more were polled by the Labour party than the Conservatives. But this was only enough to give David's party an overall majority of just three.

Now he felt he had every right to expect elevation to government office. Megan sat with him by the telephone, as he accepted calls from friends in politics and the media, many asking which office he would be given. But the Cabinet Ministers he knew remained strangely silent, and nothing was heard from 10 Downing Street, nothing from the Prime Minister he had once risked so much for. Nothing at all.

Megan seemed more upset than he was. On the third day, they knew there would be no invitation to join the government this time around. She turned to him, lips quivering.

'Didn't you investigate that horrible Alan Hoyle and his Forward gang because the Party asked you?'

'Yes, that's right.' His chest heaved as he remembered it.

'Well, you don't fool me, David. I'm sure it was dangerous. Going to East Germany, following Hoyle! Where's their gratitude?'

He stood up to make a cup of coffee. It took an effort, but as he filled the percolator with water both his hands and his voice were steady. 'Let's not be melodramatic. Alan Hoyle has dropped out of sight. My work wasn't that dangerous, and I didn't find out anything too startling about his revolutionary Marxists infiltrating the party. But that has to be kept confidential and, yes, I suppose I would like to see some sign of gratitude from the party and the government.'

Her aim was unerring as she voiced his most secret fear of all. 'But what if it was all a typical British cover-up, David? What if Alan Hoyle and Forward have made a comfortable arrangement with our rulers, and are set to be the masters? What then?'

He made a joke of it. 'What indeed?'

But that night in bed the memories came back to him. Long ago Frank Deacon had taken him to 10 Downing Street and the question of Forward had been raised. David had promised to follow Hoyle, and he had.

What had the year been? He tossed restlessly under the duvet. It had been 1971, he thought. The winter of 1971 . . .

In his uneasy sleep, the past continued to unreel. East Germany, Siberian cold, and Alan Hoyle's ruthless stare. Then the nightmare began. Same as years before. But this time, he was going to crack . . .

He came awake choking back a scream. Someone was shaking his shoulders: but he was in that room again, and this time the interrogator would break him. 'No!' He screamed it out. 'No, I won't do what you want!'

'David!' Someone was leaning over him. 'David, what's the matter!'

The bedside light was switched on and he blinked back from shock and terror. 'Megan.' He swallowed, his throat and lips gummed up. Should he tell her? East Germany, saving himself by violence, opening himself to blackmail. Impossible. 'It's you.' And yet he had to tell somebody what had happened . . .

'What were you talking about?'

He gazed at her sleep-swollen, concerned face. His wife. The mother of his children. The one person in the world, perhaps, that he could trust absolutely.

He decided he would have to tell her. But not today.

'A bad dream. It was nothing.'

Soon after New Year's Day, 1975, David reviewed his career, sitting in his cramped study in Fishguard. So far, there had been no offers of government office, and he had made many enemies on the hard Left. So much was regressing. Political violence was still on the increase, and society was gradually becoming more and more barbaric and poverty-stricken. Last year the national product had diminished, and unemployment was still rising. Inflation was still a staggering twenty-five per cent annually. The stock market had crashed again, to a twenty-year low, after the collapse of the country's second largest oil company. Was there any chance of improvements coming? Without great effort, he feared not. Everything seemed to be conspiring to paralyse sensible reforms and play into the hands of radical groups like Alan Hoyle's Forward. First they would capture trade unions, then local authorities, then entire nationalized industries, and then . . . There need be no stopping until they had seized parliament, attacked every other centre of power and influence in the nation, and suspended elections indefinitely.

Unlike America, Britain has no written constitution. A simple parliamentary majority of the elected members makes anything legal – anything at all, even dictatorship. Repeal the Parliament Act and that dictatorship could be continued indefinitely.

So David tried. He made himself available, he wrote speeches and gave interviews, he went up and down the motorways often, speaking in support of government policy to any group of people that would give him a hearing. He crossed every barrier of politics, class and education that he could, hoping it would be enough.

On taking office after the February 1974 election the new Prime Minister had established a special policy unit, under a bright, enthusiastic, curly-haired man David took an immediate liking to. Bernard Donoughue and the others occupied a small suite of rooms near the large and decorative Cabinet Room, and this little group of experts and some of the younger, newer Labour MPs would meet to analyse the problems of the day and to criticize the usually conservative response of the civil servants to each new difficulty. David became a member of this half-unofficial steering group.

Megan questioned him about his rôle now, and he had to admit that although he revelled in his position and already had some influence on government policy, it was galling to see the competition.

'Look at the Prime Minister. Admittedly, people say that Marcia Williams pushes him around – but he has a first-class intelligence, a frightening memory, and he can work twenty hours a day. The rest are impressive, too . . . Take Denis Healey, or Jim Callaghan. Either of them would make an excellent Prime Minister. Healey was beachmaster for the Anzio landings, you know. That's the competition, Megan, and it's serious.'

'But you still want to be in the government.'

'I do. Seriously, I do. And I *will*.'

Chapter Six

Alex concentrated on his newspaper as the Rolls went sedately along Piccadilly. In Cambodia, Pol Pot's Khmer Rouge had the capital city under siege. Wasn't Maggie's man supposed to be there? Then he saw a brutal photograph of war dead which carried the byline Terry Katz. Lips pursed, he read on, wondering about his own employees within the war zone. The current news from South-East Asia was not good.

Inside White's Club Alex met Hugh. Alex was determined to talk politics right through lunch. 'David's people can't do it the easy way and with consent. But this country has to change, therefore our own party has to change, Hugh.'

'But –'

'It's too late for soft options. There is no alternative!' Alex raised a hand. 'Bear with me. It has to be Maggie.'

'But, Alex!' Hugh Stanton cried.

'Yes. Maggie.'

'A bloody woman!'

The race was on, and pressures were applied. At the start of 1975 Edward Heath, defeated in three out of four general elections, had agreed to stand in a party reselection battle. The back-bench 1922 Committee set the date: 4 February, 1975, and the former Prime Minister's leading opponent was female. He might have won had it not been for a uniquely difficult contender. Alex, fascinated, saw the ballot give her an edge. Heath had to withdraw. Other heavyweight contenders threw their hats into the ring, and it seemed the contest might be long and indecisive. But the second ballot was won by a margin of almost two to one. Three Cabinet colleagues, as well as an ex-Prime Minister, had been beaten by the MP for Finchley, a former Education Minister, Mrs Margaret Thatcher.

'Cultivating your *own* garden for a change, Maggie?'

'Don't sound so disbelieving, David. That's my only plan for this afternoon. I've just finished that promotional film for the new Elton John single, and a damn fine job I did, too – even if I say it myself! Anyway, how are you?'

'Fine,' he said into the telephone. 'Listen, I'd like to meet up with you sometime, and maybe your father.'

'And talk through some Stanton business?'

There was a silence. Then: 'Yes.'

She was annoyed. 'Alex put you up to this, didn't he?'

'So what if he did?' Now David's voice was sharp. 'If we have to change things in our industries, as we must, it's better to do it with agreement. Listen, figures don't lie, and that's what I'd like to talk about.'

'Figures for Stanton production?' She remembered what Kiko had alleged. 'Stanton Industries is in deep water, David – you should be criticizing Alex, not supporting him!'

He sighed. 'I'll try again when you're in a better mood. Goodbye.'

She held on to the phone for a moment, frowning. Then she cradled the receiver, and went and threw herself into the baggy corduroy sofa. Terry, returned last week from Cambodia, was due back for lunch at one o'clock, the chilli con carne was on the stove, and she badly wanted to run through some of her thoughts with him. She picked up her current files and began shuffling through papers, knowing now there was a story here if she could gather the resources to cover it properly: it would suit either a long Sunday supplement investigation or a television programme.

First she checked her annotated copy of the Nuclear Nonproliferation Treaty, which was meant to leave all signatory countries' nuclear facilities open for inspection. But Israel, India and Pakistan, Brazil and Argentina had not signed. Nor had South Africa. Also, her researchers said that both of the Koreas and also Iraq were thought to be secretly working on atomic weapons. Japan also had a nuclear programme but, in spite of Kiko's suspicions, was nowhere mentioned as having aspirations to possess or manufacture nuclear arms. That was a relief. If it was true.

Now she glanced at some further notes concerning Japan. The prime minister, a robust, aggressive populist called Tanaka, had needed to appoint his old rival Fukuda as finance minister and publicly renounce his promise to build a new Japan because of the great cost of the oil shock, when the cost of Japan's oil imports had quadrupled. In fact, 1974 had seen the worst economic downturn in all Japan's postwar history. An article cut from a Washington paper, describing the vast expansion of Japan's nuclear energy programme, was the only place where Arigata was mentioned.

It was after two o'clock when she suddenly looked up, smelling burnt chilli. There was still no sign of Terry, nor had he phoned, and when she went to check the stove the meal was ruined. She left the pots and pans there as a reproach for him when he returned, and she spent the rest of the afternoon in a furious rage, which cultivating her own garden failed to assuage. She brooded on Kiko as she laboured with black Chelsea soil on this sunny March afternoon, feeling hungrier and hungrier.

'Hi, Maggie! I'm sorry I'm late, but the shoot went on longer than I'd—'

'That's a fine bloody excuse! Don't you ever think of me?' Maggie threw down the trowel and sprang up in the middle of her herb garden. Elizabethan odours floated around her.

Terry Katz stood medium tall. He was dressed in a light cotton suit from a Los Angeles boutique. He looked tanned and at ease, and of course that made things worse. 'Look, I'm sorry about lunch. Christ, I jumped into a cab soon's I could!' His own voice sharpened. 'And what a mess I come back to. Stink in the kitchen, and goddamn papers everywhere else!'

'Mess?' she said, injured. 'Why should *I* have to take care of the bloody kitchen, just because I'm a woman! And as for the papers, I thought you'd be interested.'

He shrugged his shoulders. 'In all those pictures of atom powerplants and stuff? Why?'

'Because it's *important*!' Her lower lip was trembling. 'Somebody's coming tomorrow. My friend Kiko. I need to know about this atomic power business and how the Stantons are tied in.'

'The Stantons?' He laughed harshly. 'Why don't you just get this obsession about the Stantons as the fountainhead of all evil out of your head.'

She flounced indoors, trailing earth and weeds.

He was angry, now. 'Alex god-damn Stanton! That's all you're interested in! Some guy who once rejected you, or maybe you walked out on, and the only person who cares about the difference is you!'

She whirled round on him, shaking with speechless rage.

'I'm being given a chance to do another book, Maggie. Just like what we did together in the Sixties. *Vietnam Nightmare* – part two. I'm going to see real evil again, Maggie. I'm going back to that war. And, you see, I had been hoping you would help me.' He stormed out of the room and went upstairs.

She watched him go, stunned. His present to her lay neglected on the sofa: the latest Little Feat album. Abruptly he came downstairs again, carrying the light suitcase he always kept packed and ready, and his old Nikon in its battered case. The front door slammed behind him, and he was on his way to Vietnam.

All of a sudden she unfroze. 'Terry! *Terry*!'

But he had gone.

A day later a new door was opened. 'Miss Akiko Hideki.'

Maggie stood up and smiled. She was wearing a Peruvian poncho and high leather boots. She briefly embraced Kiko in the doorway, then led her into the office suite she shared with Terry. 'How is Brown's Hotel?'

'Very comfortable, Maggie, just as you said.' Kiko gave a shy smile, her face gold and exquisite and immaculately made-up. 'Very impressive.' She looked around. There were recent framed covers from the magazine everywhere. 'So many famous faces,' she added shyly.

'Terry's photographs, mostly,' Maggie said, proud and sad at the same time. 'Mick Jagger in Paris. Brando. Fidel Castro.'

'Can I meet him some time?'

'Terry?' Her voice was sharp. 'Yes, some time.'

Kiko waited a moment. 'And how are things with you?'

Maggie sat down at her desk, ordered fresh coffee. 'Fine, actually. Terry's away, but things seem to run quite comfortably in his absence. Our magazine is doing well, I pick up freelance commissions from TV and the press as regularly as I want, and the London Bridge film and video complex is doing splendidly. I had this idea for short promotional films to boost singles and albums, all dancing girls and fancy camerawork and clever images, and we've done well out of it so far.'

'I have been thinking,' Kiko said suddenly. She folded her tiny hands together and looked down at them. 'You have a friend, who is almost in the government.'

'David Bryant, the MP?' Maggie asked in surprise. 'What about him?'

'Your British government has a famous intelligence service.'

'The British government also employed Kim Philby and Guy Burgess and several other Soviet-controlled traitors,' Maggie pointed out tartly, 'in its famous intelligence services.'

'Nevertheless, they could investigate international arms dealing . . . if your friend asked for it to be done.'

'I couldn't count on him for something like that,' Maggie said. 'Not favours about the government's business. I'm afraid David is a bit straitlaced about his duties. And, besides, he knows nothing about security and intelligence work, as far as I know.'

'No?' Kiko considered, lips pressed tight and brow furrowed. 'Who can help me now?'

'Me, of course,' Maggie said impulsively, reaching forward to touch her hand. 'What do you need?'

'That proof you talked about before. And friends to get hold of it.' Kiko sighed. 'What's been happening to you?'

'I tried the straightforward approach. There is a Hideki office in London, now, as well as others in Paris, Rome and Brussels. I interviewed people and spoke to an ex-employee. The Hideki Corporation has a secret interest in arms; that's about as far as I could get.'

'When was that?'

'From October to Christmas.'

'Please be careful.'

Maggie smiled at this concern. 'Of course. But I don't think we'll crack the secrecy in Europe.'

'No? Then . . . perhaps you can tell me more about the Stantons, and their involvement in Japan.'

'I'm afraid Alex Stanton works through other people, not for other people.' Maggie said smartly, going over to a locked gunmetal-grey cabinet to take out some of her confidential files. There were five folders, each with a Roman numeral, and her own hand had scrawled STANTON INDUSTRIES on each one. 'I have the facts here about the Stantons' business, inasmuch as I can get hold of them. That might be helpful?'

'Possibly. I'm trying to see how it might all fit together.'

Maggie held up one of the folders. 'Stanton armaments – or Stanton civil engineering at Arigata?'

'They might be the same thing,' Kiko said obscurely.

'You can't say more about this conspiracy to break Article IX of your constitution?'

Kiko hesitated. 'No names yet.'

'Just a few details?'

'Please, Maggie. If I said too much, I'd be giving you the name . . .' She flinched. 'The names. Perhaps I've said too much, already!'

Maggie's instincts told her Kiko was shielding somebody. She nodded approvingly.

'I am desperate, Maggie. I have found out something more about my grandfather and Arigata, and it is terrible, but I don't think we can usefully discuss it.'

'So, what can we talk about?'

'For the moment, I'd like to talk to you about the British end of the Arigata plan.'

Maggie consulted her files in detail, going through them carefully with Kiko. 'There are still three main divisions: armaments, shipbuilding, and aircraft. Profits fluctuate, but normally Alex Stanton's armaments division generates the most income.'

The Japanese accent, with its slight lisp, seemed more pronounced than previously. 'Is he committed to weapons of war with all of his heart?'

Maggie glanced up, as the coffee came in, then a big bunch of fresh flowers. 'Alex is good with weapons; with his own hands, with guns and even with swords, or so they say. And certainly he's skilled at selling the firm's products. But sometimes he talks about a new civil projects division, with equal status to the other three divisions. I believe him. But that hasn't happened yet.'

Kiko folded her hands together. 'But that is not to say he has turned his back on weapons of death?'

'No,' Maggie said, sipping strong espresso coffee. 'I couldn't say that.'

Kiko waited till the girl had gone out again. Traffic sounds came up from Ladbroke Grove, W11. 'And this Arigata project remains under the control of armaments, and therefore of Alex Stanton?'

'That's right.'

Kiko blinked, then stared into her coffee cup. 'What is he like? A bad man?'

Maggie was thoughtful for a moment. Memories came back; a sentimental tide that almost carried her away. Then she thought of Terry Katz, her man and her business partner, who had once been the second-best war photographer in the world.

An odd couple, she thought sardonically, Terry and Alex. And me in between . . .

'No,' she said at last, closing the file. 'Not a bad man, not really. Alex has a sincerity all of his own: and a kind of harsh decency underneath it. But he is ambitious and abrasive, and a very hard man, and it took everything he had to get into the family business and make them take notice of him.' She paused briefly as more memories came to her. 'But I know he has some standards – I used to *know* him, Kiko.'

'You are a strong, sincere woman,' Kiko said thoughtfully.

'Thank you.' Maggie laughed.

'Did you ever try to change his opinions about anything?'

'About everything, yes. But I can't say I ever succeeded.'

Kiko flashed her white teeth. She was very slim and lovely, and Maggie wondered why she always wore such highcut formal dresses with sleeves. 'How does he get on with his wife, Maggie?'

Maggie flinched. 'Mrs Caroline Stanton, née Ross, is the upper-crust daughter of a rather important banker. The rumour is, I'm afraid, that Alex married her for what amounts to dynastic reasons – to safeguard the interests of his firm.'

Kiko nodded, interested. 'That was a great sacrifice, I suppose.'

'You're thinking of going to Alex Stanton, personally?'

'Could I could trust him?'

'Only if he gave you his word,' Maggie said flatly.

Kiko's eyes held a dark intensity. 'Arigata is a scandal. I am sure of it. It is a means to produce heavy metals for the bomb. Like Hiroshima, Nagasaki. A black rain that falls from a despoiled heaven, a black rain that kills. I'm sure of it. And Alex Stanton has contracted to help. Couldn't his eyes be opened – unless he is afraid?'

'Alex Stanton afraid?' Then Maggie sighed. 'Look, I doubt if I could persuade him to back out of those atomic contracts now. They are worth hundreds of millions of dollars. So he would have to deny there was any link with weapons making, even if he had suspected such a thing. And your government would back him up, wouldn't it? And maybe mine would, too. So I still don't see what I can do, investigative journalist or not.'

Kiko looked up. 'Where is your man Terry, exactly?'

In unwittingly probing the gaping, empty hurt, Kiko made Maggie feel sudden pain. Terry was going his own sweet way again – and it was not so sweet for Maggie. But she spoke briskly about his current business. 'He's over in the Nam theatre of operations, taking pictures of the war again.'

Kiko eyed her carefully. 'My grandfather has offices in Saigon, you know.'

'The Hideki Corporation does business there? I wasn't aware of that.'

Kiko looked surprised. 'Many Japanese businesses are represented in South Vietnam. Didn't you know? They make and supply many items, even napalm – in spite of our home laws. But this is a little different, I suspect. I hear that, in secret, using a front company registered in France, his people have begun to recruit staff.'

Maggie was curious. 'What kind of staff would you recruit in Vietnam?'

'What kind do you think? People who know about armaments, Maggie. How to design and build and modify them. How to service them. And . . .'

'And how to use them,' Maggie finished. She sat back. 'You're trying to tell me something, aren't you?'

'Evidence,' Kiko said. 'You told me there must be evidence.'

'In Vietnam?'

'I believe so,' said Kiko. 'I have some clues: addresses and names. But it might be dangerous to go looking.'

For a moment, Maggie allowed herself to brood about going there, and about Terry, and the Stantons, and Japan – and what might prove to be the biggest conspiracy of all time. 'You mean we could trace the people who are being recruited to work for your grandfather?'

Kiko stood up. 'And follow some of the connections back from Saigon.'

'All right,' she said suddenly. 'Give me what you have.'

'You'll do it?'

'Yes,' Maggie replied. 'I'll go to Saigon.'

Chapter Seven

She experienced a great sense of release as her flight began. England now seemed a grey and uninteresting place. She felt like the old Maggie Langton as the engines' thunder began to build and the cabin floor to shake underfoot. *Have visa – will travel.* The big Boeing accelerated, pressing her backwards. Then, after one last bump, they were airborne.

Maggie settled back in her reclined seat as the horizon over Heathrow began to dip away. The 747 powered up, up, its tilt making her a little nervous, as always.

When she looked around again, it was high above the blue-grey gleam of the Atlantic, and the signs informed her that she could unfasten her seatbelt and smoke if she wished.

She reached for the guidebook to Vietnam she had bought. It brought back to her all the simplistic slogans from the sixties. 'One side right, one side wrong – vic-to-ry to Vietcong!' It wasn't quite that simple any longer, but there *was* still right and wrong. Her mind turned to Terry, who had helped make her everything she was: surely he had not meant to hurt her.

The latest quarrel was certainly something she regretted: but she also regretted all the time and previous effort they seemed to have to put into forgiving each other. They had been together a long time now; surely they had built up too much love and hate and good and bad sex to be able to part so easily. Terry was still obsessed with Vietnam – though the withdrawal of United States ground forces meant that the conflict no longer commanded the front pages – and she knew that without her his book would never see the light of day.

But now her going to Saigon and investigating Kiko's story might be the best and simplest way to make it up with Terry. In her spiral-backed notebook she had already printed: 'Secret office within an office belonging to K's grandfather, supposed to be recruiting military men in Saigon. Find company names, addresses, investigate operations. Individual testimony if possible. Find links to Tokyo .'

It was time for the Vietnam war, all wars, to finish.

Presently she slept, and did not dream.

Saigon had changed. She stared around from the blue and yellow Renault taxi, balancing two attaché cases on her knees.

It was worse.

Beggars and other street hustlers would bang on the windows every time the battered car had to stop. Not so long ago, there had been half a million American personnel here, and their presence had addicted the country to easy money and the philosophy she had always hated: 'Look after number one'. Now, only thousands of Westerners were left, and the local economy that had been a parasite on the US presence was collapsing. The shoeshine boys were frantic for business, as were all the other street traders – who would buy *Stars and Stripes* now? Even worse was the sight of the little half-caste boys and girls who toddled around. America was in their genes, and she feared for them and their future so deeply it scared her.

It was no more than 75° Fahrenheit, yet the humidity and the stench enveloping her made it hard to breathe.

The taxi took her straight to the Imperial, the bamboo-age hotel which she and Terry had usually stayed in. It looked almost empty, and at the desk they said they were overjoyed to see her and, yes, Mr Katz had been there five, six days ago and would be back soon.

She stayed three days, reading and monitoring the radio, hardly leaving her room. In the USA they were still debating how much aid to give the Saigon régime, but much of her information about that had come to her through the distortions of Washington media gossip. Here, T-54 tanks had lately overrun Song Be, capital of a whole province; only a few Montagnards and Rangers had escaped. Then, as she was entering Vietnamese airspace, the strategic town Ban Me Thuot had gone.

Still Terry didn't show up, and the military situation was clearly going from bad to something worse. Maggie felt more and more worried. Finally, remembering the necessity for mistrust, it occurred to her to check the hotel register. That was strangely unavailable for half an hour, and when at last they showed it to her the signature of Terry Katz was a clumsy forgery.

Wherever he was, he had not been staying here. So she checked out immediately and went to the Royale.

'I'm looking for Mr Katz.' She pantomimed picture-taking. 'The photographer, right?'

Here, they confirmed they had seen him, and this time she believed them. But he had departed, and nobody knew where: maybe to Hué, maybe to follow the panicking refugees on highway 7-A.

The hotel bar had a good view of the street, so she stayed there all afternoon, drinking gin with tonic water and ice, staying long enough to get drunk and berate the occasional journalist who tried to pick her up.

She awoke at three the next morning with a headache and a dry mouth. Saigon seemed strangely quiet. Then, from somewhere far off in a northern suburb, she heard several long exchanges of automatic fire – so far away it was like something heard from outside a movie house. Obscurely comforted by this, she took a drink of water and went back to sleep.

In her dream Terry came up to her.

They sat down in a café from the old French-influenced Saigon they remembered from the middle sixties. 'It's good to see you, Terry. Where have you been?'

He looked right at her, but somehow their eyes didn't meet. 'I've been getting you what you wanted.'

'Have you?'

'Look, see.'

He dealt out his own black and white photographs one by one, between the cups and saucers and two little, empty glasses of Vietnamese alcohol that tasted worse than Turkish raki.

Finally, he showed her the last photo. It was Terry himself. He was sitting by the side of a tropical road, his back to what looked like a milestone. His mouth was open, his dead eyes stared, and flies crawled on his face. There was a ragged line of bullet holes across his chest, and the blood looked black on his white linen shirt.

'You won, Maggie.'

She was only faintly surprised. 'You're dead, you mean?'

'Yes. I finally gave you what you wanted, you see.'

She was suddenly very sad. 'Terry, I don't ever get what I want.'

He stood up, ready to walk into her past. 'Don't you?'

The following morning, she thought about her dream for a long, long time.

Earlier in the spring of 1975, Kiko Hideki had bought a tiny house up in the mountains above Lake Biwa. With her new lover, she could stroll the high pathways and pick soft flowers; summer was coming. The ripening season increased their intense feelings for one another: and on weekends Tori helped her improve the first house she had ever owned.

They created their own Zen garden out of rocks, and cut the traditional bamboo pipes to bring in water from a nearby mountain stream. The outflow made a pool on her land, and she loved the music of its tinkling water. Sometimes they could drive to Kyoto and wander around the town.

'I am happy here,' she told him, no longer weary of thought, or pained by lack of harmony. 'Can't we just stay here and forget about everything else?'

Tori was somewhat younger than her, brave and fiercely idealistic – and one of her grandfather's favoured employees. 'How could we do that, with honour?' he argued.

She rolled over towards him on the sleeping mat; her hair was tied up. 'I am afraid of him. I have always been afraid.'

'Your grandfather is running something more than just a great business,' Tori said flatly. 'He teaches his selected men Bushido –

the Way of the Warrior – and all the murderous skills that go with it. What he wants for Japan is impossible. And even if it were possible, it would be evil.'

'You must find out more about his intentions.' She gave a great sigh. 'But I love you,' she added. 'So do not risk too much.'

His youthful courage spoke: 'If we risk nothing now, then we risk all of Japan!'

She wept quietly in the darkness of the mountains, knowing he was right.

It was after the happiest months of Akiko Hideki's life that Tori discovered enough to pass on. Addresses out in Saigon, where they were recruiting weapons specialists – especially people knowledgeable about nuclear arms.

But on that day Maggie Langton could not be found.

Maggie had made her way to the US Embassy's fortified compound to listen to an uplifting briefing from some USIA man. He had maps, a slide-show, statistics, teeth that gleamed with optimism. He maintained that things in Vietnam were going well; the people supported Saigon. If the South Vietnamese complained and they seemed gloomy, well, that was just their way – and besides, Thieu and Ambassador Martin were still making a pitch for increased aid from America. Here there were still millions of men under arms, and the USA had left behind the fourth largest air force in the world. It took the Roman Empire centuries to collapse, didn't it?

One of the French press contingent interrupted: 'But they were only opposed by barbarians.'

There was a long and embarrassed silence from the speaker's platform.

After the briefing Maggie ran into an old friend of Terry's called Ellis, and from him she learned where her man might have gone.

'He was aiming to get up to Hué, as far as I know.'

'I see,' she said, trying to control her voice. 'He didn't tell me or leave any messages.'

Ellis shook his head. 'What are you going to do now?'

Early next day, she set off to follow Terry.

Hué still carried the scars of Tet back in '68. The remains of broken bridge spans sagged in the middle of the Perfumed River. On the north bank of this old cultural city stood the historic walled Citadel. Going there, she remembered Terry's stories of following Don McCullin into the marine-led battle to recapture it. But something dramatic was going to happen here, she could tell.

On the Sunday morning just after Maggie arrived, the North Vietnamese artillery began to give the city a pounding. All day the shellfire intensified, and there were rumours of tank columns crossing the DMZ. Maggie checked the situation carefully. Morale in the city still seemed good, although the crack paratroop division had recently been pulled out, and she heard President Thieu promise on the radio to use every measure to defend the former capital.

Then she learned that Terry was indeed in Hué, and where he was staying.

She finally caught up with him in the old formal gardens of the north city, where his hotel said he had gone walking. Maggie hunted him down among its overgrown and deserted waterparks and lakes, in the light of a strange misty dawn.

He was wearing baggy, military-style gear and a baseball cap, and his hands were shoved in his pockets. He slouched thoughtfully, sniffing the air. There was the sound of heavy artillery, shaking moisture out of the low trees.

He turned round and saw her.

A long moment passed before there was recognition. Then his eyes crinkled and he smiled. Somehow he looked older, or maybe it was only coming back to Vietnam, where he had left his youth behind.

'Maggie?'

She replied shakily. 'This time I followed you.'

He turned his head to the right, giving him a more quizzical look. 'I'm glad, Maggie. I'm so, so glad. It just wouldn't be the same without you.'

'No,' she said, and then she ran forward to put her arms around him.

The last sounds she heard as she closed her eyes were the heavy guns.

In the days that followed, she saw for the first time here a whole city in panic. Hué was suddenly emptying, hour by hour, day by day. Everywhere she saw hatred and fear on people's faces. Terry came and went, sweaty and bone-tired, forever taking his pictures. He could remember Tet and the naval shells landing, fired by the 7th Fleet standing off the shore, almost twenty miles away. He could remember silence and calm among the imperial tombs outside Hué, the cries of the waterfowl from among the lotus flowers on the lakes, the scent of azaleas and frangipangi. He could remember so many things, now, about Vietnam.

On their last night by the Perfumed River, he showed her a map recently brought up to date by a major in the city. Terry's fingertip traced out Highway 7-B, and then he handed her the heartbreaking pictures he had taken there of the mass of refugees – the 'convoy of tears'. He did not think the end would be too much longer, now.

'They're great pictures,' she said, tearful over all that suffering, and realizing that Terry had found himself again. 'So talented.'

That night, as Hué was completely cut off, they flew out of the beleaguered city. And by the time they were settling into their Saigon hotel, Hué had fallen. It was Wednesday, 26 March.

Terry was fully alert now. All his old enthusiasm was back; adrenalin was flowing; he was young and crazy again, running with Sean Flynn and the other war reporters and photographers. 'Christ, what difference does that billion dollars Congress is talking about make now? It'll soon be over.'

He reached for another pellet of opium.

US Ambassador Martin had flown to Washington to indulge in a round of high-level lobbying. Maggie's sources soon reported back that he had failed. It was probably irrelevant to the historical process, anyway, as she wrote: the military questions were already being solved. Though President Ford was more sympathetic than Congress, Terry and most other people said it was already too late. The Vietnam War could not last many more months, or even weeks.

Maggie was woken up by a high-placed contact early on the morning of Friday, March 21.

She rolled over in the double bed, knowing there was a story here. 'I must get an interview with the Ambassador, Frank. Can you help me?'

'Not a chance, even if he was here.'

She thought a moment. 'What else is happening?'

'The defensive front around Da Nang has started to collapse. If I know the Ambassador, he'll want to take a look for himself soon as he's back.'

She frowned into the darkness. Da Nang: a name that already seemed mere history. She shivered, knowing suddenly how Terry felt. This seemed more important than chasing Kiko's demons around Saigon.

Next afternoon, after an unsuccessful visit to the embassy to gather information, she was relaxing in her room when the phone rang. It was Kiko.

'Maggie! It's really you!'

'It really is,' she said, half warm, half apologetic. 'Was I that hard to find?'

'Yes, you were,' Kiko told her. There were several clicks on the line, more distortion than usual. 'I'm speaking from Osaka. This is my fourth or fifth attempt to get you. Listen, I have some more news about my grandfather.'

Maggie grabbed her spiral-backed notebook and flicked it open. 'Go on.'

'Apparently one of his main links in Saigon is to some people *you* will know.'

'You mean the Stanton Industries office here!'

'Not quite,' Kiko answered softly. 'To Hacker-Stanton International; to their outpost in Saigon. He wants people with special military knowledge. I suspect, for the obvious reason.'

'Well, Jesus,' said Maggie, aware her speech patterns, as always after closely encountering Terry, had become more American. 'Saigon must be about the best place in the world to go shopping for that . . . So I could set about investigating through Hacker-Stanton? That'd be a lot easier than trying to infiltrate an all-Japanese set-up.'

'Are you going to follow it up?'

'I can't, immediately,' Maggie admitted. 'I'm here with Terry, and I have to be ready for a story. A big, big story.' She closed her eyes. 'You see, I think South Vietnam is about to fall.'

There was a silence. 'I see,' Kiko said at last. 'Well, keep safe, Maggie. At least my grandfather won't be selling any more napalm there. I hope we can meet again soon.'

'Amen to that,' Maggie said solemnly.

Maggie had hired a Thai film crew from Singapore.

They all flew up to Da Nang in an otherwise empty Boeing 727 that was on charter to the embassy.

Da Nang was a huge city on the coast, now crowded with refugees – perhaps a million in all, which doubled the normal wartime population. Their presence made for unbelievably crowded conditions. As their taxi made its way through the mobs of people on the streets there were military uniforms everywhere, but no obvious police presence. Maggie saw that many of the Asian faces that turned towards her were filled with hate – and she could not blame them. Then the lights would change, and the motorcycles set off in a rush, followed by cars and trucks, then bicycles.

A man on a motor scooter slapped at her face through the open window, then gave her the finger. 'Americans go home!'

She wound the window up quickly, despite the sweltering heat. Traffic fumes and dust hung everywhere. Surges of people went backwards and forwards, and she suddenly felt frightened.

'Where are we staying?' she asked Terry. Their film crew had already been placed.

He gazed around, scowling. 'South,' he instructed the driver. 'My Khe.'

It was a long slow drive there – six miles – and it turned out to be only a pretty beach fringed by trees.

'Ten years ago,' said Terry broodingly, 'this was the beach.' He shook himself. '*The* beach.'

She didn't know what he was talking about, and so she took control of the situation by leaning over to speak to the driver. 'Back to the city, please. To the American consulate.'

The hotel they chose for their last stand was aptly named: the Alamo.

Terry continued to take still photographs, in a sweaty frenzy. Sometimes he carried a gun, and she knew he was smoking opium again. In the increasing chaos, it did not seem to matter. Perhaps his photographs would be the only honest record: the images that did not lie.

It was immediately obvious that Da Nang was falling. They filmed one tense discussion in a USAID project near the harbour. The officials were talking days, not weeks.

Back in their hotel room, she pleaded quietly. 'I wouldn't mind hitting Saigon again, when this is over. I've got another story I want to follow up.'

Terry unrolled a military map on their bed.

'It won't be long now till we have to leave anyway. Look.' He fingered some features of terrain on the map, and the pencilled outlines over them. 'To the north, the west, Elephant Valley; from there the NVA 324B and 325C Divisions are moving to envelop Da Nang. In the south two other crack divisions are pressing up through Duc Duc and Dai Loc. They'll unlimber their field artillery soon, and start opening up on the city. And that'll be the end.'

That night, they saw their film crew on to the Air America plane, carrying their cans of unedited 16mm film.

Later, the shells started falling, their dull, flat explosions seeming ever closer. Maggie went up to the open window, naked. Flashes lit up the sky, and a fire had started in the distance. There was the racket of small arms from all around, though whether it came from VC infiltrators or the army shooting looters or shadows she could not tell.

They headed down to the hotel bar to find out what was happening, though they could already tell it was serious.

'Is time for you to go,' they were warned. 'The radio relay has been hit. Now we no talk to Saigon.'

She turned to Terry. 'Looks like we should try the consulate next door, or maybe get a boat out – if you're ready to leave.'

He blinked his red eyes at her. 'Right. First grab the bags. Then the port, I think.'

They decided to head towards to the harbour on foot. The local curfew had collapsed. All the lights in Da Nang had failed, but people in uniform and out of it still crowded the streets. From one nearby house they heard the short, brief bark of an M-1. People screamed and scattered, but Terry was laughing. She wondered if he was stoned again.

'Terry, we *have* to get out of here!'

Divisions of the North Vietnamese Army were tightening their stranglehold on the city, and panic had started. Maggie peered through the half-light as searchlights from the ships in the harbour stabbed at the night sky.

There were crowds also on the dockside – and too many trying to get in through the gates. Armed guards fired their M-16s over people's heads and would not let anybody in, so the crowd was howling in protest.

Even Terry sounded worried now. 'Are we ever going to get out of here?'

Navy vessels large and small thronged the harbour. Searchlights from the larger ships dazzled her regularly, but Maggie could see sampans and Chinese junks pulling away from the shore, many of them packed with refugees.

Terry turned to her, his face green in the light of the dying flare.

'There are probably Vietcong among that mob trying to storm the main gates.' Desperation edged his voice. 'There's no chance of us getting through.'

'Let's try the rest of the base. There must be *somebody* who'd let us in.'

They hurried along in the darkness. Once they passed a café from where radio music spilled out, and they could see men drinking by the light of hurricane lamps. The naval base at Da Nang was huge, but they could not seem to find anywhere to get through. There was the sound of more gunfire in the city.

'Hey, American! I can help!'

Terry halted.

The voice belonged to a navy lieutenant carrying a shortwave radio and sports bag. He was able to contact a fast patrol boat, and for 200 US dollars and Terry's stainless steel watch, he led them straight to a gate in the wire fence. There was only one guard, but he turned his machine-gun on them and snarled something in Vietnamese that clearly meant they should go away. There was a rapid-fire conversation between the soldier and their guide, too colloquial for Terry to grasp.

The lieutenant turned back to them with a mirthless grin. 'He tells me in every crowd now there are communists, dressed in our uniforms. I ask if he thinks you are communists, or I. But he says he has his orders.'

Terry's eyes were wide, his fingers hooked into the fencing. 'You mean he isn't going to let us in?'

Maggie looked anxiously along the darkened street. The ARVN marines had been getting drunk enough to start looting and shooting civilians. If they didn't get out soon, it would be too late. Behind them she saw only unlit warehouses, their corrugated iron roofs glistening faintly. Then she heard the scuffling of feet, and the guard turned angrily, his M-16 aimed at the darkened street. 'VC! VC!'

It seemed to happen in slow motion. The lieutenant's hand jerked out of his sports bag clutching a gun, and there was one sudden blast as he fired. The guard's head snapped back, then he stumbled forward and sank to his knees. Blood spilled down his face. He had been shot neatly in the forehead. A group of men carrying guns rushed out of the darkness. A huge pair of bolt-cutters snipped at the chainlink fence, and the fake lieutenant waved the men on with his free hand. All the time he trained his pistol on Maggie and Terry.

She was starting to panic. 'No,' she said. 'No, don't!'

'I might shoot.' He gave a wild laugh. 'I might, for my country. If I kill one of my own countrymen, why shouldn't I kill you?'

They had no answer to that.

When the last of the VC sabotage squad was through, he finally gestured Maggie and Terry on into the naval base. 'You tell them, television lady, we liberate. We did not kill you!'

Still terrified, they slipped from building to building until they reached the waterfront. Here they found an American in civilian dress who was barking into a walkie-talkie. Sirens wailed. After discussion, he got them on to a fast boat.

Shells were exploding in the city, and shells whistled overhead, sometimes plunging in the sea nearby. Then, at last, the engines of the boat started up with a roar; and the boat swirled to the right, heading for the open sea.

Maggie looked round at Terry. They had escaped on a mutual adrenalin high, but now she wanted this adventure to end. It had terrified her. She remembered the soldier shot at the gate. In a sense he had died because of them.

Terry stretched his legs out tiredly over their luggage. 'That was great.'

About two hours after dawn, a helicopter airlifted them to USS *Mason*. It took some talking after that, but they were able, eventually, to send Terry's pictures out through Hong Kong, and transmit her dispatches to newspapers in Washington, New York, London and Paris.

As Alex took breakfast in the tall Stanton Industries headquarters on Millbank, an early-morning mist was burned away over the Thames; it looked like a Turner seascape, but his mind was thousands of miles away. Maggie's words in her report seared him.

He threw down the newspaper. Where was any good news? Electricity prices had risen by a third, and the government had just announced that huge financial losses meant it had to take over the vast Belfast shipyard complex belonging to Harland & Wolff, where Ken McCourt had started his career.

His cousin Hugh came in, with some xeroxed proposals for setting up the civil projects division formally, perhaps with McCourt as its head.

'No,' Alex said flatly. 'I want everything to do with Hideki and our business in Japan to go through me.'

Hugh regarded him coolly. 'Alex, I'm not exactly a fool. It's become quite obvious to me you want both to keep Mr Hideki and his corporation at arm's length *and* do business with them. Do you mind telling me why?'

Alex gave a brief laugh. 'Because the less you know, the less you're responsible for – and the less blame could be attached to you.'

'If anything goes wrong?'

'Exactly.' Alex took a breath. 'Look, as far as I'm concerned, Hideki is no more than a tradition-minded Japanese businessman with a *zaibatsu* background. But I have an instinct there is much more to him than that, and if we are risking our position by associating with him, it's only right that the major risk is mine and not yours.'

Hugh collected the papers, a little hurt. 'If you say so, Alex.'

'I do.'

About an hour later Hacker rang up.

'Alex, I'm having trouble getting the State Department to see reason about our people in Nam.'

'What do you mean? They've promised refuge, haven't they?'

There was a pause. 'I don't like what's happening.'

'Right,' Alex said. 'I think I can clear my diary for Friday. I should be in Saigon by –'

'No. Alex, I'm going to fly out there myself and take care of our own.'

'Good luck, cowboy.'

It was happening quickly, now. As Hacker flew in, the North Vietnamese Army's advance was leading to the rout of the South's forces. On 3 April, order in Cam Ranh Bay suddenly disintegrated. There was panic and violence, before the NVA echelons arrived to restore order and continue their advance south. When the United States Information Agency questioned its local office about the current mood in Saigon, the reply was 'fear bordering on panic'.

A few days later President Ford addressed a joint session of Congress and the Senate. Maggie watched it on a satellite relay.

'Members of the Congress,' Ford said, 'my fellow Americans, this moment of tragedy for Indochina is a time of trial for us. It is a time for national resolve –'

Even as the President spoke, two Congressmen walked out on him.

Chapter Eight

Rumours abounded in the city of Saigon. It was said the next big attack might start the final collapse.

Terry was inclined not to believe that. 'Xuan Loc is only thirty-five miles from Saigon, so it'll have to be reinforced. It's too close and too important for the top brass to screw up this one.'

'If you say so,' Maggie said worriedly.

He eyed her, scratching at his stubbled chin. 'You want to follow up that Hacker-Stanton lead, don't you? Well, I've got some news for you.'

'Yes?'

'Just heard it from the embassy, our favourite CIA man there. Ray Hacker is in town.'

'Christ, is he? And he might,' she added thoughtfully, 'he just might be willing to help.' Here in the wreckage of South Vietnam, with millions of enforced refugees and tens of thousands dead, Kiko's story had taken a back place in her mind. When she managed to get Ray Hacker on the phone, he sounded harassed, but agreed to see her later that afternoon.

The intervening hours gave her time to make her story persuasive. In this twilight of American influence in South-East Asia there was no certainty at all that Hacker would be in a cooperative mood. Politics had always divided Maggie and him; but as the barriers between the two Vietnams were beaten flat that might make the political divides in the West even worse.

But she knew she had to try to find out more about Hideki, if only to save Alex Stanton from himself.

Under the slow-spinning fans of his sweltering office Hacker was a brooding presence. He wore a check shirt, Levi's, and his old cowboy boots. As Maggie sipped coffee, he tugged at his eye-patch and frowned. 'Just run through it all again.'

'Look, I know you and Alex do lots of business with Tokyo, but if this Hideki really is setting up an arms industry in Japan, you can say goodbye to your contracts there and say hello to the stiffest worldwide competition you can imagine.'

'That makes sense.' He nodded. 'And you think he's using Hacker-Stanton and Alex to help get his war industry off the ground?'

'That's the story, right?' She spread her hands. 'I've been told you've had trained personnel poached by him.'

Hacker sat up straight, his big fists clenched. 'Have we, by God?' He threw her a bitter glance. 'But, then, I keep forgetting we won't have too many jobs to offer here in Vietnam pretty soon.'

'Let's at least find out, Ray. Then you'll know what you're dealing with. Then you can inform Alex. Right?'

He shook his head. 'You want to keep the guy out of trouble, huh? Mother Duck or mother fuck, it's all the same to my boy Alex!'

'I don't think so,' she said primly. 'But I think we'll have to do this quickly.'

'Quickly!' He swung around in the swivel chair. The large Hacker-Stanton compound was visible through the window behind him, enclosed by its high walls. Employees and their families, fleeing from the conflict, were camping out in squalor among the huge containers. 'You're damn right.'

She could not lie. 'I'm not sorry that this corrupt government here in the South is finally on its way out.'

Hacker grimaced. 'Because you reckon those puritan bastards up in the North aren't corrupt? They might torture and murder, they might know nothing about democracy and care less, but as long as they're poorer than you and me, and don't watch Hollywood movies, they have to be saints, right? Just the sort of thing your old friend Alan Hoyle would say!'

She clasped her hands together. Alex must have passed that on. 'I'm entitled to my opinion, Ray.'

'Right. But a guy like me, rough-looking' – here he touched the scarred cheek below his black eye-patch – 'with manners as bad as his grammar, is just not as entitled to have an opinion as you, you think? Except I do. And I'm not some desk-bound capitalist, Maggie. I fought in Korea, understand: I *volunteered*. And my sister's kid died here in Vietnam. He was killed in an ambush near Tan Son Nhut just after Tet.'

'Killed for what?' she asked Ray very softly. 'Certainly not for the everyday people in the States.'

'All right.' Hacker twisted his shoulders, weariness in his face. 'Maybe that's true. But America is the big guy in the world, and I'm all for that. I don't want to live in a powerless country, and I happen to think we do a pretty good job as world policeman. Who else d'you want? But the likes of me, we pay for that position, Maggie. And we have paid in blood, in Vietnam and other places. At the very least, that gives us a right to an opinion!'

She reached for the cup of cooling black coffee, and sipped from it. 'But look at it from the point of view of the Vietnamese. The French, the owners of everything here. A corrupt puppet régime with a puppet emperor, set against a patriot like Ho Chi Minh. Then the Americans come; more white faces, more white owners. And a similar corrupt régime. That's all. A difference that makes no difference *is* no difference.'

He shook his massive head. 'My sister's kid was hardly more'n twenty when he was killed, and he owned not a thing.'

She bit her lip. 'He's dead, and that's still another thing here to be sorry about.'

He spread huge hands: his face was partly appealing, but mostly scornful. 'But you still don't see it. Listen, of course there are Communists here. I understand that. The VC inherited a lot of freedom-seekers, nationalists, whatever. But tell me this, Maggie Langton. If everybody here loves the brand of Communism north of the DMZ so much, why do so many of them head south instead of north whenever there's trouble? You and Terry have seen those convoys yourself! Or maybe you think the refugees are affected by US propaganda? Hell, you can't *really* believe that they all watch CBS and read the *New York Times* and make up their minds about the North from that!'

'There's no point in getting mad with me.'

He said it grudgingly: 'I suppose not.'

'So, you are going to help me? Just in case Saigo Hideki really does end up as your competition – or your conqueror?'

'All right,' he said. 'Nam is our turf – or it used to be. American boys bled to try and keep it that way.' He pressed a button on his desk and a buzzer sounded. 'Is Van there? Send him in.'

A slender Viet leaning on a cane came in. He looked around, smiling. He was aged perhaps thirty, though it was hard to be sure.

'Van Tien Trung,' Hacker said, 'meet Maggie Langton. Alex's old – friend.'

He offered a smile that showed red betel-stained lips and teeth: an honest smile that Maggie liked.

'Hello,' Maggie said.

Hacker flicked through some papers. 'We have your entry clearance for the States.'

'Fine,' said the man, relaxing.

'Van was once a captain in the ARVN,' Hacker said. 'Engineer.'

'Good. There's something you can do for us,' Maggie told him. 'We hear there's a firm in Saigon fishing for people with armaments experience. We'd like to find out some more about it.'

'So I'll be an expert in US arms? What do you want to discover, exactly?'

'Just some details. To see what they're up to, especially if there are links to Japan.' Maggie passed across a piece of paper. 'This is the address and the name of the contact there.'

Van looked down. 'When do you need to know?'

'I'll be back in a week,' Maggie said, then, thinking about the military situation, corrected herself. 'Less than that. You can tell me everything then.'

Hacker blew her a kiss.

* * *

The golden-skinned girl pulled back from the office window, then pointed. 'That's him. With the walking stick.'

The man did not hide. He squinted along busy Tu Do Street. 'Other side of the road, heading for the cathedral?'

She glanced out again. 'Yes.'

As the man turned to her there was a strange sense of threat in the room. 'That's the second time he's come in, hinting he has secrets to sell?'

'About Hacker Stanton International. And he says he has been in America, working on missiles.'

'You don't believe him?'

She hesitated. 'It's true he was a captain in the local army, and he has been to the States. We could check that.'

There was a hand on her shoulder. It did not exert great pressure, but it gripped. 'Next time he comes in, give him an address I'll tell you – memorize it, don't write it down. Tell him to come at noon on Sunday.'

Fear was in her. 'Anything you say.'

'As soon as you've done that pack your things and fly home to Tokyo – the very same day. Understand?'

'I can't do that! My job –' She stifled a scream.

'Just do what I tell you.' The dark grey eyes smiled in enjoyment as she gasped in pain. 'Right!'

'Whatever you say,' she said miserably, rubbing her bruised shoulder.

'Another thing,' he added. 'You won't be seeing me again, of course. In fact, you didn't meet me at all. I might be Irish, Canadian – anything. But you don't know. And if you *ever* tell anyone . . .'

'I wouldn't!' The voice shook with terror. 'Never!'

He was satisfied. 'Now, go back to work. And when that man comes again, do what I told you. Then go home to Hiroshima.'

The next morning Terry Katz and Maggie flew up to Xuan Loc in a green Chinook helicopter. Then a friendly ARVN lieutenant drove them towards what passed as the front line in a jeep.

Through binoculars Maggie could see ruined houses with blasted, bullet-pocked walls. There was confusion as they neared the action that seemed worse than ever before.

They stopped at a checkpoint and were greeted by the sight of a bloated corpse in loose pea-green NVA uniform beside the road. Everybody seemed to ignore it, despite the stench of flesh corrupting in the heat, and the swarming flies.

Terry grabbed his Nikon and jumped out. Maggie stepped down too, her stomach turning. This was the first *bo doi* from the North she had seen at such close quarters. Had he been young, as so many of them were: sixteen, seventeen? Full of youthful conviction, or just a frightened conscript for Communism? It was impossible to tell from the swollen disfigured face, and suddenly all those distinctions seemed irrelevant.

Prowling about, Terry snapped some shots. Distant crackling sounds sometimes drifted over: small arms. The crump of mortars was much louder, but irregular, and in spite of everything she could do she kept ducking instinctively at the sound.

Their lieutenant had gone into a huddle with another officer, and suddenly he called them over. He seemed very young and enthusiastic. 'The NVA, they try to outflank. You want to see more?'

'Sure,' said Terry.

They were waved through, the guards here looking grim, their weapons at the ready.

A line of empty, bullet-riddled houses faced a stream, with rice paddies on the other side. There was an ancient watchtower further down the road. There had clearly been a successful defence here. Maggie saw a few uniformed ARVN sprawled by the roadside, looking tired.

The tarmac road led up into some green and peaceful-looking hills, though the sounds of battle were even louder now. Maggie had a bad feeling about all this, but Terry was talking with nervous rapidity to the lieutenant and seemed hardly aware of his immediate surroundings.

'I was up in Khe Sanh after it was abandoned. Creepy, man. It got used as a temporary base for Nixon's kick into Laos in '71. You could walk around the old perimeter of the base where the marines killed so many and I used to watch the big splashes of light and colour from the B-52 bombings as napalm went over Route 9, which was the road into Laos.'

'I wish you could give us some B-52s now,' the lieutenant said quietly. 'Or even some gas.'

'The Yom Kippur War –' Maggie began, then shrugged. 'There're fuel shortages all over the world.'

'But here the shortages mean literally life or death.' They made no reply. Flies buzzed. He sighed, and said, 'Let's move on.'

They saw a burned-out tank by the side of the road: an American-built M-48. Shellholes were common, mostly part full of water. They passed a blown-apart NVA tank, a T-54.

A Cobra chopper in the colours of the south suddenly came up from behind some trees to their left. She saw it hover, insect-like and dangerous, biding its time before it stung. They drove on slowly, and now there were organized bodies of ARVN soldiery on both sides of the road, some huddled into lightly-dug fighting holes, some sprawled unhappily with their hands on their helmets.

Then a salvo of shells boomed by the side of the road. Her ears were ringing and dirt was flung at her face.

'Out!' Terry yelled.

They ran across the road, into some scrub. More explosions erupted behind them: huge ones. Feeling sick, Maggie scrabbled into the earth for safety and wondered if, incredibly, the North might be using bombers.

'I think it's big artillery,' the lieutenant yelled. 'The Soviet 130-millimetre field guns – very far, too far for our guns to hit.'

There was shouting now among the ARVN troops.

'Can't you use air power?' Maggie asked, wishing she had a steel helmet and a flak jacket.

'Oh, Jesus,' Terry said. 'Look up the road!'

They emerged from the green of the jungle, covered with branches tied on as camouflauge. First one tank, then two following, then three or four more: T-54 tanks. Behind them trudged men in NVA uniforms. Immediately the Cobra hopped higher and began unloading its rockets: orange-white explosions appeared among the tanks, and one veered from the road, hit. The lieutenant stood up to cheer.

Then the chopper exploded in mid-air, deafeningly. Fragments of it whistled past them.

'A SAM missile,' Terry said, snapping pictures. He sounded delighted.

There was ongoing small arms and mortar fire, though Maggie didn't think it would be enough to stop the tanks. Her head pounded and her hands were shaking.

'I take you back, away from front line. See the big brass.'

As they clambered back into the jeep, Terry suddenly waved at a passing car. His face was excited.

'Somebody you know?'

'That's Peter Arnett. A great guy. I met him in '65 when we landed at Da Nang – that beach I showed you there. He helped me out of the Marines and into this business.'

'He must be going to interview the general, too,' Maggie said thoughtfully.

The general was Le Minh Dao, who ran the 18th Division of the Army of the Republic of Vietnam. At his briefing, later, they saw him stalk about in front of a map board, gesturing and talking sometimes in Vietnamese, sometimes in English. Behind him there was an impressive row of 155mm Stanton field artillery.

The North Vietnamese were very bad soldiers, he said. Maggie, appalled, saw her press colleagues write it down. The broken spire of Xuan Loc's Catholic church seemed to quiver at the artillery shocks. 'I have beaten off six attacks in four days. I vow, now, to hold Xuan Loc, however many divisions the enemy sends against me!'

Terry leaned against her. All around them were reporters, film cameramen, photographers, treating this sideshow as something important.

Maggie lowered her voice. 'Talks a good war, doesn't he?'

Terry spat his contempt onto the soft ground. 'This town'll be by-passed, if it's likely to cost the NVA too much blood. And as soon as it's surrounded, morale here will crack.'

It seemed terribly simple.

The NBC crew filmed Maggie as she stood up to ask a question, looking particularly striking against the background of slouching soldiers, the line of guns. Abruptly a heavy machine-gun opened up from somewhere in the rubber plantation, and bullets tore through the air just over their heads. She turned when somebody screamed. A heavy-calibre bullet had hit something human – and she could tell that human was badly hurt.

It was two days before this film reached television screens in America and Britain. Viewers saw Maggie turn and drop into a half-crouch. The camera caught her shock, then fear, as the man beside her was hit. Then the camera swung, confused, to show a crazily tilting sky and then running, uniformed men.

The 18th Division fought hard, but to no avail.

Xuan Loc was doomed.

There had been nothing but the runaround for Van Tien Trung for three days. Now it was Sunday.

As a door closed behind him, Van settled on a rickety chair and glanced around the shuttered of a run-down warehouse in Cholon, the old Chinese quarter of Saigon.

Three attempts to interview the Hideki executive whose name Maggie had provided had left Van talking to the man's secretary. Finally, she had given him an address – this warehouse, owned by a Marseilles-registered import-export firm. But something in the ambience here bothered him; he frowned. Too quiet, maybe, even for a Sunday. On the wall was a tattered calendar from 1973, full of half naked girls and a French text. He suspected that the man who had let him in was a Corsican. In the old days, when the French Foreign Ministry ruled here, Corsicans had been important figures in the Saigon underworld. From outside came the occasional sound of artillery fire. Then the far door rattled and he turned to see it nudged open by a foot.

'Excuse me,' said a man, in English, backing into the room. Reaching the desk he turned around, his arms full. A tall European, with strangely commanding dark eyes. He put everything down on the table in front of him: a hacksaw, chains, padlocks, then a gun. 'Hello.' He gave a strange smile. 'You say you've had advanced weapons training back in the States.'

'Right,' Van replied, eyes on the gun. He reached for his walking stick. 'I heard you might get me into a good, high-paying, high-tech job somewhere.'

The grey-eyed man blinked. 'Where did you have in mind?'

'America.' Van smiled. 'Japan.'

The man looked at him more closely. 'So who sent you?'

Van gripped his stick between his knees. 'I sent myself.'

'You sent yourself? Only, I hear you're the one who's been asking questions about trained military personnel going from here to Japan.'

'No, no! Only questions about my own future, you understand.'

'I'd better introduce myself.' The man stood up. He had a low, casual voice. His gaze was unmoving and scary.

Van found he had to force out the words. 'Who *are* you?'

The sudden smile was terrifying. With a rush of nausea Van understood the meaning of the chains and locks, and the rusty sawblade.

'My name is Alan Hoyle.'

As Hoyle picked up the gun and cocked it with one sweep of his thumb Van Tien Trung felt very frightened indeed.

With Xuan Loc about to fall and the North Vietnamese Army continuing to make general advances from its safe havens in the North and Laos and Cambodia, the situation had become frighteningly clear. Over half the country was already lost: all of military regions I and II, and millions of people. But there was still the last act of the Vietnam tragedy to be played out.

Terry was determined to stay till the end. He had friends in the French Embassy, and other diplomatic connections that he thought led to Hanoi. That should mean safety.

'Are you sure?' Maggie reached over to touch his hand. They were having lunch on the paved terrace of the Continental Palace Hotel – where Graham Greene had set one of the scenes in *The Quiet American*. 'It sounds dangerous to me. Too dangerous.'

He sighed. 'Staying till the fall of Saigon and then beyond, if it happens . . . I must take the risk. I just have to know it's really over.'

She found she was getting upset. 'Why, Terry?'

He was staring blankly, as if into the past. 'I was here right at the beginning, Maggie, when I was in the Marines. I knew even then it was going to be the tragedy of my generation. It's been my life, my politics, my career – Nam has been everything.'

'Everything?' What about me? she wondered.

But he was no longer listening. He leaned over a copy of the Saigon daily *Chinh Luan*, his eyes full of memories. 'They call us *de quoc My*, imperialists, but I remember 1965 even though I was no more than a crazy kid and I was already regretting enlisting. We were sent into Da Nang.'

'You had to storm that beach we went to?'

He laughed strangely. Other heads turned; but there was always the sound of hysteria in Saigon, these days.

'It was about nine o'clock in the morning when we hit the beach. Everybody armed to the teeth, inside amphibious, armoured landing craft. I had my M-16, and I was ready to take a few gooks with me before I died. But you'll never believe what happened. As soon as I saw our reception I knew the US was going to fuck up and lose.'

He was angry, now, and she could imagine why. Now, in his moment of remembered pain and weakness, her compassion flooded out to him. 'It was bad. Your buddies took a lot of casualties?'

'No,' he said in disgust. 'They had schoolgirls carrying flowers for us, big banners saying "Vietnam is happy to welcome the US Marines". And the mayor of Da Nang, he had a camera. He took my picture, then he shook my hand. That was my welcome to Vietnam. And sixty thousand US dead since.'

When she phoned Hacker he invited them to his office at once.

He stared at them sourly, clearly both tired and concerned; but Maggie saw there was determination in that lived-in face. 'He never reported back?' she asked.

'No. I haven't heard anything from Van since yesterday. And all I have is an address.'

Maggie said sharply, feeling responsible, 'You could have done something already.'

He waved his arm at the big walled yard full of camped-out refugees: more than before. 'I do have a few other things on my mind, Maggie.'

Terry nodded. 'How much do you actually know?'

'He phoned in to say a secretary had directed him on to another place, a business in Cholon. Van hasn't reported since.'

'Shouldn't we get the police in on this?' Maggie suggested.

Hacker cracked his knuckles. 'I don't want any kind of publicity. We oughta follow it through ourselves.'

'You think so?' Of course, Ray had his own interest in this affair, and he was anything but timid. But she admitted, 'This might be dangerous.'

Terry stood up, turned away and swallowed something. Maggie guessed it was probably speed. 'Let's do it.'

It was hot out on the street. Hacker led them towards a battered old Cadillac. Hand on the door handle, he turned.

'Far as I know, curfew's still at 2100 hours.'

Terry nodded excitedly. 'That'll give us enough time.'

Hacker got behind the wheel and they drove through the crowded streets, where chairs and tables were still out in front of cafés, towards Cholon, the old Chinese quarter of Saigon.

The signs here were vertical; but the Chinese script was no less indecipherable to Maggie than Vietnamese. Occasionally she glimpsed the river between the run-down warehouses with quays extending beyond.

They stopped eventually, outside a warehouse: the number 7 had been whitewashed on its big closed doors. A dog was barking somewhere nearby.

Maggie looked up and down the dead-end street; it was strangely empty of people, and traffic. Only run-down warehouses; a yard full of wrecked cars behind a high metal fence topped by razor wire. A black junkyard dog was prowling up and down and barking a challenge to the world.

Hacker pulled a heavy automatic pistol out of his shoulder-holster, cocked it, and held it ready in the palm of his right hand. He threw a glance at Terry. 'Ex-marine, right? Open the glove compartment.'

Terry stared at Hacker, then fumbled and withdrew a pistol. 'A thirty-two,' he said quietly, checking the action.

Hacker climbed out and looked up and down the street. It was late afternoon: steamy Saigon at its hottest. He went up to the wooden doors of the warehouse, and banged on them with his big fist. Then he turned to the others. 'Either of you speak gook? I don't know more'n a few words, myself.'

'That figures,' Terry said tightly. He held his gun out of sight in a pocket, but Maggie stared in fascinated horror at the bulge it made. 'I'll do the interpreting, if needed. Media, you know?'

'Media!' Hacker was suddenly enraged. 'I got almost three hundred people back in the compound that need new homes where the Commies can't get them! Why don't you use that media pressure on the goddamn embassy here, and get the evacuation speeded up!'

But then the door opened. An elderly man with a Ho Chi Minh goatee looked out suspiciously. 'All finish,' he said. 'I caretaker stay. All finish, all empty.'

Then Hacker showed his gun. 'Just get the fuck out of my way! I'm looking for someone!'

The face shuttered. 'Nobody here.' He tried to close the door.

Hacker's big foot held the door ajar, and he pressed his automatic into the old man's gut. 'Where is Van? Van Tien Trung, understand me?'

'All empty!' the man protested again. He began to babble in French that the place was private. Replying in Vietnamese, Terry told him to just stay put and no harm would come to him.

Hacker barged in, gun first. Maggie quietly followed him.

The huge ground floor of the warehouse was virtually empty, except for some big empty packing cases on the right. She noticed they carried addresses that ranged from Osaka through San Francisco to Middlesbrough in England. Something scampered by her foot.

Hacker turned in a slow half circle, the gun in front of him all the time as his eyes adjusted to the gloom. A broad staircase on their left went up to the next floor. Suddenly, visibly, he relaxed. 'I don't think there's anything left here. It's just too quiet.'

She sniffed, moving forward. 'Nasty stink, though.'

'Like the rice-paddies?' He gave a harsh laugh and followed her. 'We both know how *they* get fertilized!'

'It's not like the rice-paddy smell.' She pushed through the doors at the rear. In front of her extended a narrow concrete dock with some old chairs in the shade and, beyond, the wide river itself with its countless boats. High walls hid this dock from the buildings to either side. Winches jutting from the top storey still dangled wire cables with hooks. Taking a stick, she poked through some burned papers that had been left inside a bin, finding a few animal bones underneath, but nothing significant there. An old girlie calendar and some newspapers were all else she could identify.

She sighed. Whatever had happened to Van, he was not here.

Hacker came to join her, glaring at the junks moored in the river. 'No point asking those bastards if they saw anything.'

'Ray,' she said to the big man, not unkindly, 'it's *their* country.'

'I guess you're right.' He paused, glanced around. Then, 'Let's check out the upstairs.'

Tropical light came in through the grimy windows. The wooden stairs creaked, and something else in the atmosphere made her uneasy. It was perhaps the near absolute quiet of this building; it just didn't seem right. The bad smell had intensified.

There were three little offices here, their doors locked. Hacker simply kicked the first one in, seeming to get some kind of satisfaction from the sound of splintering wood. But there was nothing to see. Empty desks, an abacus on one, grey filing cabinets probably stolen from the Americans, with drawers empty except for a few meaningless scraps of paper.

Hacker booted open the middle door.

She followed him cautiously.

'Look at this,' he snarled in disgust.

Two single beds, a table with kitchen chairs. On the table were a few tins and glass jars, pieces of rubber tubing, two dirty spoons. A candle-holder shaped like a Buddha held stubs, and a dirty syringe was beside it.

'This isn't about weapons or anything, it's shit about drugs, Maggie!'

Suddenly it made sense to her. 'A shooting gallery – addicts right here. Van must have been asking questions, too many questions, when they lured him here. And then . . .' She didn't know enough to finish the sentence.

He grunted, massive shoulders working. 'Let's see what else we can find.'

Another kick, another splintered door.

'Jesus!'

She peered over his shoulder. Flies were everywhere, huge, black, swirling torrents of them, now disturbed. Some went out of the window, some out the door, but most returned to the sticky pool on the floor.

'That is blood.' Hacker stalked over and glared at the mess, then turned back to her. 'That is blood, lady!'

She felt sick, but forced herself to be cool and competent. 'I'll check these cupboards.'

'You do that.'

The cupboards were empty, so she turned to open up the battered fridge.

Maggie stepped back, screaming. A face grinned out at her, set on a tray inside.

The hacked-off head toppled forward and came rolling across the wooden floor towards Hacker. It was bloated and disfigured.

'That's Van,' growled Hacker, looking down.

'Oh, Christ!' Maggie said out loud. 'Christ!'

'I was afraid of something like this.' He poked at the head with a toe, and it rolled over again to give Maggie a hideous, upside-down grin. 'Killed just for asking questions.'

'I have to get out of here.' she gulped. 'Otherwise I'll be sick.'

He was pointing. 'Look there. Inside the fridge.'

Written on the inside of the door, in sticky, red-black blood, was SEE Y'ALL LATER.

The Saigon police were not much interested. There had been so much blood spilled in this country that one brutal murder seemed like nothing. A quick autopsy revealed a skull fracture; while still alive though possibly unconscious, the head had been sawn off.

For asking *her* questions . . .

Maggie got Terry to accompany her and drove straight to the local office of the Hideki Corporation, a modern concrete and glass building near the National Assembly.

But the business had closed down. They would sell no more napalm here. There wasn't even a caretaker to evade them.

'Now we'll never find out anything,' she said.

'I think we'll hear more about this sooner or later,' he disagreed gloomily. 'Maybe you'd better warn your source. Van might have been forced to talk, you see.'

'I didn't give him Kiko's name!'

He glanced at her. 'No. But there can't be many people investigating Hideki. So somebody has *your* name, Maggie. And, believe me, the trail here in Saigon has gone cold.'

'But there's still a trail,' she said stubbornly. 'I don't believe Van was killed because he accidentally stumbled into some drugs business. And I know that trail leads to Tokyo!'

Saigon's CIA station chief was named Thomas Polgar. After the news of the fall of Xuan Loc, he had begun putting things in motion to oust Nguyen Van Thieu as ruler of the South, preparatory to negotiating an end to the hostilities. Maggie also heard that the head of security at the American Embassy had decided to by-pass the Ambassador and was finalizing plans to evacuate all American citizens – and as many others as possible – from Saigon. There was a full list of government officials and of employees of US and US-linked organizations such as Hacker Stanton International, and their dependents, but totalled up it came to over a million and a quarter names.

There was an all-pervading feeling it might already be too late.

They were having *pho*, Vietnamese soup, when one of the quiet men of the US Embassy had come up to them on the hotel terrace. He sat down, looking grim. 'Want your news straight?'

Maggie turned to Terry in alarm. 'Is this it? Are the VC really going to celebrate Ho Chi Minh's birthday in Saigon?'

'Sssh,' Terry said. 'Let's have it.'

He explained quietly, 'Absolutely not for publication or dissemination, but I want to give you a list. Helicopter evacuation points, right?'

'We're listening,' said Terry.

'The roof of the embassy, the defence attaché's compound at Tan Son Nhut airport, a very few other buildings you can write down if you want.'

She made her question calm. 'It's that close?'

Terry squeezed Maggie's hand, put it down. There were damp patches under his arms. 'I hear you're burning your files back in the embassy.'

The mouth under the dark glasses frowned momentarily, then softened into a wry smile. 'Like they say, Terry, a pillar of fire by night, a column of smoke by day. It'll all be ashes soon.'

'Not before time,' Terry replied flatly.

Maggie wiped at the sweat beading her forehead. She was both scared and excited. 'Is it really the end?'

'I've been over here for three tours, and except for the Tet offensive in '68, things have only ever moved slowly here. This is a *slow* Asian country.'

'Oh, come on!' Maggie told him sharply. 'This is Asia, right, but why should things always change slowly here? Just suppose you were fighting the Japanese!'

The CIA man grinned, took off his shades and reached for a tumbler of whisky. 'If we were fighting the Japanese? Hell, they'd probably be at Grant's Tomb by now.'

As the Communist armies closed in for the last time around the beseiged capital of Cambodia, all the remaining Americans were airlifted out. Most of the press went, too; their next dispatches were transmitted from US Navy vessels in the Gulf of Siam. With Cambodia fallen, could Saigon and the region around it stand alone?

The evacuation began to speed up. Thousands of people were leaving every day – but Terry flatly refused to be among them.

Things were reaching a climax. If you went out to the airport, the lines of evacuees were getting visibly longer even as you watched, and there was an atmosphere heavy with impending panic. In Saigon, the people determined to stay were stocking up with food and bottled drinking water. Maggie heard that retreating soldiers of the Republic of Vietnam had bulldozed the graves of President Thieu's ancestors: in Vietnam, that was an unbearable tragedy.

In the city, the limbless veterans begging on the streets were suddenly much less likely to be in their old uniforms. Refugees were camped out everywhere, and even the shambolic law and order that had existed in this cesspit of corruption and crime was beginning to break down.

And the army had lost the will to fight.

Even Terry's composure was cracking. He pointed at Maggie, angrily. 'Just shoot her!'

'Now?'

Maggie sprayed deodorant under her arms, not wanting to be filmed with damp patches of perspiration visible. The Saigon crowds scurried by. Nobody over the age of twelve took any notice. What difference did one more testimony make?

'Shoot her!'

Maggie moved right up to the camera lens until she could see her own reflection; what expression was that, and what did it tell her about why she was here?

'Aren't you people rolling, yet?'

'Any time you want,' the Thai cameraman assured Terry. 'Sound's okay, too.'

'You sure you have the right level?' she asked anxiously.

Terry called out to her, 'Maggie, you'll be great, believe me.' He turned to the crew. 'Roll it.'

Maggie was standing in front of the huge Marines Statue. She looked straight at the film camera as she spoke.

'Today, all Saigon heard a rumour that one of the few competent and courageous South Vietnamese army commanders finally confronted President Thieu and told him the truth: *Monsieur le Président, la guerre est finie.* Mr President, the war is over.

'The collapse may come in a week. Or the end may come after peaceful negotiations spread out over several months. Nevertheless, this is the beginning of the end, and President Thieu's overthrow or resignation will prove that to the world.

'What is the atmosphere in Saigon now? It is a blend of uncertainty, fear and panic. People know beyond all doubt that things can only get worse – until the end comes and this war is finally laid to rest.

'This is Maggie Langton, reporting from Saigon.'

It happened later the same day, at four o'clock at the presidential palace. President Thieu, in tears, resigned. 'Kissinger did not see that the Paris Peace Accords led the South Vietnamese people to death! Everyone sees it, and only Kissinger does not see it . . . The superpowers have this arranged between them. We have nothing to sacrifice, only this tiny land.'

Afterwards, Secretary of State Kissinger cabled the embassy in Saigon. On the authority of L. I. Brezhnev himself, the Russian negotiators had stated that North Vietnam had promised them not to interfere with any evacuation. In the unusually early curfew that followed Thieu's resignation speech, even more of the Americans and their clients began moving nearer to the secret assembly points.

Thieu was replaced by his Vice President, a half-blind seventy-one-year-old asthmatic.

Maggie scrawled some postcards, to her family and friends like David back in England. She wondered what her father would say now. After a little thought, she selected one to send to Alex, then could not remember his address and had to send it care of company headquarters at Millbank. She wondered if he would be impressed by her courage and journalistic devotion to duty.

Terry's hand closed around hers and his voice was gentle and remote. 'What's the point, Maggie? Unless you think the VC will send them out for you.'

She looked up from her thoughts of England. 'I guess you're right.'

She beckoned over a waiter and told him to throw the useless cards away. He remained bent over their table, nervously polishing a glass. 'These people, these many addresses . . . If there was somebody who could get me to America I would give many, many piastres.' He looked from one face to another, desperately trying to smile.

Terry's voice became even more soft. 'I'm sorry, man. I'm really sorry. For everything.'

Chapter Nine

From Thursday 24 April there came a lull in the fighting, though no one was quite sure what it meant. Perhaps the Viet Cong needed time to digest the huge territorial gains they had made; or perhaps they had stopped their advance to give a chance for a negotiated, bloodless settlement.

Or perhaps, thought Maggie as she mulled over the rumours, it was all a confidence trick, and as soon as the VC had infiltrated enough men into Saigon, the final battle would come. She tried again to persuade Terry to leave, but he merely smiled beatifically to show her the joys of opium and refused to answer.

The next morning Terry sat back in the taxi, one tanned arm hanging out of the open window. 'Oh, you'll like him,' he told Maggie over the frantic blare of car horns. 'Thought he was dead up in Hué till I saw him yesterday . . . a scholar, a poet. Believe me.'

They turned into a less crowded side-street, past a shoeshop and still another café. It was early morning and as they got out she could smell coffee and the market smells of fruit, but underlying everything was the faint odour of rot that would get worse and worse as the sun climbed higher until finally it dominated everything.

They found Tran in the back room, after a granddaughter let them in. He limped over to meet them, sunlight spilling abruptly into the room where bright-coloured birds in a dozen silvery cages warbled musically. He was a small, wrinkled man in his seventies, but his eyes were still bright with knowing and his smile was lively.

'Terry,' he said, his accent distinctly French. 'I am most pleased that you came to see me, say goodbye. Please, sit down.'

They did so, as the granddaughter came in with strong *café sua*.

'This is Maggie.' Terry said, throwing a warm glance at her.

'Madame Katz?' The old man peered at her hands for a wedding ring. 'But I thought you were . . . and a child . . .'

'In my eyes she's all of that,' Terry said quickly. He sounded proud. '*Ai cúng thích cô ay*.'

Tran nodded his head, smiling. '"Everyone likes her", I am sure. It is good to see you, both.'

'A surprise?'

'When I saw you among the bookstalls along Le Loi, yes, I was surprised. I did not think you would come back.'

'I had to,' Terry said simply. He had the beginnings of a full beard now, and Maggie noticed with surprise how streaked with grey it was.

'But this time will be very dangerous for all Americans. At the end you must not let your woman, especially, appear on the streets.'

Terry smiled, suddenly. 'We're in the presence of a great man, Maggie. He fought the French before the war and the Japanese during it, in the Viet Minh.'

The old man said proudly, 'I was one of those who had Emperor Bao Dai abdicate. But I have not had a gun, myself, since before the time of Dien Bien Phu in '54.'

Terry was excited. 'But there's no doubt whose side he's on, and he used to know Ho Chi Minh himself and he fought with General Giap, the architect of the North's victory.'

'Then you'll be safe, sir,' Maggie said. 'But I wonder if you could tell me –'

'Not necessarily,' the man said, still smiling. 'Terry knows who I know. French. Many Americans. My neighbours remember, and remind me. I have so many Americans here in my home, they say. I read the American newspapers. I even *think* American, perhaps. Very bad indictment, now.'

'But –'

'But true, Terry. Though it does not matter. I am seventy-two, almost toothless, rheumatic. An old, old man. If they imprison me or torture me when they come, I will die quickly, easily. It is no matter. Instead, let us sit down, three friends, and talk of other, happier days.'

'Yes.' Maggie respected his wishes. 'What about your granddaughter?'

'Her uncle, my daughter's husband, is a colonel. He will take her out on Sunday. He has the papers, and he has promised.' Tran stood up, with the careful awkwardness of old age, and hobbled to the near wall. 'First there is something I must do.'

'No!' Terry had jumped to stop him, but it was too late.

The old man's still-nimble fingers unlatched the cage doors quickly. Some of the birds flew out immediately, singing their songs for the last time in this room. Others lingered in the open doorways for a time before they flew away; they were not used to freedom, or perhaps they loved the hand that used to give them food so lovingly.

There were tears in Terry's eyes.

'It must be,' Tran said, very gently. He had made his peace.

When they left, the granddaughter came up to them.

'He no leave,' she said sadly. 'You make him, maybe?'

Terry shook his head. In Maggie's eyes, there was something unhuman, un-American, in his resignation. 'No. He will die here in the land of his ancestors.'

That night they walked up from the river along Tu Do Street, and crossed over near the Hotel Catinat to turn into Nguyen Hue Boulevard. They were due to meet some friends up in the high-rise

Central Palace Hotel. The streets were noisier and more frantic than ever, and they were both determined to get drunk.

'That lovely old man . . .' Maggie said, much later, up on the twelfth floor bar. Outside she saw the signs flashing: Fuji and Sony, Coca-Cola.

Somebody came in, with the latest news. Former President Thieu had been taken through to Tan Son Nhut after dusk, in a convoy of limousines with diplomatic plates, and from there flown out of the country. The last PanAm flight from Saigon had taken off days ago; now the white Air America planes and helicopters were the only regular civilian inhabitants of the sky. The last attack could not be much longer, they all agreed.

'What else is news?' she asked, slurring.

'You could file another story about the evacuation of orphans from out of Cambodia and Nam! People like that and want to hear more.'

She pantomimed retching.

Another explosion echoed over the city. Recoiling, she spilled her drink, hoped nobody had noticed.

The poker school was still arguing, as usual. Nixon, 1972. The Republican Convention turning on the veterans in wheelchairs who had come to protest the war. Terry got up, swaying. 'Fuck Nixon, and the war. Fuck crippled veterans. It's hot. I think I'll go dip my pecker in the river.'

She was upset. 'You better make it a shallow stream.'

He flinched. There was another explosion. Somebody fresh from London began to sing, 'Come up and see me—'

'I'm sorry,' she told him suddenly.

'Yeah.' He wiped his mouth, reached for his bottle of Jim Beam.

'I mean it.'

His smile was more sad than bitter.

The city was more crowded and frantic than ever, and swept by rumours that could only promote panic.

This is the way it all ends, Maggie thought, as she worked on her *New York Times* article. This was a comparison between the French defeat at Dien Bien Phu and what was happening now on a much larger scale. Then there had been a siege – a big scale and earlier Khe Sanh, with artillery grinding down the French garrison, helpless in their bunkers. Each day, the nationalists advanced a little closer. The French commander had been promoted to Brigadier General during the siege, but his general's stars and champagne were parachuted down to the Viet Minh instead.

A day before the 1954 Geneva conference, the garrison surrendered. And that was the end of French supremacy here.

That had been twenty years before, but Maggie knew surrender was inevitable again. The only question was, when? The evacuation was stepped up, and she heard that Ambassador Martin had warned

North Vietnam, through some unusual diplomatic channels, that if their forces interfered with the process, the city of Hanoi would be levelled.

So Terry waited doggedly for the end, and Maggie waited for him.

He was taking drugs again, opium regularly and LSD sometimes, and amphetamines for courage, and in the hot, darkened room she would lie naked with him for hours, curled around his curled-up body, as he stared into nothing and reminisced. He remembered all the Vietnamese girls he had enjoyed. He rambled on about children, wives, mothers. He remembered violent death in ten thousand places, napalm burning orange among the green trees, frantic doctors trying to sew together ripped flesh. Then he remembered how it had sometimes been so beautiful here. The rainwashed streets at dusk, after the rain had stopped but before the sheltering pedestrians emerged, streets shimmering with bronze and gold . . .

'Come home,' she urged him. She knew at last that she was stronger than he was, stronger and more rooted: in England she had a home. 'Terry, please come back. Let's just go!'

He had no home, he said, and nothing important to do now. He was a sixties gypsy, and he would never change. Then he got up to toast the memory of the dead of Vietnam in straight Jim Beam whisky, as the light beyond the blinds grew dimmer.

A short rocket bombardment hit Saigon overnight: and even the road to the port of Vung Tau was cut. They went out in the morning to film the last, panicky inrush of people into this city – columns of them blocking most of the highways, hundreds of trucks, buses, oxcarts, and bicycles hung with a lifetime's possessions. It was like what Maggie remembered from the newsreels of World War II.

She even scratched around trying to follow the leads Kiko had given her, but all the relevant doors seemed closed, now. People were vanishing: going back to the outside world, going north, going underground, going anywhere.

The presidency was finally handed over to a new man, Minh. Maggie, unexpectedly, found herself deeply moved by the ceremony. In his acceptance speech, the Buddhist general said, 'In these difficult hours I can only beg of you one thing. Be courageous and do not run away. The tombs of our ancestors are here, this is our land, it is here that we all belong.'

She tried to imagine some equivalent of these events happening in her own country, and felt a great throb of anguish inside herself. Was this really what people like Alan Hoyle wanted? Civil war, hatred, brother turning against brother, foreign powers interfering . . . ? Then, from outside the presidential palace, lightning flashed and she heard the slow booming of thunder, promising relief from the overpowering wet heat.

Maggie stepped outside as soon as she could, hoping the feel of fresh rain on her face would be refreshing. She stood there under the dark, lowering sky to wait for the downpour. Her head was aching. The storm seemed to be getting worse, the thunder crackling from all directions. Then, as armed guards and the rest of the press corps began to scurry around, Maggie, too, realized that she had been horribly wrong. She was hearing the sound of gunfire, coming from all over Saigon.

Terry pulled her into cover as tracers lanced up into the grey sky and explosions echoed over from the airport. North Vietnamese pilots were bombing and strafing. 'Hey,' he said excitedly, 'maybe this is it!'

'I'm tired,' she said, putting her hands up to her face. 'Terry, I want to go back home.'

'Sure,' he said, trying to pull her along with him. 'Soon.'

'But when, Terry? When?'

He did not answer. Now the combat was coming closer to Saigon, he was totally caught up in the interest and excitement again.

The last of the foreigners were now all leaving Vietnam. There were only two embassies still open, and Washington, DC had ordered Ambassador Martin not to remain at his post till Saigon fell, but to close down the embassy, ask the French to caretake, and join the evacuation. Yet still Terry was refusing to leave.

The two Stanton cousins took their guests through the Craigburn car museum. The Ferraris gleamed, but their latest addition attracted most attention – the bulletproof 1932 Cadillac Fleetwood Al Capone had driven in Florida.

Alex was persuaded to lounge behind the wheel while the Germans and French took flash photographs.

'Tax-evasion got him, gentlemen, and not an assassin's bullet,' Alex said, 'A warning to us all.'

As tea was served he moved among the businessmen. They had come to him a month before, proposing to set up a consortium to bid for the Stanton North Sea oil contracts, several of which were up for renewal. The Hideki Corporation held the contracts at the moment, but the consortium could undercut the Japanese on price. The Board – even Beauford – had given Alex the authority to start discussions.

It was perhaps another five minutes when Hugh reappeared and took Alex aside. 'A telephone call. From Dr Sidqi, in Paris. You can take it in the library.'

Alex walked quickly back to the main house, heart beginning to pound. Dr Sidqi was a Middle East fixer, based in Baghdad. Alex suspected he was a national official in the Iraqi Ba'ath Party, and he certainly had money and high-level contacts, but his background was a mystery. Some said he was an Omani by origin, others an Iranian Arab from Khuzistan. In the wood-panelled room he picked up the telephone extension. 'Alex Stanton here.'

'Alex,' the voice said. 'I was hoping we could agree to have a meeting.'

Alex grimaced. 'Try company headquarters.'

'Your secretary seems reluctant to arrange it.'

'What can I do for you, then?'

'What can Iraq do for *you*? We have oil, a great leader, increasing wealth –'

'We have North Sea oil,' Alex said, 'and a democracy here. Armaments can send you an Arabic-speaking sales team if you wish. Is that what you want?'

'Actually, there are things you can help us with.'

'Things?'

'Like in America, in 1945 and before. Understand?' Dr Sidqi was a practised conspirator; he took it for granted the international line might not be secure, and so he spoke in very guarded terms.

'No idea,' Alex said curtly.

'The little boy, the fat man?'

It flashed into Alex's mind. Little Boy, the Hiroshima bomb. Fat Man, Nagasaki. He said immediately, 'I don't think we could help you with anything like that.'

'No?' Sidqi asked, quietly. 'But some of your competitors will. The French Phénix breeder reactor went critical in August of '73, and the French have sold reprocessing technology to South Korea and Pakistan. Come, see what we have done in al-Atheer and elsewhere, see our uranium stockpile, help us. Or do you want us to see you as – not a friend?'

'I'm not the French,' Alex pointed out, 'whether I'm friendly or not.'

'Also you help Japan,' Sidqi said in feigned surprise. 'Arigata, yes?'

'No,' Alex said, deciding to hang up. 'And now I must go.'

If Sidqi, an Iraqi agent, knew about Arigata, how had he found out? And who else knew?

They were not very comfortable questions for Alex to brood over.

Maggie jerked awake in the bed.

The phone was on Terry's side and she had to reach over to grab it, hearing war thunder over the city.

'Yes?' Her voice sounded blurry even to her.

'Maggie, I'm out at the airport.'

'Christ, Terry. What time is it?'

'Five a.m., whatever. I couldn't sleep. Listen!' The sound of explosions could be heard over the phone. 'The VC have opened up on Tan Son Nhut. There's a C-130 been hit, the gym where refugees were sleeping is on fire – yes, people killed, I don't know how many. The panic has started. No planes can get off. No planes at all! *There's another hit*! A copter going down – a SAM-7 missile, I think. God, all the runways must be blocked.'

She sat up straight, the single sheet falling away from her bare breasts. 'Then how are we going to get away!'

It was as if she had not spoken at all. 'People are going to *kill* to get out of here now. I think –'

Then the line went dead in her hand.

A little later that Tuesday morning, 29 April, the latest President of the collapsing Republic of Vietnam sent a written request to Ambassador Martin to close down all military operations and send the US advisers home. Martin agreed, specifying only that a force of Marines must stay on for security reasons. Then, with Kissinger's permission, he moved to Option 4 in the evacuation plans – a last big effort, using helicopters. This was the beginning of the last chance for everyone.

In the meantime Maggie was going frantic. What had happened to Terry? The sound of the continuing bombardment could be heard all over the city, most of it directed at the airport. She tossed her head back in a swirl of red-gold hair, fright hovering inside her.

Quickly she got dressed and went to the hotel bar to hear the latest rumours. What she heard stunned her. The last of the South Vietnamese command, almost every remaining general, had turned to the US for help in getting out, and they were being held weaponless and under armed guard by the defence attaché's people out at the airport. There were stories of other officers and officials killing themselves.

'What about the airport? Will it be usable soon?'

'Maggie, face it,' somebody told her forcefully. 'This is the end.'

There came another telephone call. The tall tamarind tree in the US Embassy compound had been cut down. That would let the big helicopters land there. This was the agreed signal that the holocaust was beginning, and it was time to flee. This was everybody's last chance to get out of Vietnam before the *bo doi* and the North Vietnamese Army seized the city.

But where was Terry? In all this confusion, how could she find him again? The older hands among the war reporters seemed certain that the airport would remain closed. So the only way out now would be by helicopter.

The press man manning one of the phones shook his head as he cradled the receiver. Many phone calls now went unanswered, as the Saigon régime disintegrated.

Maggie went to sit on the balcony, hoping for a breath of fresher, lighter air as relief from this heavy humidity. She pointed below as a tiny struggling figure discarded his uniform jacket. 'Look, even the police are throwing in the towel.'

'The VC might see them as enemies of the people, so of course they'll disappear.'

'Like *we* should?'

The man laughed nervously. 'That's right, Maggie.'

There was very little traffic, although the curfew was hardly enforced. Despite the palls of smoke over the city you could see for miles if you used binoculars. She borrowed a powerful pair to scan the nearer streets for Terry. Occasional trucks roared crazily through the city with groups of half-uniformed, trigger-happy men; when she turned the glasses on them she saw that their faces were wild. At ten times they seemed so close. If the killing was going to begin here, these men would start it.

An NBC stringer snatched his binoculars away from her. 'I must take a look at the airport. Christ, Maggie, look at that!'

Even with the naked eye you could see the bombardment out there: liquid splashes of light that were followed long seconds later by the flat thud of distant explosions.

'There'll be no planes leaving from there,' Maggie said, steadily, although fear was churning through her stomach.

But the sky over Saigon was already loud with choppers from Air America and the military.

Everybody was drinking and smoking feverishly. The room became more and more packed. Some of the others listened to walkie-talkies, to monitor US and Vietnamese radio traffic. It seemed that there were hundreds of ships and boats heading out into the South China Sea to find the American armada. All were crowded with refugees, thousands, tens of thousands, maybe even hundreds of thousands. Nobody could tell, yet. The names USS *Midway* and USS *Okinawa* were mentioned, and though these names meant nothing to Maggie some of the other people nodded, and she heard one word: Cambodia.

She risked running back along Tu Do Street to the CBS office in the Caravelle Hotel. There she found Americans, frantic Vietnamese, Australians, a Frenchman. Nobody had heard anything about Terry, and there had been some bad scenes out at Tan Son Nhut airport. Much of it was supposed to be on fire.

Then someone called Ellis, a lean, gangling man Maggie knew slightly, looked over from a phone he had just picked up. 'It's the embassy here. They say everybody has to get out right now. Full-scale evacuation.'

'I can't go,' Maggie protested. 'Not until I hear from Terry.'

'Maggie, you have to go!'

'I still have to find Terry,' she repeated.

'Worry about yourself, because it could all turn really, really sour here.'

Even after Ellis managed to persuade her, it took several further calls to make the arrangements. Meanwhile a radio tuned to the American Armed Forces frequency said the codewords for the final evacuation: 'The temperature in Saigon is 105 degrees and rising.' They grabbed their kit and went outside, slipping along two side-streets, heading for one of the rendezvous locations.

Their bus, with its wire-protected windows, was already waiting. They climbed aboard quickly. There was some debate about how long they should wait, but it soon became obvious they could not delay long, even if it meant they had to leave latecomers behind. Maggie looked around, worriedly. A crowd was gathering, and by the time the bus began to lumber away, a few Vietnamese were banging on the windows, some pleading, some swearing in rage or desperation. One clung on by his fingertips for thirty yards, his face only inches away from Maggie's and his mouth shrieking words she would never hear. The face seemed familiar, and she had to turn her head away in shame. Would he live or die? Would he make it out of Saigon without them – and if he did, what about his family?

Maggie found herself in tears, but she was not the only one. And, in all this chaos, how could she ever find Terry? The bus blundered on through the city, away from the centre, presumably to pick up more foreigners. All around she saw vehicles that had been abandoned, and there were more people out in spite of the curfew. Law and order was disintegrating.

The bus stopped abruptly. People began to grumble. After ten minutes they realized that their Vietnamese driver did not know what to do next. Then the passengers really started to protest.

Finally the driver turned around. 'This is where we're *supposed* to wait!'

'What for?' somebody snapped. 'For the VC to turn up and cut our throats?'

At the sound of small-arms fire in the streets nearby, Maggie finally stood up. 'We can't stay here!'

The driver revved the engine, but more as a sign of impatience than in preparation for departure. The passengers, nervous, began to stir. From behind her somebody yelled, 'Didn't you hear what she said? Fuck you, move it!'

Suddenly she saw Terry, ducking and dodging along the roadside. He grabbed a handhold and swung himself into the bus, Nikon camera swinging at his hip.

'Let's go!' she heard him bellow. 'Straight to the embassy. The plans have been changed.'

A heavy-faced Englishman perched near Maggie squeezed his eyes shut. 'Farcical. They're going to bloody kill us!' His complexion had been turned cheesy by terror; and she knew he was an experienced war reporter. Fear like cold fingertips touched her under the heart.

The bus made a U-turn and drove off a good deal faster now. Stepping into the aisle she grabbed Terry by the shoulders, then kissed him hard on the mouth. His fingers dug painfully into her back and his stubble beard rasped her cheek, but she loved him.

'Oh, Terry, where have you been?'

'I had a little trouble getting back in from the airport,' he said casually. Then she noticed his open-necked shirt was bloodstained all down the left side. His eyes were red and his face was smoke-stained, but she could see that he was otherwise all right. They were finally on their way out of this place, and relief washed over her like cool, cool water.

The bus only made it for another four streets. Then it braked sharply, slewing across the road and grinding its side against a parked car.

She stared at the makeshift barricade blocking the street: a big, empty truck, with a dozen men around it. They wore the remains of ARVN uniforms and they carried M-16s and M-79 grenade launchers.

The man standing wide-legged on top of the truck was drunk and angry. 'Yankees! You destroy my country, now you go, leave us to VC!'

Maggie stiffened at this undeniable indictment, and exchanged looks with the other passengers. One seemed to be praying, clasping his cased typewriter on his knee.

Then Terry jumped up and went forward, turning back only once to meet her frightened gaze.

'Hey,' he yelled from beside the driver. 'You move this truck!'

The flat oriental eyes narrowed further. This man could not defeat the VC, who had now finally defeated him, but he could make his betrayers suffer. He swung the muzzle of his M-16 towards the windshield of the bus. 'Maybe I kill you, *gian-phi*.'

There was a singing in Maggie's ears. Suddenly, she remembered all Terry's photographs of the dead.

Terry drew back, then blitzed the man, shaking his fist. 'You move this fuckin' truck, because I am number one spook and I can call down thunder from heaven – Jolly Green Giant gunships, ten thousand thousand!'

For the duration of several heartbeats, the two men formed a tableau. By coincidence a helicopter did go roaring overhead, only sixty or seventy feet above the rooftops. The violence in the air was tangible.

Then the armed man began to curse in Vietnamese. Tears were suddenly running down his face. He stood back, defeated, and made one gesture to the others.

The truck pulled away, so that the bus could go by.

'What did he call you?'

'Evil-doer,' Terry said. He waved his hand. 'So I was going to call him *gián* – cockroach. The hell with it. He's right, you know. That's what we brought here, in spite of all of our good intentions. Evil.'

Dusk was settling over Saigon, the last dusk there would ever be for the southern republic. Everybody knew that this next twenty-four hours would be crucial. Terry sat down beside her and held her hand. Abruptly she began to laugh.

'I am number one spook!'

He laughed with her. 'Hey, maybe I was, you know.'

She was shocked, and hoped he was joking. '*Were* you CIA-linked?'

Terry pointed up at the darkening tropic sky and smiled. He had got something else over her. 'Only He can be told.'

★ ★ ★

Most of the US staff from all the separate agencies had retreated to the embassy by this time. But thousands of politically compromised people, police, CIA employees and senior Saigon staff, and their families – women and children and elderly relatives – remained outside the safety of the compound, scattered about in various locations far from any help the embassy could give. The Saigon docks were also crowded. Looting had begun all around the river and the people who jostled to get on to the escape barges heard shots in the city.

Their bus turned up behind the Caravelle Hotel and parked by the high-rise buildings. Terry and another man left the vehicle to check pedestrian access to the US Embassy, which was a couple of blocks away. A bearded man went off, too, to try to call up the embassy staff by phone.

'I don't like this,' the plump Englishman said.

The hubbub could be heard from a long way off. There was a raging sea of people, hundreds or thousands strong, in front of the Embassy compound.

Terry stopped, he was so appalled. People climbed up the walls, throwing themselves screaming on to the barbed wire that lined the top; but the marine security detail pushed them back down. Floodlights were on, and the sky overhead was dark except for the riding lights of the evacuation traffic. Everywhere he saw guns – and lots of fear.

The man beside him turned. 'Let's get out of sight. This is going to get much, much worse.'

'Just wait till they figure out Uncle Sam isn't taking them to safety. They'll crucify every one of us.'

'Do you blame them?'

Terry jogged back to the bus and jumped aboard. 'I don't think any of us can make it into the compound. Maybe if one guy tried to sneak through . . .'

'Terry, somebody's trying the phone! Let's wait and see if there's any news.'

He looked at her, his face hard to see in the low light inside the bus. They had no place to go, and he was scared.

The United States 7th Fleet, standing off the mouths of the Mekong, had begun sending in its big helicopters in relays. Full darkness was falling now, and as the big machines twisted and turned above the river, the darkened land and Saigon itself there were flashes of small-arms fire and the occasional frightening strumming as rounds hit the choppers. They flew only to the Embassy or the US compound out at Tan Son Nhut; there was nothing else American left.

Maggie was getting desperate, wondering if her luck was exhausted. They had been parked here for only a quarter hour, but Vietnamese had begun to gather near the bus, jabbering and pointing. Some of them were armed. Fright again bubbled in her stomach. It was dark here, which made things more frightening, and she gripped Terry's hand tightly.

At the embassy there was confusion and fear, but the sound of helicopters was ever-present now.

The bearded man came rushing out of the café where he had been using the phone. 'French Embassy,' he said. His chest was heaving, and not just from exertion. 'Christ, it took them ten minutes to pick up their phone! If we can get there, the French have a gate into the US compound.'

Maggie stood up. The lightning flickered briefly and it began to rain. 'And what if we can't get there?'

A brief, panicky discussion ensued, and they decided to move in small groups, ducking from doorway to doorway. Maggie was in the third group.

It was just before nine when the last of the busload had made it to French diplomatic territory, then through the gate to temporary safety in the US Embassy.

Maggie looked around, half stunned, as Terry fired off more photographs. He looked like a crazy man, his hair flying everywhere. The noise of the helicopters was like rising and falling thunder. Nose searchlights glared on abruptly, dazzlingly bright, as the choppers dropped the last forty yards through the dust-filled air. She felt dazed and thirsty and badly in need of a shower. The sounds of the mob outside became louder. She thought briefly of her father being taken wounded off the Dunkirk beach: he had never talked about it. She felt confused, and exhausted, and afraid. Was this what it was like, being part of history?

There could be upwards of a thousand people left here. Inside the building the burning and shredding of documents was reaching a crescendo of panicky haste. When the VC came, the friendly names compiled by the CIA and other agencies could be as good as death-warrants.

One of the State Department staff came limping up. He looked shell-shocked. 'Terry, a flash message from the fleet – they want to stand down before midnight and restart operations after dawn.'

'What?' Terry exploded. 'They must be crazy! We can't spend the night here!'

The man's drawn, long face was suddenly only tired, not haunted. 'I told them that.'

By midnight, the US compound at the airport had been emptied of evacuees. More helicopters could now be dispatched to the embassy, where the lines of people waiting for the airlift were getting shorter. One queue led up stairways to the roof, where only the smaller CH-46 choppers could land. The other snaked around to the car park, where the vehicles' headlights had been carefully arranged to light up a makeshift landing field. They watched the evacuation for a while, sipping from a Thermos of black coffee.

'They say,' Terry said thoughtfully, 'that the SAM missile warning lights are on in the cockpits all the time.'

She tried to make sense of that. 'What?'

He explained. 'The VC could decide any moment to open up . . . and that'd be the end of the evacuation.'

She buried her face in his shoulder. 'Oh, Terry, Terry.'

He moved the Thermos to his right hand, hugged her with his left arm. 'Of course, if they do that the Commander-in-Chief Pacific will give the order to obliterate Hanoi.' He shivered suddenly. There was shouting around them and the choppers did not seem to be landing so often, but at least the lines were moving. 'It really is all over, isn't it? I can't believe it, Maggie. I can't believe it.'

She looked around, and listened. She could believe that it was over.

It was long after midnight. The sky shone red from fires all around the city. Tracers arced lazily in the air, and sometimes the noise of explosions could be heard even above the din of the choppers. The air tasted of smoke and burnt paper and gasoline fumes and unpleasant chemical odours.

One of the security detail came up to her; a sergeant, with an M-16 rifle.

'You have to go inside, miss. They might start shelling the embassy.'

'You mean – stop us getting out?'

His face was harsh and smoke-stained. 'They've hit the airport, and they're shelling our evacuation ships off Vung Tau. You have to take shelter.'

As she followed the other civilians inside, she could hear the screaming of the crowd at the gates. They realized now that they were going to be left behind.

For a time only the Marines remained outside, on perimeter guard, using rifle-butts and fists to prevent anyone else joining the evacuation. Then people began to trickle outside. Some were weeping openly. Everywhere smoke was curling, from flares and burning documents; the air was sweaty and foul, and ash drifted down on their heads, making everyone cough and itch. The embassy was now surrounded by despairing people still struggling to join the evacuation.

Maggie knew this vision of Hell would never leave her. The end of April 1975: the retreat from empire.

She sat down under a tree and felt about three thousand years old. It seemed like several centuries later when Terry sat beside her. His four days' growth of beard was heavily touched with grey and he looked exhausted.

'It's April 30,' she said dully. 'I hope we live to see May Day.' He said nothing. She started to cry. 'Let's go home, Terry. It's time to go. *Please.*'

He squinted at her as if he saw a stranger and his thoughts were a million miles away. 'Home?'

The tears came faster now. Tears for all the loss and pain in the world. 'Our home, Terry. *Our* home.'

He studied her closely for a long moment, and then he nodded.

Finally, they joined the line to leave Saigon.

They were flown out in a packed Chinook sometime after three in the morning. Below them it all went by: Saigon, the silver tracery of rivers, the green of the paddyfields, lit up by the occasional falling flare.

They had no problems getting to the delta, then out to sea. By then, the Asian dawn was breaking, immense and slow. In other circumstances, Maggie thought, it might even have been beautiful. They left the war behind with wonder and sadness. It was the biggest helicopter evacuation in history, and might never be repeated.

After them, the last people to leave the embassy compound were the US Marines, some time after dawn. But left behind were hundreds of loyal Vietnamese who had been assured they would get out.

Terry didn't care. Maggie held both his hands, lovingly, and they were on their way home.

That was enough.

Chapter Ten

Television screens throughout the world were soon filled with those last images of the frantic helicopter evacuation from Saigon. Watching, wondering if Maggie had discovered anything there, wondering if she had even lived, was Akiko Hideki.

She was in San Francisco, staying with some friends involved in the ecological movement, as South Vietnam entered its death agony. The phone rang early on May Day. Somehow, her grandfather had traced her. He brusquely told her to pack her things and return to her own country.

'If you wish it.'

'I *order* it.' His voice was harsh. 'Already arrangements have been made for you.'

It seemed unlikely that Maggie could have made any connections in Saigon between Saigo Hideki and illicit weapons. But her lover Tori still worked at the Hideki Corporation head office in Tokyo, a man of courage and initiative; he would find out more things for her, till the damning trail from wartime atrocity would be seen to lead straight to her grandfather.

It was a long flight, clear across the Pacific, and Kiko felt nervous, restless. What did her grandfather want? He had seemed to ignore her for so long, and on the rare occasions when they did meet, she sensed his cold disapproval.

The quiet man who came to collect her from Haneda airport had nothing to tell her. She emptied her mind of worry, and began to read the English-language *Japan Times*.

By-passing central Tokyo, they drove for a considerable time, on a highway offering glimpses of beautiful, rugged mountains, though the route led through smoking areas of heavy industry. Her country, its twin souls revealed.

This day, the last day of Saigon two thousand miles distant, grew hotter and more humid. Eventually they reached a higher region with poppies dotted everywhere like splashes of red blood. As everywhere in Japan, mountains lowered menacingly.

Kiko had tried to make conversation with her hard-faced escort, but received no reply. Finally she recognized the high wall of grey stones which they skirted.

The ancient gatehouse she saw next had a red-tiled roof like a pagoda, but the powered gates were modern high-grade steel. They opened before her, then closed behind with a snap, like a man trap. The car braked sharply. In front of them was another set of tall spiked gates – a security trap, so that any car that had crashed through the first barrier could here be riddled with bullets.

Men stared at the car, stared at her, expressionless. Then they were waved on through.

To her surprise, Kiko was not driven up to the great house itself, but along by the lake and over a low wooded ridge, then down to the flattened grass of the training ground. Here the car stopped. Kiko laid down the newspaper, fascinated.

The fifty men ranked before them wore the armour of seventeenth century samurai: warriors from the time of the great *sei-i-tai shogun*, the barbarian-conquering lord general Iyeasu Tokugawa. The driver unlocked the passenger door and gestured with a thumb.

'Out,' he said curtly.

She obeyed, holding her carryall in one hand.

Faces concealed behind their warrior masks, the men could not be recognized. Kiko wondered if they were staring at her. Something lurched inside her stomach. Then there was a shouted order, and every man flourished his long, killing sword. Steel glittered frighteningly in the sun. She heard the car drive away behind her.

A chorus went up. 'Hideki! Hideki! Hideki!'

Then, through the hot, sticky air, they began to advance towards her. She stood her ground until the first row of men was only fifty feet away, then thirty, then twenty, and finally right in front of her. She hid a sudden pang of real fear, and lowered her gaze demurely. She could smell the sweat of these men, hear their ragged panting breaths. They had been exercised very hard, and taken to a plateau of tiredness and fierceness that made them inhuman – made them true soldiers.

'Hideki! Hideki! *Hideki*!'

Three horsemen came galloping out of the trees, one holding the standard of Hideki's company, a banner with the slashing strokes of a Japanese character. They reined in beside her, their horses' nostrils flaring.

Her grandfather dismounted slowly, with the careful awkwardness of age. He stood before her, holding the bridle, sometimes patting his horse's head to quieten the nervous beast. 'My son who died a hero's death on the bridge of his warship, my son Ito who was killed by the *gaijin*, he had a daughter,' he announced, looking over her head towards the blue sky.

'You summoned me, grandfather,' she said politely. The masked samurai still stood before her, killing swords raised.

'She bears my name and she is my heir.' At last he turned a baleful look on her. 'For the moment.'

'I came here as you ordered. I obeyed you!'

'Yes,' he said, a small, fierce man, with sweat stains under his arms.

Her chest heaved, and she choked back a sob. She had never seen him look so savage. What was he about to do?

Hideki turned to his men, raised his arms, and his voice. Here in Japan, they would work only for him all their lives. They had to be loyal. 'Make good use of my swords. I want only the warrior spirit in my company. Now, we must defend *ourselves*. After the fall of Vietnam, the American shield is proved to be worthless!' He lowered his arms. 'You, and you – come with me now.' He handed the bridle of his horse to his standard-bearer, and stalked away towards some buildings near the lake shore.

Kiko and the others followed hastily, past the stables and into the large barn-like structure where the men would train when the weather was too bad outside.

She saw at once there was another man here, a samurai somewhere in his mid-thirties, with a shaven head, black waist sash and a grey kimono. Though burly, he balanced easily on his feet.

'You can't really wish to turn your employees into soldiers, grandfather – not even as a game?' Oh gods, she thought, even to me my voice sounds weak. How shaming.

He turned to stare at her with dislike. 'I provide work to a quarter of a million citizens of the Land of the Gods. Am I not entitled to my retainers? And what is wrong with what I do? Is there something disgraceful in the history of our land which means we alone in all the world must wipe out our own past and always be ashamed of it?' He spat on the floor, and withdrew his own long sword from its scabbard, his eyes fixed on her. 'You know this sword is from my ancestors – from *your* ancestors also? You know what it means to unsheathe it?'

Her eyes met his, though she understood nothing. These were male things, brutal and unnecessary. 'Yes,' she said nevertheless.

'It's a masterpiece. A killing sword, understand?'

'As you say, grandfather.'

He ran a fingertip parallel to half the length of the steel blade, carefully not touching it. 'I am proud to hold this sword, proud to have inherited what it represents. *I* am not a traitor to my race: I celebrate the Land of Nippon, and its traditions.' Suddenly, he spoke in English, so quietly that only she could hear him. 'You must respect that in me. Respect is what I want from you, living daughter of my dead son!'

Her eyes were wide. 'I do respect you.' She made it sound like an appeal.

'Then why have you been trying to interfere with what I did in Vietnam!' He looked enraged. 'Don't you know that in the Pacific War Vietnam was ours, from Hanoi clear down to Saigon! We, too, have rights!'

'Pardon my ignorance, grandfather. But I have never been to Vietnam.'

Hideki gestured with the sword – raising it in the sunlight slanting down from the skylights.

She felt great fear at the sight of that gleaming blade. 'Forgive me. I know nothing without you. I am nothing without you.' She bowed her head in submission.

After a moment he lowered the weapon and turned away, speaking again in brusque Japanese. 'You two, take off your helmets.' He pointed.

She watched them hurry to do it. The first man was Takahashi, her grandfather's aide. The other was Tori, her lover, and her source of information within the Tokyo office. He was young and slender, and looked around in suspicious puzzlement, one hand on the hilt of his sword.

Takahashi spoke venomously in English: 'No traitors in *our* country.'

Hideki stepped back. But his sword instructor stepped forward, his muscle-heavy arms swinging. He grinned.

The threat he represented was ugly. Kiko caught her breath, eyes widening. This could not be happening. Not simply because she had provided Maggie with an address in Saigon.

'Young man,' Hideki began severely. 'Nakarama Tori, you have betrayed the great trust my company had placed in you. Now you must redeem your honour in blood. Your own, or that of another.'

Tori shook his head fiercely. He answered in workable English. 'Who do you think you are? Just because you pay my goddamn salary! I'm doing nothing to anybody.'

'You will acknowledge my authority!' Hideki blazed.

'This is crazy. Listen, I'm getting out.'

The burly swordsman pulled out his own long sword. It hissed as it left the leather scabbard. Gripping it in two hands, he swung it high over his head. 'You will not leave here without facing me, coward.'

Kiko saw the young man – her young man – laugh. Tori threw his sword on the ground in front of them. 'That's what I think of all your games. Maybe my sense of honour is different! There is no way I will take part.'

The master swordsman moved once, in a blur of motion.

Kiko shrieked. The cut, perfectly aimed, had slashed her upper arm.

She moved to squeeze together the lips of the three-inch wound with fingers that trembled uncontrollably, but there was already blood all down her arm, soaking the white sleeve of her jacket.

Tori picked up his sword and stepped forward to protect her, anger moving in his face.

'Good, coward!' The other man sneered. 'You will protect your whore, if not your honour.'

The two men began to circle one another warily, like Siamese fighting fish.

'No,' Kiko wailed, taking a step forward. Horror and fear began to fill her. 'I don't want this. No!'

Takahashi, smiling, punched her in the stomach. She doubled up. He grabbed a handful of her hair to haul her back from the fight, then held her upright so that she had to watch. Her grandfather stood close by, hands on his hips, lips pursed with concentration.

The swordsman feinted almost too quickly to follow, left, right, swaying from the waist. Steel rang briefly on steel. Tori kept up his guard carefully. His face was a blank mask of concentration. He was young, lithe, and he threatened the swordsmaster with little cuts towards the head, then struck suddenly at the face.

The parry came at the last instant, and sweat sprayed as the heavy man jerked his head sideways. Tori pressed forward, then stopped.

'What does shedding blood prove?'

Still Kiko cried, 'Stop this, grandfather; please.'

Tori was triumphant in his generosity. He lowered his killing sword, his *katana*.

'Enough of your game,' Hideki said sharply to his swordmaster. 'Make it real.'

The instructor grimaced agreement. His eyes were evil. 'I have toyed with you long enough, boy. Now you will see that I have only been torturing you with hope.'

Screaming out his aggression he came forward rapidly. Tori fell back, as the master again and again hacked at him, each two-handed sword-slash coming a little closer to the flesh. Steel clanged on steel as he pressed on with overwhelming ferocity.

Tori made the mistake of changing his balance to step back.

The other man hacked straight down, raising his sword again instantly.

She flinched from Tori's scream as amputated toes fell away from his sandal and the blood streamed, red and terrible, into the dirt. Face distorted with rage, he hacked at the head of the other, hard and quickly, but with less skill. The two swords rang as they met in mid-air, once, twice, three times.

Sweat was pouring from Tori's face.

'See how we treat traitors, granddaughter,' the old man said. 'Learn from it!'

She saw that Tori was steadily losing blood and strength and courage. He would die – die publicly shamed. 'Grandfather,' she pleaded, 'I beg of you . . . please.'

Hideki said only, 'This is the Japanese way, which I will never retreat from.'

Tori, grim-faced and desperate, did not look away from his opponent as he cried out to her. 'Kiko, for you! Don't follow your ancestor. No matter what happens to me, don't give up the fight!'

She could not even make that promise in her heart, for she could see only disaster in front of her. She could not oppose her grandfather again. Not if this was the price!

Tori's opponent was easily his master, and over several minutes taunted him with continuing small hacks at his body. Every scream made Kiko shudder and blame herself, as Saigo Hideki intended.

By now, Tori had lost one ear and two fingers, and deep slashes criss-crossed his heaving chest and shoulders, welling blood.

Kiko shrieked and tried to pull away from Takahashi. 'No, stop this! I'll do anything.'

Her grandfather nodded, pleased. Tori stepped back, panting. For a single moment he turned to Kiko and their eyes met. His eyes were wide with terror.

Then the burly swordsman hacked into his left leg.

Tori toppled over, shrieking, both hands reaching for the wound. Kiko saw bone somewhere in the surgically-opened mass of muscle tissue, and wanted to be sick. On the ground, Tori rolled on his right side, face distorted, still howling, but also asking for mercy, mercy that would not come.

Hideki stepped forward, holding his own seventeenth-century blade in both hands. He raised it. 'The unsheathed sword.'

Tori's eyes bulged. His mouth gaped wide, without dignity.

Hideki struck once, powerfully.

The head was severed, and Kiko screamed again as the last beats of the dying heart sent blood spurting everywhere. The head she had so often embraced flopped loose. There came a sour stench from the steaming urine that poured out between the shuddering legs.

She had only a faint awareness of the swordsman dragging Tori's body away by its heels, as she fell to her knees, dizzy, to retch in the red carnage in the middle of the large room.

Then the others were summoned from outside. Hideki's chosen ones, still stern and anonymous behind the metal masks of samurai. Unless you instantly obeyed Hideki, you would never be a power in his huge conglomerate of companies.

In front of them all, Hideki shamed her.

She was still kneeling among Tori's blood and pieces of his torn flesh, weeping hysterically, arms wrapped around herself as she rocked from side to side.

Hideki pointed his finger. 'This woman Akiko, though a Hideki of my blood, is a traitor and a coward. Until further notice, I forbid you all to have anything to do with her. No longer treat her as my son's daughter, nor as my heir.' Still in the bloodstained costume of a samurai, Hideki stared around the crowded room. Nobody moved. 'Now, go, and remember what loyalty is all about – and the price of failure.'

Kiko was taken back to the main house overlooking the lake, then along passageways into a white tiled room. There she was scrubbed clean in a piping-hot shower, and her wound was stitched and then bandaged. She was in shock, weak, defenceless.

As she was led down another corridor, a shoji screen was slid back by an unseen hand.

Here, her grandfather knelt at a low teak table, in a room walled with folding screens from the days of the shoguns. The floor was polished wood. He grimly told her to kneel beside him.

As if in a dream, she did so, noticing that there was only one photograph on the walls: the atomic-age dome of Arigata in Niigata province, rising up from an autumn sea-mist.

'I wish now for peace between us,' Hideki said quietly.

The sun was setting over the lake, and the colour reminded her of blood. She gagged, then looked down, trembling with the shame of her weakness.

'This will not be a true *cha-no-yu*,' he told her, naming the ancient tea ceremony said to promote perfect peace and harmony. 'You are not worthy.'

She turned towards him, bowing her head low till it touched the floor, humbled, hoping complete submission might save her life. 'You are my ancestor.'

Hideki did not reply, as he measured out an exact quantity of the powdered green tea called *gyokuru* into a priceless earthenware teapot. An ancient iron kettle hissed, and then he poured its bubbling boiling water over the green tea. He sat over it for three minutes, in the starkly tranquil, spotlessly clean room. There were wild flowers scattered on the polished wood of the floor, giving the room a touch of natural colour. There were two tea bowls on the table they knelt at. Hideki gently poured out the steaming, fragrant liquid, then whisked it quickly. He offered her tea with stately grace.

She took the bowl in her right hand, then laid it on the palm of her left, automatically bowing twice – once to her grandfather, the master of this tea ceremony, and once to the Lord Buddha. She turned the bowl to reveal its more beautiful side to her grandfather, then sipped noisily. The tea, of course, was perfect. She wiped the edge of the bowl, then turned it again.

Even this truncated ceremony was giving her some sense of tranquillity. In a calm part of her mind she was almost deciding to surrender to him. What alternative was there, anyway? He had mastery here. He was Japan.

She and her grandfather shared the little rice cakes that were also part of the ritual. Only then, finally at peace with himself, did he turn his gaze upon her. She was pale and beautiful, fierce and true in her own way, and he wanted so much to be understood and honoured by her.

Nevertheless, he could not use the affectionate tone that might have won her heart.

'My granddaughter, you have been consorting with foreigners – is this not so? In America and in Britain. You have been urging them to interfere with my plans. And as a result, a man working for Hacker-Stanton came to one of my establishments in Saigon.'

'Did he?'

'Sent by a woman, Maggie Langton – your friend!' He suddenly sounded enraged. 'Oh yes, we had him questioned, before he died.'

She stared back at him, no longer afraid. Today, he had taken away her honour, and she had nothing more to lose. She picked up the Chinese fan laid out for her on the table, opened it with a flick of her wrist. 'What was his name?'

'He was a nothing and he died for nothing. Your fault – because of your friends!'

'I think much of all my friends, grandfather. Very much.'

'Foreign friends! Foreign values!' His lips peeled back in rage. 'You must not associate with foreigners. You must make your home here in Japan. And in future, you must not work against me!'

She bowed, hiding her face behind the fan. 'I understand.'

He continued his indictment. 'You learned things from that young traitor Nakarama in my head office, and after you slept with him like a dirty foreign whore, you told the foreigners company secrets – *my* secrets. But that woman Langton cannot help you. She could achieve nothing in Saigon; and she can do nothing here to stop me! I will be Japan, and Japan will be me.'

She concealed her alarm behind the fan. 'What do you mean?'

'That is my business,' he told her curtly.

The fan flickered. 'But why do you work so closely with Stanton Industries?'

This he seemed prepared to talk about. 'Outside of America, it is the greatest concentration of military production there is. And what they do not produce themselves, they can provide – including uranium ore and nuclear fuel. But Stanton Industries will eventually become the armaments division of my corporation. That is, the armaments division of Japan.'

'But surely the Stantons would fight you, if they discovered your plans?'

'I already have a third of that company and will take more, if I choose.' He raised the bowl of tea to his mouth, quaffed from it. 'But Alex Stanton is in my hands. He has given his word, and he needs the money from Arigata. He knows that, I know that. Know it as well, woman! And Stanton Industries along with Alex Stanton and his companies control something like five percent of the North Sea oil reserves. Don't you see how brilliant it is for us? I use that company to give me access to the British and European markets, including access to NATO. I still have the merger papers. When signed, all will be open, most especially the North Sea oilfields.

'And given sufficient time, I will weaken their industries so that they *must* buy from me – and that will give me long-term control of the biggest arms-makers outside of America, and enough politically secure oil to run all my businesses here.' He took a breath. 'And Arigata. They will help me with Arigata because I will make them do so.'

'What will Arigata give you?'

'Power,' he said simply. Electric power, and the power to blackmail every Westerner associated with it, he thought. And one day – military power.

She said humbly, 'I am sure you are right, grandfather.'

His eyes flashed. 'But you must keep my plans as you would keep a family secret – as I have kept *your* secret for so long.'

She bowed her head. Her secret, so shaming.

'And do not think there is anyone on the face of this earth who could help you now against me and what I plan for this land. I have amassed wealth and power for this. My will is pure. Nobody in this degenerate age can withstand me. There is nobody powerful enough to help you now, granddaughter!'

Except, she thought, hiding a flicker of hope, just possibly one man...

That same warm and star-filled night, Takahashi prowled through the estate from the edge of the lake up to the main house and the adjacent stables. All this could be seen as a Japanese equivalent of Craigburn: but this family was without a true and obvious heir. The lady Akiko could never be accepted as such, and Takahashi considered the other possibility, Hakagawa, as ignorant of the world and perhaps too old.

It was hard to suppress his feverish excitement. He knew he was feared in the labyrinthine Hideki empire, and he also knew the old man had trusted him recently with some of his most secret work.

Takahashi stared at the lighted windows of the house. I will be master here, one day. I am ready to be inducted into the old secrets, yet I'll be a modern man – one day none greater in all Nippon! I'll use everything I learned in America, everything I learned from home, to be supreme.

At ten o'clock, he was summoned. He dressed quickly in traditional clothes: kimono and sandals. Then, heart beating quickly, he was escorted to his master's lair.

'I bid you welcome,' Hideki said formally. Hakagawa was at Hideki's shoulder, his chosen man, and some said his intended heir – but Takahashi himself desired very much to be in that position, and he was much younger. He bowed low.

The three men kneeled at a low, lacquered table. On it were four heirlooms: a brass mirror; a glittering and ancient sword half-drawn from its inscribed leather sheath; a poem in manuscript; and a faded and stained document with a sword drawn on the cover.

Hideki spoke quietly, eyes fixed on the sacred symbols. 'I am a descendent of the great Shogun Tokugawa, who first brought order to all Japan. Order in the name of the Emperor, but profitably and ably administered by himself and by his family. That order and discipline is just as necessary today. More so, as Japanese history has become a fouled and polluted stream.'

'There must be a cleansing,' Hakagawa said fiercely.

'There will be a cleansing,' Hideki prophesied. He drew the sacred sword with ceremonious slowness from its scabbard. His gaze turned to his employee for a moment. 'Now, Takahashi Mutsuo, you are a young man, and so there are many things you do not remember. Let me speak openly to you of the time of war, as I have never done before. In my training school you have seen the film of the trials in Tokyo, with Tojo stoutly justifying himself and the policies of his Emperor. We must follow his example, being faithful to death and beyond, and unashamed of those things we were obliged to do for this favoured Land of the Gods. We tortured and executed our prisoners? It was our way. We had no democracy? That was to prevent little, selfish people from interfering with great plans made for the nation's good. It is *still* our way. So it was when my businesses were running Manchuria; so it will be when my businesses are controlling America and Europe and all the world.'

Takahashi was transfixed by the expression on Hideki's face. It had the intensity of one taking part in a religious rite. It was the face of a man fully capable of burning cities, or committing seppuku, the ritual suicide of the samurai. Takahashi, overawed, had no doubt of that.

Hideki continued, 'All my life I have struggled to make Japan great. I supported the League of Blood and other patriotic organizations. I wanted us to take Korea and China, and drive Russia out of Asia. We have never been defeated, not in our hearts. In the great Pacific War the heroic defenders of this land were overwhelmed by mere industrial power only. Therefore, we must now achieve that same industrial power for final victory, and for a final solution to the problems of the world. We fought till 1945 and our spirits were never broken – *never*. Then, our Emperor wisely commanded us to surrender to save the home islands from invasion and to spare such of our cities as remained.' He turned to the much younger man. 'Remember, the Americans used napalm on Tokyo, and atomic bombs on Hiroshima and Nagasaki. They are murderers; they can claim no moral superiority over the civilized Japanese.

'So, the Emperor spoke. Two weeks later occurred the official rite of surrender on the battleship USS *Missouri*. Then the Americans came; an occupation army of hardly more than a quarter of a million, and only after a blessed interval. In that interval, we Japanese could secretly burn evidence about the past and prepare for our future. Of course the Americans began polluting our women's bodies and our culture. MacArthur tried to change our ways, and he was the conqueror – or seemed so.

'Some of our leaders were executed; many more were purged from public life. Communists were allowed to agitate. But behind the scenes the Japanese way continued, just as it did before.

'With patience, we persuaded the Americans to leave, to give us back our Okinawa, and to let us grow strong under their nuclear umbrella. We made a fortune here out of the wars in Korea and Vietnam; but both times the Americans spilled blood and lost a fortune.

'In 1945 no more than ten interconnected families controlled almost three quarters of industry, commerce, and finance. The House of Mitsui alone employed over three million by the end of the war. These great combines powered the war machine: Mitsui, Mitsubishi, Hideki and Yasuda. They made our islands great. The Americans think industry is to benefit the little people, the citizens, rather than the nation, and so they tried to break up these great combines, including my own. For a time there was even a thought that I would be brought to trial for what they called "war crimes". But naturally I arranged for the evidence and for certain inconvenient people to be disappeared.

'So I am still the Hideki of the Hideki corporate combine. But my country has been subjected to "psychological disarmament" – to pollution, that is, of the minds of our youth. That shame, too, must be obliterated.

'In my youth I was a supporter of various societies like the Great Japan Military Virtue Association, and other patriotic and anti-*gaijin* organizations. But after the war miscarried for us, I came to realize we would need patience and a new approach to create our co-prosperity zones. And I was not the only one to think so. We needed time and secrecy to work behind the scenes. We had to sheathe our samurai swords for a time, and smile at the foreigner and seem to obey him. This we did, but secretly we kept our swords, knowing that one day we would unsheathe them again.'

He passed his hand over the document. 'The Unsheathed Sword Society Manifesto describes how it would be. I hoped I would live to see the day when our industries would be great again – and I have. I hoped to see again a strong, armed Japan, and I shall. Our next steps will involve taking over foreign firms and buying foreign property. Then Japan will truly be *ichi-ban*. By 2000 AD, the world will be ours. I hope to see that, too. But now, even more so, we need to keep to the old ways. I am the secret head of the Unsheathed Sword Society, and I will take responsibility for Japan – *whatever weaklings and enemies say!*'

Still kneeling, Takahashi gazed down at the manifesto. He realized suddenly that many of the greatest men of Japan were secretly members and had signed their names. 'And what of Stanton Industries and Arigata – ?'

'They are all part of my plan. Arigata is a fast breeder reactor: which means that we will have the power.' He beckoned Takahashi closer, writing brush in his other hand. Then he held out the mirror. 'See into your soul. If you are unworthy, do not sign.'

Takahashi gazed at himself.

Then Hideki read the poem:

> 'The chrysanthemum flourishes
> Has always flourished
> Linking the future to the past . . .'

'I understand,' Takahashi said softly. The poem meant that the spirit of Japan had survived, must survive, and ought to prevail. 'I will be worthy.'

Hideki sighed as he leafed through the aging document. He had composed most of it late in the winter of 1944 after the first fire raids on Tokyo. 'In October 1945 we all signed this document. Signed it in our own blood. Now, take the sword, cut one finger. Bleed into this dish. Then you may sign the manifesto of the Unsheathed Sword Society, as we have done.'

Takahashi cut himself, bled for Japan, and solemnly put his name to the document. He wondered if this small act, even more than all the larger, more violent things he had done, would one day make him Saigo Hideki's heir.

Chapter Eleven

This building was in Mayfair, London. Gilded letters by the discreetly armoured door said Hacker-Stanton International, giving other addresses in Dover, Delaware and the Cayman Islands.

A closed-circuit camera set above the door swivelled from the stone steps towards the pavement as a tanned Ray Hacker stepped from the company's Mercedes-Benz 350 SE. Alex Stanton's bodyguard John Reid had driven him from Heathrow airport. Hacker touched the bell-push, then went inside.

Alex grabbed his hand, his face splitting in a grin. 'Ray, you were a bloody hero!'

'Everybody got out of Saigon.' Hacker looked tired but very proud. 'Every last one of ours, anyhow. Let's have a drink to celebrate.'

After greeting the staff they made their way to the big private leather-upholstered office at the rear, where Alex poured out malt whiskies on the rocks.

'Saigon.' Hacker shook his head. 'That was the end of somethin', boy.'

'I imagine it was.' Alex sipped his scotch: peaty and dark, and a man's drink. 'What about that killing? Maggie Langton seems to think it was down to Saigo Hideki.'

'She's been talking to you about it?' Hacker unloosened his tie. 'I don't know, Alex. Can't make sense of it, although I'm not exactly at my brightest at the moment. Van couldn't get to speak to the guy whose name Maggie gave.'

'So that puts Hideki in the clear?'

'Well, somebody working for Hideki's firm came up with an address. Apparently.'

'Who was that? And what address?'

'Van didn't say. A secretary, I think. I don't even know if he saw her face to face. The address was the warehouse I told you we visited.'

'Some visit,' Alex said drily. 'Some discovery.'

Hacker swallowed Scotch, grimaced at the memory. 'A human head.'

'No more clues? What do you think?'

'Maybe it was just bad luck. I saw needles in that place, and you didn't need to be a forensics guy to see the import-export business down there involved drugs. Might be that Van just happened to walk into a major drug deal. I don't have to tell you what that means.'

'No.' It still preoccupied Alex. 'But do you think the murder *could* be traced back to Hideki?'

'You can bet he wouldn't be personally involved.' Hacker shook his head. 'Van didn't have to do that for us. I'd got him a green card. He had an in to the States.'

'And now he's dead,' Alex said grimly.

'But to kill a guy like that,' Hacker argued, 'makes it very serious. And what could Hideki be into, in Saigon?'

'I suppose you're right.' Alex sighed, remembering the pictures of the last helicopters rising from the US Embassy. But he wanted to know, very badly. 'We can hardly go back to Saigon and shake the place down for evidence.'

'That's true.' Hacker finished his drink.' 'Lots of loose ends were tied up for good, in Saigon. Or cut forever. So what's the new plans?'

Alex opened a briefcase, both locks clicking at the same time. 'It's all working out brilliantly. As long as we can stay ahead of schedule, Arigata means big money – which I have lots of uses for. In the North Sea, much of that oil will be ours. The shipbuilding division produces exploration rigs; the aircraft division has a subsidiary company that runs choppers out to those same rigs. It's going great. And when the first oil reached shore, a government minister held up a bottle and said it: "I hold the future of Britain in my hands."'

'And our futures, maybe – and for sure a good part of Stanton Industries' future.' Hacker nodded. 'Anything else?'

Alex hesitated. 'I may as well tell you. Remember the Franco-German approach to us, to undercut the Japanese?'

'The guys you took round Craigburn? Sure. It went to the Board and you started secret discussions.'

'The Hideki Corporation hit us last meeting. Re-sign with them immediately, or there would be "technical difficulties" in all our North Sea operations.'

'I see.' Hacker scowled. 'Beauford was all for it, I suppose?'

'He certainly was. Very well briefed, very articulate. The Board went with him. Hideki gets the contracts again.'

Hacker nodded. 'I wonder how much Hideki paid the noble lord.'

'Short of taking over his bank and inspecting his private accounts, we'll never know. And, naturally, no decision yet on Tokyo buying our Mark VIII tanks. Anyway, I need to start modernizing the Armaments Division, and I've started making informal approaches to the unions and other interested parties. As soon as the profits from Japan flow in, I'll make a start.'

'Profits from Arigata? Maggie was telling me all about that.'

Alex was exquisitely polite. 'Was she?'

Hacker's single eye glinted. 'Sure was. So maybe it's time *you* told me about it, too.'

Maggie had returned to England, by herself, after a week in San Francisco. The warm May weather there had left her hot and discontented. Kiko had vanished from Frisco and Maggie could not find her, and the absence of war and its terrors in America and Britain felt strange. In her dreams she still heard heavy artillery, approaching. In her waking hours she felt a crushing sense of anticlimax, and a strange guilt for escaping.

Then, suddenly, she woke up to England, her England, heading towards summer – and there were programmes to edit for television, articles to write, her magazine *Capital Life* to run. Then, wonderfully, a real holiday.

On her return from Granada, at his request, she went to see David Bryant. He met her in a pub on the main road through Pimlico.

'Maggie!' He stood up to embrace her, kissing both cheeks. 'God, you look wonderful!'

She touched her red hair. 'Flattery will get you everywhere, David.'

She was tanned and rested and clear-eyed. Freckles had begun to break out over her nose and cheeks, and her wide-mouthed smile was as infectious as her laugh. Her holiday in Spain had done her the world of good.

He continued staring at her as if some kind of legend had materialized in that wooden-floored public house. 'I can't believe it. My oldest friend, the last woman out of Saigon . . . How was it?'

She closed her eyes for a moment. The convoy of tears. The panic in Da Nang. Terry and his increasing drug habit. The shameful flight from Saigon. She opened her eyes and touched his hand. 'It was beyond me, David. I still don't know what to say. A whole country, or half a country, going down. Millions of people. It was history – too big for me.'

He nodded, and for a while they shared a reflective silence. 'Would that last morsel of American military aid really have made a difference?'

'No.' She sighed. Then, 'So how's it going here, David?'

'That remains to be seen,' he admitted. He took a breath. Unemployment was up, and the oil shock and the consequent inflation had hit Britain badly. 'Politics aside, I'd like to give you some figures.'

'Oh? Figures?' She watched him drain his Guinness. 'What about – politics aside?'

'Stanton Industries. The armaments division.'

'You're acting as Alex's errand boy again?'

'Errand boy?' he said sharply. 'You're bloody irritating sometimes – if I may say so.'

'Just like any other woman,' she said sweetly. 'All right. What is it, exactly?'

'Some facts and figures,' he told her, 'about productivity in the Stanton armaments division, an O&M report. First I show you, and you check. Then I show your father.'

She looked at him for a long time. '"Facts" about the Stanton tank factory in Newcastle?'

'Yes. True facts.'

She said nothing for a while, drawing lines with the spilt beer on the table, then looked up. 'You give these figures credit, and you've checked yourself?'

'Yes.'

'Then I'll pass them on to my father.'

'Excellent! And we're going up to the factory to see for ourselves.'

'You and Alex?' Her voice sounded strange.

'Me and Alex.'

During a long and successful meeting of the Board of Directors, McCourt reported back on their expansion in Japan. It was late the same evening when Maggie rang up Alex in his St John's Wood home. His wife Caroline had already gone to bed, so enthusiasm and single malt and the prospect of an attentive audience got the better of him, and he proceeded to explain some of his plans to his former lover.

'Arigata is an incredible feat, and McCourt's just come back from the site. Japanese standards of work have been an inspiration to us. Stanton Industries can match the Japanese in terms of investment, but we must match them in productivity, too.'

'You never talk about Arigata in public,' she murmured. 'I was hoping I could persuade you –'

'No, of course I don't talk about Arigata in public.' He bulled on, changing the subject quickly. Arigata had to stay as secret as possible. 'Welcome back from Saigon, anyway.'

'Everything still seems strange,' she said softly.

'What about that murder you stumbled on?'

'Stumbled on?' There was a pause. 'I asked a Vietnamese called Van to go to the Hideki Corporation. I had the name of an executive in Saigon who was supposed to be recruiting for military R&D.'

Who had provided the name? Alex made his voice indifferent. 'You say "supposed"?'

She sighed. 'I'm not concealing anything, except the name of my source. I don't know the real story. Yet. Van didn't even get to speak to the executive! It might all have been a coincidence . . . violent death wasn't exactly a rare event in Saigon. But I still say you shouldn't be doing business with the likes of the Shah and Hideki!'

'I have to,' he told her. 'If I don't, thousands of your father's union members are out of work!'

That silenced her, but only for a moment. 'Anyway, how's business otherwise?'

'Oil is the thing at the moment, and MacKenzie's shipbuilding division is profiting from it. Each of the rigs they're working on represents a £25 million contract – profit and experience for the company, work for your father's members.'

'So everything is going well?'

'Superbly well for me as an individual.' He had already made large personal investments, together with Ray Hacker, in companies like Lasmo and Ranger UK, as well as profitable offshore facilities. But that also meant he now had the exact figures to compare British and foreign methods and productivity. 'Some specific problems, still,' he admitted. 'Things need to change in our operations, I'm afraid.'

A pause. 'What do you mean by that?'

'We have to bring our working methods up to date. Improve training, cut down on strikes, breaks and absenteeism. Has to be done. As of now the North Sea has generated maybe two hundred thousand jobs in the States, against a quarter of that figure over here, and—'

'That's the fault of your workers, I suppose!'

'Management,' he said crisply, 'has its responsibilities, too. But firms abroad have higher productivity, lower manning levels throughout, and they complete projects more quickly and with less disruption. I can give you examples, if you want.' He paused for breath. 'McCourt has given me some ideas based on what he's seen in Japan. Take our Tyneside tank factory, for example. A run-down site. Old-fashioned machinery. And, even worse, inadequate work practices. Umpteen different unions in the same factory, all in competition, representing so-called skills I've never heard of – like what the hell is whitesmithing, or rough painting, and I'm damn sure all these boilermakers on the tank factory payroll don't actually make too many steam boilers these days!'

She had gone quiet. Then she asked him, 'So what are your plans, specifically?'

'I intend to start looking around some of our plants myself. I'm going to remake this company.'

She said derisively, 'The bright lads from London head office just don't do that.'

'That has to change,' he said crisply. 'Ask David about his plans for the country. And you can tell your father from me, we're going to get more graduates and technicians into the factories. After all, some production engineering skills can't be learnt on the factory floor.'

'So when does all this start?'

He found himself telling her.

The dark Rolls-Royce crossed the River Tyne on a bridge high above the water. Far below, the river gleamed: like glittering nets sent twisting across lead-grey on this sunny Monday morning. In the back of the limousine sat Alex himself, Ken McCourt, and a sober-looking David Bryant.

David glanced out of the window. 'The home stretch.'

The bridge took them above the roof of the shipbuilding division headquarters, which had been burned out in the aftermath of the '71 strike. Now, restored, it fronted the historic cobbled Quayside, not far from the Custom House with its royal coat of arms, just as it had done for over a century and a half.

'I'm sure friend Hoyle was responsible for the fire there,' Alex said, meditatively. 'Though we'll never know for certain.'

'Not now, we won't,' McCourt said, seated opposite them on the pull-down seat. He opened his black dispatch case and started looking over some plans. 'Now to start catching up with Japan . . .'

David Bryant suddenly turned to Alex. 'Are you sure all this is wise?'

His large, ironic eyes glanced away from the handsome façade of the city's Central Station. 'Mr McCourt, myself and you taking a look at the tank factory – what's wrong with that?'

'Nothing, as such.'

'Well, then?'

'Except, as we both know, the next step they'll expect is bringing in the time-and-motion people – and probably gutting the old factory. You could have tried convincing the workforce the changes were necessary, or giving Langton time to study your figures.'

Alex gestured towards the sign which read SCOTSWOOD ROAD. 'Cue for a song, do you think?'

David had a terrier's instinct; he never gave up. 'Alex, there isn't the money in your company treasury for major changes here, because everything has already been committed to Japan and your push into the North Sea oil business. You've told me that yourself.'

'True,' Alex replied. 'But so what? Looking is free, isn't it? So is planning ahead. Maybe by 1976 we'll be cash-rich again, and we *will* be cash-rich as soon as we finish Arigata. And if we bring the Mark IX tank into production, I'd like state-of-the-art facilities. And whose bloody factory is it, anyway?'

'The union might regard your appearance as provocative.'

Alex shifted on the leather seat. 'So?'

'So the men – and Maggie's dad there in the regional union office – know you must complete the current Iranian tank contract by mid-year, or face financial penalties.'

'You're saying the firm, or at least the armaments division, is vulnerable?'

'Exactly. And known to be vulnerable.'

'Okay, point taken. But this visit is a complete surprise. Almost.'

'Almost?'

Alex shrugged. No point in mentioning his phone conversation with Maggie. 'If we're going to have some kind of confrontation I'd just as soon have it now, before impartial witnesses.'

'Me, you mean?' David asked sharply. 'Just in case I get into government one day?'

Alex said nothing, only smiled.

Having left the city centre behind them, and heading west, the car was now passing the tall, monolithic structures of council flats up on the slopes. Then old pubs with curious industrial names were on the right, and on the left they saw high walls protecting long Victorian sheds with tall chimneys.

The Rolls drew up at the main gates. A uniformed security man gaped at them as Alex's driver got out to explain who his passengers were.

'Works manager is called Cooper,' Alex explained tersely. 'He's on

Teesside today, meeting some chaps from Foster Wheeler, a subsidiary of a big US company which has built more offshore deep-water platform modules than any British firm.'

A man in a cloth cap could be seen vanishing inside the nearest of the vast, tarry sheds. Then a factory hooter began to blow; others, at different pitches and powers, soon took up other throbbing, foghorn-mournful notes. Their driver climbed back in and the steel arm across their path was finally raised. The Rolls glided forward perhaps twenty yards, then stopped.

'Trouble,' David said tersely.

Men in greasy Stanton overalls began to appear, filing out grimly from the four wide-open doors in the structure in front of them. Others surged round the corner from other parts of the factory complex.

'Jesus,' he continued. 'There must be thousands of them.'

Alex stepped out of the limousine as they began to form up in loose ranks, many producing cigarettes. Some gestured at the Rolls, others jeered; and one man even spat in their direction. A few Forward placards were brandished by some of the younger men.

David could sense the hostility of the workers as he followed McCourt and spoke quietly to Alex. 'The Rolls was a mistake. They think you're flaunting what you are.'

'Yes,' Alex said grimly, his eyes flickering about. 'But what I'm flaunting is only this: that I'm a Stanton.'

McCourt nodded towards a burly man in collar and tie who was marching towards them. 'Looks like the confrontation starts here.'

Alex recognized the regional power in the engineering workers' union, a powerfully built man in his fifties. His face was craggy and his thick hair greying now.

'Will Langton,' Alex said, unsurprised. 'Maggie's father . . . so that's how they mobilized so quickly. He knew I was coming.' He grimaced, realizing that he had failed to apply one of the central maxims of the great Chinese strategist Sun Tzu: Always surprise an enemy. Gazing around at the thousands of men who stared straight back grimly, Alex, silently cursing, realized that this time his customary audacity would not be nearly enough.

'A good morning to you,' Will said, tabloid newspaper tucked firmly under his arm, smiling.

Alex gestured with his thumb. 'This isn't quite the reception I was counting on.'

Langton pulled a comic face. 'There's nothing wrong with the lads here seeing their ultimate boss, is there?'

'I only run the armaments division. Cousin Hugh is still Chairman of the group.'

'I think I know who runs *him*,' Will said, eyes twinkling. There was something very warm and human about the man.

Alex said only, 'I have a feeling your people don't want me inside.'

'We don't, lad, and we outnumber you about three and a half

thousand to three.' He glanced at David Bryant. 'Though I'm not quite sure whose side you're on.'

'We only came to look around, Will,' said David, trying to find a consensus and make peace. 'We don't want trouble. And we certainly don't want a re-run of the '71 strike all over again.'

'Quite right. I don't want the same kind of closures and redundancies here in the tank factory. And it isn't Alan Hoyle and his Marxist gang you're facing now. It's the lads here, and me. Out in the open, fair and square.'

Alex had begun to seethe. 'Your daughter told you I was coming, didn't she?'

'What if she did?'

Alex unfastened the buttons on his grey Italian jacket. Thousands of hostile faces were still fixed upon him. 'I could probably force my way in.'

'If you take just one step into the factory, or send in your damned efficiency experts, we'll all be out. Right? Thus buggering up your contract with your friend the Shah. And I have the notion you can't afford that, young Stanton.'

'Not so young now,' Alex said, fighting a familiar battle. The Rolls really had been a mistake, he realized.

'We've closed down the plant,' put in another, younger man. 'It'll stay closed as long as you and yours are on the premises.'

Alex was inclined to brazen it out, though a light rain had begun to fall. But David Bryant tugged at his sleeve, hissing from the corner of his mouth, 'Let's just leave. Please! You're only making it worse by hanging on.'

The assembled men jeered loudly at the Rolls and its passengers as it reversed out of the gate and drove away.

'And they think they've won a bloody victory,' Alex said in disgust.

David sighed, hands folded tightly. 'That's the great British tradition, I suppose. An ongoing family quarrel. And what we can do about it I really don't know.'

'It's an unbelievable situation,' McCourt grumbled. 'The chargehands – the foremen, the most skilled people we have – are forbidden even to *touch* any of our tools or machines!'

'What's the idea of that?'

Alex shook his head. 'It's a trade union agreement, apparently. A madness the Japanese wouldn't tolerate for a moment.'

'I can't defend it,' David admitted.

'And we have brand-new machines nobody will operate.'

'Why is that, Ken?'

Alex explained for him: 'That time we couldn't get a union agreement . . .'

'Why not? Maggie's father Will isn't so unreasonable – well, he's no more pigheaded than you or I.'

Alex spread his hands. 'They wanted too much money.' He glanced at David. 'Look, I'm getting worried about the production side of the firm. I'd like to visit some more of the factories in person, or at least send people in to get the measure of the situation – which I don't like. Too many of the managers seem indifferent, or downright defeated. Everybody assumes their job is safe, and also certain to be quite mediocre as a career, so why struggle or take risks that can't bring you any significant reward? And if there are problems, they're insoluble by the individual, so you need to go to the government and get the taxpayer to bail you out.'

David was shocked. 'Things are as bad as that? Even in *your* firm?'

'This situation can't go on,' Alex told him soberly.

Their eyes met. They both knew it was true. Stanton Industries – and the nation – could not continue to follow the old safe and comfortable paths. There was no alternative: change had to come – unless it was already too late.

The postcard depicted the Marines Statue in Saigon and had a date on it from just before the evacuation. Langton showed it to Jackie Sutton, his troubleshooter in the region's union office, then put it back in his wallet, feeling a long way from his daughter and her concerns. She moved among Americans and talked about world affairs, whereas he was still a rooted man, dominated by the old struggles of Great Britain.

Another man sat down at their table in the smoky bar room. He had a black attaché case with him.

'Afternoon,' said David Bryant tersely. He looked tired.

Will Langton shook his head. 'Cheer up, lad. I'm here, just like I promised Maggie, and the next round's on me.'

'I've had a bit of thinking to do.'

'Thinking?' Jackie Sutton said.

'Testing what I believe against experience, over and over again. Testing what I used to believe about Stanton Industries – about all our industries.'

'What was that?' Langton said, still amused.

'That it was a piece of the old greatness here that's still great.'

Jackie Sutton raised a glass to his lips. 'Lost faith, have you?'

'In a whole lot of things.' David remembered his 1971 visit to Eastern Europe: at first hand, a grey-on-grey bad dream. He sighed. 'Remember when our fathers and grandfathers would talk about Russia? It would come back second or third hand and the message would be: I've seen the future, and it works. In Russia now, or the Eastern bloc, who would say that?'

Langton shrugged. 'Did the past work there, either? Think about that, bonny lad!'

It was small comfort. And a part of Stanton Industries, here and now, was heading for trouble. 'Read the report for yourselves. Maggie's researchers can guarantee that the figures are accurate.' He pulled papers from his case and handed them to Sutton. 'You won't like the conclusions any more than I do.'

Will took another mouthful of beer from the dimpled glass. 'I don't think Alex Stanton liked being turned away from the factory.'

'Nor did I,' David said.

Langton turned back to Sutton, who had glanced through the report now. 'What do you think?'

'It's a hell of a case, Will. Seems like the factory, if compared to its Japanese equivalents, *is* obsolete. But to improve the factory'd cost jobs, and we can't go along with that.'

'But if we don't,' David said, 'it could eventually cost the country the whole of Stanton Industries.'

After Saigon, Terry had flown straight to Washington DC to cover an old story that was finally breaking big.

Senator Sam Ervin had set the ball rolling back in August '72 when he'd indentified the dirty money that had paid off the Watergate burglars. By May of '74 the source of that money had been established as one of America's biggest defence contractors. In November, two of America's giant oil companies came clean to the Securities and Exchange Commission about their corporate slush funds.

Public hearings were demanded by the Senate, and both Terry and Maggie went. By June the chairman of Northrop, the US aircraft manufacturer, had been called before the subcommittee. Maggie listened carefully as he began to unload blame on his giant rival. In her spiral-backed notebook she underlined one name several times: Lockheed. That was particularly interesting because she seemed to recall that Alex's partner, Ray Hacker, had first made it as a salesman for the Lockheed company . . .

That night there was a telephone call. Terry handed her the phone. 'Somebody wants to speak to you, won't give their name.'

She pressed the phone to her, and heard traffic sounds and faint conversation. A public phone. 'Hello?'

'Maggie,' the Japanese voice said. 'It's me, Kiko.'

Kiko Hideki. Maggie remembered the unreturned phone calls, the mutual friends who had not seen her since Saigon fell. 'Where've you been?'

'Nowhere good,' Kiko said flatly.

Worry became accusation. 'I was getting scared.'

'Listen, I'm glad you got out of Saigon, but now we must talk quickly.'

She sat up in bed, mind clearing. 'Right.'

They exchanged information. Then there were questions about Alex Stanton, his morality and politics, his power. Maggie answered with complete honesty, then Kiko had to hang up.

Maggie felt disturbed. Was Kiko hiding something? And what could possibly interest Kiko in a man she had never met? It was a mystery Maggie had to sleep on. But a bad dream came. Saigon, and Van's head rolling in slow motion across the floor, grinning at her, and she found herself waking up mumbling the words in blood that had said SEE Y'ALL LATER.

In another two days, on a sweltering August afternoon, she burst into their Georgetown apartment, bubbling with excitement.

'You'll never believe it! Lockheed just admitted twenty-two million dollars worth of bribes!'

Terry smiled. 'This is some story.'

Each revelation from the Senate hearings came across the Atlantic like a shockwave. In his high castle in Millbank, as he worked in secret on his Japan-style modernization plans, Alex had watched as public figures in the Netherlands, Italy, and Germany, became implicated. The highest in the land, brought low.

He felt uneasy. This was coming too close to home. Arigata, and his own link to it, could not withstand public exposure; but he knew his family firm was in urgent need of Hideki's money.

The second round of Lockheed hearings brought with it allegations of a million dollar bribe to Prince Bernhardt of the Netherlands, whose public offices were hastily discontinued. As elections were under way in Italy, the Communists made great play of the involvement of the prime minister and two former defence ministers. In Germany, too, federal elections were thrown into confusion when it was revealed that twelve million dollars had been siphoned into the right wing party of the rotund Bavarian, Franz-Josef Strauss. Which country would be next? One of the Middle East states? Great Britain itself? Or, worst of all, the United States and its military-industrial establishment?

Alex got on the phone to Hacker in Texas who told him happily, 'No, we're in the clear, but just wait till they prise the lid off of Japan, Alex. They'll find a real crock of shit.'

The economic situation grew more serious. The oil shock of 1973 had sent inflation ballooning everywhere, but the more powerful economies could cope with it. Germany and Japan continued to prosper, but David saw Britain falter. In his political career he had been especially open about the necessity of Britain's staying in Europe, and he had opposed the unholy alliance of the far Left and far Right who demanded a 'no' vote in the upcoming referendum. The magazine *Forward* ran an especially vicious campaign. The language it used was meant to alarm and intimidate, and it all too often succeeded. Nevertheless, when the EEC referendum was held on 5 June, 1975 it produced an overwhelming 'yes' vote for Britain to remain in the European Economic Community.

Fortified by this, the Prime Minister decided to take on the hard Left team at the Department of Industry. Anthony Wedgwood Benn, who preferred these days to be know simply as plain Tony Benn, was moved to a more harmless post, and other ministers were sacked.

David Bryant was hopeful. As he had taken a well-publicized interest in industry and trade, this might possibly be his chance.

Nevertheless, no promotion was offered to him.

It was worse than frustrating, he explained to Alex. 'I feel I have solutions, have learned things from you and your people inside Stanton Industries, and also from Germany and Japan.'

Then, on the 30th, as the Prime Minister was eating strawberries at the Royal Agricultural Show in Warwickshire and talking down the economic crisis, the pound began collapsing again. At an emergency Cabinet meeting that continued into the next morning, the Treasury view gained the upper hand – there would, after all, be an incomes policy, backed by the full force of criminal law. But it seemed to many that new ideas were called for in the government.

Early the following morning, David Bryant was finally summoned.

He was driven the four hundred yards to a side-street off Whitehall, and left on the doorstep. Once inside, he was escorted to the Cabinet Room where the offer was put to him by the Prime Minister in person. He accepted immediately. It was his chance to step on to the ladder that might one day lead to great heights.

He used a telephone in Number 10 to ring his wife.

'I've been—' Excitement choked him for a moment. Then his voice grew deep and strong. 'I've been appointed Parliamentary Under-Secretary of State, Megan – I'm *in*!'

'Oh, my God,' she said, rocked by the news. She had not expected this so suddenly. 'Which department?'

'I'll be working under Peter Shore at the Department of Trade; I'm taking over from Monday.'

'Can I tell Uncle Frank?'

'Of course you can, and tell him I know how much I owe him, and thank him for me, please.' He hung up, looked quickly around the lobby, and grinned at the doorman.

'Good news, sir?'

'Oh, yes,' he said as he passed. 'Absolutely wonderful news.'

He met Alex for a quiet drink in St John's Wood. The atmosphere between the two of them was subdued, as they both recognized the magnitude of the problems, but also purposeful.

'I feel I've come into my own, Alex. I feel . . .' He spread his hands, lost for words. He could not explain, even to himself, why he felt so happy.

Alex was smiling but restless, leaning on the huge mantelpiece for a moment. 'I know exactly what you mean. There's something about getting the opportunity to do great things. Even the merest chance of greatness. It's uplifting.'

'Do you think we can do it? Modernize the firm, modernize the country?'

'Let's drink to it.' They did. 'Now,' Alex said, 'I know you have doubts about nuclear power, but there are some things about the Arigata project I hope you'll be able to help us over.'

Alex was casually smiling; David's expression was reserved. This was an important moment.

'I expect I will,' David said at last, 'as long as it's all done through the proper channels. I don't like back-door politicking.'

'As you say, Minister,' Alex said, his charm undiminished.

Despite its rather forbidding modern exterior of glass and concrete, there was something about the Department of Trade that David Bryant had taken to immediately. Perhaps he was remembering the days when he had visited its corridors to collect statistics for Frank Deacon, though he thought it was more probably the atmosphere of positive effort he could find here.

Now, he had an official car, and secretaries at his disposal, interpreters, telex links – everything he needed to help him plough through the papers that piled up daily in a red leather despatch box stamped with EIIR in gold. He found he was quickly at home among his civil servants, mastering the figures.

Megan had soon found she had a formidable rival for David's time and affection. In the Kennington flat, and in the family house in Fishguard, she found she was taking second place, not to David's ambition, which she could have complained about, but to his conscience. She found to her surprise that she was married to an intensely patriotic man. David's new world fascinated him: his sober-suited staff, his foreign and domestic contacts, and his hundred-million-pound decisions – a new aluminium smelter, aid for North Sea exploration, or increased tax credits for industrial investment? All were thoroughly compelling questions. Most of all, he was interested in the overriding philosophy of industrial competition, so that whatever the Japanese and Europeans had, he intended to make sure Britain had, too.

'It all seems a little *dry* to me,' Megan said, driving him back to Fishguard station.

David laughed. He felt relaxed and expansive, listening to Mozart piano music on the car radio. 'Of course, as a junior minister my powers are quite limited,' he told her regretfully, 'but I want to be an ideas man for this government, if I can. Suppose I *can* help get Stanton Industries into shape . . . And I get a real kick out of the weekly, monthly and quarterly figures – it's almost like gambling: pulling the handle of a one-armed bandit and seeing what comes out!'

'Don't you think it's funny they call you "puss"?' Megan said.

'Parliamentary Under-Secretary of State,' he said with satisfaction. Then he saw she was teasing him. 'It could've been worse than "puss", you know. I could have been in American politics, and been an Assistant Secretary of State.'

'And I'd be an ASS's wife,' she said humorously.

He gave a short laugh. 'You think I'm taking it all too seriously – and myself? It's just that the job's so' – he sought the correct word – 'absorbing, and utterly crucial to the future of this country. I want to involve myself in long-term schemes: industrial investment, sound money, training, flexibility. I want to see an industrial policy that promotes *change*.'

'Now you're really beginning to sound pompous,' she said, looking at him quickly before returning her attention to the traffic. 'I only hope that you remember politics is about people, David, and that you have to carry the people with you.'

'And the activists?' he asked her, a little bitterly. 'All Alan Hoyle's friends, and those Marxists who really ought to be in the Communist Party – or really *are* in the CPGB, and have been all the time! I think about Alan Hoyle quite a lot. And about what would happen if there was ever blackmail from East Germany.'

He saw her hands tighten on the wheel. 'Alan Hoyle is dangerous and despicable; and if I thought he was a real socialist, I'd stop being one!'

'I know, dear,' he told her, loving her moral rectitude.

After a while, she asked him about Alex.

'Maybe marriage agrees with him, Megan.'

'He's not a happily married man! I won't believe it!'

David laughed, touched her knee. Suddenly the atmosphere had eased. 'There isn't a limited quantity of happiness in the world. With luck and good planning, there might be enough to go round for everybody. Isn't that what *our* politics is all about?'

Alex Stanton saw Great Britain's year was ending on a depressing note with over one and a half thousand million pounds of government money being used to prop up all kinds of ailing industries: the country's biggest car producer – and even Burmah, the country's second largest oil company.

Stanton Industries, however, was still growing stronger.

Alex had worked hard at creating the right management structure – the single most important asset any company could have – and he knew that once the machine was oiled and gleaming, he could set about achieving an ambition he had been nursing for four years. To talk again with Hideki.

The following week he invited David and his wife over to St John's Wood for dinner. It was Caroline's birthday, and the caterers she used surpassed themselves. Twenty-two people sat around the oval table in mellow candlelight and thoroughly enjoyed the French cuisine. Afterwards there was music. In one corner of the reception room, near the tall windows, an Austrian quartet played light classical music, mainly Strauss from Vienna's long-lost golden age.

Later that night, as Caroline busied herself organizing coffee and trays of black chocolate peppermints, Alex went up to his old friend and after a little idle banter came to the point.

'I was wondering if you'd seen Maggie lately.'

David, in his dinner jacket, raised an eyebrow. 'You're not in touch?'

Alex looked into the fireplace. 'Not on that kind of personal level.'

'She's reconciled herself with Terry Katz, you know.'

'Permanently?'

'Now that's a hard one to answer, Alex.'

'Do you mean to say I'm prying?'

David looked him straight in the eye. Alex had few personal secrets from his old friend. 'I suppose I'd call it a legitimate interest. I was at their Flood Street place for dinner late in June, just after they had come back from the Senate corruption hearings. But he mainly talked about Saigon.'

Alex shook his head. 'Trying to stay on after the north took the city . . . Russian roulette, David.'

'The whole US adventure there was exactly that,' David said impatiently, then began toying with his sherry glass. 'I remember saying something like that to Alan Hoyle, years ago in Oxford.'

Alex gave a cold smile; that was an opponent he both respected and hated. 'Come, come, David, I know you. And your memory. You remember *exactly* what you said to comrade Alan Hoyle. And I can also tell you know that treasonous Marxist bastard a damn sight more intimately than you ought to!'

David lowered his voice. 'That's over, Alex. Now somebody else has to oppose Hoyle that way. I've got a wife and kids.'

'It was appreciated, David.' Alex spoke quietly, eyes sweeping the room to make sure he could not be overheard. 'Stanton Industries would have gone down, if it wasn't for you. I wouldn't ask you to do anything like that again. It's bad judgement to push your luck too far.'

David swallowed the last of the sherry. 'Terry Katz was certainly riding his luck in Saigon.'

'It made good copy, didn't it?'

'I don't think he was risking his life out there just to get an exclusive story and pictures to go with it.'

'No?'

'I think he was also risking himself to prove something to Maggie.'

That was all Alex needed to know. It was as he had suspected. Deftly he changed the subject. 'They say Saigon is going to be known as Ho Chi Minh City.'

'Indeed. Therefore I'm more interested than ever in getting to grips with Japan.'

'Why? Because Saigon fell? What's that got to do with Japan?'

'That's only the second time an Asian nation has defeated a Western power – and the first time was when Russia lost to Japan in 1905. The world has been shifting on its axis, and it's about time we in the West looked into why.'

Alex nodded briskly. 'You're the government minister. I'm the man of business. We both know Hideki. Let's investigate.'

His eyes glinted. David recognized the greatness of his courage, and his will. Solemnly, they shook hands.

'Let's hope my fellows on the Stanton Board of Directors agree with you, David.'

'What do you mean?'

Alex lowered his voice. 'I heard from Langton. We're going to meet up at the tank factory.'

'You have plans for it? More expense?'

'I always have plans,' he said toughly. 'And I hope I'll always have money.'

Sitting in the back of the silvery Rolls, Alex Stanton had to crane forward to see into the rear-view mirror. That confirmed it. He was still being followed.

He continued to speak into the radio telephone. 'Hideki's people will soon have the contracts ready to sign; but I'll need an appointment with the Minister to get official approval. Exporting uranium and plutonium is a serious business . . . Get on to David Bryant's private office today. Then chase up the architects. I want those designs in absolute apple-pie order before I apply for government assistance. This has to be done right first time.'

As soon as the Silver Shadow turned into Newcastle's famous Scotswood Road, Reid pulled over to the kerb and climbed out. It was a wet morning, and a grey drizzle fell.

The passenger door was opened.

'Thank you, Peter,' Alex said as he got out. 'Tell the family I'll be back at Craigburn for a late supper.'

The very ordinary blue Austin Princess that had been following them drew up behind the Rolls. Its driver got out also. Alex took the Austin's keys and changed places with the driver, then continued westwards along the Tyne.

Rows of tall council flats soon gave way to battered pubs, and on the left could be seen a sprawling, decayed industrial complex of tarry sheds and steaming ventilator stacks. There was faded lettering on some roofs, but he could not read it, so long had dirt and rain and time been working to efface the name. Along the crumbling brick wall that parallelled the road, some Geordie joker had painted a slogan – SEE SCOTSWOOD ROAD AND DIE.

At the works gates the security man directed Alex to a small cobbled yard and telephoned a message ahead. No sooner had Alex got out and slammed the car door, holding a hand above his head to try and ward off the rain, than a balding man of stocky build was by his side. They moved quickly to take shelter under a projecting roof. This man was George Cooper, the works general manager. Another person was with him – the man Alex had really come to see.

Cooper's puzzlement was obvious as he looked from the blue Princess to its driver. Rain drummed over their heads.

Alex half smiled, pleased that his decision not to arrive at the factory in an intimidating Rolls had been justified: *keep 'em guessing* was a good motto. A travelling office complete with radio telephone and a ride smooth enough to do paperwork was marvellous, but this was not the time for it.

Alex turned to shake the rough hand of the other man too. 'It's been a long time since we had discussions face to face.'

'So I think there must be something important on your mind, Mr Stanton,' Will Langton told him.

'There is.' Alex turned away, ducking a trickle of water spilling from a broken gutter. Then he entered the echoing Victorian workshop of the Scotswood Road site. 'Gentlemen, let's take a walk into history.'

It was dark inside, as many of the lights did not work. At this end of the huge, cold workshop two men, puffing on cigarettes, sat by an ancient machine that hammered thin steel plate. They stood up guiltily as Alex and the others walked by. There was no continuous covered way between the many buildings, and they passed through eight of the twenty-three workshops on the site, getting wetter as the downpour intensified. The old building let in water and leaked heat at every seam.

After his ambitions to match Japan and its clean efficient factories, the sights here depressed Alex. Everything – buildings, working methods, equipment, attitudes – was at least thirty years out of date. He looked around, frowning. 'And the politicians ask why the Germans and Japanese are able to deliver the goods whilst we're not!' he said.

'This place is clapped out,' Will Langton agreed gruffly, rubbing his hands together for warmth.

'That's right,' Cooper added. 'It was mebbe good enough for '39 to '45, but it's not good enough for the economic war now, Mr Stanton.'

'At least your humour's dry, Mr Cooper.' Alex shook the raindrops from his raincoat and folded it over his arm. 'Let's see if it stands up to what I have in mind.'

It took a long time to get to the office that Alex wanted. Lathes screamed. All around were many disconsolate men in Stanton overalls. Some pulled faces at the sight of the senior management. Others seemed entirely indifferent, glancing up from newspapers or simply turning their heads away. Eventually the three of them passed the first huge and almost completed Mark VIII-C tank – another destined for the Shahanshah of Iran.

'I'm surprised you take the time to come here,' Langton said truculently as they walked. 'You must be the first man from Stanton's Board of Directors to pay a visit in years.'

'No wonder, after my reception last time!' He wondered, bitterly, how his equivalents would be received in Japan – with respect, interest and enthusiasm, no doubt. 'Look at this place!' Alex said, gesturing at scrap piled high in a corner of the pressing plant. He made chopping motions with his hand. 'Rust, decay! It's beyond belief. Twenty-three separate workshops, eight of them abandoned years ago, none of them purpose-built. It's like an overgrown garden that's gone to seed. We've got seven different staff canteens and a heating system that costs half a million pounds a year but still doesn't work properly.'

Langton shook his head pityingly. 'It's living history, man. Think what your great-grandfather achieved! The historian of this city says that the growth of Stanton's factories—'

'—was the chief romance and pride of Victorian Tyneside,' Alex finished, then said fiercely, 'Do you suppose I don't know that? What do you think I want?'

'I know what the men I speak for want. I don't think you want that.' Langton glared at him belligerently. 'I hear rumours you've had your people around here, preparing for a close-down.'

Alex shook his head, continuing to meet Langton's gaze. 'No.'

'No? Then what *is* your plan? What do you want here?'

'What I want, Mr Langton, is to make this firm great again.'

Langton stared, thrown by the announcement.

'But I need help to do it.'

'Oh aye?'

They entered a linoleum-floored corridor, with dingy offices to either side. Typewriters chattered, and somewhere a salesman was shouting apologies into a phone.

'I do have a plan – for a brand-new factory that will be the most efficient armaments-production facility on earth. With it, I will be able to go to Japan or any country. Every contract I win will represent work and wealth for this nation. This city, the men who work here – again, leading the world.'

'By God, I believe you mean it,' Langton said.

'I do.'

The din abated as Cooper finally closed his office door, but the warm, oily smell of industry still permeated the place.

Alex glanced around before he took the seat offered. Faded photographs of past glories hung on the walls; the sepia men who stood in them looked like ghosts. In one framed photograph he saw President U. S. Grant shaking hands with Sir Samuel Stanton.

'I've been here since the forties,' Cooper told them both. 'That was the time to be here. Great days, when the defence of the realm depended on us, and all hell was breaking loose in Europe.'

'No doubt.' Alex regarded the man thoughtfully. He made his decision. 'I want you to know that I've the highest regard for your past record as a manager . . .'

Cooper's demeanour changed. He stood up, a hopeless anger colouring his face. 'I understand. You want your own man in, now that you're boss. Well, I can't say I haven't been expecting it. Ever since the Rolls-Royce collapse and the mass redundancies in the shipbuilding division, I've known that the axe would have to fall here some time.'

The union man watched silently, measuring, as Cooper plucked his framed thirty-year service award off the wall.

Cooper slammed it on the desk top. 'But I'll tell you this, Mr Alex Stanton, you'll not change anything by making a scapegoat out of the likes of me and those poor buggers down on the shopfloor. When this Iran order finishes, that's it! There's no more.'

Alex smiled, causing Cooper to stare at him in angry frustration.

'Perhaps that's the best time to make changes. But you're right about one thing, Mr Cooper. I do need my own man running things here. We have a fifty-acre site. It's damned nearly unmanageable.'

Will Langton said furiously, 'Very tough, Mr Stanton. You bloody dismiss the manager of the whole site in front of my face – the first of many, eh! Then you're going to tell us that the easy option is to close it all down and forget about it.'

'I have no interest in the easy option.' Alex put the sheaf of papers on the desk. 'And I'd value your help, George – I *need* your help. I want to see this company survive, and I'd like you to assist me. You will have to oversee great changes. But I have the confidence that you can do it. It's either change everything – or closure. There is no alternative. Because, rest assured, if I have to go to Japan or Korea to get the services I need, I will go there.' He looked at them both. Force of will poured from him. 'But what I want, what we all want, is to do it here. Now, can you do it for me?'

Cooper was shaken. He was a bulky man, not afraid to get his hands dirty, but he collapsed into his chair like a child and held his head in his hands, and when he looked up again, there was a strange light in his face. 'Thirty-eight years, now,' he said. 'Yes, I'll help you.'

They worked through lunch hour, sending out for coffee, leaving it undrunk when it arrived. The sheaf of papers that Alex called his 'preferred solution' contained a far-reaching plan. He showed the others architects' drawings; a view of the Tyne with a long, futuristic factory along its shore that seemed to be made of red plastic and glass, with trees in the neatly landscaped gardens.

All three men pored over the proposals together.

'It's a pioneering move,' Cooper said. 'For as long as anyone can remember no one's thought seriously in terms of reconstruction in the industrial North-East. It's like a jump from 1945 to the year 2000 – this is incredible!'

Alex chuckled, pleased by the enthusiasm. 'I think it's very credible. And I have the figures to prove it.'

Langton was rubbing at his chin, a dubious look on his face. Cooper saw it, and his own lips tightened.

'New working practices and cost-cutting – fine ideas in principle, Mr Stanton. But will the unions stand for it?' Cooper was once more grave. 'They've got pride in their own areas of influence. Each trade has its own domain, and they're jealous of one another's power.'

Alex turned to Langton. 'The whole deal turns on that, Will. Either you wear the idea of a single union – your engineering union – or we can't go through with the preferred solution.'

Langton frowned. There was perspiration on his brow. 'You've put me in one hell of a position, man. I have to turn my back on tradition, help you knock out other unions, and then I have to convince my members that they must accept redundancies and new working methods or it's closure.'

'I face opposition from a major shareholder, but I'm fighting him, and I want to see you fight, too.'

'Beauford?' Langton threw him a shrewd glance. 'I've met him.'

'What did you think?'

'I like him about as much as cancer. He's lied to me and the union, and as you can imagine I don't think much of his politics. He'll try and stop this modernization programme, won't he?'

'He won't be in favour,' Alex said. He sighed. 'There are some problems in the aircraft division, now. But we must make the change. There really is no alternative. Japan has shown us the way and we *must* follow.'

'I could be called a traitor for this!'

'So what?' Alex pointed straight at his chest. 'As long as *you* know you're right.'

Langton watched Alex, impaling him with a look that questioned his sincerity and his ability.

'Don't doubt me, Will Langton. It's change or closure.'

'All right,' Maggie's father said at last. 'I'll push for change.'

Maggie was on another continent, and too busy to worry about anything as she covered the presidential election primaries for the first months of 1976. Between February and June these would be held in twenty-nine states and the District of Columbia. For the Republicans, Nixon's inheritor President Ford had an edge over Ronald Reagan. But the Democrats' long race to the convention in July offered the excitement of a genuinely open contest.

Compared with the dark, jowelly Nixon of the five o'clock shadow, the grating voice, the recorded obscenity on those Watergate tapes, the Democrat who became front-runner was as different as could be: smiling, Southern, Christian, and transparently honest. She met him, liked him, cultivated him.

'He's called Carter,' she told David during a transatlantic phone call. 'Jimmy Carter – from Georgia.'

'Carter? Who's he?'

'Apparently,' she said, not able to keep a straight face, 'he used to run nuclear submarines and the State of Georgia – and farm peanuts.'

But in the 1 May primary, Texas gave ninety-three of their ninety-eight delegates to the likeable, good-natured man from Plains, Georgia. He would face Gerald Ford in the presidential election.

Things, Maggie knew, were really changing – and she was involved.

Chapter Twelve

As Alex had feared, the next Stanton Board meeting was unusually rancorous. The aircraft division had been crippled for several weeks by a major strike in the Bristol factories, a strike that was threatening to spread, and had already caused the loss of a major order for the Swedish air force. It took them five hours to work through the agenda to the last item: any other business.

Then Lord Beauford abruptly turned on Alex. 'There is a member of this board whose judgement I must again call into question!'

Hugh, mopping his forehead, said nothing.

Alex waited for half a minute, cold contempt on his face. 'I think you'll need to be more specific.'

'This business about an entire new factory—'

'Don't you think it's necessary! Besides, the expense is already agreed in principle with this board. The new works and the union's agreement to updated working practices will slash our costs by upwards of thirty percent.'

Sainsbury looked up from some abstruse calculations. 'If the factory is built. And union leaders can't deliver their members. We've learned that lesson painfully time and time again.'

'I want to bring Will Langton round to my way of thinking,' Alex said, 'and he's a man of his word. He'd sweat blood to keep a promise.'

'Yes, William Langton and his beautiful daughter,' Beauford said spitefully. 'Gentlemen, I seem to remember a very undignified headline: UNION LEADER'S DAUGHTER IN SEX-ROMP WITH BOSS'S SON.'

Alex flinched from the polished boardroom table, aware that some of the others were trying to conceal smiles. 'Maggie Langton and me? It was very enjoyable, and no crime,' he drawled. 'And, by the way, I've never been the boss's son. I've earned this position.'

Lord Beauford had rocked him, though, by trading on his vulnerability over Maggie. Alex knew some people still said he loved her. The merchant banker stood up suddenly, then leaned over the table. 'I think we should have a greater degree of mutual trust on this board.'

'Hear hear,' said one of the others.

Hugh threw in with a calming comment. 'I'm sure no one could accuse any of us of not being wholly on the side of Stanton Industries.'

'You say so?' Lord Beauford asked, peering at the Stanton who was

Chairman of the company. 'But what would you say about a director who went behind the backs of all of us on major matters, and was then proved wrong?'

'Oh, come to the point,' Alex said.

One of the new non-executive directors glanced at him, then looked away – clearly intimidated, Alex realized.

'Is it true you will soon have to come to this board for an extra twenty-five million pounds for the Arigata reactor?'

Beauford obviously knew it was true. No doubt his contacts in Japan had given him the figures privately, and Alex wondered if Tokyo saw him as some kind of threat. 'We may need more money,' he temporized. 'Just to finish this stage of the Arigata project. But it will still be within budget.'

Sainsbury's eyes opened wide. 'I didn't know we would need so much, so soon.'

'And what about these civil projects in general?' Beauford threw up his pudgy hands. 'Over one hundred and fifty million pounds invested so far, with little return.'

'As yet, certainly, though we're already close to covering our costs. But we need to expand out of defence-related work; that has already been agreed at board level.'

'But why does everything have to be done through your own armaments division? Why do *you* have to stay in sole charge?'

Alex hesitated, then spoke firmly. 'As these matters are still controversial, it is only proper that I take full personal responsibility.'

The peer was scornful. 'I think you're rash and ill-advised to pour our money into Japan, and foolish to miss our next Board meeting to go there in person. Do you really think Saigo Hideki wants our firm doing business in Tokyo?'

'I'll make him want it,' Alex said coldly.

'And the new factory here will really be completed on budget and on schedule – without you having to ask this board for more money?'

'It will!'

'So what will you do if you are proved to be wrong?'

Alex stood up, too. He noticed Hugh's shocked face but he knew there was no alternative: he had to commit himself.

'That factory *will* be completed on schedule, and our business in Japan *will* be successful and profitable. If I am proved wrong on either of those issues, I will offer my resignation to this board.' He began to turn away, wondering if his career inside Stanton Industries was soon to be over. 'Good day to you, gentlemen.'

When David was called to 10 Downing Street he sat down for a brisk meeting with Harold Wilson and Peter Shore, his ultimate and immediate superiors. The trade crisis was not mentioned, to David's surprise. Instead they asked him, as their Under-Secretary for Trade, to fly to Tokyo to represent British interests at the Trade Normalization Conference.

'Might even take two or three weeks,' the Prime Minister told him jovially as he lit a cigar; the famous pipe was for the cameras. 'A talking shop, maybe, but it's important for national prestige that we're represented – and talking sense. You're good at that.'

It was a duty David was very happy to perform, though he still had to work night after night as well as day after day on his plans, and going to Tokyo would be time-consuming. But then again, he mused, as he posed in his new Pierre Cardin suit before the mirror, especially with Alex around, there might be the chance of a little fun among the fragrant flowers of the Orient . . . But also he secretly thought of his mission itself in rather romantic terms. This, after all, was the world stage at last.

As the British Caledonian jet flew the last stretch of its long flight, David Bryant was chatting with Christopher Paulin, his private secretary.

'Land of the Rising Yen,' he joked, pointing towards the distant coast of Japan. 'Inscrutable Orient.'

As he found out on his arrival at Haneda airport, the reality of this new Japan was very different from temple gardens and pagan shrines. He had asked not to be met: instead he and Christopher took an ordinary taxi, and he spent the drive peering out and taking note, awed to be in Japan at last. He could remember Alex Stanton's stories from five years previously. Even he had failed to penetrate this city successfully.

Tokyo was no romantic place. Its air was both urban and industrial, with a bitter taint. It was a relentless conglomeration of buildings, people and traffic that ran on overdrive twenty-four hours a day. It was actually a little frightening, and it took them hours, it seemed, to get through to the embassy. David arrived there jet-lagged and exhausted.

The car swept along a dual carriageway, skirting a park where the moated splendour of the Imperial Palace could be glimpsed between flowering trees, and finally it drew into the embassy precinct. Up above, the Union Jack hung lifeless in the still air.

David climbed out, stiffly. Paulin was clutching two bulky cases of briefing documents as they were received by a staff secretary.

'Thank God,' David said, blinking. 'I want a shower, a cup of tea, and about twelve hours sleep.'

Instead, he got a formal meeting with Sir Oliver Gregory, Her Majesty's Ambassador to Japan. As Ambassador, Sir Oliver was obliged to deal respectfully with a Minister for the Crown, to call him 'sir', and to defer to him without too much obvious irony. However, David knew he would be a fool to stand on ceremony and ignore the experience and knowledge of the man on the spot.

The First Secretary was called to the main office, a conspicuously old-fashioned room. No telex or computer terminal, only one telephone, and leather upholstery that might have been Victorian. David frowned at the dearth of technology, but the diplomats did not seem worried by it. Annigoni's celebrated portrait of the Queen hung in reproduction on one wall.

'I hope you had a comfortable flight, Minister. We have booked you both into the conference hotel.'

'Excellent.'

'Incidentally, I feel it would be best for you to presume that the suite is not completely secure.'

David pursed his lips. 'Secure?' he echoed.

'The hotel may not be – how shall I put it? – one hundred percent information proof.'

'Do you mean *bugged*?'

The First Secretary smiled. 'I'm afraid the Japanese are very serious about international trade. Their Ministry of International Trade and Industry is apt to take things a bit far.'

David looked at the man. 'Well, it may be thought un-British of me, but I don't see anything wrong with playing to win. But thank you for the warning.'

As he opened his briefing, he wondered how he could raise his next point. Paulin met his eyes. David had thought the description of his duties unduly sketchy – even for a junior minister. On the plane, his suspicions had been further aroused.

'I understand that no other Members of Parliament will be attending, though there will be several representatives of British industry?'

The First Secretary consulted the finalized list. 'That's my understanding also, sir.'

'Then I'd like to add Alex Stanton of Stanton Industries to the British delegation.'

'No need for that,' said the First Secretary. 'He turned up here last week, and said that you'd be expecting him to join you.'

David shook his head, his expression admiring. 'That's Alex Stanton. Expect nothing from him except the unexpected.'

'As for the conference . . .' the diplomat began, drily.

David decided to speak his mind. 'I'm a little concerned about my precise rôle here. The Prime Minister has said almost nothing about what he expects from the meeting. I've already had dozens of highly technical background briefing documents from the Japanese, and a starting date, but nothing else. No list of attendees, no agenda. I don't see how fourteen countries can reach any proper formal agreement inside a mere ten days, and in any case I have no authorization to agree any changes on behalf of Her Majesty's Government.'

The First Secretary settled back in his chair and clasped his hands together.

'Mr Stanton put this to me: our chance of reaching a satisfactory trade liberalization agreement with the Japanese – "a deal with teeth" – is virtually zero.'

David, his fatigue now completely forgotten, sat up straight. He was shocked by the comment. Suddenly it all became clear; he flushed, feeling a complete fool.

'Then, to put it bluntly, I've been sent out here to nod and smile and to pass the time in civilized English fashion, while everything of significance goes on exactly as before?'

The First Secretary unlaced his fingers. 'Yes, Minister,' he said. The man added sympathetically, 'Sometimes the inscrutable Orient is a difficult place to deal with. In the wake of this frightful Lockheed business everything here is in a ferment. The ruling party is *very* embarrassed – to the extent they've postponed their spring elections.'

David was crestfallen and hurt and his mind began to run over possible reasons why he had been got out of the way by his masters, but he forced himself to keep calm. He knew he had to work with these people, so they must continue to give him respect. He thought hard, studying the diplomat's bland, pale face which gave nothing away.

Over cocktails, David discovered that the First Secretary was an Eton contemporary of Alex Stanton's, and knew him also from Oxford. David was glad that he had found a link with this man. In a more relaxed mood now and glad that he had made tentative allies here, David began to tell a story about the Prime Minister, Concorde, and former President Johnson.

He did not return to serious business until they were again in private, sitting at the conference table. The First Secretary was now accompanied by a Second Secretary (Trade), a bluff, heavier man.

'I intend to do a good job, here, and I'll need your help to do it. I'll need information. Alex Stanton does business here, and he's explained to me the many difficulties. Now you tell me the Japanese *talk* of trade liberalization, but they don't actually mean it?'

The First Secretary touched an earlobe. Tall blue and pink flowers shivered in their window box behind him. There was a view of the embassy garden beyond. 'The conference is merely window dressing: MITI's response to US pressure.'

'I see. And their real intentions?'

The Second Secretary answered. 'It's become my own view that they intend to build their trade surplus ever higher. They're conscious of the technology gap between themselves and America, and they are reinvesting in key areas at a terrific rate in an effort to reverse it. They won't lower their barriers until they're sure they're ahead.'

David sat back. 'You mean they won't compete fairly until they're certain they'll win?'

The First Secretary shrugged. 'They may make promises, all couched in suitably sincere-seeming rhetoric, but they will nevertheless continue the programme as before – keep up trade barriers and undervalue the yen to keep their export drive fully fuelled.'

David stood up, disturbed. 'Then my being here seems to be a total waste of time.'

'I wouldn't put it quite like that. There *will* be a trade conference. And there it will be your duty, Minister, to push for the interests of the nation.'

David reached forward to shake his hand firmly. 'Now *that's* the kind of language I understand.'

Suddenly the telephone rang, bringing a hint of crisis into the room. The other men exchanged glances. The First Secretary answered it. For the first time, the man's composure seemed to crack. He put the phone down.

'Minister, I think you should know,' he said. 'That was news direct from Whitehall.'

'Yes?'

'The Prime Minister has just resigned.'

Alex Stanton had come to Japan with one overall objective in mind: to get the new Arigata contracts signed and take away the money due.

Supplying uranium and plutonium fuel for the nuclear complex would provide the income he needed to build the new tank factory back on Tyneside, as well as the shipyard. Otherwise, he wanted to check out some of the other business he was doing in Japan, and discover as much as he could about the Japanese economic miracle. Then he would shamelessly steal as much of that miracle as possible.

He intended to open a bigger office here for Stanton Industries and do more business; and he hoped he could take advantage of Saigo Hideki's influence to smooth the path. But even though he knew Hideki, too, had a great deal invested in Arigata, and was therefore vulnerable to pressure, Alex had no illusions about how difficult it would be to become big in Japan.

After Alex's earlier failure to break into Tokyo, in the middle of 1973 the Hideki Corporation had bought the rights from Stanton aircraft division's avionics subdivision to manufacture, under licence, a limited number of aircraft instrumentation, radar and navigation sets. The Stantons had developed the sets from the military originals they had first supplied to NATO. In Japan civil aviation was set to expand, and the deal would give Hideki the right to sell to their own small domestic market, a market from which Japanese bureaucratic red tape had excluded Stanton Industries itself.

All seemed well in the lucrative local aircraft market, though he was surprised at how few units Hideki's firm had sold – or *acknowledged* they had sold. Alex had decided to build on this cooperative success to propose a joint attempt to freeze out Mitsubishi and monopolize Japan's 1978 armaments budget, which was set to soar far above previous levels.

Alex had arrived in Japan three days before David Bryant, with an itinerary already arranged. McCourt, fluent in Japanese, was with him.

They would meet Hideki's senior executives before the conference itself opened, and try to extract down payments on his guaranteed supplies of uranium from Stanton Industries' mining subsidiaries abroad, and reprocessed plutonium from the government reprocessing facility in Cumberland.

By coincidence, their tour began with the two famous cities A-bombed in 1945. Nagasaki, the great port on the island of Kyushu, came first, and they went straight to see Hideki's largest achievement so far.

'Good God!' he said at the edge of the dock. 'It's vast!'

He turned to McCourt, who shielded his eyes to survey the enterprise. 'In Belfast I used to see Harland & Wolff at night,' he said. 'The arcs of the welding torches looked like a constellation. But this –'

As far as the eye could see, cranes and gigantic handling equipment lined Hideki's 990 metre long Kozagi dry dock – the biggest, most modern in the world. Inside the great dock, thousands of busy workers swarmed over the leviathan bones of the one and a quarter million ton tanker they were building for Esso. Alex's initial surprise gave way to respect. 'It makes you ask yourself whether it's possible for us to compete with this, Ken.'

Studying the monster, McCourt shifted his weight from one leg to the other. 'Well, yes, but I'm sure that's what the Japanese who visited your great-grandfather's foundries before the Russo-Japanese war asked themselves.'

Alex nodded. 'You're quite right. The tables have been well and truly turned within three-quarters of a century – despite their losing the war. *We've* got to think about the next seventy-five years just as positively. Wait till the tank factory is complete; *that* will show them.'

'The dry dock here was constructed on a partially man-made island. It was opened in 1972, under budget and ahead of schedule. For almost twenty years now, Japan has dominated the world shipbuilding market.'

'It's a lead they'll be reluctant to give up,' Alex acknowledged tersely. Could MacKenzie's shipbuilding division ever match this, North Sea expertise and income or not? The Kozagi dock awed him. 'No restrictive practices here, no overmanning, and everybody who works here feels about his company with the same intensity as he does about his country.'

The manager who had been delegated to show them round picked out one of the workers and beckoned him over. Dressed in white overalls and a bright orange hardhat, he bowed quickly. There came a quick three-way burst of Japanese, then the worker said to Alex, 'I at Singapore in war. Great victory for Japan over your country. Now no more war.'

Alex wondered if he had a single shipyard worker who spoke Japanese. 'No more war,' he repeated.

'All people in Japan most proud of Japan country.'

'Of course,' Alex said.

'We have great respect for England, Queen.'

'Thank you – *domo*,' Alex said, endeavouring to look grateful. '*Nippon sukidesu.*'

The manager stared at Alex in surprise and then opened his mouth to respond, but Alex raised a hand. 'I'm sorry, I don't speak Japanese as Mr McCourt does. Just a few words from the phrase book. *Eigo de hanashimasho.*'

The manager continued in English. 'Few English people make an effort to learn Japanese,' he said. He was frowning in concentration. 'English is extremely hard also – the speech, thinking, writing – gives headache.' He gave a short laugh. 'Our law says English must be learned in all school. If I go your country or America, I can travel, learn things by myself. I can sell goods to anyone.'

Alex nodded, feeling uncomfortable at this. He knew that here in Nagasaki, as much as anywhere else in the Land of the Rising Sun, the Second World War had never really ended.

He considered it carefully, lying in bed that night. In schools all over America and Britain political history was taught: how Japan and Germany had lost World War II. But the equally important fact that they were winning the economic contest that followed was disregarded.

A day later they moved on to Hiroshima, and there visited the Hideki Corporation's Azu factory complex. The name Stanton meant something to them, so Alex and McCourt were conducted round with scrupulous, cloying politeness. But the visit was frustrating; they saw so little, and had failed to penetrate the skillful PR of their escorts.

Alex looked at the row of women at a long, tidy workbench, assembling electronic systems. The factory was clean, and soft music played in the background, and there was an all-pervading sense of purpose and efficiency.

Outside again, they were bowed away in farewell.

'Well?' asked McCourt.

'Bloody impressive. An inspiration.'

'For the new tank factory?'

'Exactly.'

But something bothered Alex about the way they had been treated.

As they went into Sogo, the huge department store near the city centre, he was silently trying to figure out precisely what it was that alarmed him. The elevator attendants were young girls in formal uniforms and neat white gloves, who repeated Japanese courtesies at each floor as they rode to the roof. There, on the top of the multistorey block, big colourful fibreglass children's rides had been set up. Tiny children in one-piece quilted suits laughed as they went round in giant Disney animals, their delicate, delighted faces making Alex smile too.

Then it clicked. 'They're hiding something from us – something their Tokyo office told them to hide.'

McCourt stopped. 'What could it be?'

'That,' Alex said darkly, 'is the million-dollar question . . .'

They moved across to the racks of bonsai, which were being watered by an assistant. Alex examined a particularly convoluted, hundred-year old spruce in a green vitreous pot. Then he pulled out his American Express card.

'I didn't realize you had a fancy for these gnarled, tortured things, Alex.'

'I'll have it gift-wrapped and sent to my London home. It will serve to remind me of the twisting and turning of which I suspect Saigo Hideki is capable. I'd give a lot to know what his corporation is really up to.' The Hideki head office had been unable to schedule the intended face-to-face meeting, claiming Hideki was unwell. Alex had wondered: A diplomatic illness? 'I'd call their attitude extremely polite, but thoroughly unhelpful – even though they're licensees of ours.'

McCourt agreed. 'You noticed we were conducted through only the older part of the factory, and none of our technical questions were answered straightforwardly?'

'They're not normally people to hide their light under a bushel, Ken. We've been round enough of their factories to know that.'

'Yes, they're normally bursting with pride – keen for us to know just how *ichi-ban* Japanese industry is. But not this time.'

'They were certainly anxious to keep us away from the production lines where they make the avionics equipment. Everything was strictly under wraps, and the newest part of the factory complex was quite definitely off limits to us.' Alex remembered the reports he had had about Hideki's private musings. 'Maybe they're putting our units to military use, in spite of Article IX of their constitution. Maggie had somebody investigating in Saigon, and –' Alex grimaced. 'She thinks Hideki had him killed.'

'*Murdered*? Surely not. What could he be concealing that needs blood to hide it?'

'I don't know,' Alex said. 'Something to do with arms, Maggie suspects.'

McCourt glanced at him. 'What if we don't get the Arigata supply contracts signed, with some payment in advance?'

Alex hesitated. 'That'll do grave damage to our cash-flow – and possibly leave me at the mercy of Lord Beauford.'

The Ulster voice said quietly. 'Do you think you'll get much mercy from him?'

'No,' Alex said flatly.

Leaving Sogo, they crossed the bustling street and entered a neat, tree-lined park in the busy town centre. Thirty-three years after the bomb, only one ruin crowned with a skeleton dome remained of the original city. It had been at 'ground zero' – directly under Little Boy when it had exploded – and was justly regarded by the Japanese as a miraculous and fitting memorial to the horror. Close by was the infamous bridge where the outlines of bomb victims had once been engraved by a light as bright as a thousand suns. A stainless steel plaque detailed the event in five languages. Now there was nothing to see except the plaque; the bridge was laid with minutely-finished tarmac, executed with more neatness and pride than any equivalent in England. Strange, Alex thought, how such small details could become the yardstick of a culture, the measure of its vigour and its intent.

'Look at it from their point of view,' Alex said at last. 'South Korea, Taiwan, Malaysia are all hard on Japan's heels. They waste no time in restructuring to meet new conditions. They're all adaptable, and they all resist the temptation to rest on their laurels.'

'Mmh,' McCourt mused, rubbing at his chin. 'So where does that leave us?'

'If I was Hideki, I'd fully automate my production lines. Maybe that's what they don't want us to see. Automation is something we in Britain have been avoiding. The unions fear it will cause job losses; managements won't find the money. I'm beginning to understand that unless we get into the computer age and automate soon, there won't be any jobs left at all.'

'It seems like a big investment for so small a market,' McCourt said.

'That's what worries me, Ken. Maybe they know something about the avionics market that we don't. Unless –'

Their eyes met. McCourt said quietly, 'Unless they've been turning out more of our navigation units than they've paid us for. *Or* they've made improvements and they're selling them as their own work.'

'That's happened before,' Alex said bitterly. 'My mistake. I should have insisted on unlimited rights of inspection – and I will, next time I do this kind of business with Hideki.'

McCourt watched Hiroshima's office workers and shoppers, a thousand black-haired heads bobbing along the busy street, and he said nothing.

Tall and fair, Alex stuck out here in the crowd like a nailhead. 'You don't think we *can* do business with them, do you?'

McCourt repressed a sigh, and nodded towards the stark girders of the dome over which, thirty-one years ago, the atomic age had begun in violence. 'Alex, doesn't it send a shiver down your back?'

'Yes,' Alex said, now lost in thought. What was Arigata really for – and all those new uranium-supply contracts? If they were signed, they meant he would have to provide Hideki with enough fissionable material, as one of his scientists had pointed out, to blow up a continent. 'Still, incredible to rebuild so quickly and so well. Hiroshima and Nagasaki and Tokyo may have been razed to the ground, but look at them now. Incredible.'

'And speaking as an engineer,' the Ulsterman added, 'the progress in engineering is incredible, too. I'm starting to think that by the eighties they'll be ahead of us.'

Alex nodded. This was the competition, and he respected it. 'With industrial robots they'll be *impossible* to compete against.'

Later that afternoon they headed for the train station. McCourt had booked them tickets on the bullet train to Tokyo. Alex needed to be there by Monday, for the start of the conference, but he wanted to meet David Bryant before the official opening. He needed to think through his plans, and David was ideal to bounce ideas off.

They waited together in Hiroshima's railway station, standing tall in their spotless Burberry raincoats, clean shaven, very well groomed. Alex was impressed by the commercial hive of the provincial rail terminal. It looked more like Selfridges than King's Cross, a sanitized block of marble and glass. No prostitutes nor aggressive drunks; no ruined telephones nor filthy corners full of litter.

After a short silence, McCourt asked. 'When will we get to meet Mr Hideki, I wonder?'

'When it suits him, of course.'

McCourt opened and closed his copy of *Asian Defence Review*. 'So you have no idea whether or not he'll see us?'

'None whatsoever.'

McCourt smiled. 'In Japan, to admit curiosity at this point would be considered weakness.'

Alex stared stonily down the tracks. 'The hell with them,' he said.

In the Stanton Tokyo headquarters, Alex held a top-level meeting, bringing together McCourt, Fujiko their administration manager, and the top man at the Arigata site. The office's legal team, an American from Harvard and a Japanese from the University of Kyoto, were there. Alex discussed the Arigata project in detail. Things were going well, there.

'So,' he said. 'It's time to arm ourselves with the draft contracts, and maybe some suspicion, and see the Hideki team. But I want to emphasize this to everybody: I have already committed money on the basis that we will receive from the Hideki Corporation what they promised us. If there's going to be a battle, we must win it.' He looked around. 'Let's go.'

Alex headed for the company's white Rolls-Royce, a massive Phantom VI with air conditioning. The others followed, the lawyers in another car.

They took the expressway towards the Ginza, past the Aoyama cemetary. As always, the Tokyo traffic was heavy.

They arrived at the huge interconnected buildings that formed the corporate nerve-centre of Hideki's empire – bronze, glass and concrete, and gigantic. Far larger than the local Stanton building here.

Takahashi and a junior executive met them outside one of the canopied entrances. He gave his familiar exaggerated grin. 'Mr Stanton!'

Alex shook hands, and there was the usual round of introductions and exchanges of business cards as they entered the lobby. Lesser mortals bowed as they swept by on the way to the express lift reserved for the highest officials in the corporate bureaucracy. Alex gave a grim smile, remembering that Japan was supposed to be a model, classless society.

The uniformed lift girl sang out the floor numbers in a high and feminine tone, though it was obvious the tone was forced. The atmosphere in the lift was not quite comfortable. Alex talked to Fujiko as an equal, knowing this would upset the Japanese men and their rigid notions of protocol. He was determined to take the initiative right from the start. If there was going to be a power struggle, he wanted to bring things to a head quickly, to take advantage of the international conference on which some of the world's attention was fixed. On the fourteenth floor they all stepped out, Alex waving Fujiko ahead.

The meeting room was large and lined in cream-coloured leather. Alex sat down without waiting for an invitation, and waved his team down, too. He wanted it obvious that he was displeased. He looked round. 'I understood Mr Hideki would be present.'

Takahashi touched his moustache. 'Mr Hideki may attend later.'

Alex took this as: *Mr Hideki will reward you with his presence, if negotiations proceed to a satisfactory conclusion.* Typically Japanese, the Hideki men's faces remained impassive. Alex looked around at this inscrutability, deciding it did indeed make them impressively difficult to deal with.

Alex decided to disconcert them once again by coming straight to the point. 'I have the contracts, Mr Takahashi, drawn up as we discussed. From Australia and Canada, uranium ore; from British reprocessing facilities, once we get the Arigata waste, comes high-grade plutonium and U235.' He laid a blue folder on the long table.

'I see.' Takahashi drank from a glass of water, and glanced at the two men beside him. Fusao Hatoyama, like Alex once of Harvard Business School, who worked out of head office here. The older, round-faced man was called Ito Katayama, the nuclear power plant specialist who would be in charge of Arigata when operational. His plump, bespectacled face remained blank as he turned back to Alex, saying nothing.

Takahashi said softly, 'We may need to take a more active interest in your company, just to make sure the contracts are dealt with properly.'

'You're demanding a seat on our board as the price for doing what you've already agreed?' Alex realized he was having to refight old battles. And the Japanese would know from Beauford that he desperately needed their money to rebuild his tank factory. He tried a shot in the dark. 'We were shocked about the outcome of our avionics agreement, and the units being produced by the Azu factory . . .'

Takahashi's lips tightened. 'What do you mean?'

'Military uses,' Alex said. It came with a blaze of realization. Hideki *was* recruiting men for weapons research and development, and that was why Van had been killed in Saigon – for investigating Hideki's secret ambition. 'Extremely surprising. Are you doing military research, in spite of your Constitution? Even more surprising is the lack of the previously agreed royalties.'

'Military uses?' Katayama scoffed, apparently genuinely. 'Military research? That is just not so!'

Alex turned to Hideki's chief aide. Takahashi was completely taken aback, eyes shifting about as he groped for something to say.

So it was all true. Alex gathered up his papers and stood. 'Mr Takahashi, the question is, will we be content to continue keeping your secrets – for no reward?'

'But –'

Then Katayama said something; there was a rapid exchange of Japanese as the Stanton party were walking out.

None of them spoke till they were settled back in the Rolls.

'You're taking a big chance, Alex,' McCourt said. 'Putting on pressure like that, even in private, might backfire.'

'There'll be more pressure,' Alex prophesied, 'unless they come through with what they promised. Hideki's going to keep his word! I need that money for the new tank factory, and I need Hideki to get Lord Beauford off my back.'

'That's a hell of a risk.'

'I know,' he said quietly.

There were no further overtures from Hideki.

Next day, Alex decided to turn up at the conference. He wanted to see what was happening before he watched David's own presentation in the afternoon.

Downtown Tokyo seethed with people. The buildings of the Marunouchi district, where the financial powerhouses of Japan were situated, showed a serious concern for practicality, efficiency and progress. All was modern. His Rolls-Royce Phantom VI, one of the very few to be found in Japan, moved effortlessly forward like a great shark. The Nissans and Toyotas that schooled around it were so many colourful tropical fish, dwarfed by the power and elegance and handsome lines of the British car.

The Trade Normalization Conference was taking place in a huge luxury hotel. There were fourteen nations represented here at governmental level. Eight others, including the USSR and China, had sent observers. He sat down to watch just after eleven.

Every nation had its chance to make a statement about each day's topics, but there was little real debate, and no opportunity to pass resolutions. Mountains of irrelevant statistics were put to the delegates. Low-ranking Japanese officials continually made dissembling noises about the trade gap, saying things were changing, or might be changed, or could be changed under unspecified circumstances. None of them said things would be changed.

'This morning's session was especially heavy going,' David Bryant told him angrily in the conference bar at lunchtime, after a quick handshake.

'I agree. Layer upon layer of ultimately meaningless platitudes, empty promises dressed up as business. It's a charade.'

'But as we know, the Japanese can be the most efficient, to-the-point people on earth when it suits them. Still, they're a trading nation, Alex, so in the long run free trade is the only thing that can really suit them.'

Alex shrugged. 'They have free trade already. They're free; we aren't.'

David regarded him. 'How is your business going, here?'

'Badly, at the moment. I feel let down. There've been none of the post-Arigata contracts they used to assure me about.'

'By God . . .' David said angrily. 'They've been freezing you out?'

'They most certainly have.'

David took a deep breath. 'Well, I don't think they're going to like what I have to say to them.'

David's determination not to allow himself to be fobbed off by Japan's bureaucrats impressed Alex.

David Bryant had been instructed not to report by telephone, and to communicate with London only by coded telex or diplomatic courier. There had been no response to his first report except a terse, unsigned message from the Prime Minister's private office that said only: PM ASKS YOU TO CONTINUE THE GOOD WORK. It was almost an insult, he felt: he was exiled, kept away from the contest to select the next leader of the party and Prime Minister, and his activities here in Tokyo were being ignored. After Alex's description of how he was being treated here, David became lividly angry.

Late that afternoon, though he had still received no new instructions from London, he chose to take the podium and make an unambiguous statement that quickly became an angry denunciation.

'There must come a point,' he said gravely, leaning into the microphones, 'when the meaning of "free trade" comes under scrutiny by other industrial nations. Japan's business samurai seem to think that if they continue to smile and apologise while they stab their foreign competitors to death, then they will be allowed to get away with murdering our industries. I have to say now that this cannot, and will not, be tolerated any longer.'

There was a stir in the auditorium. The cameras caught his stern expression superbly; a man of goodwill but strong character, speaking from the heart.

'I believe in free trade. I want to see all the nations of the world grow richer together. Therefore, I have no intention of staying here any longer, unless some *real* business is done.'

He walked off slowly. To his surprise, there was a scattering of applause that grew stronger.

Outside the conference hall was a sleek Rolls-Royce, and beside it stood Alex Stanton.

'Well, David, I'm glad *somebody* finally told them . . .'

In the conference hotel that evening, Alex came up to David and made a point congratulating him in public. David responded warmly.

They had already agreed on their own tactics. Now they discussed the Japanese reaction in guarded terms. It had been low-profile but noticeably anxious.

Alex said, wickedly, 'I think we've found a language they understand.'

'Do you think they'll crack?'

'To avoid embarrassment during this international conference? I'd lay odds.'

They were joined by Akira Nanwara, the slight, smiling, head of Nippon Electronic – NE, whose electric signs were everywhere in the world. Televisions, stereo systems, computers and peripherals: a gigantic concern. Alex took to the soft-spoken man, and not only because of his impressive record as a businessman. There was nobody who knew more about the economic miracle that was Japan, so Alex began to question him.

'Where does your success come from?'

'Many things, Mr Stanton, Mr Bryant. We think hard about products, and spend much of our company's income on research and developing new lines. Also, loyalty, hard work. In Japan, taking a holiday is like – a sign of weakness.'

David questioned Nanwara about the Japanese lifetime employment system, and asked what he would do if he found he had to make a large proportion of his workforce redundant.

'They are family. We have to keep them.'

'Keep them loyal, you mean!'

'Of course,' Nanwara explained patiently, 'that is part of it. In your country, a manager might have a year, two years at most, to make short-term profit. Short-termism is bad, and un-Japanese. Also, your executives have selfish mobility, company to company. What is important to them is short-term profit, short-term career. With lifetime loyalty, you see, *everyone* thinks long-term – to have company that is great and strong in thirty, forty years, not just today and tomorrow.'

Alex had to agree that was sensible.

'Here, market share is the thing; profits follow. We do what we must to increase market share.'

Like subsidize your industries, and make use of other people's ideas, Alex thought. But then, wasn't that what successful capitalism was all about? Free exchange of ideas, free competition? He decided to be blunt. 'In other words, you're prepared to use government subsidies to copy our techniques and steal our markets.'

'Copy technique?' Nanwara wagged a finger. His English grew more fractured. 'In especially European industry, if somebody have idea, they proud of that. But idea itself doesn't make sense unless it is utilize in business way. Anybody can have idea – but very few people make idea into industry. We can, and we will.'

'I see,' Alex said. 'But don't your shareholders press you to cut costs to increase their profits?'

Nanwara said, as if it was obvious, 'We think long-term. Our task, you see, is to utilize good ideas from anybody, even if it takes five years, ten years, fifteen years, before there is profit.'

'And that's the secret of your success in Japan?'

The older man looked at them, considering. 'No.'

'Then what is?' David asked, fascinated.

'The secret is, *to have the desire to succeed*.'

David looked at the man. 'Aren't you afraid that we'll take your working methods and ideas back to Europe, and compete against you more effectively?'

'I think not,' Nanwara said, with frightening certainty. 'I talk to British, Americans before. They will not see necessity for change.'

David was shocked. 'That's a terrifying indictment of the West.'

Alex pressed for more practical details. 'So what do you give priority to?'

Nanwara looked at David and considered his answer carefully. 'Production engineering. In the West, you appreciate scientist – Nobel prizes, clean hands. Sometimes you don't appreciate engineer.'

David admitted it. 'In England, nobody wants to go into industry. They want to be actors or writers or social workers and things. Or civil servants. Or lawyers. At best, accountants.'

Nanwara smiled. 'Of course.'

'Why "of course"?' David asked.

'Then they are safe from foreign competition.'

Alex agreed. 'But if you are in industry, it helps to have your government behind you. MITI for example.'

Both Englishmen knew that MITI – an acronym which they pronounced 'Mighty' – had sent its own representatives to the conference. The powerful Japan Ministry of International Trade and Industry was obviously keen to monitor progress, and their three impassive senior men in dark business suits mingled and small-talked at every opportunity. They exuded an aura of intelligence and a remarkable political grasp; their calibre impressed both Alex and David.

Then a younger man appeared, who spoke English with a marked East Coast inflection – Harvard Business School, David guessed. Alex introduced him as Paul Takahashi. He seemed familiar to David from somewhere. It clicked when Nanwara asked, 'How is Mr Hideki?'

Alex threw David a look. Was this the approach they had been hoping for?

'I have just left him. He is well now, and keen as ever to do business.'

'That's a relief,' Alex said sardonically, and took Nanwara aside to let David operate.

David considered the man's probing and responded carefully. Surely Mr Bryant wished the conference to succeed, in a pleasant and productive atmosphere? Not if there was nothing to be gained by it, David told him. He was a busy man; important government business.

Takahashi looked shocked. Then David was prepared to walk out from the conference isolating his nation from all the other, true friends of Japan who would remain behind?

No, David said. He indicated that other attenders at the conference were displeased, too. There had been talk of tariff barriers . . . David smiled, then bowed shortly, remembering his first meeting with Saigo Hideki five long years before, and left the man; afterwards he refused to acknowledge him at all.

David calculated his actions carefully.

He made several public mentions of his great respect for Alex Stanton, and then arranged to dine with the Dutch, French and Italian delegates in the hotel restaurant. He spoke here about his concerns and described Japanese methods, making sure his voice carried. Afterwards, he extended invitations to the American, West German and Canadian representatives for drinks in his suite at ten thirty. The Japanese reacted as he hoped.

They found Alex Stanton, and this time they were ready to do business.

Chapter Thirteen

David drew Alex to one side and whispered, 'Watch Takahashi. He's Hideki's man, isn't he?'

'Hatchet man,' Alex said.

'He tried to pump me earlier. Then he tried to get me to back down. Some chance!'

'Nasty piece of work, isn't he? Smokes Dunhill, and that's an affectation out here. But you're too late, he's already got to me.' David's interest showed. 'He asked me point-blank to shut you up, David. I think he presumes you're like the politicians here – in the big businesses' pockets. His masters are worried that your ideas are contagious.'

'I hope my ideas are contagious,' David said gruffly. 'What do you get in return?'

'The promised bloody big import deal with Hideki Corp. We provide uranium ore, refined reactor fuel, reprocessing facilities for up to a thousand tons of spent fuel, plutonium. Not just for Arigata, but for other parts of the Japanese reactor programme as well.'

David whistled. 'How much?'

'I think we could push them up to twenty-five, maybe thirty million –'

David's eyes widened, his lips began to curl upwards at the corners. 'Thirty million?'

'Per annum.'

David tugged on Alex's tuxedo lapel. 'That much? Take it.'

'Eh?'

'Take it. You need it to support your armaments division modernization! I just wish it could have been something other than nuclear power . . .'

'Come on, David, you can't give up now, you're giving them diarrhoea.' Alex looked about, his face like the Cheshire cat's.

'You might like to see them squirm on this public stage, but we have to be practical. Thirty million a year is much more than we'd get for your company by formal negotiation, *and* it might take a year of chat. Just tell them I've agreed to drop it, get your agreements initialled, and I'll say no more.'

'You'd agree to stay silent?'

'Yes, completely silent.' He grinned, winked. 'That is, for the moment.'

Alex pursed his lips, well pleased with David's suggestion. 'Yes, minister,' he said.

'Let's go and have a word with the Germans.'

Alex and McCourt were quietly invited back to the Hideki headquarters, and this time the atmosphere was very different. Takahashi was willing to please. In an hour, the contracts were finalized and signed. Another ninety minutes saw a down payment of five million pounds placed in one of Stanton Industries' London bank accounts.

Alex returned to the conference hall, well pleased, and even more impressed by the Japanese sense of purpose.

'So we're going ahead with the bigger Tokyo office?'

Alex looked McCourt up and down and produced a wry smile. 'We are. Japan seems more anxious to do business now.'

'You think David pulled it off for us?'

'Dead right.'

McCourt spoke even more quietly. 'I wonder if Takahashi means what he says about the import contracts.'

'We just put it in writing, didn't we?' Alex said impatiently.

'In Japan, it would be advantageous if Hideki himself signed. It's a matter of face.'

'As long as it's a matter of enforceable international trade law, I'm quite happy.' Alex smiled.

'Takahashi seemed very ready to agree,' McCourt said.

'Why shouldn't he be?' Alex asked sharply. After a success he liked celebration, not doubt and self-criticism. 'Listen, two years' profit on that deal will pay for the new tank factory.'

McCourt looked abashed. 'You seem determined to get beyond our present toehold in Japan. But even if Hideki really wants Arigata, and really wants the uranium deal for it sewn up, they're normally watertight here; they just don't let people in. Importing into Japan has been made almost impossible by a series of tariffs and, worse, by invisible but impenetrable non-tariff barriers.'

'So we need a big deal with one of the Japanese corporate giants, some *zaibatsu* or other, to smooth the way – and I think we have one. Don't forget, Japan needs uranium for their nuclear power stations just as much as they need oil. Our Australian mining subsidiary is important to them – and I think I can tie in our British fuel reprocessing facilities too, David permitting. Hideki knows that.'

'But they agreed so suddenly, Alex. It *must* have needed more than that.'

Alex smiled broadly, feeling sure he knew why they had caved in: David Bryant's pressure, from a sovereign government which could influence others, even America. 'Do you think I've become overconfident – that they've tricked me, or something?' Alex paused. 'I think not.'

'Then why –'

'Well, perhaps my old friend David made them an offer they couldn't refuse.' He turned around as he heard an excited murmur. 'Looks like the political news is in.'

A look of concern passed over Alex's face as he went over to read the lines of print coming off the wire service – the latest news from around the world, brought direct to the conference hall:

1976, APRIL 5, 1425 GMT
LONDON, ENGLAND
THIRD AND FINAL BALLOT FOR LABOUR PARTY LEADERSHIP –

'So who got in?' Ken McCourt asked, over his shoulder. About a dozen people had grouped around.

'The next Prime Minister is –' Alex tore off the long strip of paper, waved it at his audience.

CALLAGHAN 176, FOOT 137.
JAMES CALLAGHAN TO BE APPOINTED PM BY HM QUEEN AFTER PUBLIC ANNOUNCEMENT.

'Sunny Jim!' It could have been worse, Alex thought. He remembered his brief, secret battle when allied to David, against Alan Hoyle. There were plenty of far Left extremists in the country; and they were dangerous. If the Left's choice Michael Foot had got the vote, all hopes of maintaining a stable exchange rate would have been dashed, and billions wiped off the London stock market overnight. All that money would flood abroad, leaving devastation behind.

'Unexpected?' asked McCourt.

Alex was still thoughtful, going through the ramifications. As the Japanese knew only too well, political stability was a prerequisite for industrial, and therefore financial, strategic planning. The deal David and he had been trying so hard to set up could have been cut to ribbons by a governmental upheaval at home. But now Alex felt the way ahead was clear – and he only hoped that Hideki was really prepared to finalize things. 'Not at all. Callaghan means business as usual, and for us his arrival means hard work.'

The long bar here on one of the upper floors of the conference hotel was dimly lit, air-conditioned. The odour of spirits hung in the air, coming through the faint, clashing perfumes. Here journalists, diplomats, industrialists and exporters could meet on equal terms. But David, standing with the trade secretary from the embassy, looked over his shoulder at a group of three Russians. An older, square man with hacked-out, stony features, not familiar to David; beside him, the KGB resident here in Tokyo, in a blue-grey suit.

But David stared at the elegant, tall correspondent for *Pravda* with them. Memories of East Germany flooded back, with a terror David had to swallow to repress. David had also met Oleg Kerensky in London once or twice since that time. Now he raised a glass to him.

His escort from HMG Embassy spoke in a very low voice. 'See the rough-looking man behind the other two?'

'A glimpse. It's as if they're hiding him.' Realization came to him. 'That's what they're doing, isn't it?'

'Indeed.' The trade secretary swallowed some tonic. 'Anatoly Glykov, fresh from Moscow. Foreign Ministry cover.'

David observed the man without seeming to. 'Who is he, really?'

'A general from the First Chief Directorate of the KGB. We think he runs a Far East department – the whisper is, much of east Asia, probably excepting China.'

'Vietnam, Korea – and Japan?' David said, wondering if Australia was considered to be Asian. Not quite yet, he thought, though when the Japanese began to buy up Australian land and assets and move their own people in . . . 'Why are they here?'

'Fishing for secrets? Trying to suborn one of us? Who knows?'

Trying to suborn one of us . . . David felt a fist clench around his heart. Then he saw Glykov turn away, to brood out of the window with the lights of Tokyo flaring below him.

Then there was a little stir at the doorway. The Japanese backed away, as three hefty bodyguards sauntered in, staring menacingly around. Saigo Hideki followed them, chatting with another greying but powerfully built Japanese. A woman glided behind them, as tall or taller than the men because of her high heels. David could not quite make out her face.

Heads turned, and some people bowed.

Those two men had presence. David felt it like electricity. 'Minister Hakagawa,' the embassy aide whispered, 'and—'

'I've already met Hideki,' David said. In this context, with his dark, sharply designed suit and his fawning entourage, Hideki suddenly looked dangerous: a *yakuza* gangster, or a Latin American politician who did deals with cocaine smugglers and ran death squads as a hobby.

They came over, their expressions a strange combination of bland friendliness and icy disdain. Hakagawa's eyes were dark and did not change no matter what the rest of his face tried to do.

Hideki spoke: 'Please, not to rise. We are here casually, as friends. All peoples to be friends with Japanese, yes.'

'Whether they want to be or not?' David could not refrain from saying.

Hakagawa, just for a moment, glared at him. Shaken, David realized both the power of the man's personality and that he understood some English at least.

Takahashi was among them immediately. 'Mr Bryant's little joke, right? I just love that English sense of humour – and of course they get a lot of practice laughing at themselves.'

Alex had drifted over. He stood sometimes watching the Japanese, sometimes watching the KGB diplomat contingent. He had the uncanny ability to be absolutely still and blend into the background.

But Hakagawa had already noticed him, and said something which Hideki rendered as, 'The famous Stanton of the Stanton Industries. We may have business for you. Perhaps your famous tanks.'

'I'd be honoured,' Alex said shortly, having heard it before.

Then there was a shadow. David looked up.

If there were ugly Americans, this was the Russian equivalent. Glykov. His voice ground out, heavily accented. 'Mr Stanton. Mr Hideki, and Mr Hakagawa. Things in common?'

Hideki's face was blank and arrogant. Hakagawa's eyes showed brief ferocity.

'You were both in Manchuria, I believe. Kwantung Army.'

Hideki said nothing, but Glykov nodded. He seemed to be making his mind up about something. 'You are very important men in the new Japan – as in the old.'

It was no question, but Hideki chose to treat it as such. His face wrinkled with disdain. 'We are, Mr Communist. We are.'

Glykov stiffened. 'I was in Manchuria – what you called "Manchukuo". And in Tokyo in 1936. And I was at Nomonhan in '39, with Marshal Zhukov. Do you remember Nomonhan, or is that something else – like the Rape of Nanking – that is missing from your history-books?'

The Japanese were aghast. Then Takahashi was at his elbow, trying to usher him away, but he shrugged off Hideki's aide and stalked away with Kerensky.

Minister Hakagawa and Hideki left shortly afterwards.

'I wonder what on earth that was about,' David said. He still felt disturbed by the sheer, hardly-concealed savagery both sides had shown.

'A testing of mettle,' said Alex. 'I have a feeling there's more going on here than we understand – something between Moscow and Tokyo. What do you know about the dates Glykov mentioned?'

David said softly, 'We're talking the 1930s, with Hideki around forty and Hakagawa younger. In their prime. The Kwantung Army was an élite Japanese force that started its own war with China. It grabbed Manchuria, which of course was once annexed by Czarist Russia. "Manchukuo" was the name Tokyo used; the Japanese had the last emperor of China, Pu Yi, as their puppet ruler. I think 1936 was one of the times the extreme right in Japan staged a coup d'état – and almost brought it off. Do you think Hideki could have been involved in that – the League of Blood and the officers' plots?'

'I don't know, but I believe I've heard of Nomonhan.' Alex said. 'Siberia, I think. Zhukov's Red Army beat the Japanese. And everybody knows about the Rape of Nanking.'

'Except the Japanese, maybe,' David said. 'Don't forget those censored schoolbooks. What Glykov said about that is true.'

'So all that history involves Hideki and Hakagawa?' Alex said thoughtfully. 'I didn't realize they went back such a long way together. Interesting.'

'According to a story I heard in the embassy here, the army and high bureaucrats worked closely together in what they called "Manchukuo" with "patriotic" businessmen.'

'Such as Hideki?'

'As you can imagine, the historical record isn't exactly unbiased and detailed, but there was a military theorist called Colonel Kanji Ishiwara who wanted a "national defence state" and made his name lecturing at war college on the forthcoming "final war" – the war between Japan and the United States, that is. Anyway, apparently occupied Manchuria was run by a proto-fascist régime into social control and supercharged industrial growth.'

'Christ,' Alex said, 'like a blueprint for today! And Glykov was involved, on the other side – Stalin's side! No wonder he sees Hideki and Hakagawa as people likely to smash Russian ambitions.'

David swallowed. 'You mean the KGB have some kind of ongoing plan for Japan?'

Alex smiled mirthlessly. 'Most certainly. And – they may well see Japan as an ongoing threat.'

David glanced around, as one of the American delegates approached. 'And they may be right,' he said.

'I'm sure they can't be as bad as you sometimes try to make out, David,' Tom Kalbach said. He was a Washington lawyer; now Deputy Chairman of the President's Special Commission on International Trade. 'They don't *force* us to buy their products, we choose to do so. That's what free trade is all about.'

David murmured, charmingly, 'A very American self-confidence.'

Kalbach beamed at them, straightened his bow tie. 'And why not?'

'Because it isn't that simple,' David said immediately. 'This is Tokyo: they mean to win. We must learn from them.'

Kalbach laughed. 'I think it'll be a while before the US of A needs to worry.'

Alex threw in, 'Tom, a little worrying now might save a hell of a lot of heart ache later.'

Kalbach's shrewd eyes went from one man to the other. 'What do you mean?'

David said, quietly, 'Suppose I told you there was a meeting at the Ministry of International Trade and Industry here in Tokyo last week, with the powerful bureaucrats, the big industries and the political bosses all represented. Subject: in the next twenty years, finish the conquest of the car industry in Europe and America. Where will that leave Ford and GM and the rest of Detroit?'

Suddenly Kalbach looked shaken. 'They really do it like that? God . . . that's really their plan?' He gulped more of his drink.

'Of course,' Alex said, impatiently. 'We told you. They mean to win.'

'How did you hear about the meeting?'

'I didn't,' David said calmly. 'I made it up.'

Kalbach spluttered into his glass.

Alex laughed, patted his back. 'They sent people to check on rival shipbuilders: and they've come close to finishing off the British industry, which till the fifties built half the ships in the world. You think America is immune? Believe me, they *will* hold such meetings, probably under very innocuous-sounding names – and outsiders, *gaijin*, will never get to hear about them.'

'Oh, you can't be certain of that. I mean, sure, they've been doing very well –'

'Tom, MITI *runs* Japan,' Alex said sharply. Without effort he commanded their attention. 'In Britain we build our strongest institutions round Royalty, in America it's the Constitution, in Russia the sacred ark of Communism – if you doubt that the Japanese are first and foremost interested in strong industry, take a look at MITI, and I'll give you some notion of how it works.'

From the barroom window in the hotel they could all see the unprepossessing ten-storey building which housed the ministry.

A slender Japanese woman, dressed in exquisitely stylish Paris fashion, saw David's wave directed at the MITI headquarters. She moved unobtrusively to stand closer to them.

'It doesn't look like much, does it?' David said, turning to Alex. 'Yet we know it's the most prestigious ministry in the entire Japanese system. Finance may have the power, but MITI is *ichi-ban*. Number one.'

Kalbach plucked at his black bow tie. 'Oh, come on. The Japanese have done well, but a little Asian country hardly bigger than a large US state taking on the entire US economy – that's ridiculous!'

'Two of my friends were in Saigon last year,' David said. 'Remember Vietnam? Another little Asian country taking on the United States?'

There was dead silence.

Now Kalbach looked concerned. 'How does it work here, David?'

A soft feminine voice said clearly, 'As it always has since our leap out of the past and into the future, which began in the nineteenth century. By a kind of war. What you call MITI was always the powerhouse: but originally it was the Ministry of Munitions. Of course, we gave it a politer name after our defeat in 1945. It is merely another route to the absolute Japanese triumph.'

Alex's eyes opened wide. He saw a face, as beautiful as any he had ever seen. Her eyes, deep and guileless, met his, and just for an instant there was a spark between the two of them.

The Japanese woman spoke in a quiet voice, aware that she was being surreptitiously watched by Takahashi. Her English was as excellent as his, though her accent seemed more French than New England. 'So now MITI organizes Japanese firms into cartels which don't compete with one another for the benefit of the consumer, the citizen here in Japan, but instead cooperate to carve up the world market to their mutal benefit.'

'And when foreign firms are in the way?' Alex asked.

Her eyes met his and she spoke with devastating directness. 'The cartels effectively loss-lead until the opposition goes out of business.'

Alex felt shaken. He knew somehow that he had met his equal – for the first time, in a woman, since Maggie.

'But don't you have anti-trust laws here?' Tom Kalbach asked.

Her laughter was genuine, but she kept her voice low. 'Japanese legal obfuscation, selective interpretation, exemptions for "trade associations", loopholes you could drive a Mitsubishi truck through!' Takahashi came within earshot, so she turned to him and gave a meek look. 'Constructive footdragging is part of our cultural heritage. Is that not so, Mr Takahashi?'

Paul Takahashi gave her a bland smile and a short bow. Alex stared at him until he stepped back from the contest, then gave up and went away. Victorious, Alex turned to the woman again.

'It costs money to loss-lead a product for years on end,' he objected. 'A fortune. Believe me, I know.'

'Ask about sugar import licences, Alex,' David said.

She nodded at the point. 'The Japanese government has to maintain the appearance of a free market economy, but in reality it gives grants through MITI equal to the cost of dumping goods abroad in unprotected foreign markets like Europe and America.'

'And it raises the money through the mechanism of granting sugar import licences?' asked Alex, beginning to catch on.

'To name just one. Why else would companies like Toshiba and Hideki hold sugar import licences? The Japanese housewife pays a great excess over the free market price on every bag of sugar she buys. There is also a twenty-five percent levy on gambling, which is something we Japanese like to do very much. Billions of yen have been quietly diverted in this way. Naturally such sums never appear on the balance sheets of the companies concerned, but they are subsidized secretly to compete ruthlessly against foreign firms.'

'But that's cheating!' Kalbach said.

David said sharply, 'What if we retaliate?'

Kiko tossed her head, still staring at Alex. 'Most Japanese believe the West is too morally weak to make Japan a trade pariah. And soon it will be too late to fight back.'

During the exchanges which followed, David saw how Kiko watched Alex, and how he returned her looks. He had picked up a discreet but powerful attraction operating between them. He wondered if Alex knew who she was. She certainly seemed to like the way he had dealt with Takahashi.

Alex was curious. 'You feel strongly about improving your country?'

She said fiercely, 'Japan is effectively a one-party state, and it is run for the benefit of industrial producers – for the powerful industrial and political dynasties.'

'Don't you have the vote here?'

'Votes mean nothing; there is only one party in power, without policies except "business as usual" while ordinary people die from overwork. We *cannot* vote for change in my country. We can only consume what is set before us. Whereas we would all like larger houses, green parks, leisure, better and more convenient transport – it is sickening to be shoehorned into the bullet train, sickening to have to commute for endless hours – we cannot use democracy to get what we want.'

'What can you do?'

She turned her head to him. 'You are Alex Stanton. What can *you* do?'

He said nothing, thinking.

Her eyes met his and she spoke in a whisper. 'Later. You agree?'

He nodded. In spite of himself, Alex had kept turning to glance at that beautiful Asian face. Without high heels her head would come up no higher than his chin. She seemed quiet, demure – a very Japanese woman, in fact – but he could tell there was powerful emotion in her, a great well of feeling, and something in her eyes told him this again: I am your equal, Alex Stanton.

It was a strangely refreshing, disturbing feeling. He wondered what she was like, what her politics were, who she was – and how good this woman would be in bed.

David saw his preoccupation. He nudged his old friend. 'Take it easy, Alex. Don't you know who that is?'

'No idea!' He laughed, feeling a long way from this room and the seemingly casual, probing chatter.

'That's Kiko. Kiko Hideki.' He decided to make Alex's next drink a double. 'Old man Hideki's sole surviving grandchild and heir presumptive.'

'Hideki's granddaughter!' It was like a shower of ice-cold water. 'Enemy, you mean?'

David saw her clutch her glass of mineral water to her chest and look, again, at Alex through lowered eyelashes. He remembered how outspoken and honest she had just been. 'I don't know, Alex. Not our enemy. Maybe.'

Maggie Langton relaxed in the hired Bentley, on the way to a charity concert for Bangladesh in London.

'What about 10 Downing Street, Alan?'

Hoyle lounged back, frowning at her. For a man of self-confessed austerity he certainly enjoys his luxuries, Maggie thought. Then she looked at his watch. It was gold, Swiss, and obviously very expensive.

'I had my constituency people pushing hard against Healey and Callaghan. I wanted Foot in.'

'Michael's heart is in the right place,' she acknowledged, then worried aloud. 'I don't know how well he'd come over on TV, though.'

He snorted. 'That doesn't matter at the moment, Maggie! We're in for years of Callaghan now.'

She had to admit he was sure of his ground. She glanced at him again: the gold watch, the immaculate suit, the expensive aftershave. Yet this was the same man who had once appeared at her house in a battered Ford Cortina that looked ready for the junkyard, and used to address far-Left meetings in sweaters and faded jeans.

'Alan,' she said after a while, 'how do you make a living these days? Freelance journalism doesn't pay that much, not Left-wing journalism. Or does Forward pay your bills?'

He sighed. 'Maggie, did it never occur to you that the rumours are true? I freelance out terrorism.'

She twisted on the seat. 'What?'

Hoyle grinned. 'I work in the Middle East and elsewhere for anybody who'll pay well, and I personally subsidize the Forward movement out of that. Iraq has been especially generous. And another country I'd rather not name. I'm a gun for hire.'

Horror reached inside her. 'But – you can't –'

He started to laugh, slapped his knee. 'You believed me, didn't you?'

'Of course not,' she lied. There really was something about Alan Hoyle, presence, and under the good looks something raw and male, a little like Alex . . .

Traffic in London was heavy, so they decided to walk the last two hundred yards. Alan admitted he did not want to be photographed leaving her hired limousine, then changed the subject as they walked through Jubilee Gardens by the river, the Thames flowing beside them.

He wanted to talk about Alex Stanton, and Stanton Industries' activities in Japan.

Maggie told him what she had learned from David.

'David's in Tokyo?'

'At some conference,' Maggie said. 'I suppose you, with your contacts in the party, must have heard why David was shuffled off to Japan during the voting.'

'I reckon his friends in the cabinet wanted to keep his head below the parapet of the trench. It was a vicious campaign, but they wanted to keep David Bryant safe.'

She heard the loathing in his voice and did not understand it. Jealousy? What? 'I thought you used to work with him.'

Alan turned his head away and it occurred to her that he had something to hide. 'He's a right-winger. A traitor, and that I can't forgive. Remember Lord Acton's dictum?'

'Power corrupts?'

'Yes. It's corrupted him.'

Maggie tossed her head, jingling her big round earrings. She thought of the reeks of corruption that were drifting all round the world, and shook her head.

'Oh, Alan – David's decent through and through. You've got to remember he's working inside the existing system. It must be hard.'

'He's lost his courage and his revolutionary principles. I still remember '68 and after. He's a coward. And a racist. I support radicals in Iraq and other places, I'm a hundred percent behind Saddam Hussein and Pol Pot, but *he* seems to prefer Americans. You know the first thing he said to me after he was elected was "sorry, Alan, old pal, but thank you and goodbye"!'

'Was that cowardice?' she asked him softly, taken aback by this ferocity.

He turned his gaze on her. In the gloom she could not quite see the expression on his face but for a moment she was frightened.

Alan vanished again after that night, hinting that he had earned a lot of money in the Middle East and would use it to empower his organization, Forward. A few whispers came to her over the next week or two. It seemed that some people were scared of Alan Hoyle.

General Glykov and Kerensky took a cab back to the USSR Embassy, went through security and into a suite of rooms that had already been checked for listening devices. This was the KGB residency, and in the background telephones rang and teletypes chattered Moscow codes.

'Come here to the table, young man,' Glykov put his attaché case between them. The old KGB man smiled, but not entirely pleasantly; as if to a favourite son, who had somehow failed to please. 'I have things to show you, things to tell.'

Oleg Kerensky sat down. He stretched his legs under the table, careful to show a deferential face. 'As you say, Comrade General.'

'And you can wipe off that look and listen to me for once, Oleg.' He raised a hand, speaking in slurred, colloquial Russian. 'And no squirming about, no injured innocence! I know what you think of me: an unsophisticated old bull of a Chekist, with bullet wounds in him from the Germans, who smells of blood from the days of Beria and Stalin. Well, that may be. I am a simple man, of simple loyalties.'

Their eyes met.

Kerensky risked showing a little outrage. 'And I am not?'

'And you are not.'

The old general leaned forward to open the case. Kerensky was suddenly very frightened. As the locks clicked he felt for a moment that the old general had suspected him, tried him in his own mind, and had come to Tokyo to execute the sentence personally.

His voice was hoarse. 'Of course I am loyal!'

'So you say.' The old man grinned, and slowly opened the case.

Was there going to be a gun, and instant execution of a sentence predetermined in Dzerzhinsky Square, KGB headquarters? Had they realized from the increasingly sarcastic tone of his reports that he was losing faith in the Marxist monolith, or did they know that all the easy Western women and easy friendships had corrupted his original beliefs?

Kerensky forced himself to look inside the case, and caught his breath. It was not anything like what he had expected.

'Good, eh?' the old man said.

There was a chilled bottle of vodka, an exclusive brand, and little snacks of cheese and bread and caviare to go with a drinking session. Under that, in translucent plastic covers, official papers in Russian with KGB headings on them.

'Listen, Oleg. I think of you almost as a son. Of course you are loyal – but are you *simply* loyal, like me? I fear not.' He spoke over Kerensky's spluttered protests. 'Now, don't misunderstand me. I know that you are brave and well-trained, and you have done good work for us in Tokyo and London. But you do not have that fierce cutting edge of dedicated loyalty to the party and the state and the organs of the state which I look for. You must acquire that if you hope for great things in your career serving the State Security Committee.'

Kerensky watched the deft movements of the old man's gnarled fingers. Vodka, glasses, plates and their drinking-snacks, all were quickly arranged.

'If there is something more I could do . . .'

'Be less Western; less weakly cynical. Let me tell you, you are becoming too much like all the other slick, sleek and well-connected young men we have with us today. Now listen to this.' With some ceremony, the general lifted the first folder of papers. There was a Moscow Centre designation printed there. 'A report of yours, from four months ago. Let me see.' He fumbled for his reading glasses. '"Comrade Leonid Ilyich Brezhnev's thunderous speech with its mastery of fact and logic made a profound impression on government circles in Tokyo, and our informants there were almost overwhelmed –"' The general shrugged, his mouth a compressed, bitter line, and laid the papers down.

'Well?'

'Oleg, you and I know Tokyo does not pay any attention to the General Secretary, let alone to his speeches! It is polite to pretend in your reports that the country you are observing does. But do not do it in such an aggravatingly cynical way! You sound as if you are making fools of the comrades on the Politburo –

and only a very stupid and very arrogant young man would do that.'

Kerensky breathed a little easier. This was a very important but very unofficial warning from the old man. His life and his career were still safe. 'I understand. Forgive the tone; I have been away so long from the heartland.'

'Yes.' The old man returned the papers. 'We are thinking of moving you.'

He jerked upright. 'Moving me?'

'Yes. A London base, and again journalistic cover, but this time working for the Near East department, not the Far East.'

'But Japan is –'

'Do not worry about the yellow men.'

'But they are becoming so rich, so strong!'

General Glykov laughed. 'Toys and consumer goods. How can that be strength?'

Kerensky looked at the old KGB man, shocked. The general did not understand at all. He found himself gabbling through an explanation. 'But I think they plan to use all their economic success, their income, to use industrialization as a base to – to compete—'

'I told you, comrade, I am not interested in their little toys.'

'But I thought you wanted to know more about this Arigata atomic project.'

The gnarled old face became harder. 'Yes. But you are not our only agent. By no means! Now, be cautious when you are in London. The English are of no account now, as we hope the Americans will be diminished by the year 2000, but once they were cunning. Make contacts there with diplomats and industrial people, especially exporters and arms-makers. We need people in Stanton Industries especially, because of their links to the Middle East and the Shah's Iran.'

'I do not feel I have completed my work in Tokyo. And please, do not underestimate them. They fought the Czarists to a standstill in 1905.'

General Glykov grunted. The old eyes, which had seen all the leaders back to Lenin, glittered.

'I think there is something happening here in Japan.'

Glykov replaced his reading glasses. 'What do you mean?'

'Hideki, and the one he pays for or works with, Hakagawa – I haven't quite worked out the relationship—'

'What about them?'

He hesitated, wondering if what Kiko Hideki had been hinting to his contact was really correct. 'I think they are really looking for plutonium – for nuclear bombs.'

David could not bring himself to use the false, Western name. 'Why did you bring me here, Mr Takahashi?'

Their car stopped outside an eleven-storey building; white stone, glass, in quite extensive grounds. There was another, similar building alongside it, this one more like an apartment block than offices.

The man twisted his body round. He would be smiling, David knew. 'I'll show you outside.'

David got out of the car, automatically looking up at the high, spiked walls, guessing there were surveillance cameras here. A long black car came out of the building, pausing beside them for a moment. Automatically he turned his head away, not wanting to be recognized or photographed.

'You have not been here, ever?'

'No,' David said, puzzled. He turned up the collar of his jacket as it began to drizzle, though the thin rain quickly made even the smoggy air of Tokyo sweeter. 'What is it – the Hideki head office?'

Takahashi barked out a laugh, kept on laughing.

David was annoyed. He was alone with this man in the middle of a dark night in Tokyo, someone else's city, and it was making him nervous. 'I said something funny? What is it, then?'

Hideki's man spoke the syllables carefully. 'It is the embassy of the USSR.'

David felt his stomach contract. In the light of a streetlamp the other man smiled and opened a silver cigarette case. 'Dunhill?'

'I don't smoke,' David said stolidly. The rain grew worse, but he could not break away from this confrontation. 'What do you want?'

This time the voice was ugly. 'I want to serve Hideki-*san*, and my country.'

David sighed, feeling alone in this strange land. 'Please, enough histrionics, enough ritual. What do you *want*?'

'Your help, Mr Bryant.'

Thunder boomed, echoing back from the tall, earthquake-proofed buildings of Tokyo. 'Go on.'

'Mr Hideki could prove you have connections with Alan Hoyle.'

'Had,' David said automatically. 'Had, as you know. It was a long time ago. Now I'm an MP and—'

Takahashi raised a hand, the steel wristwatch gleaming. The East Coast accent sharpened. 'Hey, I'm not asking anything dishonourable, though your association with that traitor, which he is, and terrorist, which he is, has dishonoured you forever in Japanese eyes.'

'I will answer for what I have done in my life in another place.'

Suddenly the other man laughed. 'I like you, Mr Bryant. You never give up, do you? Listen, this is all unofficial; my idea, right? I thought I could help hush up this Forward business for you, and in return . . .'

This is it, David thought. The price. For a moment he closed his eyes, realizing afterwards that Takahashi would have seen this moment of weakness. 'In return, what?'

'We can offer Mr Stanton much in the way of business. Those atomic contracts, for example. Much more than that is possible.'

'Well, we had to lean on you to get those!'

The laugh, again. 'You are very naive. We need that uranium and plutonium.'

'Then why didn't you sign the agreements before?'

'We signed them here, now. The same contracts.'

'But – you delayed, Hideki didn't appear, and we were starting to think . . .'

'Yes, you were starting to think. So you put public pressure on Japan, at an embarrassing time. So now our government will subsidize us heavily during our association with Stanton Industries.'

It hit him. 'You mean the Hideki Corporation is pleased by what I said to the conference?'

'Of course, as long as no government follows you – and they won't, not even your own. So now our government in Tokyo will give us money so that we can give some to Alex Stanton to keep you quiet. Of course he will give you money, too.'

'I don't take bribes.'

'No?' the man said, clearly not believing him. 'There might be money directly from us – say, a hundred thousand US, paid into a secret Swiss account. None of your high Socialist taxes, Mr Bryant. No taxes!'

'The answer is still "no". Now, I repeat, what do you want?'

'Stanton Industries is a power inside Iran, is it not? Armaments, and lately the oil business?'

'Yes.'

'Excellent. Then I can tell Mr Hideki that you and Alex Stanton will use your goodwill on our behalf, in Tehran as well as in New Delhi.'

'If the price is right, of course we will.'

'The price'll be right,' Takahashi said. 'Do you know that we plan to modernize and re-equip all our armed forces by 1985 when our new government will—' He stopped for a moment, then laughed.

'What new government?'

'Never mind that! Just think of Mr Hideki's power. Oh yes, the price will be right.'

David could not help asking himself the key question. Right for whom?

It was long after midnight when he was returned to the conference hotel. The streets had been crowded with Japanese businessmen even though it was late, and most of them were staggeringly drunk. He saw two or three of them, dishevelled, throwing spasms of yellow vomit into the gutters. Others sang to themselves or talked, fists clenched, though there was nobody to hear. David wondered if it was their way of escaping the incredible physical and mental strain of living in the minutely-controlled pressure cooker that was Japanese society: here good manners were utterly necessary, but the code was so rigid it could be a torture.

A policeman in a long coat, stationed by the automatically opening glass doors, gave him a nod of recognition. He felt warmed by the acknowledgement. This was the international stage, and after so long, he had arrived. He felt joy. He had not been corrupted, and he refused to be threatened, and he still had so much to say and the power to make people listen.

He crossed the huge lobby, going through a great jungle of tropical greenery where live, caged parakeets flapped their wings in throbs of bright colour and squawked at him. He saw cracked sunflower seeds around the cages. David felt pleasantly intoxicated by relief, and he paused to listen to the musical sluicing of water down the artificial waterfall. Here, a Zen grotto had been created by some inspired architect, right in front of the registration desk. There were still many people about, Europeans and Asians intermingling now, and he looked about for Alex Stanton's familiar face. He did not see his old friend, but there was a ripple of recognition from other people, including Tom Kalbach and a reporter from the *Washington Post* he knew vaguely.

David loosened his tie and rode the elevator up to the penthouse bar. There was an audience there, and malt whisky on the rocks, and toasts to be drunk. The Tokyo skyline was all bright, lit-up jewels. He felt in a wonderful mood and he began to talk.

People gathered around, impressed by his eloquence and his grasp of detail, as he described a wonderful future where the Eastern bloc nations disarmed and the West followed, where the burden of debt was lifted from the Third World, and where the globe's resources were for the first time in human history spent on all the peoples – all – of the world.

'That's a wonderful vision,' Tom Kalbach said.

'Fusion power is clean power. Imagine that, clean water and decent housing for everybody in the world – and it can be done.'

Other people became caught up in his ideas, and suddenly they were all here not to lie and cheat and hustle for career interests, or for their own national interests, but to remake the world.

He went to his room at two in the morning. He had not seen Alex, nor Kiko Hideki. The thick pile of the ash-blonde carpet muffled all sounds, but he was humming to himself, one of those old Irish laments Maggie used to sing till her own sad, sweet emotions choked her up with tears.

'Mr Bryant.'

He turned quickly, key in his hand. It was a woman, tall and well-made, her hair long and golden and her eyes luminous and green and a little like Maggie's. Her voice had a German huskiness. She wore a dark, strict business suit that was surprisingly sexy.

He took an unsteady pace forward. 'You know me?'

'I'd like to know you better.'

He went over to stand beside her, vaguely aware of a door in the other wall, to his right, that was a couple of inches ajar. She had a guileless smile and she touched his hand for a moment.

'Are you a journalist? What's your name?' He could smell an exotic, musky perfume.

'Yes, of a sort. And I want to interview you. After the film.'

'Film?'

Then the other door opened and two men came out. They were big men, much bigger than he was, and they were entirely sober. They crowded around him quickly, even though the corridor was still empty. David braced himself against the wall behind him but he knew they could take him in a moment. Then the German girl had opened the door to her own room and suddenly they were all inside.

It was a comfortable room with expensive hotel furniture and a double bed. He swallowed, sobering by the minute. The men moved quickly, one to block the door, the other to take the balcony.

There was a metal-legged shape humped under a white cloth. He presumed it was a camera. He looked at the girl, every muscle in his body tensed. Was this going to be blackmail, or violence?

'You're very handsome, Mr Bryant. And very sweet.'

The accent was definitely German. East German, he decided, giving her a wide smile. 'And you're very, very lovely. By the way, what is your name? Your real name, as well as your Stasi rank?'

She folded her hands together. Her pinstriped jacket was tight on her splendid body. 'What does that matter? I know who you are, and here we are.'

He put his arms around her and kissed her once.

She smiled at that, only a little surprised. 'A chaste kiss, but you don't want to perform with me.'

'Not in front of witnesses. Not in front of a camera.'

She laughed, then a big hand on his shoulder pressed down so that he had to sit on the bed.

'Cigarette?'

'No.' For the first time he was feeling really frightened. This was the tenth floor, after all. A long way down, if he defied these people.

So this is it, he thought. *What I did, East Berlin and Hoyle, escaping, it's finally coming back to haunt me. Here in Tokyo they make me pay for it . . .*

He had never felt more frightened, open now to blackmail, to exposure, to ruin. He would resign first, if he had the option. It came to him again: ten floors down . . . Then the girl turned off the light and the only sound he could hear was his own hoarse, desperate breathing in the darkness of the room.

Chapter Fourteen

The eight-millimetre film was projected on to the wall. The black and white images hardly flickered. David could see himself, five years previously. He saw the State Security man sitting behind his desk. On it were scattered his own leather wallet and passport and the pictures he still carried. Megan and the children. Maggie, years ago in Oxford.

The soundtrack was low-quality, but it was obviously, and perhaps provably, his own voice. He watched and listened to himself in a dream, his fists clenched so the nails dug into his palms.

The Stasi interrogator leaned over the table. We got you into your Parliament . . . what will you do for us in exchange? What would you do to get out of this place, now?

Then David saw himself dive across the desk and batter the other man's head on the wall. He flinched at the violence. The man resisted feebly, until his eyes glazed over and there was blood everywhere on his face and on David's hands. Shuddering now, he saw himself stand up, face pale and appalled, and flap his hands to try to throw off the wet blood.

He felt sick to the stomach. The advertising lights outside blinked on, blinked off.

The film ended and the lights in the hotel room were turned on again. He squinted, at the sudden shock. There was silence for a minute.

'If this was publicized –' A breath. 'You would be ruined, David Bryant.'

He remembered what had happened afterwards.

There had been laughter, as people had crowded round him excitedly in the long back garden full of ramshackle outbuildings. Then he realized the socialist state's security officer, in a place like this, would have almost unlimited power. No doubt he had exercised it, and been hated. David stood there, shivering, emotionally drained.

The laughter continued, even when the East German was taken away on a stretcher with bloodied bandages around his head. There seemed every chance that the man was dead, and still they slapped him on the back before they led him to the black car where Alan Hoyle was waiting to meet him.

'Now, you go back,' the girl with a face like Stalin's told him. 'But now, comrade, you are one of us.'

One of us . . .

He huddled up miserably on the back seat, Hoyle sitting beside him. A set-up, so they could blackmail me . . . When David looked up again, he was back at the guarded gates of the Potsdam '71 conference building.

Hoyle had embraced him, then pushed the car door open. 'So you were dead wrong, David.' His breath was steaming. 'You got out scot-free. In the future, trust me absolutely.'

David felt overwhelmed. Hoyle looked almost drunk. David was frightened enough to gabble. 'I only doubted you for a moment. When the lights blinded me.'

Hoyle patted his shoulder, then leaned forward to stare into his eyes. He was speaking with a dangerous quietness, now. 'You doubted me? That's because you're weak. But if I thought you'd ever betray me, David, I'd . . .' He took a breath, then grabbed David's face in both hands. His thumbs were digging in painfully below David's eye-sockets, and he finished in something like a snarl, his eyes bright. 'I'd tear your fucking eyes from out your face. And then I'd suck your brains out through the holes.'

'I'll never turn against you,' David lied, meeting Hoyle's gaze desperately. 'Never.'

Hoyle was suddenly expansive, pushing him lightly away, then hugging him. 'I'm sure the footage of the cross-questioning will do nicely. For blackmail.'

In Tokyo, now, David Bryant's thoughts were cold, clear. He was not frightened, though he knew much more than his own career was now at risk. 'Why was that man sacrificed?'

'He was a long-standing British agent, an expendable traitor recruited to the cause of imperialism in 1946. By a man called Deacon.'

'I've often wondered . . . So what is it you want with me now?'

She sat down on the double bed with him, a big-boned German girl with plenty of flesh on those big bones, and in all the right places. Her smile was an invitation. 'You know we have excellent sources in your country. It seems you are well thought of, there. For permanent cabinet rank. Even as prime minister, perhaps. In your position you could help the cause of Socialism very much.'

'And in return?'

She smiled into his eyes and stroked his hand. 'I think you would find that we had a great deal to offer.'

He was powerfully attracted, in spite of everything. 'I see. The other man, the Stasi – he died, I suppose?'

'Of course,' she said quickly, too quickly. 'I could show you the papers, the autopsy and everything!'

His instinct never failed. He took a breath, looked her in the face, and knew she was lying.

He concealed his joy. 'A flickery old film, though. What does it prove?'

She smiled.

He stretched his legs out. He felt weak but entirely clear-headed. It was strange, he thought, the sobering power of a profound shock. 'I don't believe it. Somebody who looks like me . . . so what?'

She put a hand on his knee, this time. 'It could be proved, you know.'

'I think not,' he said harshly.

She recoiled at this unxpected and forceful resistance, one hand going to her long blonde hair, the other reaching for a cigarette.

Immediately, he was there with his engraved gold lighter, offering her its flame. 'Even if there was any proof, I think I'm immune.'

'Immune?'

'I could blow the lid off. Don't you understand? Hoyle showed me, he *told* me. All about the links between the KGB, the German Democratic Republic, and terrorism – Forward, Alan Hoyle, Franz Schaller and his Stanton Industries spy, everything. And that includes the training camps in Finsterwalde and elsewhere, for people from abroad. Red Brigades, IRA, Arabs. I know much more than you think. Much more.'

Two spots of high colour had appeared on her cheeks. He turned the power of his personality on her. She felt the weight of his anger and she looked away. 'And another thing, tell your masters in East Berlin and Moscow that I've written it all down. If I ever end up dead in some mysterious road accident it'll make very, very interesting reading.'

She recoiled. 'But that would—'

'Embarrass me? I'd be dead. In any case, I can write very well, and it would make such a good, touching story. I saw the light, you see. Or rather I saw the darkness, when I went to the part of the world *your* people control. So I turned my back on '68 and the Revolution and the great god Marx. No doubt my family would do very nicely from the royalties. Especially as my death would rather tend to prove my case, don't you think?' He stood up, brushing absently at his lapels. 'Thank God for a free press, eh? Can I go now?'

She seemed stunned, but she could manage to wave the man away from the door.

He locked his room from the inside and left the door jammed shut. His hands were trembling and he had a headache. Nevertheless, he felt exhilarated, although tension had given him a pain in the chest and turned his bowels to water. The East Germans had made their move and he had walked away from it, unscathed.

I walked away. I walked away from them. He lay in bed, thinking of the future. I walked away.

★ ★ ★

Kiko, shyly, had wanted to undress in the dark.

Alex Stanton lay naked in bed, waiting for her, trying to read what was in this woman. There was blackness smeared over her left shoulder and part of her left side and he wondered what it might be. Tattooing, something Japanese, like the tattoos of the yakuza gangsters? Or dark oils? He knew better than to ask her. She stared at him, hands clasped, all her confidence suddenly gone.

But she was still beautiful.

He knew what she needed, even before love-making. He got out of bed. Broad-shouldered but athletic and light on his feet, he padded towards her. Her small breasts were neat and prominent, and he saw nervousness on her face. He took her in his arms. 'You are very lovely, Kiko Hideki.'

She closed her eyes and he kissed her.

'Come,' he said, excited, hard, bending to put his mouth on each erect nipple for a moment.

But she pushed him away.

He asked with a gentleness that surprised her, 'What's the matter now, Kiko?'

It was said fiercely. 'Are you a bad man, Alex Stanton?'

He thought for a moment. 'Not in my own eyes. Nor in the eyes of the people I know and respect, by and large.'

She took a breath, fierce, sincere. 'Let me tell you what I have heard. You have sold arms to everybody. You once sold to Arabs, terrorists you then had killed. There was a Kurd, in Iran, that you murdered yourself. And others!'

He nodded, calmly. 'I sell arms to governments the West approves of. As for terrorism, I've gone up against those people, hard, and I've paid.' His hands had made big fists. He tried to relax, but he saw the Jewel House again, the aquarium light, and the bodies of the Italian schoolgirls lying in bloody ruin on the floor . . . If he ever learned who had done that, they would be made to pay in blood, in their turn. 'As for the rest of my career, I'm not ashamed of it: some of my employees and my friends paid for our efforts with their lives – and I take the same risks.

'The Kurd? I admire the Kurds, and they deserve a country. That story is only partly true. It happened in Iran, when Washington and the Shah were helping the Kurds against Iraq and I was channelling arms over the border towards Kirkuk . . .' It came back to him, hideously. He said harshly, 'He tried to kill me, and an Iranian colonel called Azari, with a machine-gun. Only I was lucky and a little too fast. I shot him in the shoulder. And Azari, he wanted the full story from that Kurd, and the names of his relatives so that they could be killed, too. So he nailed that man to a board, Kiko Hideki. Wrists and feet. He crucified that brave man and fed him into a central-heating furnace – feet-first. I saw him burn and I smelled him burn. And Azari wanted more, Kiko. More agony, more fear.'

She touched him, bringing him back from terror and horror across the gulf of years and thousands of miles. 'Why do they say you killed him?'

'I shot him again, Kiko, killed him for the sake of mercy.' He remembered Azari's powerless rage; the uniformed soldiers pushing back, afraid, as he stood there in the filthy cellar with the smoking gun in his hand, daring them to do something. 'I shot him for no thanks and no glory, just to stop that screaming.'

'That is not the story they tell.'

'No,' he said heavily. He felt sick over the recollections: burnt human flesh, the mouth wide open and screaming as Azari asked more cruel questions, smiling. 'But it's the truth.' Then, 'Are you crying, Kiko Hideki?'

'Just hold me!'

She was shaking, inside the embrace of his arms. In the daylight she had seemed stately and almost tall, but now she was like a girl. 'You want to go to bed now?'

'Carry me there.'

One arm under her shoulders, one arm under her folded-back knees, he carried her to the double bed and laid her down. He ran a finger down from her chin, between her breasts, to the faint blur of pubic hair. A lovely, perfect doll that did not move. Then she rolled over, and he massaged her slim buttocks, feeling the muscles under the babysoft skin. 'You're very beautiful, Kiko Hideki, and there's nobody like you.'

'And you're very much of a man, and unique.' She twisted on to her back, her eyes glinting at him for a moment. Then she sat up suddenly, reached for him; a woman, alive, wanting. She held his dangling testicles cupped in her two hands, weighing them. 'Very much.' She leaned forward, her tongue licking out.

He stiffened at the feeling, grabbed her hair as she spread his thighs.

'I have to know you,' she said, her voice coming up from his groin, muffled and perhaps tearful again.

He touched the top of her head. 'I'm here for you.'

'And I'm ready, Alex Stanton.'

They moved again, and he was on top of her, weight supported on his elbows so that he could take her head and kiss her hard on the mouth. 'Then why wait longer?'

He slipped into her easily, smiled, lost himself inside her as he began the first slow strokes. She was mumbling endearments: then perfumed sweat sprayed away from her skin as she bucked beneath him, making long, low moans in her throat.

He kept going. A pulse was beating in his head, harder and harder. This meant so much to her that it could not have meant more to him. This was wonderful.

On the bed, later, Alex rolled away from Kiko's shadowed, golden body, sated. Her long, straight hair was streaked with the unfathomable blue of a blackbird's wing in this dim light. She propped herself up on one elbow and began twisting her delicate finger in the hairs of his chest.

'Ouch.'

She was grinning and totally relaxed and he knew that he had greatly pleased her. 'You know, Japanese men have smooth, hairless bodies, but you're different.'

'Of course I'm different,' he said out of the heart of his own fierce determination. 'I'm different like you.' He smiled at her, then kissed her brow. 'Kiko . . . To think I'm in bed with the great Hideki's granddaughter.'

Her eyes were alight. 'An honour?'

'A supreme pleasure.'

Outside, the night air of Tokyo stretched across miles of suburbs to the jewel-box of Chiba, and the mountains beyond. Many of the city-centre buildings were clad in brightly coloured animated signs that built up trademarks and corporation logos over and over.

This was Japan, he realized again. Different. Alien.

'So muscular and fit and strong,' she said, musing. 'So many honourable scars. So hairy on the chest.'

Alex laughed. 'What would your grandfather say if he thought you were in bed with a gorilla?'

'I don't care what my grandfather thinks,' she told him sharply.

'Then you're one of the few people who are powerful enough to defy him.'

'Powerful? No. I have to hide what I believe from him, have to be demure and obedient. After tonight I will have to lie even more. But I have inherited his courage! Tonight I will tell you things I have never told another living soul. I am past thirty, now, and I have been waiting for this day all my adult life.'

'That's quite a compliment.' She had a touching and impressive seriousness to her. 'Why did you decide to trust me, of all people?'

Her voice was husky. 'Perhaps I know of you, Alex-*san*. Perhaps I have already spoken to those who know you.'

His first reaction was to freeze, and reveal nothing. What if she was really working for her grandfather? 'Is that so?'

'I spoke to one who knows you better than anybody.'

He smiled, touched. Did she mean David? Presumably, as David had known who she was. He couldn't quite remember who had made the original introduction, but that hardly mattered now. 'God, but you're beautiful.'

She rolled over and placed her hand over his heart, but she was on a different wavelength entirely. 'We are in a room I paid for only an hour ago.'

He heard the tension in her voice. 'What *is* this?'

'I was not followed, I have checked the room. Nobody can listen in.'

'Especially your grandfather?'

Her nipples were relaxed now, and he felt a sudden impulse to kiss her there, but she pulled the satin sheet up under her chin.

'He's a very dangerous man, Alex. You know that, don't you?'

'Yes. We've crossed swords before.'

'Crossed swords!' Kiko gave a harsh laugh. 'The government listens to him. He has tremendous influence. And he exerts it. The Lockheed scandal here has created a power vacuum into which grandfather hopes to move. Part of it is that he thinks he has solutions to our oil-supply problem, and to Japanese deficits of $10 billion and more to the Gulf states. One thing is to have more and more atomic power. Like Arigata. And the other thing also concerns you.'

He jerked upright. It was what he had half-suspected since 1971. 'You mean he intends to rearm Japan – and start a big armaments industry here?'

'Exactly. Then he will sell to the Gulf countries himself. The only thing standing in his way now is Article IX of Japan's constitution. He intends to renounce it, when he has the power. And he will tear up all of our democratic constitution to do so!'

'What?' Alex was suddenly cold. He knew the Japanese constitution was supposed to prevent Japan having a fully-fledged army, navy and air force. 'He's going to work on the Tokyo government and—'

She laughed, harshly. 'Alex, don't you understand? He already has the Hakagawa faction of the ruling party in his pocket. He will *be* the government – unless he is stopped.'

'By who?'

She did not answer, except with a kiss.

He said worriedly, 'Why are you telling me?'

She looked into his ice-blue eyes and sighed again. 'Because I believe in peace, and my grandfather does not.'

Alex felt a chill. 'What do you mean?'

'He will make guns and bombs, but there is more, and I think you know it.'

'More?' He shifted uneasily in the bed.

'My grandfather, the great Saigo Hideki, will get uranium and plutonium, enough to make nuclear weapons.'

'Nuclear – You can't know that for certain!'

'No? My grandfather struggles for the soul of the nation. He has faith in the pure blood of the Japanese, in the samurai virtues only. His plan has been started. He has agents all over the world, some very high-placed. Effectively, your Lord Beauford is his agent, and so are many others.'

'His agent!' Alex said grimly.

'Grandfather has brought down companies and individuals who opposed him. He has committed acts of violence. Violence. I know!'

Alex felt the blood draining away from his face. Many things made sense, now. 'Does the name Alan Hoyle mean anything to you?'

'He has used that man; he has used others.'

Alex twisted away, not wanting to believe it. But one more thing had to be asked. 'And Saigon? Did your grandfather secretly recruit armaments specialists there?'

'So I heard. And I told your friend Maggie.'

He thought of Van Tien Trung, Hacker Stanton's employee, dead after Maggie had persuaded him to ask questions. He sighed. 'Maybe you have the wrong man. What do you expect me to do? I signed up to help build Arigata – I gave my word. I believe in nuclear power, and I already make guns and bombs.'

The voice was low. 'I must find a man who is something like my grandfather, and has similar power and wealth, to oppose him. But I know of the Stantons – know you, Alex. You are strong, ruthless, but I think you are decent. Think of what my grandfather plans. He has approached three countries for uranium. Iraq, I know, will supply him if you do not. Working with Stanton Industries, he has secretly begun the manufacture of arms. Soon he will tear up our American constitution.'

'He's really started to work on guns and tanks?'

'Military avionics you have already guessed about, I hear.'

'You hear a lot!'

She shrugged. 'He will pay you well, now you have guessed. But whatever you think of what I have said, I tell you this: if you continue to work with him, you are cutting your own throat! He will take your business! If you don't believe me, go to the Azu factory in Kanagawa. Ask about tanks. That will change your mind.'

Alex lay back on the bed, smelling her warmth and nearness. Now, he felt sure he had solved the riddle of the Azu aerospace factory. Kiko was right. Hideki was making experimental electronic systems for warplanes. 'You say he's going to be the government – how can I possibly stop that? You must know I'm doing business with him and that, Christ, contracts are already arranged, signed by me personally, so it's too late to back out.'

'Where's your courage?' She threw a leg over him, straddled him. Her hair and her small, perfect breasts hung down as she stared into his eyes. 'Why do I ask you to help? Because you are powerful, Alex Stanton, and you are not afraid.'

'I'm not afraid?' He snorted. 'Why is that important?'

'I will tell you, afterwards. Now, go to Kanagawa.'

Next day, David found Alex extremely preoccupied. They drove to the airport together, but Alex did not say much.

'Listen,' David said eventually, 'I was with Takahashi last night. He's a smart one. So is his boss.'

'I know,' Alex said.

'Watch yourself.'

David spent much of his return flight from Tokyo speculating: would Stanton Industries really get to help arm Japan, and build the reactor at Arigata?

On landing at Heathrow he was almost assaulted inside the airport; a pack of photographers jostled to take his photograph, then as he and Paulin walked through the crowd he found himself recognized by a party of returning businessmen.

'You tell 'em,' one Wolverhampton man told him.

'We're as good as those people abroad, Mr Bryant,' another said. 'Speak for the nation.'

David paused to shake a few hands. 'I intend to. Thank you.'

At home, Megan produced a file of press clippings. 'I thought you might like to see these.'

David looked through them, and saw that his remarks in Japan had been covered in detail. The papers had him protecting the national interest in a resolute manner: BRYANT SPEAKS FOR BRITAIN.

'It's pretty rare for a trade secretary to make quite such a big splash,' Megan told him. 'I think you came out of all this very well.'

'That remains to be seen,' he said gloomily. 'I've been rocking the boat; they don't like you doing that in this country.'

Early next morning, David went to the House and found a note waiting for him. He went in to the new Prime Minister's office tentatively, worried about the controversy he had caused. However, the PM was courteous and pleasant about everything; this high office clearly suited Mr Callaghan.

David was still hurt that he had been excluded from the battle to select his leader, and the nation's.

'It wasn't a question of keeping you down, David. Your friends, and I include myself among your allies, were protecting you. There was nothing to be gained by letting you set your stall out publicly against the far-Left wing of the party. And we thought you'd benefit by a trip to the East. It's always good to see things at first hand, and make contacts. Nobody expected you to let rip like you did, though.'

David tensed, prepared to defend his actions to the hilt. Both the moral and practical aspects of his decision were important points of principle by which he felt he must stand whatever the political cost – up to and including resignation.

'I did what I thought was necessary.'

The PM chuckled and sat back from the table. 'It's a damned good job you did over there. How would you feel about taking on a little more responsibilty within the department?'

The man from the US Embassy in Tokyo shuffled the papers on his desk.

'It's been a long time since Saigon, hasn't it?'

'Right, right, Mr Stanton –'

'Alex, please.'

'Sure. Alex. Anyway, any friend of Ray Hacker's—'

'Quite.'

It was a large office, with a view; a faint odour of bourbon hung in the air. The man peered down at his desk. He seemed worried, too worried for this kind of minor favour. 'This is all entirely unofficial, of course.'

'It's strictly deep background as far as I'm concerned,' Alex said.

'Hideki . . .' The man drummed his fingers on the desk. He still looked nervous, and Alex wondered suddenly if the Japanese industrialist had any hold on this man or secret links to the CIA. But that, surely, was impossible. Or almost. 'I can't say too much. State sees him as an ally.'

'They would,' Alex said cynically. 'But I'm also interested in his granddaughter.'

'Kiko.' The man's face brightened. 'The lovely Kiko Hideki. I think I begin to understand.'

Alex raised a hand. 'Strictly deep background.'

'A very beautiful lady. Hideki's only living descendant. Aged thirty-three, single, born in Nagasaki –'

'Presently unmarried?'

'Never married.'

'Why might that be?'

'Well, she's a little difficult to handle. Quite outspoken, and sometimes she's involved herself with ecological movements, things like that. Very inappropriate for a high-born Japanese lady. There's been nothing in the press about that lately, though.' He took up another file, hesitated.

Alex sensed there was something more. 'There's something else, isn't there?'

The other man gave a twisted smile. 'Enough to reduce marriage prospects.'

Alex shifted in the comfortable chair, unable to shake off the fear that Kiko was using him in some intrigue of her grandfather's. 'Tell me, please.'

'The American A-bombs we had to use here . . .'

'Yes?'

'She was under one, as a child. Serious burns, and radiation. The Japanese have a word for people like her – *hiba-kushi*: and they're almost unmarriageable. For obvious reasons.'

Alex was shaken. Now he remembered the dark shadows across her shoulders. Kiko, so beautiful. A victim of war. Scared to have children because of the blast of radiation she had received at Hiroshima . . .

Now, he believed that she was a sincere opponent of militarism, and her grandfather. He got up to go, thanking the CIA man.

There was still one last check to make.

That afternoon, he made it. McCourt, following instructions, drove

Alex in a rented Nissan to the front entrance of another huge factory, this time in Kanagawa.

Alex was eating lunch; a hot dog. He had been amused to find out he was dining on what the Japanese would call a *hotto-doggo*.

'You must be pleased now, Alex.'

'Mmh.'

'That share of Arigata, signed, sealed and delivered; the supply and reprocessing contracts; and also a half-promise of all that armaments work.'

'A half-promise, yes. But I'd like to see anybody get half a brass cent on loan from the likes of Lord Beauford on that basis.' He wiped his hands carefully as McCourt parked and then flourished a couple of business cards.

'Do we really need these forgeries, Alex? It seems a little cloak-and-daggerish to me.'

Alex looked round him quickly. 'I want this kept secret, strictly secret, for as long as possible.'

The luminous sign was in Japanese. Indecipherable. The thing that lay under wraps in the far corner of the company's site was still there. They got out of their car and strolled over to the uniformed gateman. McCourt said something in Japanese, then the two men were conducted through automatic doors into an air-conditioned reception area. It was clinical inside, almost sterile.

'I'm from the United States, name's Frank Pohl,' Alex said, smiling. He flashed a business card that said *Indiana Agricultural Plant Co*. 'I'm expected.'

It did not take long to reach the office of a Mr Kodama, the firm's head of sales. Alex looked keenly at the graphs and charts headed up in terms of sales and profits and market share. Mr Kodama, in physique like a pocket-sized sumo wrestler, talked them through a range of products. This division of the Hideki Corporation made road graders, construction plant and agricultural machines. There was an exchange of pleasantries as Kodama expressed how cheaply such vehicles could be produced, and how easy it was to export from Japan.

Then Alex asked about the vehicle that was covered up in the yard. Through McCourt, he said that he had seen it was a tracked vehicle. Kodama admitted it was a tank – a single prototype the factory had made, to test how easy it would be to tool up for such things.

Alex's face expressed surprise. McCourt worked hard to translate Kodama's words. 'It is true that, since 1945, General MacArthur's constitution has been recognized. But already it is possible to manufacture arms here, and in two or three years or so, maybe we can export also.'

Alex nodded again. 'This tank – may I see the specifications?'

Again, McCourt translated smoothly. 'We have based it on a successful Western model, one of which we obtained in 1974. It was more effective than the Soviet T-72 by far, and we have improved it. Only the gun would have to be imported. But' – McCourt's head turned away, turned back – 'we wish to know if your interest is serious, as we must act confidentially.'

'I understand the need for secrecy perfectly,' Alex said. He managed to keep too much sarcasm out of his voice. He already had a good idea which Western tank Hideki had based his designs on. He gritted his teeth, hoping the expression would pass as a smile. 'But my company is associated with another, operating in Iran, which would be interested.'

Iran: that name made Kodama take real notice. He rang down for the details immediately.

Alex read rapidly through the fractured English of the provisional brochure for the new product line, checking the listed details for the 'A1' tank: engine power, armament, range, and so on.

McCourt blanched as he saw the anger rising in Alex.

'It's extremely cheap,' Alex admitted. 'I suppose it would be hard for your price to be matched in America or Europe?'

McCourt spoke: 'He says, he will guarantee this is the cheapest and the best. It will be sold only on that basis. If you find otherwise he promises to match the opposition, less ten percent.'

Alex stood up, towering over the shorter Japanese. Alex shook his hand and said heartily, 'I'll be in touch.'

In Japanese, Kodama asked, 'When?'

Alex's control almost snapped, but he remained blandly uncomprehending until McCourt translated and he could make an offhand reply. 'When it suits me.'

In the car, he sat back to think, hands folded on his lap. Kiko. And her grandfather. And what she claimed about his secret plans . . . It all began to whirl around inside his head, and he did not know what to do.

He feared there was no alternative except to take Hideki on, and in his estimation he could not fight Saigo Hideki head-on. If he did that, he would lose. Then Alex turned to McCourt and spoke with unconcealed anger. 'Kiko was right.'

'What?'

'That was a Stanton Mark VIII, Ken! Hideki *is* rearming.'

McCourt's face cleared. He jerked a finger over his shoulder. 'You mean they . . .'

'An exact copy. Or as near as damn it – it's minus our composite armour and it's been refitted with Japanese electronics and auxiliary power.'

'Good God!'

They were further along the road to Tokyo when Alex spoke again. 'But here's the only big difference between his product and ours, Ken: that man can deliver his version of the Mark VIII, anywhere in the world, for twenty per cent less than I could deliver ours to our own factory gates. We have to get a new tank factory up and running, because if they can do that over just a quarter of our product range, Ken, we're dead, dead, *dead*.'

Chapter Fifteen

There was more change in the ministerial ranks. Trade and Industry were combined, and now David Bryant had cabinet rank. With that came the spacious, brown-upholstered office overlooking Victoria Street, in the new Trade and Industry complex, and a large personal staff to keep him informed and back up his decisions. But in spite of everything that the new government began to do, the trade situation could not improve immediately, and after one night in June 1976, Britain woke up again to a pound that had slipped six cents against the dollar. What if all the foreign banks who held sterling began to sell? Some did. With inflation still at twenty percent, Britain was in crisis again.

It was then that Alex Stanton came back from Japan.

David frowned at him from his swivel chair. In moods like this, Alex looked dangerous even to his old friend. On David's desk this morning a newspaper headline proclaimed ARIGATA REACTOR: BRITAIN'S SHARE. Nevertheless, neither Alex Stanton nor he were smiling.

Alex had been stalking about restlessly: he was fresh from Tokyo, in a white Yves St Laurent suit. 'Never mind about my business, David, what about the country – this exchange-rate crisis?'

'It's been disastrous,' David admitted, pained. 'From March and April till now – do you know how much money we expended to try and prop up sterling?'

'Tell me, David.'

'A third of our foreign currency reserves.'

'A *third!*'

'Now the cupboard is almost empty, Alex.'

Alex's face was thunderous. 'We have to make this country work, David. We have to make people do it right. We're dying of a disease called deindustrialization, we must be cured, and it's much too late for the cure to be painless.'

'You always think answers are easy and straightforward, don't you?'

'No.' Alex turned around, heavy arms folded tightly in front of his chest – as if he was trying to restrain himself from violence. 'But there bloody well are right answers, David. The Japanese have them – I've seen it, you've seen it. We must change; make things profitably, and do anything that's necessary to sell them. Now if only I can improve on that foothold in Japan . . .'

'You didn't expect to get that big part of Arigata, did you?'

'A project like that? Not in my wildest dreams! Think of the scale of it. Building and initial fuelling, well over one billion dollars. Then . . .' He shrugged. 'Running costs. Uranium fuel. Reprocessing. Add on the costs of decommissioning in twenty or twenty-five years. Another quarter of a billion, maybe. Two thousand million dollars! Or more!'

'Astounding sums.'

Alex's voice was raw. 'This will be the making of our Civil Projects Division, when I formally set it up. With the help of you government boys we're going to get inside the castle of Japan. Arigata will be completed before 1978 – ahead of its schedule. I guarantee it, no matter what Beauford says.'

David looked at him with a blend of admiration and uneasiness. Alex's ambition and energy might be admirable: but it all meant pain for himself and for other people. David now felt sure it was all a product of his friend's early exclusion from the Stanton family and the firm. In Alex's mind the huge Stanton Industries empire should have been open to him from the beginning. Because it hadn't been, he had given everything to become the dominant voice in one of Europe's largest companies – and he was still hungry for more.

David glanced at his watch. 'I'm sorry, I've only another five minutes to spare. I'm going with the Chancellor to a meeting at Number 10. We'll need to speak to the International Monetary Fund again – and we desperately need to get our story straight.'

'Cap in hand,' Alex said harshly. 'A huge trade deficit and a declining currency. And this was such a great country, once! Till we threw it all away,' Alex said savagely, 'scared to compete, scared to change.'

'There's nothing for nothing in this world, after all. And it isn't too late to change.' Insight came to David. 'You're still making angry noises about Japan, aren't you? Look, what exactly happened over there between you and Hideki?'

Alex twisted his head towards the window, then back. 'I think I've been made a fool of, David, and I hate it.' His underlip jutted out.

'What do you mean?'

'Two things. Remember when the old board of directors wouldn't back my mission to Japan?'

'Osaka, and your tank battle – the one Maggie described?'

'Exactly. I personally imported tanks to Osaka, including one of our new Mark VIII-Cs with the composite armour. Then I staged a mock-battle there, against a couple of Russian T-types I'd persuaded my friends in Israel to sell me.'

'A good piece of showmanship.'

'I thought so. The new electronic fire-control system showed up spectacularly well – now Stanton tanks can fire over 360° with pin-point accuracy, and the gun is fully stabilized. But those Tokyo government people – they just weren't going to buy.'

'I remember you telling me. But isn't that the risk you take,

Alex? Win some, lose some.' David looked at his watch again and straightened his silk tie. 10 Downing Street demanded his best.

'I hate losing, David. But that's not the worst of it. I arranged for all tanks to be scrapped after the demonstration, but I obviously didn't oversee that personally.'

'So?'

'So Hideki copied my Mark VIII, David. Exactly. And he can produce my tank for over twenty percent less than we could on the Scotswood Road.'

'Twenty percent less!'

'Yes.'

'Couldn't you . . . ?' David was thinking furiously. 'Look, maybe I could help with government grants and union backing for some big, big changes. Suppose you demolished the Scotswood Road site completely? Then we could change *everything*, to compete with the Japanese.'

'If that's possible.'

'Maybe we could make it possible,' David said, suddenly excited.

Alex smiled at him. 'I've engaged your interest, have I?'

'Yes.' There was a pause. 'Listen, let's meet up again to discuss this. You really want to compete with Japan?'

'Like I want women to make love to and air to breathe. I've been challenged, now.'

David hesitated. 'Hideki, through the Japanese government, has been making overtures.'

Alex's eyes narrowed, and he came to stand over David. There was no elegance in Alex Stanton now, only a fierce intensity. 'For all practical purposes Hideki & Co. *are* the Japanese government. What's he been proposing?'

David said thoughtfully, 'Arigata would only be a start. But I feel dubious about it, and the party conference won't like it at all.'

Alex's blue eyes had lit up. 'What do you mean? What do the Japanese want?'

'Wider technical assistance with their reactor programme, and they'll give us a chance to bid for reprocessing all their spent fuel.'

'Sounds good to me. What's the problem?'

'But don't you know what we'll be extracting for them from their reactor fuel?'

'Not exactly.'

'Plutonium.'

Alex said only, blank-faced, 'I'm not an engineer.'

David wondered if he really knew nothing. 'Plutonium. As in the nuclear bomb,' David said simply. He hoped he was planting the idea in Alex's head; then Alex, perhaps, might do something. At least, he thought, I might be able to keep my own conscience clear . . . 'And I really must go. I have a country to run.'

* * *

As David Bryant had expected, there was no good news at the 10 Downing Street meeting in the cabinet room.

They sat around the highly-polished oval table, sweltering in the hottest summer for years, listening.

Almost every new statistic they were given meant a downturn. David was grimly fascinated to watch the nation's economy disintegrating, and he decided to speak out in spite of his status. In his time at the levers of power he had pushed through many development schemes, helped bring North Sea oil ashore, and worked with the Foreign Office to improve the international side. But he had grown increasingly dissatisfied with the British system. It was simply not geared to aid anyone wanting to see the country reshaped as a dynamic industrial nation. It was not a system that tolerated 'trouble-makers' who wanted change. To the established order, silence equalled consent, and that was called consensus.

'This country desperately needs to earn money abroad; we must solve the trade-balance problem.' He looked around the table; crystal tumblers, white blotters, some faces politely expectant, others self-concerned, remote. Many of his colleagues now seemed to think there was only the choice between Britain becoming an economic desert, or adopting rigorous, Eastern bloc-style Socialism. Only David believed in a third way. 'I think I do have some answers – we must have progress, economic progress, drawing on the unlooked-for bonanza of North Sea oil.'

The Prime Minister tapped his glasses back in place. 'It sounds good, David, but your specific proposals are so expensive—'

'Do we have a choice? We must retool, we must reinvest.' The fact that no one else was preaching that doctrine drove him almost to despair. 'Let me talk generalities – and why not? We can't run this government entirely on a day-to-day basis. What about the long term? We keep talking about redistribution of wealth; a few percentage points here or there. Well, in my opinion, the real problem is efficiency – making Britain work – in every sense. It's the only answer to the relative decline that has now lasted almost a century.'

Another minister said half humorously, 'Fresh ideas, eh?'

'Exactly. We must have an open, competitive society; too much of politics here is about protecting vested interests. It's too late to be comfortable. *We must have change.*'

'There are all kinds of problems. In the House, and elsewhere,' the Prime Minister reminded him kindly. 'We're in a minority. Perhaps later . . .' Then there was a knock on the door, and a messenger came in. Mr Callaghan read the note quickly, then looked up, grim-faced. 'The International Monetary Fund has just sent us its terms for the new loan HMG has requested. You may remember we have asked for a minimum of 3,500 million dollars.'

There was a long pause. David glanced quickly at his colleagues. He knew there would be no discussion of the broader issues today.

'Well, Jim?' Michael Foot asked. 'What's their pound of flesh this time?'

'They want more cuts – up to five thousand million pounds.'

There were gasps. This was the crisis indeed. David could not help speaking his mind. 'This is the price of economic failure. Death, by a thousand cuts.'

The State Opening began when the priceless regalia were dispatched by coach from Buckingham Palace: a crown set with 2,783 diamonds, and the sword of state. David waited in the crowded Commons chamber with his colleagues, his mind's eye seeing the cheering crowds in Parliament Square and the dipping and waving Union Jacks. The Queen herself would come in the gilded state coach, step down in front of the imposing Victorian bulk of the palace of Westminster.

Queen Elizabeth II walked with conscious dignity into the Royal Gallery and so to the Lords' chamber, where she sat down, glitteringly jewelled on a gold throne. Lords looked on, robed in ermine, the law lords in eighteenth-century wigs. Archbishops, dukes and marquesses, earls, viscounts, bishops and barons, in descending rank; then life peers and officers of the chamber.

'My lords, pray be seated.'

The nation's peerage settled on to the red leather benches. Then the gentleman usher known as Black Rod was sent to summon the government and other members of the House of Commons, preceeded by cries of 'Make way! Make way!'

David saw the doors to the packed chamber slammed in the face of the Queen's man. There was an amused stir among the Labour members around him, but with his knowledge of history he took the ceremony more seriously: a civil war had been fought to establish such rights as this – the right of the Commons to refuse the Queen's messenger, and so the Queen's writ.

David, in his twentieth-century suit, craned to the right as the usher in his knee-breeches and gold chain was allowed in after being made to knock three times. 'Mr Speaker, the Queen commands this honourable house to attend Her Majesty in the House of Peers.'

The Prime Minister himself stepped forward to head the long procession, Mrs Thatcher as Leader of the Opposition walking beside him. In pairs, ministers and their shadows followed, David taking his own place and other MPs crowding behind in an excited, disorderly mass, the ghosts of past centuries going with them.

In the Lords, David looked around. Gold everywhere, in this splendid Pugin interior; but not nearly enough seats. Suddenly, he wondered at this ancient, absurd ceremony. Which is it? he asked himself. Either the State Opening is enjoyable, harmless pageantry, preserving the necessary rituals of government. Or it's a time-consuming nuisance that gets in the way of the busy MP, and still another example of pomp holding up the administration of what should be a modern industrial nation . . .

He thought of his own position in the government. Trade and Industry was the most crucial office, in his opinion. But the traditions of Her Majesty's Government meant that the highest pay went to a lawyer, the Lord Chancellor. All the traditional officers of state outranked him – and so did Environment, the Lord Privy Seal, Social Services. It was absurd and, worse, it was obsolete.

The Queen began to read out the speech outlining the government's intentions.

'My Lords and Members of the House of Commons,' she began. By a quirk of the antique, unwritten constitution, the speech was prepared by ministers but delivered as if the Queen herself made policy. 'My government will in this coming session seek to . . .'

It was no news to a government minister. David's attention wandered elsewhere.

'My Government will reintroduce the Bill to bring into public ownership the aircraft and guided weapons, shipbuilding, shiprepairing and marine engine industries . . .'

Stanton Industries, among other firms. He smiled grimly. Was nationalization and control by politicians, civil servants and trade union leaders really the best way to compete against the likes of Japan? He was not at all certain, now that he met all three types every day in Westminster.

'. . . the extension of industrial democracy in the private and public sectors of the economy . . .'

In other words, more power to the union bureaucrats. His smile became even grimmer.

He looked at Queen Elizabeth II, and thought of Elizabeth I speaking so stirringly so many centuries before. It all endures, he thought, it all continues, but it has to *change*.

Only, where will we start? Where, and when? And how?

And even more importantly, who?

Chapter Sixteen

Alex decided he had to investigate the changes, now that the presidency had Carter's name on it.

After the inauguration ceremonies, Alex stayed on in Washington, DC. Even with the Stanton lobbying office pushing hard it took days to set up a meeting with the new White House staff, and then the atmosphere inside with them was as cold as it was out of doors. At the end of a freezing January made worse by petrol shortages, Alex went south to Texas for a meeting with Ray, face to face. There had been a renewed flood of rumours coming out of Washington he did not like, though Hacker had not seemed too concerned.

In their Dallas office Alex came to the point quickly. 'I came to get US back-up. I'll need it when I see the al-Saud princes and the Shah again. Instead of approval I got the cold shoulder. I know you don't take it seriously, but this thing called détente, Ray—'

'I was wrong.' Ray spoke brutally: a big man with a big anger. 'Yesterday I made some calls, right? Jimmy Carter means it. The army, navy and air force get de-balled.'

Alex slammed down the tumbler of bourbon. 'As bad as that?'

'Yes. And the CIA gets the same treatment – just when, after Vietnam, the Russkies think they have us on the run! There's gonna be a lot of guys tramping the sidewalk and they'll be the only people, the *only* people *we* have, who know about places like Iran and Saudi and even our Latin friends south of the Rio Grande. It's crazy. And we get your friend Maggie in the *Washington Post* saying what great peace-loving guys this Carter and Cyrus Vance are!'

'She did help the campaign,' Alex said quietly.

Hacker would not be diverted. 'How can you get peace if you throw down your weapons in the face of your enemy and raise your hands and say "please"? I'll tell you, I'm going to get that man out of the White House if it's the last thing I do. We have to get somebody patriotic, who looks good on TV, next time. Because, believe me, there are people out there in this world who will make Carter pay for this weakness – and the rest of us in the West, too.'

Alex gave a grim smile. 'You don't think the KGB will do much budget-trimming in response?'

'Damn right I don't! And I bet you that guy at the head of the KGB, you know—'

'Andropov,' Alex said flatly, remembering. 'Yuri Vladimirovich Andropov; the chairman of the State Security Committee.'

Ray grimaced. 'I suppose he'll get value for money.'

'Yes. But I don't suppose, Ray: I *know* he will. Because I know him.'

Ray stared at him, his shoulders hunched. 'You know the top man in the KGB! Alex, you're kidding me.'

'No. It was in 1956.' The memories came flooding back to Alex; so long ago, now. 'I remember it clearly. A conquered country, struggling and bleeding to be free. Hungary. Security policemen were hanged from their own office windows. When the Russians came back, afterwards, unarmed men were shot down by the Red Army tanks. See, after my father Michael Stanton was killed, his brother Edward adopted me, and he was seeing Noel Barber, a chief correspondent in Hungary then – and Sir Edward was also a personal friend of the British Ambassador in Budapest. When we visited, guess who was his Soviet opposite number? Andropov.'

The Texan looked at him curiously. 'What's he like?'

'Impressive. That man is cunning and cold-blooded; a heavyweight Stalinist pretending to have a human face. But in the '56 rising Andropov was a bastard, no mistake. He called in the Red Army, and that was the end of the freedom-fighters. Blood.'

'The son of a bitch!'

Alex remembered the monochrome fifties, the grey, harsh postwar men. 'Andropov is tough, puritanical, sarcastic and clever. Tall, grey. Hard eyes behind spectacles. He speaks fluent English and several other languages, and he has been a ruthless part of the machinery of repression for decades.'

'And on our side, a sweet-natured Georgia peanut farmer.'

'They aren't going to give up. But neither are we. One man in the right place can be worth more than an army in the wrong place. As we both know.'

'You're right, Alex, but there's nobody knows that better than the Soviets. Not even us.'

'If we can keep the Red Army out of Iran and the Gulf, that'll be something – and I for one plan to keep the house of al-Saud sweet on the West, and safe. Whatever your man Carter says.'

Hacker laughed. 'You and me both, brother. When'll you go there and give 'em your sales pitch?'

'Soon after I come back from Japan. You see, unless I make sales – more sales of the Mark VIII to Iran and Saudi Arabia at least, and maybe one other country – Hideki will have me over a barrel.'

'And he'll know it.'

'Yes,' Alex acknowledged. 'As long as he has Lord Beauford as his man on the Board, he'll know it.'

Hacker nodded, leaving the rest unspoken. 'Now, what you doing with Stanton Industries?'

Alex put on a down-home accent: Hacker's. 'Preachin' salvation, boy.'

'I hope you succeed.'

Alex reached for his attaché case again. He thought of Japan. 'So do I.'

Alex and David Bryant both flew to Tokyo on February 14, in a Stanton 727 jet decked out in black and gold. They arrived to hear of violent protests by anti-nuclear groups that had involved tear-gas and broken glass.

Late the next evening, even as they were winding down the day's discussions at the Ministry of International Trade and Industry, the Stanton Industries building was petrol-bombed.

The Japanese apologies were numerous, and seemed sincere. Alex went to see the wreckage next morning, riding in a large white car MITI had supplied, rather than the company's distinctive Rolls-Royce. Fujiko went with him.

When the car stopped, he pushed his face up to the steamy window. The burned-out skeleton was roped off, and in front of it broken glass and wreckage had been swept up in heaps, restricting access to the three-storey wreck. Square-shouldered men in blue police uniforms eyed the ranks of the onlookers. Alex noted the immaculate neatness of their black belts and boots, the caps with white trim and the white lanyards running to the holstered pistols.

He stepped out of the car, and immediately a murmur from the hundred-strong crowd attracted his attention. He frowned as he recognized the dislike in the expressions. Flashguns detonated light, and as he realized the pictures would make him seen hard and aggressive he turned quickly away to help Fujiko out of the car. A policeman hawked out of his throat and spat near Alex's foot. The gob of saliva steamed in the slush as Alex moved his polished shoe away. He hoped it was Japanese manners, not English ones.

He looked at the ruin, smelling burnt wood and paper, and an icy dampness: the aftermath of extinguished flames. He was glad he had made sure the office had fireproof Swedish safes. 'Terrible, Fujiko.'

'A bad setback; we lost computer records, files, and lots of the paperwork needed to import things here.' Fujiko lowered her voice, her breath white in the bitter air. 'Also, we have heard the police made little attempt to save the offices.'

He was concerned. 'What? Hell, the Tokyo riot police are well-trained, aren't they?'

'Of course, Mr Stanton. After the terrorism of such as Sekigun, or even the battle for Narita—'

Alex leaned closer to her. 'Sekigun?'

'The terror group run by the woman Fusako Shigenobu. What you will know as the Japanese Red Army.' She bowed and smiled as a senior policeman went by. 'I hear they have issued threats against Arigata – and you. So have other terror groups.'

'Threats? Why wasn't the office better protected, then?'

She looked at him, fragile, beautiful; her eyes seemed full of sexual longing. She was almost lost in a full-length coat of silvery fur, and he saw gold gleaming at her throat and wondered who had bought it for her. 'Nuclear power is very controversial here. And so the authorities are not unhappy to see a foreign firm identified as promoting atomic power and providing our Self-Defence Forces with modern armaments.'

'Christ,' Alex said. He wondered if he should help Kiko get publicity for the truth, here. 'What exactly have the papers been saying?'

'Oh, that a change may be necessary for this land. A more actively patriotic government, for instance.'

Alex stared hard. 'Any names been mentioned?'

'Minister Hakagawa's, among others.'

The embassy helped with discussions that meant a new and extremely confidential memorandum of agreement was drawn up: at the official opening of Arigata in September both the British government and Stanton Industries would commit themselves to further assisting the Japanese nuclear programme.

They all went out to eat Japanese-style that evening. It was a tiny but highly recommended place off Chuo-Dori, crowded and steamy. On one side of the long table were two HMG diplomats, David Bryant, Alex himself, lively and charming, and a dour, cagey McCourt. Opposite were some of the polite men from MITI and the corporations involved in the Arigata reactor.

Fourteen people sat talking and drinking. English, Japanese, French and German phrases were tossed around. Alex dined lightly, unrelaxed, picking over delicious *nigiri sushi* and *oshi sushi*. Sometimes he listened to the increasingly drunken conversation, and sometimes watched the amazing antics of the *sushi-ya* chef, whose arms whirled all the time though he never stopped grinning. There was great energy in the Japanese: and yet, supposedly, some of them lacked stamina, and to Alex it had been obvious since the 1976 trade conference that they could not hold their drink.

At the end of the evening, they all went back to the embassy.

There was another meeting here, though it was almost one in the morning, in a room David insisted should be swept for bugs.

A diplomat shifted about uncomfortably. 'The Ambassador here has often cautioned me not to expect the worst.'

'Let's make sure,' David said calmly. 'I can't help noticing the domestic staff are all Japanese.'

It was fortunate Alex had brought his security department's latest equipment from London, because he found an electronic eavesdropping device hidden under a table. It was no larger than a cigarette packet. Alex dropped it on the floor, and crushed it under his heel.

The First Secretary's face screwed up in disgust. 'What do they think they're doing in the Tokyo government? We do business together, we're *allies*.'

'You're *sure* it was the government here? Might have been the Soviets, might have been a big corporation . . .'

'The Russians?' McCourt asked, surprised.

'Why not?' David said. 'They've fought the Japanese in two wars, and they'd certainly want to keep an eye on Tokyo's nuclear programme. It's no secret why we're here!'

'Secret! I'll be in tomorrow's papers, the bad guy selling tanks and Arigata to peace-loving Japan! And besides,' Alex added quietly, 'that might well have been a government-approved tap. Maybe they see things differently. As a winner-takes-all competition, for instance. What do you think, Minister?'

David was already having second thoughts about everything. 'I bet they do see it like that. They're competitors, not allies. I think they seek mastery, not cooperation. It seems to me Stanton Industries is a stalking-horse here, that's all; a British company being used to attract a lot of the flak nuclear power is going to get in Japan. Hell, we've only sold one reactor here that's completely British, that old Magnox back in the sixties!'

'We're committed to Arigata, now.'

'Yes, I suppose we are.' David sighed. 'I'm sorry, Alex, but to me the thought of Japan really opening up for business is unbelievable. And my opinion may not change even if you do make your arms sales, and I'm certainly not counting on that.'

'We'd better be good to them,' Alex said, 'because we need to count on doing well here. Unless we can keep ahead of schedule the work we're doing at Arigata will barely be profitable for us. It only makes sense if it will lead us to better things.'

'That means Hideki has a stranglehold on you.' David looked around. 'Why are we really here?'

The Ambassador sighed. 'I think we're all going to have to look a lot harder for those answers, Minister.'

One of the embassy people shifted about. 'There've been some rumours we can be optimistic about. Interior Minister Hakagawa is supposed to be pushing hard for a strong nuclear future here, and they say he's very determined.'

'A nuclear future,' Alex said, thoughtfully.

The next day, they were taken to see the Arigata site. Things there were nearing completion.

It was a bitingly cold but clear day. The silvery dome of the reactor containment building glistened in the sun and the single big cooling tower gleamed white as they drove up the main road to the huge peninsula site.

McCourt met them at the main gate, with Paul Takahashi. As trucks passed and curious Asian faces stared, they all went up to a board that held a map.

'As you can see,' McCourt said politely, 'a river flows through the site, a river used for cooling purposes. Here is the quayside, for the reception of heavy equipment. The central dome here contains the reactor: when fully powered, it will generate up to 900 million watts – enough to light up a city.'

There was a busy, efficient atmosphere as they walked through the site. External construction had long since finished, and the first reactor fuel had arrived a week ago.

After the surface installations had been inspected, they were all taken underground. A massive steel door closed behind them.

David shivered. 'Is this necessary?'

Takahashi stopped and said quietly, 'Keeps us safe, down here. Just in case something goes wrong up above, with the reactor.'

'Is that likely?' asked Alex.

'No way, Mr Stanton!'

There were surprisingly few people around. All were dressed in yellow and wearing hardhats.

'It must take a hell of a time to train people to use all this,' David said, waving a hand.

'It does,' McCourt acknowledged, 'but every expensive minute is necessary. This is nuclear power. It *can't* be allowed to run wild.'

Alex glanced around. 'Silent agreement, eh?'

'Let me show you something else.' Takahashi led them back. There were closed doors here. 'I can't let you into the control room till all the instrument boards are installed and sealed. At the moment even dust could be dangerous.' Takahashi went down a different corridor and opened another door. 'It's the project museum.'

This was not yet much. A mere room with blueprints, photographs of the original site and buildings under construction. A scale model of the plant. A corner of the exhibition showed photographs of Hiroshima and Nagasaki, after the bombings. They gathered here silently for a moment.

'And here,' Takahashi said, 'please.'

At the other end of the room was an armoured glass window with some pieces of silvery metal behind it.

'Not exactly the Crown Jewels,' Alex murmured, remembering.

Then Takahashi clicked off the main lights. Their gazes all turned to the glass wall, from beyond which came a faint glow. As their eyes adjusted to the dark, that glow became an electric, unearthly blue.

David said hoarsely, 'Is that actually, ah, plut –'

'Polonium,' Takahashi said harshly. 'Element 84 on the periodic table. It is five thousand times as radioactive as radium; the blue glow means that alpha radiation has ionized the air around it.'

Alex was standing close. 'It is safe, I take it?'

'Quite safe, behind that barrier,' the emotionless voice said. 'Incidentally, polonium is used in nuclear weapons as the initiator of the chain reaction.' Takahashi clicked the lights on again. 'Let's go.'

They felt glad to emerge into the open air again, even though the sea breeze was very cold.

'Did you read Maggie's last article on nuclear power?' David asked. He waved a thumb at the concrete mountain of the dome. 'There's a sleeping demon down there, locked up inside that radioactive core.'

Alex raised an eyebrow. '"The Demon Sleeps" – that's something from a lurid paperback cover.'

'This,' David said, 'is no joke. And what if that demon wakes up?'

'It will wake very soon,' Takahashi said coolly. 'The reactor fuelling will begin within a month, on an experimental basis. Then the chain reaction will commence.'

'It will indeed,' Alex murmured.

They were to have a French-cuisine lunch in the restaurant building, and had reached the stage of coffee and cognac when they sensed a little quiver of excitement run through the executives seated in crowds at the tables. Men patted their lips with napkins, straightened their ties. Then the double doors that led out to the snow-covered balcony were opened, and, preceded by two bodyguards and an interpreter, Saigo Hideki marched in.

Everybody stood up.

It would have been rude and conspicuous not to, so David and Alex had to rise, too, with their guests.

Hideki bowed briefly, left, right, centre, then waved his arms. Everybody sat down immediately, except for the visitors.

Alex said quietly, 'What upstanding people we are.'

David was smiling through gritted teeth as he pulled his chair towards his legs and sat down. 'He's made us feel awkward and very isolated.'

'I dare say that was the idea, David,' Alex said coolly.

The great man and some of the entourage joined their table. There was coffee or green tea for everybody.

Hideki sipped tea thoughtfully. 'You have strike in your Windscale reprocessing place?'

David answered. 'I'm afraid that's right, Mr Hideki.'

'Led by your friend Maggie Langton's father.'

'He's regional secretary of the engineering union. He has to interest himself in all such disputes. It's part of his job.'

'I see.' Hideki turned to Alex. 'Very bad problem at Windscale. I hear BBC has predicted disaster.'

David hid his doubts. 'There's really nothing for anybody to worry about. There's no immediate risk of catastrophe. Even the BBC can be alarmist on occasion. Besides, a cabinet decision has been made. Supplies will be taken through the picket line by force if necessary.'

'Good,' Takahashi said, smiling. 'Because that's a huge contract we're thinking of giving you, or giving your BNFL. Be a pity if we had to go elsewhere. To the French, say.'

David, though annoyed that they were discussing this in public, had mastered his brief. 'I think you'll find their Cap la Hague reprocessing facility is booked up for years ahead.'

But Takahashi had been briefed also. 'Perhaps not – if we offered a much better price.'

Then Hideki stood up and began to speak, smiling at his two guests. All heads had turned. A squat man in heavy-framed glasses translated smoothly.

'We want to bid you welcome here, where Arigata will be your triumph, not ours. We are conscious of the honour, to do business with the English government and that firm supreme in English history, Stanton Industries. We hope to work together with your firm and others, in Europe, America, and all the world, a partnership in the great co-prosperity that will expand and expand until all the world is engulfed. It is destiny we serve here!'

There was immediate applause. Alex glanced around, only his eyes moving. The executives' faces were shining; there were actual tears in some eyes. He wondered what the speech had sounded like in Japanese. Even more martial, he guessed.

He looked at David, and there was an indefinable change in his friend's gaze.

David stood up and raised his teacup, wondering if they would realize he was mocking them a little. 'I thank that great man Saigo Hideki, lord of Japanese industry. What a vision he has presented us with! A great partnership, to spread investment and industry throughout the world. A wonderful vision, and a wonderful partnership – and as long as we are equal partners, my friend Mr Stanton and I will celebrate too.'

Hideki bowed low, then straightened up. Gold teeth gleamed, and he answered personally, in hissing English only a few of the people in the immediate area would understand.

'Equal partners. I buy you, your firm. Tanks, everything. Equal partners.'

They could not help wondering if he indeed meant 'buy', or only 'buy from'.

On the way back, David was able to persuade their entourage to let them drive up to a nearby snow capped hill and park. In the car, they had both been reading a *New York Times* article about the Japanese space programme.

'A nip in the air,' Alex said, quietly ironic. He folded the newspaper away.

'Very soon, sir,' their driver replied through the opened partition, not quite understanding – or understanding only too well.

David grinned, ruefully.

On the summit of the hill he got out by himself to stand looking at the plant and consider the huge investment it represented. A thousand million dollars, and more. In its nuclear hearth, new, deadly elements would be smelted – elements like plutonium, and uranium 235.

Alex followed him, limping slightly, waving to the chauffeur to stay at the wheel.

The frigid wind was western, blowing from Siberia and Manchuria over the cold Sea of Japan. David was preoccupied, hands clasped behind his back, and his face ached with the cold. 'Funny, but even now I think of Japan as tropical; hot, sweaty, jungles. It isn't, quite.'

'It's in the same latitude as Greece and Turkey and parts south. Or Iran. And believe me, the middle of Iran in the middle of winter is literally Siberian.'

'Iran literally Siberian?' David asked, cocking an eyebrow. 'You really think it might come to that? One day the Shah might fall?'

'I hope not!'

There was a stir among the Japanese officials behind them. It was obvious they did not like the opposition's government and industry getting together like this, not out of earshot. David turned around and, scowling like an over-acted Othello, waved them back. 'Our Japanese friends really want everything, don't they?'

'Do they? But at least they're polite about it – unlike your Left-wing friends, David.'

He sighed, chilled to the bone. 'I suppose it's true they steal with a smile, as Ogden Nash put it. "So *sorry*, this my garden now."' David drew breath and smiled dazzlingly at their escort.

Alex was whistling tunelessly between his teeth. 'Maybe we're misjudging them, David. I mean, Hideki is a very impressive and competitive man. But when he said "I buy you, your firm" I'm sure he only meant to say that he'd buy *from* us, and from the firm. Kiko has to be exaggerating about his rabid nationalism and ugly career in Manchuria and ambitions for armed conquest. Hell, this is the twentieth century.'

Then David turned around and said in a harsh voice, 'Do you *really* think this reactor is our toehold in Japan?'

Alex put his hands into his pockets and began to walk down the surprisingly steep and poorly-made road, the two limousines following them at a discreet distance. 'I don't know, David. We are doing massive work for the project, it's true at a low price if we slip behind schedule. But our Australian subsidiary alone stands to make a considerable profit on the uranium fuel arrangement.'

'Ore, fuel? It's a truism that Japan takes in raw materials and exports finished goods. And reprocessing the spent fuel in England will be a dangerous and polluting business, profitable or not.'

'You also heard Hideki hint that if we continue to help with their nuclear power programme, they'll buy arms from me.'

'It's not in his gift. He isn't the Japanese government, yet.' David walked on. It was below freezing, and snow was shining on the mountains. 'Perhaps we ought to consult other citizens of Japan. I wonder what Nanwara thinks of Mr Hideki, for example. The longer I stay here the more convinced I am that the Japanese, at least some of them, *want* us to stay ignorant.'

'Maybe you're right.' Alex felt they were very alone here, and almost invincibly ignorant. He had spent hours of his valuable time studying Japanese, but he could not match even David's smooth but very limited attempts to speak the language: he had mastered a few phrases and a little of the history and culture of Japan, and that was all. 'I keep asking myself about our hosts. I mean, they *must* be pleased with us. The Japanese government have invited us both back for the formal opening of their new international airport at Narita. So surely they must –'

David turned around, his voice sharp. 'Why are we fooling ourselves like this? The situation doesn't feel right to me. Nor to you.'

Alex ground a fist into one palm. 'Then what are they doing? What do they really want?'

There was no answer from David Bryant. Not even speculation.

Alex said finally, 'I'll have to try other sources of information.'

Chapter Seventeen

They walked together down the busy road called Sanjo-Dori, Alex Stanton and Akiko Hideki, towards the famous temple pagodas of Nara.

Kiko had brought Alex to Nara, the eighth-century capital. In the wooden temples here Chinese monks had first taught Buddhism to Japan. This was where the old Japan met the new. There was no litter here, but the cramped road was full of noisy traffic whose fumes choked, the pavements were crammed with pedestrians, and the modern buildings seemed shoddy and ill-designed.

Alex found all this unpleasant, and also there were the annoying stares at the tall blond *gaijin*. 'How can you find anything revealing in this, Kiko Hideki?' he said accusingly. 'This is just tourism, and uncomfortable tourism!'

'In a little while,' she said, haltingly. She seemed worried and uncertain. 'I beg you to wait, have patience. In Nippon you must look *into* things, not at them.'

Alex limped badly today, after hours of touring, but had brought no stick to walk with. Endless exercise on the road and in the gym meant he could run almost as quickly as before the Tower of London bombing, and he was more muscular than he used to be: the grim pain he had to live with.

He followed her towards a temple. Buddhist nuns with shaven heads went by in procession, straw hats on their shoulders. Alex followed them all inside.

In the echoing stone hall the chanting had gone on for a long time. Alex watched the monks in the yellow of the Buddha. In a sense, he reflected, the chanting had been going on for centuries.

Kiko, listening carefully with her slender arms folded, translated.

'—the human body is temporary, frail, and mortal; the human body is a bubble that soon bursts; it has no permanence, it is like fire; it has no consciousness, it is like the stones—'

To a people who believed that, Alex reflected, death would hold little significance and no terrors.

Even the pilgrims to the temple sometimes stared at them. The tourists, often bespectacled, always with expensive, complicated cameras, were quite blatant.

Alex touched her shoulder, and leaned forward so as to keep his voice low. 'Will your grandfather find out we are seeing each other?'

She dropped her gaze. 'I hope not. But probably that can't be concealed for long.'

'He isn't bothered?'

'I imagine that he would be, as you are a foreigner, and *you*. But I do not know his mind. We have not spoken much, these last few months.'

Alex turned to concentrate on the chanting, low, strangely powerful, ominous. 'I must know more about your country, Kiko. And what your country wants.'

She smiled demurely. 'I will make you very welcome here. I will try to educate you.'

Head bowed, he remembered their journey: by road, in another white car. The area around Nara was mostly polluted and brutalized by heavy industry: you saw concrete slab architecture and smoking factory chimneys for miles. But he could not find it in him to criticize Japan for that. In its Victorian heyday, he suspected, Tyneside had been very much like this – and hadn't the city fathers of Newcastle once torn down much of the teeming remnant of the medieval city, to make way for the railways and the station and progress?

She led him out of the temple, back into the crowds.

He looked around fretfully. 'Why are there so many people here?'

'Nara is our heritage,' she explained carefully. 'We have seen defeat and so many, many changes. We come here to seek for ourselves and our meaning. We listen to the ancient words and think of our future, and how we may achieve harmony between past, present, and the years to come.'

Alex nodded. '*Wa*. Harmony. That must be a key concept here.'

'That is so. If we *all* do what duty says, everything will be harmonious. That is one reason why we do not like the world outside Japan.'

Alex thought of the rich variety of the world and its peoples, which he so much appreciated, and threw her an appraising glance. 'You make me feel very Western, Kiko. Do I make you feel very Japanese?'

'Very much a Japanese woman, actually.'

In the huge public park they were approached again and again by grinning and insistent sellers of hot food, paper hats, and badges made of antlers. Alex had trouble brushing them off, and even the tame deer roaming everywhere annoyed him with their greed and persistence. Kiko and he bought roasted sweet potatoes from a wheeled wooden stall. As they ate them, piping hot, more people came up, demanding in broken American English to do business, buy, sell, buy, sell.

Alex was glad to reach the fragrant peace of the botanical gardens. Here, she smiled at him, large-eyed. He had forgotten how very lovely Kiko Hideki was. 'I have much else to show you, and you must stay. There are the three thousand lanterns of the Kasuga shrine, and also—'

He laughed. 'I'll stay.'

Finally, after more tourism, she took him into the great hall of the Todaiji: 200 yen each, for startlement.

The immense wooden structure which they entered was made from hewn trunks of gigantic trees. The great bronze Buddha inside, looming above the heads of the crowd, was over fifty feet tall. It had been commissioned, she told him, by Emperor Shomu in the Christian year 743. Alex was overwhelmed: sheer brassy bulk. They circled the bronze mass with difficulty, holding hands. Once in the same spot again, Alex finally pulled out his own camera – a tiny model, well-adapted for industrial espionage. He took a couple of snaps, then posed Kiko.

'Stand there, on the left. What's that statue?'

'Komukuten. He is trampling a demon.'

He took her picture. 'And on the right?'

'Tamonten, doing the same. And, do you see, there is a hole cut in the base of the pillar.'

He saw people, often children, squirming through. 'Why are they doing that?'

They went closer. The hole was quite small.

'It is said if you can struggle through you will have a place guaranteed in heaven.'

Alex was tempted for a moment, though he was quite a tall man, with broad shoulders.

'The last notable person from the West to do so was your Prince of the Wales, in 1922.'

Alex turned away from the pillar. 'I'll give ground to royalty.'

'If you had been here only a few weeks ago, in mid-December, you would have seen the great festival of *On Matsuri*. There were some men from my grandfather's household here, dressed as samurai.'

'A taste for military matters, eh? No doubt he visits the Yasukuni Shrine.'

'He would say, only as private citizen. Only to remember friends, and his son my father, dead in the war.'

Alex nodded, filing away into his capacious memory still more facts about Saigo Hideki.

Next, they drove to a tiny traditional inn, a *ryokan*, far away in the hills near Kyoto, another former capital.

It was a cold, crisp day, but after he followed Kiko's instructions and parked the car he found the pine smell of the trees invigorating. They walked together along a forest track. More snow began to fall, feather-light, melting as it touched their faces or the earth. He took her hand. He felt comfortable with her, very comfortable, but he wondered what the night would bring – and he still had so many questions to ask her.

He glanced at her sidelong for a moment. Kiko was heart-stoppingly beautiful, so beautiful he found himself resenting the power she was already beginning to exercise over him. They had been together one day; it seemed longer, and their attraction was mutual and very powerful. He felt renewed.

The *ryokan* itself was lovely, even from a hundred yards away: a sloping roof of red tile, supported by ancient carved beams. The windows were all shuttered, the plastered walls pure white, and the varnish on the wood gleamed bright.

She turned to him. 'This place is almost private; guests are always friends of friends. I do not think any Westerner has ever slept here before.'

'Never?' He bowed. 'I am honoured.'

'I had to tell them . . .' She hesitated. 'I had to tell them that in a manner of speaking, we are man and wife. I hope you are not offended and will maintain my honour for me: otherwise I will lose face, greatly.'

He caught her shoulders and looked into her opaque eyes. 'We will spend the night together?'

She kneeled before him on the rutted track, melting snow glistening in her dark hair, on her golden skin. 'What else?'

He felt both embarrassed and deeply touched. 'You don't have to kneel to me. Here.'

He reached out a hand, hauled her up. She was so light she hardly existed. He continued to hold her hand.

'I must show respect, Alex Stanton. Because I hope you will one day show that respect to me.'

He spoke with sincerity. 'You're a wonder, Kiko Hideki. And I really don't know if I'm worthy of that.'

She laughed, and slipped her hand from his. 'I have faith.'

Below the covered, wood-pillared porch a maid in a kimono met them, bowing. After taking off their shoes and putting them below the step they replaced them with house slippers, and were escorted inside. Alex saw there were many rooms of different sizes under the steeply pitched roof. Warmed air rose from the suspended floor, adding to the heat produced by the traditional braziers.

Here was the proprietor, a middle-aged woman with a wise, worldly face, to welcome them. They all exchanged bows, and Alex tried to master the pronunciation of her name.

Alex listened carefully to the two women speak, as he was conducted to his room – or to one of their rooms, rather. Here were more tatami mats, in the austerely furnished space; bare beams, walls of coloured paper. Flowers, arranged in a blue porcelain vase, were a fountain of colour on a low table in one corner.

'What do you think?'

A floor-to-ceiling alcove contained a hand-painted scroll: ink and brushed colours on silk, a few precise strokes creating a mountain landscape.

'Absolutely exquisite.'

Following her example, he changed into loose Japanese robes, and was given the wooden flip-flops known as *geta* for excursions into the grounds. Then a paper wall was slid aside with much ceremony, to reveal an inner, private garden.

Alex caught his breath. After the maid had glided away, Kiko explained to him how to admire the flowers and rocks and tiny, flowing stream that bisected the ornamental garden outside. He stared meditatively, arms folded. Kiko softly chanted a Zen Buddhist mantra; and for a time, here on the hills where the air was clear and fragrant, you could think yourself far away from the twentieth century.

The maid returned with green tea. Alex tried his crude Japanese: '*Domo*.'

He needed Kiko to translate after that, but he could tell his politeness had pleased.

When the tea was drunk the maid conducted them to the baths: a series of stone rooms built on to the *ryokan*. Again, they heard noises, but their own room was private. There were hot and cold faucets here, and several wooden stools with holes in the middle. Here another maid, this one an older, muscular woman, took over.

Alex was obliged to be undressed first: as a man, he naturally took priority here. The steamy room was blood warm, and he felt no shame in revealing his muscular body to these women. He sensed its trim fitness pleased them, and if there were some scars, what of that? He was a man, and he had taken part in a man's battles.

The bathhouse maid first scrubbed him briskly, then shampooed his hair. Kiko waited patiently as he was rinsed off completely, then towelled dry. The woman led him to a massage table and began pummelling at the muscles of his limbs, then at his shoulders, then buttocks, and finally at the base of his spine.

She said something Kiko translated as, 'Much muscle, and many scars.'

He laughed. 'Much good luck, too. I'm still alive.'

It felt very, very good. He almost dozed for the few minutes it took for Kiko to receive the same treatment. The sound of splashing water and the steamy, confined heat of the room made him drowsy. He felt very comfortable like this. He wondered vaguely if it might be possible to live here, in Japan. He had a half-dream that he became Japanese: he married Saigo Hideki's granddaughter, became the old man's heir, and changed Japan entirely for the better, and for all time.

He stirred, restlessly, sweating in the Turkish-bath atmosphere. He was half-American, and was often there; he had American relatives, and many American friends. Yet he wondered, given everything he had inherited, if he could ever have been entirely happy in the United States. He moved his head on to folded arms, his eyes still closed. He remembered Ray's invitation from years before: come to America, be anybody you are capable of being, defy history, and be free.

He sighed. Maybe that was the point. He did not believe people could be free, entirely, except by denial – and he still had much too much loyalty to deny his own heritage, and far too much appetite and curiosity to turn his back on the world. Over in the new continent they had made themselves free of history by denying it. They had

had their revolution and renounced the authority of kings, renounced the past. Their pioneers had come to a lightly-inhabited, green world, and in the name of freedom they had abolished the continent's first native inhabitants, as well as their own past histories. America was a new-found-land, and all about escape, self-realization, and the future.

In comparison, England and Japan had similarities. Both were lands dominated by the past, by the loss of empire and the hope of empire, and – in Japan, now, much more than in England – both peoples were controlled and inspired by subtle conceptions of duty.

'Alex.'

He opened his eyes, raised his head, and looked dubiously at the steaming water in the huge, sunken tub. You had to be wholly free of soap before you could step in. Kiko, entirely naked now, slid down into the hot, deep water, sighing with pleasure.

The maid made an inviting gesture. Alex stepped in more gingerly than Kiko. 'My God, this is hot!'

'Of course.'

His legs were turning red with the heat, but he gritted his teeth and slowly eased down until the water reached his chest. He panted, hoping that would cool him down. Then, after he stopped moving, the temperature of his skin suddenly felt tolerable again. He smiled. They soaked together, at peace. Kiko's eyes flashed pleasure at him, and he knew now there would be much in the night to enjoy.

'We will have fun, Alex Stanton?'

'Tai-fun.' He touched a bare breast, his hand rippling out of the water. 'We will.'

But he still remembered that he had come to her for answers. Pleasure was a bonus.

When they returned to their room the thick sleeping futon had been unrolled. They took off their slippers ceremoniously. Alex saw they had both been given the usual leathery excuse for a pillow, but he shoved his aside.

Kiko made conversation as they ate a light meal in the privacy of their two adjoining rooms. They kneeled around the low Japanese table, and she served him, using lacquered chopsticks. There was raw fish, seaweed, tempura, rice both plain and spiced, and more of the green tea, agari.

'Where is your friend now, the government minister?'

'Flown home a couple of days ago,' Alex said, sipping warmed saké and hiding a grimace. 'He has affairs of state to attend to. And besides, his party does not have a working majority in our equivalent of your Diet; his vote is needed.'

'So much that he must leave Nippon so quickly? A strange way to run a government!'

Alex shrugged.

'But he is a good man.'

'Yes,' Alex acknowledged. 'One of the finest I know.'

She spoke hesitantly now, long eyelashes fluttering. 'I believe my grandfather will be sending men to England. They will tell your friend that unless he uses his influence to get your government to do what we want, you and your Stanton Industries will suffer.'

Alex was shocked. 'What a terrible thing, to use David's loyalty to me to make him act against his conscience.'

She said, 'They will do that terrible thing. And much more, far worse.'

Alex's brow had furrowed with concentration, but after a minute he gave a wan smile. He could not have his relations with the Hideki Corporation upset; not even if the sole heir to the business was responsible. 'They will be very foolish if they underestimate my friend.'

There was a long pause between them. Alex was becoming more and more aware of the small body in the silk Japanese clothes. So different to Maggie, or to Caro, his full-fleshed wife.

There was a silence.

'You wish to know more about my grandfather, and Hakagawa?'

'Yes,' he said. 'Will you tell me?'

'Only later, and only if you promise me one thing.'

He did not like making forced promises, so he did not. 'Go on.'

'Promise to believe me.'

He grinned crookedly. She was very trusting, wasn't she? 'I promise to believe you, Kiko,' he said.

I'll believe you, maybe, but will I act on what you tell me? That, Kiko, I cannot say. And any promise I was forced to give you about that would be a lie.

Another maid came and cleared away the dishes. Silence settled upon the *ryokan*.

After Kiko had undressed she stood before him naked, but not as a Western woman would stand; neither brazen nor ashamed, but as simply beautiful as bars of pure gold.

'Tell me, Alex Stanton,' she said, lisping slightly over the 'x'. 'This woman you have married.'

'The former Caroline Ross; Lord Ross's daughter.'

'The rich banker.' She said it without expression. 'Somebody important's daughter . . . Is she one with you?'

Alex was carefully folding his clothes away. 'What do you mean?'

'Is Caroline your other soul? Does she share your interests, support your ventures – love you?'

Alex shook his head. Her body gleamed in front of him in the light of the bedside lamp. 'I couldn't say she does, Kiko Hideki.'

They made love for half an hour. But Kiko's question about Caroline resonated in his memory until, after a long time, he slept.

Early the next morning Alex raised his head, instantly awake as usual. Morning light wafted into the room through a paper blind, lighting up the masterful landscape in the alcove. Alex lost himself in the minimalist coloured strokes; he was impressed.

There was a book on the low table beside their futon. It was *Madame Bovary* in French, and Alex sat up and turned the pages curiously. Was this some insight into Kiko's soul?

When she stirred he smiled down at her and replaced the book. 'Kiko.'

'Alex of the Stantons.'

'That's me.'

'Will you stay?' she asked him, her eyes large with pleading.

'Of course.' He touched her cheek. Soon he would ache to get back to work: Stanton Industries had become his life, and he doubted she could change that. 'Not forever, but I will stay.'

She sighed, and held his hand against her soft face. 'Be here till *sakura* time. The cherry blossoms are the soul of Japan. It will happen soon. They do not last for more than two weeks, but you must see that flood of colour.'

It was the first commitment he had made to her. 'I will stay that long.'

They went driving in the rugged mountain country once again, though he kept away from the high passes, some of which could still be snowbound. He drove on the left, as he did in England. There was little private traffic, as if the people here were deliberately kept immobile, and he was still surprised at the poor construction of the minor roads and bridges. Obviously the government here had chosen to invest chiefly in industry, and in direct support for industry.

His hands tightened on the wheel, and he changed gears brutally. He could not deny it. The Tokyo government had done what he would have done, had he the power – done what governments in Britain and America should have done, but had not.

'Are we going to talk about your grandfather's plans, Kiko, and what you want me to do?'

She touched his arm. 'If you had been here before Christmas, you would have seen a landscape still beautiful as fire. Autumn comes to the Land of the Gods in warm colours, russet, gold, brown: autumn lingers for a long time.'

'Very poetic,' he said drily, swearing for a moment as the car slewed through a water-filled dip in the road. 'But just at the moment I'm hungry, and I'd rather have a big Mac than poetry.'

She laughed.

The landscape was ruggedly beautiful, though. In the last two days almost all the snow had melted; it was the beginning of spring, fresh, clean, renewed, exactly as Alex himself now felt. There was something exhilarating about Kiko's company. He drove for a long time, heading east and north. They could go to Osaka, then perhaps take the historic Tokaido road towards Yokohama and Tokyo.

They could have a week. He wondered how much she knew about her grandfather, and how much was mere suspicion and prejudice.

Then he put the question directly: If Hideki really wants to arm for World War III, can I live with myself if I help him? He drove on. Do I really have any choice?

He feared he had no alternatives at all.

In one village she obviously recognized Kiko had him stop. He parked the car, looking around thoughtfully. There were paddyfields stretching out, with farmers in traditional dress working in them. Birds called in the green wood behind. They walked together down the street, and he tried to ignore the horrified stares at the *gaijin*, and the giggles and the embarrassment. These little houses with overhanging roofs could have been from the seventeenth century, if not for the ever-present television aerials.

She took him to the last house, and called out. An old man with a gnarled, kindly face emerged, and greeted her with a bow and a long burst of Japanese. All Alex could recognize in the sounds was her name.

They were soon indoors, kneeling around a low table and sipping saké. Alex managed to put together a few polite sentences and the old man stared at him and then said something in rapid-fire Japanese.

Alex concentrated. '*Yukkuri kudasai.*' Slowly, please.

The man smiled, then clapped his hands. Two tiny Japanese children came in and sat down. The old man waved a hand over them, mouthed, then waved at Kiko and Alex. '*Wakarimasu ka?*'

'Do I understand? I think so.' Alex smiled at Kiko. 'A storyteller, right? For children especially. *Wakarimasu.*'

He bowed low to Kiko, and began to tell his story.

It was an adventure handed down for centuries, since the days of the Shoguns. There was a princess, held captive by an evil stepfather. The storyteller pulled faces, gesticulated, mimicked the characters' voices and expressions. Alex listened entranced, though he needed Kiko to translate the slurred, old-style language. Kiko spoke quickly, lightly. The princess was alone, and in trouble . . . Who would dare to rescue her? Could it be done at all?

She stopped speaking suddenly, and choked. Alex turned around.

Kiko was crying.

The old man gaped. The boy and girl chewed their knuckles, their eyes big with surprise.

'It is all dying.' Kiko got up to go, shockingly quickly; but the peasants forgave her her bad manners, because she was so upset.

Outside, when she turned to Alex, there were still tears in her eyes. 'All the old ways are dying.'

He thought of England, and spoke to her with compassion. 'I know.'

Then they went together to Osaka. Alex remembered his Stanton Mark VIII tank, gun thundering as it outraced and outfought the Russian T-types General Dayan had helped him obtain. This city was still the same; commercial, full of neon light, bustle, money – and traffic-choked.

They checked into a hotel. Their room was on the fifth floor, overlooking the city lights. Alex climbed into bed, as she sat brushing her hair in front of the mirror. The strokes were long, calm, the brush ivory-backed and expensive. Alex considered her naked shoulders. Some of the women in Japan wore their hair in artificial, beehive-style mounds; it looked painfully old-fashioned and artificial to him, like a poor imitation of the 1950s.

Kiko was real.

'Come to bed,' he told her, low in his throat. 'I want you right now.'

He kissed her hard, several times. Even in the low light of the room her eyes were shining. Was this love? He spread her thighs, running his fingertips down the smooth golden abdomen to the opening pink crevice of her sex.

Their bodies talked.

After she had showered and thrown scented talcum powder over her shoulders, Alex knew it was finally time to speak, though he wondered if bed was the right place to ask these questions.

'That was so good, Alex.'

He caressed her bare, rounded shoulder. 'How do you see me? Another of the *Kichiku Bei-Ei* – American and British devils, come to pillage and rape?'

Lying on her back in the double bed, she threw him her devastating smile. 'There has been no rape tonight.'

He regarded her solemnly. He saw beauty in the delicate bones of her face, and the strength of will in her. In possessing her he had sometimes felt he was possessing the soul of all Japan. Oriental, strange, and great. She did not avert her gaze. Instead, her eyes widened so that he seemed to see a hint of purple in the black, and finally he had to look away.

'Will you help me stop my grandfather and Hakagawa trying to change this country back?'

He answered her question with another question. 'What do you need?'

'Now? Fifty thousand US dollars.'

He whistled tunelessly a moment. 'Let me think about it.'

'But you are rich. You could afford it easily, to stop my grandfather, and surely you have the courage!'

I could give you money, Alex thought. If money alone and your efforts could do it. But you know that probably won't be enough. So, pacifist or not, there is another suggestion you can make to me . . . That I could stop your enemies – with a bullet.

He said nothing out loud but he stared at her. Also, he thought, if I do give you help and your grandfather finds out, I will have made an enemy – and he must be one of the most powerful and ruthless men on the planet, master of an industrial empire that has a larger budget than most Third World countries.

'You ask me for money.'

'I do,' she said harshly.

'Better tell me how you would spend it.'

Her head fell back on to the pillow. There was silence for a long time. Then, when she spoke, there was rueful humour in her voice.

'Am I just helping you get a better bargain from my grandfather? What more can I do to convince you that he must not win?'

'Tell me what you would do.'

'I would give your money to the other parties, to the ecological movement here, to the better factions in the government. I would prepare the ground for when grandfather and Hakagawa move. You won't read the Japanese papers, but you are beginning to get the blame for Arigata. I could help generate a genuine debate. Then the public would know.

'Also, I would spend your money investigating them, and give reports to your office in Tokyo. You would have extensive dossiers on my grandfather and his chosen man Hakagawa. That would give you power, Alex. Power for good! When grandfather's firm ran part of Manchuria in the war, that man Hakagawa worked for him, or with him. He has a very bad reputation. You could make use of that to weaken his position. I could make use of it to stop Hakagawa ever becoming Prime Minister.'

Alex relaxed, as he brought his mind into focus. 'What are his secrets?'

She stared at the ceiling, her face inscrutable. 'What can be proved about our Hakagawa – now that he is Interior Minister, and such a powerful man?'

Alex rolled half over and put his arm across her bare stomach. 'Tell me, can we use even what we *know* is true? Would your nation listen even if we had the proof?'

Her face was averted again. 'Our society is not totally obedient. When Prime Minister Kishi Nobusuke pushed the Security Treaty through our parliament, the Diet, the country was in uproar – and that was as long ago as 1960. Of course, Nobusuke was an abrasive, unpopular man, dogged by rumours about his career in Manchuria during the war . . . Diet members held a sit-down strike. There were demonstrations, with violence. Four thousand students tried to storm the Diet building. Hundreds were injured, one killed. Over five million people took to the streets to oppose the government.

'If things came to that point, now, to stop Arigata or something similar, it would be much, much worse for our rulers. Even something as comparatively harmless as the new airport at Narita has been held up for years by people's actions.'

He needed the money from a completed Arigata, but it would not bother him if it never functioned as a breeder of fissionable material. What Arigata implied had begun to scare even him. 'You think Arigata could be stopped, just by civil disobedience?'

'I do. Only a couple of years ago our rulers tried to make use of nuclear energy to power the ship *Mutsu*. But two hundred and fifty small fishing boats blockaded it in port, for months. It took an August typhoon to scatter the boats, and a Maritime-SDF escort to protect the ship when it sailed at midnight, under auxiliary power.'

'And what happened?'

'As soon as the reactor was brought to criticality, during sea trials at the end of the month, a leak developed. Neither borated rice nor old socks served to make impromptu repairs, and—'

'Rice and old socks! Rice and old socks. You must be joking!'

'No,' she said, hurt. 'Emergency repairs to the reactor; to stop leaks or some such. It's in the public record. Believe me. And so the ship drifted for forty-five days. The crew feared for their lives, if they dared to make port.'

'So,' he said, thoughtful now, 'people here do have the power to stop things.'

'Yes,' she responded fiercely. 'But don't use that fact to salve your own conscience!'

'No,' he said. 'Of course not. But you think that your grandfather and Hakagawa are vulnerable to such pressures?'

'Enough pressure, and anyone is vulnerable. As for Hakagawa, well, he takes money. I can now prove it. From grandfather and other right-wingers.'

'How do you know that?'

She closed her eyes. 'From Takahashi. He wants to be my grandfather's heir; but at present I am the heir. So he cultivates me, sometimes.'

He felt a flash of absurd rage; then jealousy reddened the anger. 'You cultivate him, don't you? To get information?'

'Yes.' She turned away. 'And, yes, I have slept with him. On several occasions. That is how much all this means to me.'

It hit him like a fist. Perhaps that was the only reason she was sleeping with him, Alex, here and now. Simply to get and give information. He ground his teeth together. I don't want to believe that, he thought. I want to mean something to Kiko. And I want to build bridges, just as she does.

'Hakagawa's family is from one of the northern islands the Russians took. He hates Russians racially, as well as for being Communists. But then, he hates everybody who is not Japanese. I have a tape-recorded secret speech where he justifies the Pacific War, justifies Pearl Harbor and – worse things than that.'

'Do you now!' Then he suddenly felt it polite, and more Japanese, to keep the triumph out of his voice. 'There are still a whole lot of "ifs". If we could prove all that, if the papers would print it—'

'Our newspapers exposed the Tanaka scandal, didn't they? He will go to jail; an ex-Prime Minister. Everybody here knows of the black mist of corruption around our politics. When the time is right, there will be a lot of mud to be thrown at my grandfather and Hakagawa. I have seen to that.'

'That's very brave of you.'

She answered with a shudder, remembering Tori hacked to pieces in front of her. Blood and pain, and no dignity at the end. 'It is!'

'And what has your grandfather done, exactly?'

A silence. Then, a small voice. 'He has spoken of rearming.'

'I'd gathered that.'

'With, according to Takahashi, nuclear weapons.'

'Jesus!' Alex jerked up in the bed. 'But you can't be sure that's their policy – can you?'

She shrugged. 'I am sure. Nuclear weapons. Which your firm will help to provide.'

'My firm!' Alex's heart began to beat faster. 'Would people here stand for that?'

She turned her face away once more. 'I told you, we are not as well-drilled as you might think. We would not follow Hakagawa as prime minister, not all of us. There are already terrible rumours about that man's war.'

'Excellent,' Alex said. Then he saw her face, and his smile died.

'They say he made his prisoners turn cannibal.'

'Christ!' Alex thought it over, remembering Hakagawa's brutal face. Then he remembered what Imperial Japan had meant, all the way through till '45. Nanking in China, where women and children were bayoneted and hacked to death. Across all the lands the Imperial Army conquered, women forced into prostitution, and narcotics supplied. Allied prisoners tortured to death, according to the Way of the Warrior.

'But is he *really* in a conspiracy with your grandfather to change the government and rearm with nuclear weapons?'

She writhed about in the bed. 'Yes, yes, yes . . . and they must be stopped, Alex.'

'Your grandfather? How, exactly?'

'The people must know!'

'Supposing publicity and argument isn't enough?'

Her voice was flat, dead. 'He must be stopped.'

'And must I—?'

'I beg you to help me, Alex Stanton.'

He touched her, but said nothing.

'We must have peace.'

He looked down at her compassionately. Kiko Hideki's poor tortured heroic soul did not know much peace.

Later that night, as Kiko slept, Alex studied the translation in front of him. Article IX of the Japanese Constitution of 3 May, 1947:

Aspiring sincerely to an international peace based on justice and order, the Japanese people forever renounce war as a sovereign right of the nation and the threat or use of force as a means of settling international disputes.

In order to accomplish the aim of the preceding paragraph, land, sea and air forces, as well as other war potentials, will never be maintained. The right of belligerency of the state will not be recognized.

The words touched him in a curious fashion, though he knew that if these sentiments were ever adopted worldwide, Stanton Industries would be out of its first business – and that he still needed the money arms-making brought in.

He thought of what Kiko had told him. Was it really true? And even if it was, what could he do about it?

He did not sleep well.

They were in a topless hostess bar in Tokyo. A naked girl writhed in a gold cage, to the boom of US soul.

'Tell me more,' Takahashi said. 'I'm fascinated.'

'Trust me. I know how these things are done.' Alan Hoyle smiled widely, drunk. 'Have the courage to go all the way. Attract as many journalists as you can.'

'Do it all in public?' The pink light played strangely on their faces. The girl danced ecstatically. 'Have journalists there with their telephones and cameras?'

Hoyle leaned forward on his stool, voice low and intense. 'Keep them there.'

'Ah! As hostages?'

'Exactly!' Hoyle sipped more imported Scotch, hearing the ice chink inside the glass. 'Hundreds of innocent witnesses. Now, who would dare to bomb *them*?' Hoyle chuckled, wiped his lips with the back of one hand. 'The government would have to kill many, many civilians to recapture the site. Not politically possible, right? Even if the Russians became involved, they wouldn't dare do anything, either. I mean, think of it, people screaming over the telephone to New York and Los Angeles and Paris and Vienna and Delhi, screaming out "here come the Russian bombs". They'd not dare. I know them, believe me.'

'You're brilliant,' Takahashi said, meaning it. He smelled the Scotch on Hoyle's breath and decided he would switch to a Highland brand, and never drink Suntory whisky again.

Hoyle closed his eyes. 'Then you will have power – the only power that counts. Listen, some of the people with the oil wealth want an Islamic bomb. Smash America, smash the West—'

'You mean Iraq? Libya? Or do you keep the details to yourself?'

Hoyle waved a hand. 'The point is that the Hideki Corporation could make billions, if your nerve holds.'

'It will hold. Who can stop us now?'

'So your local politicians are out of the game,' Hoyle said. 'But what about the Stantons?'

'We have them in our hands,' Takahashi said simply. He stared at the girl in the cage. Her oiled body was writhing, and as she rubbed her hands over her breasts he wondered if her nipples were erect. Excitement stirred in him, but he finished making his point to Hoyle. 'Stanton Industries will be nothing more than an agency of the Hideki Corporation. They've lost their battle – as Alex Stanton is going to find out.'

Alex made some phonecalls from Osaka, then flew straight to Tokyo and took a cab to the Hideki headquarters.

He relaxed in the car, wondering what the great man wanted now. Fujiko had said the permission had abruptly come through for the new, permanent office, and then a very senior Hideki executive had telephoned to set up a meeting. A favour, he remembered Hideki saying, for a favour.

He was met at the great bronze doors and escorted inside after bows, to the executive elevator.

The door slid aside automatically. They all rode up together, but Alex was left by himself at the door to Hideki's apartment.

Inside, the huge room was carpeted by rich green grass. Water tinkled down one wall, which was made of grey boulders. He went forward, surprised. This was the country in the city. Opposite the waterfall ancient wooden beams made a frame for a single scroll painting. He paused before it. Ink, gold, green-coloured pigments: a door into a green, garden of Eden world. He had already glimpsed a stupendous view over Tokyo, but the modern world suddenly seemed far away.

'Like it?'

He turned around quickly, annoyed that Hideki had surprised him but not showing it. 'Very much.'

To Alex's surprise, the old man sat alone, on a rough-hewn wooden bench. He stood up slowly, his face grave, and extended a hand which Alex shook.

'Sit with me.'

'Mr Hideki,' Alex said pleasantly. 'By the way, thanks for your help in getting our new office set up.'

'A favour for—'

'I understand.'

The ancient eyes regarded him sternly. Hideki looked tanned, lean and hard. Like most Japanese businessmen of his generation, he dressed with extreme formality: an undertaker, in a black suit. Tea was served by a deft woman in a kimono.

Then, 'You have excellent contacts in Tehran.'

Alex was surprised. This was the favour? 'Major Coombes, our representative there, has been in the country since 1941. There is nothing he doesn't know about the political process in Tehran.'

'Very pleasing.' The eyes flashed. 'And he knows the Shah, and can get access?'

'Indeed he can.' Nothing more was said, so Alex added, 'We're always pleased to be of service. Was there anything more?'

Hideki sat back, folded his hands together in his lap. He regarded Alex for a long time. 'We understand the Shah of Iran is in trouble. We also understand that President Carter will forbid the Saudi Kingdom to buy modern arms.'

'Rumours,' Alex said, lightly.

'Diplomatic reports from Japan's embassies,' Hideki said. He smiled. 'Your country is poor. But Japan can still afford new tanks.'

'Can afford *my* tanks, you mean?'

Another grin. Hideki enjoyed negotiating from a position of strength. 'Of course is possible. A favour for a favour.'

'Anything else?'

'Your British Nuclear Fuels Limited.'

'BNFL is not mine. It's a government business.'

'Government!' Hideki's lips twisted. 'Even though your good friend Bryant is now part of the government of Britain, BNFL is still waiting for approval from the government for its new thermal oxide reprocessing plant.'

'It'll be specializing in highly radioactive fuel,' Alex said. 'Japanese fuel, if the contracts go ahead. Some three thousand tons of it.'

'We want those contracts to go ahead. Can't you pressure Bryant?'

'I can ask him for a favour, yes,' Alex said.

Hideki smiled at what he took to be a circumlocution. 'Excellent. Then do so. Because what we get back after our fuel is reprocessed,' Hideki said calmly, 'is refined uranium 235, and plutonium.'

'That's to your advantage.'

'Indeed.' A grim smile. 'To help with my plan. For a new, powerful, unashamed Japan, that can say "no" to anybody.'

'A rearmed Japan, with nuclear power to make you independent of the Middle East and OPEC? Well, you've already bought from my armaments division.'

'I want much more.'

Alex led him on, wanting him to be specific. He felt a sudden impulse to tap his fingers on the attaché case, but resisted it. 'I'll supply. Don't you worry about that. If the price is right I'll supply all the tanks and planes and artillery you want.'

'What if I wanted nuclear weapons for Japan?' The eyes blazed. 'You do not seem shocked.'

Alex fought to appear calm, and said, 'Would you expect me to be shocked – and, if I was, to show it?'

Hideki nodded. 'I am glad you don't make a pretence with me. Almost from the start, you must have suspected. Yes?'

Alex shrugged.

'Example. I know you have sometimes met my granddaughter. After the Tokyo trade negotiations, and I think later. I have no doubt Akiko told you about me, though she has denied it.' Gold teeth flashed in a smile. 'But I have confidence you respect reality. So, I tell you what is real. Whatever you think, say, or do, I will get what I want. *I will not be stopped.*'

'I understand perfectly,' Alex said. Surprising that Hideki would be so frank.

'I am sure you do. If you were in my place, it would be your ambition, too – to be *dai-ichi* one day. Isn't that so?'

Number one. Alex spread his hands.

There was a silence between the men, filled by the babbling water. 'Remember, you are in effect working for me now. Beauford, on your own board of directors, is mine. You yourself have already signed agreements to supply me with atomic fuel. You are committed.'

Alex decided to make Hideki feel safe. 'If I expose you, I ruin my own good name?'

'So you must be loyal!' Hideki wheezed, seemed to relax. 'But I wish also to say this. Forget my urgent ambition. For a Japan to be truly strong, as I wish, we will have to wait. Twenty years. Thirty years. You need not worry now, and you need not concern yourself now. I tell you this, on my honour.'

'I understand,' Alex said gently.

The old man rose. He was tiny, and aged, and dressed in a black and painfully formal suit: but his presence was truly imperial. 'Now, you may go home.'

In the Stanton office Alex took McCourt through the door with a stylized male outline on it. He bolted the door, looked round. 'I don't think anybody would bother bugging here, but I'll check carefully for listening devices anyway.'

McCourt watched him work. 'Satisfied?'

'Not with Hideki,' said Alex, putting the electronic detectors away.

'No tank sales?'

'I didn't even ask. Unless there's a major political change here, they won't be buying. I'll have to ask the Embassy for advice.'

McCourt nodded, then asked curiously, 'What did Hideki say, exactly?'

'It wasn't exact at all. First he admitted he is interested in nuclear arms. Then he said that was only a long-term ambition, and he probably won't be alive to see it realized.'

'What was the truth?'

He made no reply as he opened up his case, jacked in an earphone, and wound back the tape. 'It wasn't quite a confession from Hideki, but it might do . . .' Then, listening, he began to curse under his breath.

McCourt's eyes widened.

He looked up. 'The tape has been wiped. Hideki's office must be protected from eavesdropping devices. All that's left on the tape is useless distortion and hiss.'

McCourt said glumly, 'I'm so sorry he's won.'

Chapter Eighteen

Alex got in touch with Hugh from the Embassy, by coded cable. Lord Beauford had renewed his rumbling, public discontent in London. Hugh did not like it.

Then Alex flew back from Tokyo, stepping down from the plane into Kiko's arms.

Osaka was soot and clatter and big buildings. Industry, not romance. Obeying her instructions, he drove through the permanent traffic jam: there were things to see here, she told him. But already Alex itched to return home, and he knew many international flights left from Osaka. He wondered whether or not Saigo Hideki had told him the truth, and what he should do now.

She turned to him. 'You said?'

A crooked smile. 'I was being Japanese.' He had been thinking about her grandfather. '*Shigata ga nai*.'

It can't be helped.

On their way to the famous Kabuki Theatre they passed a public park, and he left the car here to go for a stroll through one of the very few green lungs of the city. Kiko gasped at the trees.

Alex turned to her. 'I don't know if there'll be time to see the castle now.'

Spring had come early; some of the cherry blossom was pink, and picknickers with hampers and bottles were coming into the park.

'One more day?' she pleaded.

In spite of his preoccupation he could afford to be that generous with his time.

'Of course. Or two, if you wish.'

Early the next morning they took an ANA flight south to Shikoku Island. It was a more rural place. He drove. Just after noon, they reached an ornate wooden gate. Here was the famed shrine to Kompira: the demon-god brought good luck to those setting out on long and dangerous voyages – a suitable target for his own prayers, Alex thought.

It was a long walk, and the path was steep. The sky was a flat, luminous and perfect pearl-grey. It made Alex uncomfortable – like an alien roof over his head. As they trudged up the mountain slope to where the shrine perched on the high summit, he wondered about Kiko. She was dressed in ski clothes and was merry and melancholy by turns. He reflected. As Hideki had pointed out, he was an old man. His heir was Kiko. Was it really possible for Alex himself to stay here in Japan, joining their great adventure and perhaps changing it? He looked at her sidelong. Kiko loved him. And perhaps with her beside him he could make a life here and, like the country, strive for greatness. As the cold winds swirled around he shivered and wondered what the twenty-first century would bring. Which Hideki would have more influence over the Japan that by then would be number one power in the world, Saigo or his granddaughter Akiko?

It was tiring, and some other pilgrims began to give up. Rain sifted down. There were ancient stone steps, here, but over time countless hundreds of thousands of feet had worn them hollow. Alex had to pick his way carefully, pain beginning to gnaw at his leg. He was glad he had brought his silver-headed walking cane, but he winced occasionally.

'I hope this will be worth it, Kiko.'

'It is,' she said, turning round to gesture at the horizon. 'Look!'

He turned, and saw the rainbow. It was a great pale arch of colour across heaven. A promise of something: but what, he did not know.

Kiko Hideki or Saigo Hideki? he asked himself, again.

He winced suddenly and leaned over to rub both hands over one calf.

'There is much pain?'

'It hurts sometimes,' he said tightly, his self-control shaky for a moment, 'but it's better than the alternative.'

Her face was full of compassion. 'What happened to you?'

'I was caught up in a terror bombing in London. People were killed – a bunch of Italian schoolkids and Hacker's wife Angie and an American TV guy called Bloom.'

'Bloom?' She had stopped walking and her face was stricken. 'Someone killed Irving Bloom, and almost you?'

'Yes, that's right. Weeks in hospital for Ray Hacker and me. For others, death.' Then every sense in his body came on the alert: he rasped in a breath. Kiko knew something. Instantly, he was back in the Tower. The explosion, so loud it was a massive blow, not a sound. Himself, flying on fire through the air. The horror and pain of the hospital . . . He took her by the shoulders. 'What do you know?'

Her eyes were huge. 'I think—' She struggled, beginning silent crying, but could not say it. 'I think—'

Alex read her mind. 'It was your grandfather, wasn't it?'

Her eyes were squeezed shut. 'I heard Takahashi talking once. I told you that he likes to keep in touch with me, in case I do inherit . . . It was about somebody writing a book, I think in England, who had found out too much about my grandfather's past . . . And Takahashi said to my grandfather over the telephone, "Hoyle solved the problem of that man Bloom, didn't he?"' She opened her eyes. 'I'm so sorry, Alex!'

He pushed her away. He was shivering, his teeth chattering. Was it true? Could it really be that simple? But his instinct told him it was.

He knew from David that Hoyle hired himself out as a terrorist, and had worked for Hideki at least once before.

So that's the answer. Bloom knew too many Japanese secrets, and Hideki had him killed. The children, Angie Hacker, me, we were all just accidents, random casualties . . . He felt a great anger welling up. Saigo Hideki giving an order to Takahashi; then a link to Hoyle's terrorist freelances.

'So you can't work for my grandfather now!'

But he had no alternative. He gave a grim smile, balling up his fists, the big muscles in his shoulders working. 'I think I have to, for a while. But there'll be some kind of reckoning, Kiko. There'll be a reckoning.' He looked at her. 'I'll give you that money. We'll do it so that it can't be traced back to me. Then I'll really have to go.'

Their last night together was full of love and philosophy. They lay sprawled on a futon, naked, their arms and legs intertwined.

'You must leave me?'

'Yes, Kiko. I must. Back to England, to see things through.'

'It is your duty?'

'Exactly.'

Kiko opened her eyes wide. 'My grandfather has information from very high in your company. From the Board of Directors.'

'Our friend the noble lord,' Alex said grimly.

'I have learned another thing to help you. My grandfather is still paying that man Lord Beauford, who is deeply in debt.'

'Oh?' Alex said lightly. Beauford in debt: interesting, very.

'He hates you, of course. You know that?'

Alex's eyes closed. Lord Beauford, peer, banker, old Etonian, uncle to the City. The man who was the best friend money could buy. If he could ever get access to the secrets of Beauford's bank, he would find proof of the treachery.

'Alex, I pray you will help me, and that we will succeed. Japan must not rearm.'

'But *I* can get my hands bloody, making and selling arms?'

She touched him, lightly. 'That's not my wish. But I would trust you to do that more than my grandfather.'

Alex rolled over, still feeling restless. 'On Tyneside the new factory will soon be complete, and then we'll be tooled up for the Mark IX light tank. And your Ground Self-Defence Forces – your army – will be in the market by Christmas.'

'Don't sell to them. Don't help them with Arigata, and don't go there. Just don't!'

'Kiko, I *have* to. It's all I can do.'

She placed her bare hand on his sex. 'I want you so much, Alex. You could be a great man. I just don't understand why you have to deal in death!'

He snorted, not wanting to respond to her close, warm body. 'A Japanese asks me why I must follow the traditions, even if that involves blood and suffering? I don't understand *you*, Kiko. Or I don't understand Japan.'

'Japan is schizophrenic. Sword in one hand, chrysanthemum in the other; our souls have two faces. Our actions are brutal, unambiguous. Our words are poetry, sly, elusive – as you English speak. You wonder if we can ever reconcile thought and action, language and life? I do not know, Alex Stanton. Is there a middle way of compromise here in the Land of the Gods? Who can know for sure – until it is found?'

He thought over what he had learned of Japan, its past and its present, and the future Kiko feared. 'It must be difficult to compromise in Japan.'

'Oh yes. There is no middle way in Japan, no debatable way – all such matters of right and wrong are things only *gaijin* would debate. In Japan, there is only the Japanese way, forever.'

'Which you hold to with fanaticism.'

'Yes. You must fight to the end, never surrendering, never compromising; that is *Yamato-Damashii*, the spirit of Japan. When the Imperial Army defended Aitu Island ninety-nine out of a hundred were killed there. The Yamazaki Regiment died almost to a man.'

'Then it is just as well the bomb made you surrender in—' He realized what he had said as she stiffened in his arms. He hugged her, feeling the faint roughness of the skin on her shoulders. Scars from 1945. He could have bitten out his tongue. 'Kiko, I'm sorry. I didn't mean it like that.'

She did not relax. 'You deal with planes and bombs and guns, and now atomic power. Well, know the price, Alex Stanton. *Know the price.*'

He raised himself up on one elbow and kissed her forehead. He felt the Hiroshima agony she remembered. His own body still carried painful scars from the Tower of London bombing. 'Kiko . . .'

There was a long pause.

'I am sure grandfather and Minister Hakagawa still have their great secret.' Her voice was curiously hollow. 'It must be atomic power. There is always talk of uranium and reactors, and Japan's desperate lack of oil. OPEC, foreigners, could strangle us! But I fear they want the nuclear bomb for themselves.' She turned to Alex. 'But that would not be possible, would it? Even for money and after threats, nobody would *sell* nuclear weapons?'

He hugged her. Arigata would both need and produce plutonium and uranium. 'Of course not. But who would buy, after 1945 here?'

She was a million miles away. 'You know who would buy, and what they would do.'

'And you know that you have to bring me and the world proof before we will believe that.'

She turned her head even further away. 'Proof.'

'It would be against the law here, to have the bomb. Surely it would destroy the reputation of everyone associated with it, because of 1945.'

'A disarmed Japan. That was our price, for losing, but we deserved to pay it. I have always wondered if I heard the broadcast,' she murmured, 'there in the little hospital without drugs, doctors, or even bandages. I think I did, after my grandfather found me and carried me through the burning streets. Though it may only be the memory of a memory . . . Everything is confused, when I look back. I remember being a little girl, but things were so different then. The big modern villa in the city. Then the ancient life in the country, in the three-hundred-year-old house. I don't even remember the names of my friends, but I remember what we would do.'

'Go on,' he said, wanting to show her he was interested.

Her accent was stronger. 'The sun was always shining. We used to trap cicadas using long sticks dipped in rubber gum, and afterwards put them in bamboo cages. They would trill for days, till they died. We used to try and capture dragonflies and butterflies, running after them through the long dry grass.'

'I used to do that too,' he said. 'Sometimes near Craigburn, our home in Northumberland; sometimes in Central Park in New York.'

'I never caught any.'

He laughed. 'I did, I'm afraid. The instincts of a hunter – straight into glass bottles with them . . . What else do you remember? Did you really hear the Emperor's surrender broadcast?'

'Oh, no question that I have heard it. Did I hear it on 15 August, 1945? That I do not know. Emperor Hirohito recorded it the previous day. He spoke in the very formal, archaic language of the court . . . not to the point, you know.' She turned to Alex. 'We are not an outspoken people. We are like the English. We do not speak the things in our heart, not directly.'

Alex felt her gaze on him. He looked away. 'Yes,' he said grimly, 'I know all about Japanese circumlocution. How did Hirohito put it? "The war situation has developed not necessarily to Japan's advantage".'

'Is that all you have to say, Alex?'

He reached out for her. 'No.'

'No?' she asked. He sensed her in the darkness, fierce and strong. His equal, or even more than that. 'I cannot give you my love, Alex, nor tell you the truths that I know, if you wish only to serve my grandfather.'

He said only, 'At the moment, I need his money to build up my company.'

'Money! Are you not rich enough?'

He took a breath. 'Kiko, I promise you this. If I take his money, it's because I have to. If I build Arigata, it's because I have agreed to. But one way or another, Arigata will not give your grandfather power, nor atomic weapons.'

She was rigid and unyielding in the bed. Then, 'You promise me, faithfully?'

'I promise you.'

In the darkness, she touched him. And though he was in the darkness, he was not alone.

The Board of Directors met on the same afternoon Alex came back from Japan. He was dog-tired and he had spent a great deal of time thinking over what Kiko had told him. But he was also aware the success of Arigata was vital to the firm. It was the biggest single contract they had, and he knew they needed it. As Hideki had reminded him, he was personally committed to completion by signed contract: the Stanton empire was committed, too.

'Fourth of July, boy,' Hacker said to the oval table, the chandelier from St Petersburg glittering above the directors' heads.

Hugh said warmly, looking around, 'Every division is in profit, in the case of shipbuilding and armaments substantial profit: the subsidiaries likewise. Things have finally come good.'

MacKenzie, Head of Shipbuilding, turned to Alex. 'And Arigata is up to schedule again, I hear.'

'More or less,' Alex said. That was true enough. 'Fast breeders using liquid sodium are still one-off projects. But we're doing it.'

'And the final payment goes straight into the company treasury as planned?'

Alex said nothing, glancing at Hugh.

Lord Beauford scented blood. He grinned. 'Suppose the Japanese project does fall behind schedule . . . then you lose the final completion bonus, don't you?'

MacKenzie began to press Alex: 'Look, is the money from the Arigata contract going to be available for our expansion or not? And I include the £65 million completion payment in September. We need that money to support the shipyard modernization programme, and I have two other oil-rig contracts to fish for.'

Hacker said quietly, 'Alex, you already have the finance for the new tank factory, don't you? Or did the Hideki Bank withdraw – without you or Hugh tellin' us?'

'Everything's going to plan,' Alex said, tight-lipped. There was no point in anything less than complete honesty with himself. Whatever Kiko might find out, he was committed to Arigata. To pull out now would be a hammer-blow to the firm. He tried to shake off his forebodings and he said with a smile, 'The tank factory is ahead of schedule, so is Arigata, and the Hideki Bank of Nagasaki is still backing us.'

These statements were true, at the moment.

At ten in the morning the next day in Newcastle-upon-Tyne, Alex was picked up by Reid in a rented Ford. They left the Central Station and drove straight to the city end of the Scotswood Road. Alex said suddenly, 'John, I might have to send you to Japan. Will that be all right?'

'It's on the firm's business?' The broad shoulders shrugged. 'Aye. Any particular reason?'

'In strict confidence,' Alex answered quietly, 'I'm getting worried about the Arigata situation. And Hideki. I want trained men available.'

'Trained like me?'

'Yes.'

Reid drove along slowly, heading west, the multistorey towers of Elswick looming over the slope. He stopped outside a mesh fence: here was the factory site. They had given no advance notice of their visit.

It had been a while since Alex was last here. He got out, thinking of his great-grandfather firing his newly-invented torpedoes across the Tyne: that man had changed history, and Alex wondered if he could achieve anything as ambitious.

The long and narrow Victorian site here on the northern river bank had already been cleared. Hundred-year-old tarry sheds and machinery dating back to 1916 had been obliterated, and the site was being made ready at breakneck speed. Earth-moving dozers roared over the scene; he saw construction crews in yellow hardhats move about quickly, purposefully. Maybe they could keep abreast of the only industrial competition now worth worrying about: the race with Japan. He winked at John Reid.

'It's looking good,' he decided. 'It's cost me a fortune, but it's looking good.'

Alex had decided to keep his single-union plans quiet, because Langton had to act in secrecy. Alex knew the older man was risking his position as a union leader and as a power-broker in the Labour movement, and he had to admire big-hearted courage like that. After all, Alex had seen Japan, and knew there was no alternative. For Maggie's father, rooted in an older world than Alex's, change must have been painful.

As planned, he met the older man that night in a restaurant near the Quayside. They ate their meal with relish, sparring a little about politics before turning to personal matters.

Abruptly, Alex pushed his cutlery aside and offered Langton an expensive cigar.

Smoke soon wreathed Langton, grey and pungent, and he beamed. 'Cuban, I suppose. The pleasures of Marxism, eh?'

'About the only one.'

Langton continued to smile. Alex studied him unobtrusively. Maggie's father still had a strong-featured face, but good nature and good living had left their marks there, too. Chatter from the other diners rose around them.

'How's your grandson doing?'

'The Stanton apprenticeship? Fine. The lad's clever and good with his hands, and he has ambition. It must run in the family.'

'Speaking of ambition . . .' In the same light tone, Alex asked, 'How's your Maggie, these days?'

Langton brutally stubbed out the cigar. 'Still running after bloody money and that bloody American.'

'You don't think that's working out?'

Langton scowled: a big man with a big anger. 'I don't think he's much of a man, if you want it straight. I don't have much use for self-indulgent men who think they're bloody young lads!'

'He took some risks to cover Vietnam, though.'

'Yes, and risked my Maggie's life in the process – you know she only followed him out because they had split up?'

Alex looked at him. 'Isn't that loyalty?'

Langton gave him a direct, unafraid look; Maggie's look. 'She always was stubborn. Like me, I suppose. But she's made a mistake there. Thank God there's been no marriage and no children.'

Alex thought of his own relationship with Caroline.

Langton reached for his whisky. 'Terry Katz isn't going to make her happy, you know.'

'No,' Alex said. He sighed. Their eyes met. In a simultaneous movement, they both raised their glasses in a toast.

The long, low boat was being poled across the lake. Water-lilies dipped in the swell, and the huge, hanging moon was reflected in the dark water.

'I now prefer Scotch to Suntory,' Takahashi said, as a servant opened the hamper. He remembered Hoyle. 'I've changed.'

'And why not?' Hideki grunted. 'They do what they do best, we do what we do best.'

'Yes, grandfather,' Kiko said submissively.

The old man eyed her, thinking of the uncouth blond foreigner pawing her and more, sickened by his imaginings. Kiko was painfully attractive. 'So. Alex Stanton will do nothing?'

'No. I pretended to be a little interested still in ecological things. He laughed. He is only interested in business,' she said, genuine anger making her voice high. 'Finishing Arigata and taking the money, nothing else.'

'He absolutely must have the contract payments,' Takahashi reminded Hideki. 'The Lord of Beauford – still our man on the Stanton board – has assured us of that. It was discussed at the last meeting.'

Hideki nodded, then toasted the moon hanging over the private lake once again. 'Go to London, get it all settled. Then we will have won.'

Kiko knew with horror that slowly mastered her terror that he was right.

David sighed, not looking forward to seeing the Japanese delegation. 'Will this be counted as a trade matter or a foreign relations one?'

'For protocol purposes, the FO will be in charge,' Paulin said.

'I suppose the Foreign Office people will insist on holding the meeting on their territory?'

His private secretary examined a fingernail. 'Leopards rarely change their spots.'

David spent time rehearsing the facts, but he went to the dowdy grandeur surrounding the Foreign Office quadrangle in a dubious frame of mind. Tokyo wanted to reopen several questions legally-binding contracts were supposed to have closed, and none of the people they had sent were actually government ministers.

There was a gracious welcome, some talk about the long flight and hotels. Then they all sat down around an oval, eighteenth-century table, whose high gloss reflected their faces. A stenographer produced pencil and shorthand pad.

David stared at the five hard, Japanese faces, wishing he had more support. Lambert, a Far Eastern desk linguist from the FO, his own man Paulin, and a spokesman from Energy, a bluff Yorkshireman who had managed a coalfield.

The meeting began. 'Mr Takahashi,' David began, warmly, 'it's so good to see you again. And may I call you—'

'Very happy to be here, sure,' Hideki's man said quickly, 'and of course I don't use a Western name. I am Takahashi Mutsuo, in Japanese style, and proud to be so.'

'Fine,' David said, unsettled by the lack of the usual Asian politenesses. Had something happened in Tokyo? He glanced quickly at the others: a grey-templed, silent man in his forties from high up in MITI, two representatives of other giant Japanese combines, and a secretary-interpreter.

There was some inconsequential sparring. Then Takahashi congratulated him on the progress of the new Stanton works on Tyneside. It was obvious he knew about it in minute detail. David felt unsettled. Had Hideki seen blueprints? How much would a similar factory complex cost in Japan?

'A great, great achievement. Almost Japanese, in fact. And your very good friend Mr Stanton will want a market for all those tanks.'

David made himself sound confident. 'The Mark IX is so good technically it's sure to do well.'

'In Iran or in Saudi Arabia, Mr Bryant?' said the man from MITI, turning one hand over to examine his palm. 'Not so certain, I hear. If I were you, or Alex Stanton, I would continue to cultivate the Japanese market.'

David shifted in his chair as cream tea was served. Paulin directed that operation very smoothly, keeping the guests distracted. But they were coming to the point quickly, now. Tension had gathered in the room.

The Foreign Office official at David's elbow had spent six years in the British Embassy in Tokyo, where David had met him as

First Secretary (Trade). David subtly gestured Lambert into the conversation.

'Excuse me,' he said, scrupulously patient and polite, 'but I'm rather wondering how official your mission is – and how official is your attempt to link Stanton Industries to HMG's attitude to what amounts to nuclear proliferation.'

The Japanese seemed to sit closer together. As ever, Takahashi answered. 'Very official, completely so – in a half-official way.'

Very Japanese. David stared him right in the eye. 'You mean you are all deniable?'

Takahashi straightened his tie and laughed. 'Might be, might be, but don't fool yourselves. This mission is fully authorized by the Tokyo government, under the especial authority of Minister Hakagawa. And as soon as the present prime minister resigns . . . you get the picture?'

'In full colour, with stereophonic sound,' David said drily. 'You represent the coming men.'

The man from MITI began to speak but Takahashi silenced him with an upraised hand. 'Exactly.'

'And you wish to add items, if possible, to the agreements already signed about providing you with uranium for Arigata and your other power stations?'

'Right. And to help us with our nuclear programme in the next fifteen, twenty years we wish to sign a billion-dollar agreement.'

'A billion dollars?' David knew how much that could mean to the country.

Takahashi gave a juvenile grin. 'For you to reprocess our nuclear waste. So, a binding agreement valid till the year 1995 – and from that reprocessed waste we want to import from you high-grade plutonium, of course only for peaceful uses; that is, plutonium which is pure to ninety-eight per cent.'

'What!' David was staggered. 'But that's weapons-grade plutonium, man! *Weapons-grade plutonium!*'

The tense moment of silence stretched out. Then David heard the antique French clock, ticking away on the mantelpiece: time, counting down. The man from MITI settled his glasses more firmly on the bridge of his nose. He smiled at David, and spoke through the young Japanese translator.

'Ah, we feel the contract should be sufficiently profitable to you to counteract any embarrassment over nuclear non-proliferation treaties and so forth. We want it to be signed by you, Mr Bryant, when Arigata is opened.'

'I have to go to Arigata and sign?' David said, taken aback.

'You want us to continue investing in your country?'

'I mean, through prejudice or cowardice you don't want to deal with us?' Takahashi said, his eyes glinting sardonically. He delivered his low blow looking at the Foreign Office man. 'There're always the French, you understand.'

'I understand perfectly,' David said crisply, though he suddenly felt cold. He tried to maintain a bland exterior, however: he did not want them to know he now believed there was a conspiracy in Tokyo, and they did intend to rearm – and the conspirators had no intention of doing any long-term serious business with Stanton Industries, because they wanted to make their own arms, so as to equip new armies, navies and an air force. He blinked his eyes. Was it just a coincidence they were advancing into space, just as they took the first steps towards making atomic weapons?

He fought for time. 'We don't have to decide on the details immediately, do we?'

'No. As long as you commit yourself, for your government and also personally: you have to be willing to deal.'

David looked at Takahashi. He did not know the man, not really, and the little he did know he did not like. He licked his lips, then hated himself for this rare lapse in actually showing his nervousness. They were virtually blackmailing him. If he wanted to help support the factory that Alex and Will Langton had sweated so hard for, he had to say something now. 'HMG will look favourably on this scheme, subject to fulfilling the conditions of the nuclear non-proliferation treaties.'

The MITI man's face was stone. 'You need not worry about the plutonium. We are peace-loving. And besides, we are probably years away from bomb-making technology, so there would be nothing at all to worry about in the short term.'

'But what about the long term?'

'Don't worry.' Takahashi shook his head. 'You would be out of government, perhaps, dead, or in another country. And besides, you in the West never think about tomorrow: only we take the long view.'

David believed it.

For the record, he had to accept the assurances they gave in exchange for his signature, but David could not stop worrying. He wondered whether or not he should take his suspicions to a cabinet meeting: but it did not seem possible that the British government, unassisted, could prevent the remilitarization of Japan.

The next day he summoned a confidential meeting of his advisers, and put the questions to them plainly. First, was this rearmament plan something which should be stopped?

They felt it should not be encouraged.

'In that case,' David said bleakly, 'is there anything we can do to stop it?'

Nothing occurred to them.

David wondered, grim-faced, if Maggie might be able to use publicity, but that seemed unlikely to be effective. And on this occasion there was no use asking any of the Stantons for help and advice.

He remembered what Alex had hinted about. The thought of that kind of right-wing conspiracy was terrifying.

He rang up Megan from his office, and made some smalltalk about family business, family friends and enemies, anything to take his mind off this problem.

'And what about moving back to London, then?'

He temporized, his mind still on Japan. 'We can think about that later.'

'I've been talking to Uncle Frank. He seems to think Hoyle the chief troublemaker is stuck abroad.'

He scratched his chin. He wanted to give it a little longer, but that indeed was Lord Tytryst's opinion. 'If my friends think it's safe in another six months, we'll think of getting a house near Westminster then.'

Then the only possible answer to his problem came to him in a kind of blinding flash of inspiration he could not help but associate with nuclear power, and his hand tightened on the telephone.

'Oh, David, that's wonderful! If we can afford it.'

'What?' He turned his attention to the conversation again. 'The money is no problem. Look, my love, I have to go now.'

He regretted, now, that he could not have consulted with Alex, because only this one means of stopping the conspiracy had occurred to him: but now he could say nothing about his idea to anybody, because some people might give his last desperate plan a blunt name.

He said the word to himself. Treason.

Kiko was taken to a Kentish town flat owned by one of Maggie's researchers.

'This is Sally,' Maggie said. 'I trust her absolutely.'

'That is good,' Kiko said tiredly. She looked at the younger, blonde woman. 'Because what I am doing is dangerous, what we are all doing is dangerous, and Arigata is a scheme very close to my grandfather's heart, and if he ever suspects . . .' Kiko gave a delicate shudder. 'He is deadly, and I am afraid of him.'

Maggie touched her hand. 'Sally knows how to keep quiet. Don't you?'

Sally swallowed, gave a nervous grin. 'Most of the time.'

Maggie sat back in the battered sofa. 'So, what happened?'

Kiko said slowly, 'It went well, I thought. For a time. I persuaded him to help me with money. I think he was annoyed by the bad publicity in Japan . . .'

'Alex has an obvious interest in keeping Saigo Hideki out of power,' Maggie said dryly. 'Hideki in power means goodbye to Article IX, and Japan as an arms-exporting nation. But he'll be happy enough otherwise to help a man with a big chequebook!'

'There's no need to be sharp with me,' Kiko said, 'just because I have slept with him. Are you jealous or something? He is attractive and powerful; it was worth trying.'

'Of course,' Maggie said, after a while.

Kiko turned her pale face towards Sally. 'You have the facts, I think.'

'She does,' Maggie said. 'So, from Friends of the Earth, and several libraries, Sally— ?'

Sally opened the file. 'Officially nuclear power is safe. That's the line taken by governments everywhere and all the firms involved.'

'Is it?'

'No, Maggie.' Then she glanced at Kiko. 'Edited highlights. So, this country. On 8 October 1957, up at Windscale, a technician doing a routine operation without the pile operating manual ignited the graphite and uranium core of the Number One Reactor. Incidentally, this reactor was apparently made to produce plutonium for weapons. It wasn't noticed till a couple of days later – I know that sounds incredible, but it's true. By then, eleven tons of uranium, and all that steel and graphite, was blazing. So, radioactivity spewing out. Fortunately, and against opposition, a man called Cockcroft had insisted on having filters installed in the smokestack. Some radioactivity was filtered out; more escaped. At this point, naturally, the public had not been informed.

'They tried to extinguish the fire, which was raging out of control and getting worse all the time and threatening to crack the concrete containment vessel, which would have been an absolute disaster – dead people all around the Irish Sea and over the north of England and the Scottish lowlands. Dead quickly from radiation burns or dead slowly from cancer. First they tried carbon dioxide gas. That failed. Eventually the public were informed, plans for evacuation were cobbled together, and three men stayed by the reactor to try and extinguish the fire with water – risking an explosion that would have split the reactor wide open.'

Maggie's imagination showed her. 'Terrifying.'

'That worked, fortunately. But nobody really knows how much radiation escaped. Radioactive isotopes were spewed all across northern England and the Irish Sea – probably much more radiation than came from Hiroshima and Nagasaki combined.'

Maggie felt a little sick. How far was Tyneside from the Windscale plant? Eighty miles, or less? 'Go on.'

'Lots of people will probably have died prematurely from that event, though the government never collected any figures.'

Kiko shifted uneasily, then reached for her tea cup. 'A very serious incident, but is it directly relevant to us, and to Arigata?'

Sally was leafing through her ring-binder. She looked up. 'Try this. Arigata is a sodium-cooled fast-breeder reactor. So was the Enrico Fermi 1 reactor, sited at Lagoona Beach in Michigan – and no more than an hour's drive from the one and a half million people who live in Detroit. Now, the thing about fast-breeders like Arigata is that the core has to be much, much smaller than a power-generating reactor. About the size of a drum, say. Also, it has to be compact in such a way that a fairly small distortion could make the core go supercritical—'

'What does that mean?' Kiko asked.

'Blow up!'

'And my grandfather is building this in Japan,' Kiko marvelled. 'What a risk!'

'Incidentally, sodium, the coolant, can explode on contact with water or air . . .'

'This is terrible,' Kiko said glumly. 'It's worse than I thought. And Arigata is a fast breeder of a similar type!'

'It didn't explode – did it?' Maggie asked. 'Nobody could cover up that kind of incident . . . could they?'

'A bit of the reactor assembly broke off and blocked the flow of coolant – molten sodium is opaque, so you can't see what's happening. A part of the reactor melted down. The operators tried to scram it, shut it down by sending extra moderating rods into the core assembly. That only worked in part. The big fear was, with an unstable mass of melted uranium lost somewhere in the reactor, any disturbance might accidentally create a critical mass, and so an explosion . . .'

Maggie stood up suddenly. 'I don't think I want to hear any more, just at the moment. In fact, I feel sick.'

Kiko was looking at her, hands still folded together. 'We must hear more. Sally, what does a fast-breeder do?'

'It makes more fissionable material than it burns. You get the used-up nuclear fuel and you can extract plutonium and uranium 235 from it. With that, you fuel more reactors. Or you make bombs.'

'Bombs?' said Kiko, outraged.

'The rumour is that the British government is going to reprocess the fuel. Lots of countries are involved. That means Maggie's friend David Bryant will have to give fissionable material to companies in Japan.'

'Supposedly for power stations, but perhaps for bombs?' Kiko spread her hands. 'Maggie, we must do something to stop Arigata.'

'Not so easy,' said Sally. 'Here the Atomic Energy Authority police are all armed – pistols and machine-guns. It'll be the same in Japan. And there are governments involved, countries, as well as some of the most powerful companies in the world.'

'Nevertheless,' Kiko answered, 'we must stop it. Somehow.'

Chapter Nineteen

Alex stretched his feet out comfortably, as the black car with the royal crest sailed past Speaker's Corner on Park Lane, following the road around the spot where the Tyburn gallows had once stood.

What to do about Beauford, whose presence on the Board compromised all of Stanton Industries? And how could he get out from under, in terms of Japan?

Alex was just in time to switch on ITV's ten o'clock news, the over-amplified sound momentarily blasting through his huge, empty house.

As he undid his tie and threw it over the back of a chair he saw that the *Amanya Seville*, a Stanton-built supertanker no more than half a dozen years old, had been wrecked late that afternoon off the coast of Brittany.

He sat up very straight. Most of the 230,000 ton cargo of oil was lost and hundreds of miles of coastline were going to be polluted. The black filth was flowing everywhere, and he grimaced at the montage of film-segments: holiday beaches would be ruined from Cornwall to Normandy and beyond.

He happened to be sitting near the phone and he picked it up and dialled Maggie's Flood Street number. She answered almost immediately, a little breathless: either she had been fighting with somebody, or she was expecting an important call.

'It's me. Alex.' He realized he was more than a little drunk; and suddenly it left a bitter aftertaste. He quickly mentioned the disaster.

'Look, about this oil spill. I could give you transport facilities, if you want to cover the incident. It's been a quarter-million-ton ecological disaster, Maggie.'

He never forgot how she replied, and he had no good answer, then or later.

She snapped, 'You still encourage nuclear power, you are still building Arigata in spite of everything, and yet you call the spillage of something organic disastrous!'

'It's only oil, Maggie,' he said quietly. 'Not the end of the world.' There was a pause. Then he continued, 'Terry away again?' Her silence answered. 'So's Caro.'

In a brisk voice she told him, 'Alex, I know you've talked to Kiko.'

'Not recently,' he said sadly. Two weeks, now. 'She's turned her

230

back. I've tried phone calls, a couple of cables, even a letter sent by courier. No response.'

'How much do you care?'

'Of course I bloody care! What do you think I am?'

'I didn't mean it like that.'

'Yes, you did,' Alex said gruffly. 'All right, she was, is, a source of much useful information – but she was a source of so much else, too. Ah, I hope she's happier, doing whatever she's doing now.'

'It couldn't have been her grandfather, warning her off you?'

'I wouldn't think so. You'd have to put more fear than the fear of God into her for her to give up a man she really believed in.'

Maggie made no reply, so Alex replied for her. 'Of course, that takes it for granted I was once a man she did believe in . . .'

'Do you blame her for being annoyed and disappointed? You know Arigata is dangerous – and that anything which gives more power to Saigo Hideki and Akira Hakagawa is bad.'

'Listen,' he said toughly, 'I'm a businessman. You give your *facts* about them to David or to the world, and something will happen. Mere guesses and speculation won't do it!'

'You're still the same!'

'Just like you?'

He went to bed tired, sure he had said the wrong thing to her once again. Was this business about plutonium really so serious? Serious enough, he thought, for eight countries to have approached the armaments division over the last year for uranium ore or advice on reactors, or worse. Dr Sidqi of Iraq was still on the scene, too. He felt anguish, staring at himself in the mirror. Clearly Maggie thought it was vital, and he had rarely disagreed with her instinct about what was important, though they had often argued over morality. He remembered what Hacker had said about Van Tien Trung's mysterious death in Saigon, and he realized now that Maggie must feel responsible. Could Hideki really be doing half of what his granddaughter claimed?

It took him a long time to get to sleep, and he was disturbed when Caroline arrived very late and went into one of the spare bedrooms. He came completely awake and lay on his back, considering whether or not to invite her into the king-size bed. He sighed, and rolled over again. It hardly seemed worth the possible trouble.

They met over the breakfast table. She spooned in cereal, the diet clearly forgotten. Without make-up she looked like a plump, petulant teenager.

There was silence, interrupted by occasional, barely-polite words. Then Caro said, 'How long will you be away this time?'

'A week, I hope. I'll probably have to hit the Middle East again. I have a good deal of business to transact.'

The spoon clattered. 'I thought it would all be different when we were married. I'm afraid I have expectations, Alex.'

He forced a smile. 'I understand that, but I'm completely tied up at the moment. If I fail, there are going to be thousands of people unemployed here – and much worse elsewhere.'

She threw her head back as he rose from the table. 'Your business is all very well, but what about me?'

He smiled diffidently. 'I'm sorry.'

She stood up, too. 'Well, we may as well say goodbye now.'

Suddenly, surprised, he felt terribly alone.

He felt strangely preoccupied as he went through his correspondence, his digest of the world's press, and the divisional figures. Hugh had coffee with him at eleven, complaining that somebody at board level had again leaked price-sensitive information about the company to a competitor, this time in Taiwan: and he suspected Lord Beauford. But to Hugh's surprise, Alex hardly raised a flicker of anger.

There was something familiar to Alex about the name of the wrecked tanker, and during the afternoon he paced about his huge office overlooking the Thames, trying to remember where he had heard it before.

'Patricia, can you get me details of stock-ownership in the company owning that wrecked tanker? – oh, and check the source, ownership and destination of the cargo.'

Even with all that information displayed in front of him Alex could not make the connection. Nevertheless, the incident had started off a chain of thought that was suddenly completed a couple of days later when he picked up a rumour that Lord Beauford was indeed in financial distress.

Now, abruptly, he remembered. Heat flooded him. Beauford *was* associated with the sunk ship.

Within the hour, Alex had formulated a plan. He asked his secretary to unearth an old friend from his Eton days who was now a Lloyd's underwriter. Lloyd's, the three-hundred-year-old marine insurers whose agents are in every corner of the globe, and whose registers report the movements of almost all vessels on the world's oceans, was the connection that had brought Lord Beauford into Alex's mind.

'Hello, old man,' he said with hearty geniality down the phone. 'Yes, fine – and how are you? A favour. Well, as a matter of fact, yes you can . . .'

His friend asked around, and rang back later. After they talked for a while about Hambros bank and Beauford Cleves, Alex had his memory confirmed: by a mischance, Lord Beauford had both been a major investor in the cargo of oil, and by an unlucky coincidence also a lead name in the Lloyd's insurance syndicate that had underwritten both the ship and its cargo.

'The loss of the *Amanya Seville* must have personally cost Beauford up to a quarter of a million pounds. Quite a blow.'

Alex considered carefully. As he well knew, Lloyd's had extremely strict rules. Its members had to accept unlimited liability for losses, even if that took them into bankruptcy . . . 'That's a fortune he stands to lose.'

'And think what a vulnerable position it puts him in.'

'I have thought.'

If Beauford was taking a financial hammering, Alex knew some of his shares might have to be put on the market at a distress price. He rang Kintyre and asked for the discreet services of his stockbroker. 'I'd like you to buy whatever he's selling. Either Stanton Industries shares or his shares in Beauford Cleves.'

'To get that fearful old creature Beauford out of your hair? I'll oblige. If he'll sell.'

Alex laughed: the Scots accent, the warmth of Kintyre's friendship. 'What a big word is "if".'

His old friend murmured confidentially, 'I'm sure you've thought of ways of making him sell.'

'Indeed.'

'He really tried to take the company away from your family?'

Alex remembered the battle: the summer of 1974. 'Yes; but we won the day, as you'll remember. With fighting spirit and foreign gold.'

'How did you work that? You've never spelled it out before.'

He smiled, remembering the flash of gold ingots under the spotlights. 'Iran owed me a favour or two. And further, after the stock market slide in '74 I convinced them the shares were a bargain. The extra shares we bought went to Hugh and I personally, and to the family trust; and the shares held by the Shah of Iran and his associate banks are, by a binding agreement, voted by me.'

'My goodness me, that means you have a huge public company virtually as your private domain!'

Cameron was so openly admiring that Alex felt touched. 'Yes, but then, so much of our business requires strict privacy. And with Beauford on the Board of Directors we will never have that privacy.'

'It must be galling for you to have that man on your board.'

'Certainly. I hate him; he stands for everything I despise. But Lord Beauford is still the owner of record for several million Stanton shares. According to the company's rules he can demand representation on the board – and if Hugh and I tried to change the rules he'd certainly create a scandal.'

'And he knows too much for the scandal to blow over quickly?'

Very astute. 'Something like that. But this is important to me, Cameron. It might give me the chance to get Lord Beauford off my back, and for good.'

There was now a very good reason why he wanted that to happen.

Cameron, the Lord Kintyre, touched briefly on other affairs. 'What else has been happening with you, Alex? Charles was hinting you're not getting on too well with Caro.'

'A few stresses and strains,' he murmured, his hand tightening on the telephone for a moment.

'You know we've been involved with the Arigata reactor over in Japan? Well, the official opening is coming up . . . and so is my best chance to pull off the arms deal of the century.'

Kintyre was clearly surprised. 'Sell your tanks and artillery to the Japanese? How very strange!'

'In what way?'

'We've just had an indirect approach from your Mr Hideki, actually, through a chief aide called Takahashi: one of his companies is proposing to set up an exhibition of avionics and armaments-related hardware here, and they've sounded us out about the finance and foreign exchange end.'

This time Alex saw the knuckles of his free hand go white, and he glanced at his desk calendar. Not long now till the next board meeting. Not long at all till the showdown. 'That's not the only thing they're planning.'

Next, he rang Maggie, to persuade her to attend the opening of the Arigata complex, which was now set for 1 September, 1977. 'I'd like you to get that information about the fat man, now. The banking information. Money no object, Maggie, if it'll help your investigations.'

'What do you want me to do with it? Remember, the truth can hurt.'

'Just get it in the press and make sure the link is to Switzerland.'

'Will that get rid of – our friend? Completely, not just off your own board of directors?'

'If we do it right, he'll be exposed for what he is. So, you'll do it?'

She agreed.

'And if you could put in a good word for me with Kiko, I'd be obliged.'

'All right,' Maggie said, then rang off hastily.

Alex was satisfied. For the first time in some years, he was on close speaking terms with her once more, and even in their brief business conversations over the phone she had been as lively, forthright and attractive to him as ever.

For some reason he hated to think of her, but then he did not have to, as there was much else on his mind. Until Arigata was all paid for, Stanton Industries would be badly over-extended – and he could not prevent Lord Beauford from knowing most of the details.

Alex stared down from the huge window in his office: sunset over the Thames and the Chelsea rooftops, and over Maggie's house in Flood Street. There had to be the chance, Alex felt sure, of provoking Lord Beauford into more indiscretions and errors – enough to make him vulnerable. But whatever happened, he was dangerously well informed about Stanton Industries, and he had to go.

He sighed. He had computer screens here still displaying results from all the Stanton Industries Divisions, and he was pleased but not complacent. So near, he thought, and yet so far from huge profits; and so many enemies.

If only he could get rid of Beauford, and find some kind of hold over Hideki . . .

Patricia came in, the automatic door sliding away, then looked up from the communications desk near the drinks cabinet. 'Our relay centre, Mr Stanton. A telex from Tokyo.'

He went back to the massive leather swivel chair set behind his own desk. 'Copy and switch it through.'

The teleprinter chattered maniacally.

TOKYO HQ HIDEKI INDUSTRIES
ATTENTION ALEX STANTON, LONDON, CODE 2458462:
URGENTLY REQUEST YOU ORDER YOUR TEHRAN REPRESENTATIVE MAJOR COOMBES TO ARGUE OUR CASE WITH SHAH'S GOVERNMENT THERE. STILL NO AGREEMENT FOR FINAL HAND-OVER OF THE OIL-REFINING INTERESTS HIDEKI INDUSTRIES IS PURCHASING FOR OVER 200 MILLION US.
ACKNOWLEDGE ACKNOWLEDGE ACKNOWLEDGE.

He tore off the message, scanned it in one glance. Though Alex crumpled the paper casually in his hand, there was suddenly a blaze in his soul. This proved Hideki could make wrong moves. He had gone into Iran at the wrong time, and for the problems described here had to go to the Shah's court and his intelligence agency SAVAK. It was a tiny weight to counter the massive amount of money and power Hideki could turn against him, but it was something.

'Acknowledge it,' he said tersely, 'then copy it to Tehran HQ without further comment, usual high-security codes. When Major Coombes asks what he should do, tell him verbally to put the whole issue on the back-burner – but tell him to make a little noise about it, so it sounds as if we're taking action.'

So Hideki, too, could overreach himself. That was a great comfort. And better than that. This was his chance.

It was a long-distance call next, McCourt speaking from Tokyo.

'I wanted to get straight to you.'

'I'm listening.'

'I just heard this from a US embassy source –'

'I know. *Him*.' Hideki, not named for security reasons.

'He has to deliver that business in Iran. A big contract with the government; it's just been made public, I presume by Hideki's enemies here.'

'I understand.' *Has to deliver.* 'Thanks.'

David took a break from his governmental work to see Alex off from the airport. Stanton Industries was the name written in man-sized letters on the side of the Boeing 727, and the plane was painted black and gold. They talked quickly, as Alex could not fall behind schedule.

'I need the government to grant us access to Hong Kong, David. Stanton Industries *must* be involved in building their rapid-transit system.'

David straightened his tie, nervously. Alex sounded overbearing. 'I'll see what I can do. Anyway, good luck in Iran and Saudi.'

'I may need all the luck I can get,' Alex said, 'though I'd prefer active support, ideally from HMG.' He looked almost savage, squinting against the blazing August sunlight that made all the colours of Heathrow strangely washed out, his fists swinging as he came up on his toes. Huge engines roared: airliners clawing into the blue sky on sheer power – and petroleum.

'Alex—'

Alex answered fiercely. 'Do you know what's wrong with Britain? A taste for self-criticism is not at all the same thing as a burning desire for self-improvement. And that is what we have lost in the twentieth century. We must change.'

'I hope you do good business, Alex.'

'So do I.'

There are over three thousand princes of the al-Saud line. Some do nothing. Some let others work in their name; others work for themselves, or for the government; some at different times do all of those things.

After the huge cargo door was opened, burning hot desert wind gushed over Alex and the crew. Immediately his throat was dry. It might have been merely hot in England, but Saudi Arabia was scalding. Riyadh was much hotter than Japan would be; the sun here was like a burning glass.

An old friend had left a message at the British embassy for him, and three retainers in a silver Range-Rover picked him up from there before dawn the following morning. He was driven into the burnt-yellow desert, away from the pink sunrise. The air was cool and not yet swept clear of stars.

They drove for an hour, into the Nafud Dahy. It was open, sun-blasted desert.

Then, there were camels to ride. He mounted, tasting dust. Like the others, Alex rode in loose light-coloured robes, with a burnoose on his head and water-bottles and a Colt AR-15 in his saddle-bags.

They stopped at a Bedu encampment, far in the desert. It was blisteringly hot. There was Arabic coffee, thick and strong, and polite, inconsequential talk. Then, later in the afternoon, the Saudi prince took his friend outside, to be private.

They squatted down in the shade of a column of rocks. Heat devils danced around the sun-blasted landscape – the sunlight so intense it threatened to give Alex a headache.

The royal held a falcon on his right wrist, stroking it, cooing at it. Lean brown fingers stroked the hooded bird of prey. Alex watched, patient, fascinated. Flies buzzed even here.

The old prince with the leathery face sighed. He spoke the courtly English he had learned fighting Turks for the British and the future Arab nation during World War I. 'This is a bad time, in many ways. I have been disappointed.'

'Even you?'

He squinted at Alex. 'I expected much more than this, when I rode into Damascus with your Lawrence of Arabia and my Hussein of Mecca's son Feisal. Now, this land is ours, but then it always was. And we are all rich from oil.'

'Is that bad? Surely it must be as God wills?'

He spat and Alex saw his saliva sizzle on a particularly hot stone. 'But our youth have turned away from the old ways, turned to the West, to whores and white powders. And drink. Nothing manly is in that. And such hatred among we Arabs still, some of us rich, and some not. And more hatred against the Jews, though they esteem Abraham as their father and they are, just like us and Christians such as yourself, people of the Book. I feel that while I have grown old in hatred my people have never grown up, and now . . .'

Alex had known other disappointed old men, not least his adoptive father, Sir Edward Stanton. He spoke compassion. 'Now, you do not wish for the sword, any longer?'

Laughter wheezed. 'So you think? Ah, it is worse than that. The new men in Washington are putting pressure on us. My son is not authorized even to talk about your tanks; and Prince Sultan will be stopped from buying, it seems. But *I* wish for the sword, Alex Stanton.'

'That's good.' Alex chuckled. 'I have many swords. As always. And the very best. Necessary, too. After all, other people can buy swords, you know. Israel, Iraq. Iran.'

'Iraq, and those blood-gorged Ba'athists? Saddam Hussein?' He spat again. 'Listen, you may not be as successful as you think, dealing with our other rival, Iran.'

It was over a hundred degrees Fahrenheit but for a moment he felt cold. 'No?'

'That upstart on his peacock throne! I hope that one day we will buy from you again, Alex Stanton, whatever America says. Soon, if I have my way. But that man will not have the power to!'

Alex was genuinely shocked. 'But the power he has, the Shah!'

'Is power security? No! What power has your royal Queen? Little, or none. But she is *secure*. In the Middle East today, who is secure?'

'Nobody,' Alex admitted. 'But the Shah of Iran—'

'Would be finished, if the people of his empire ever thought that God had turned against him.'

It was frightening, even to think of it. What would happen then? Would the whole region collapse into chaos and Islamic fundamentalism, with the Soviet Union picking up the pieces? 'I see. I understand,' Alex said. The Shah of Iran, with his huge, loyal army and air force, his incredible oil wealth – under threat.

'I will hunt more today,' the Arab said, scratching unshaven cheeks. 'We will speak again on Sunday, if you are returned from Tehran by then.'

Alex risked directness. 'What will we talk about? The Mark IX tank?'

It was rebuffed. 'Or maybe I will send you my son.'

Tomorrow, he would go to Tehran personally, and try to negotiate a sale for the Mark IX – but a sale on terms as close to cash as he could. He sighed, still not really believing it. For a time the credit of the Shah of Iran had been better than the credit of the British government. Now that, he had been told, was all changed.

The old Arab turned. *'Salaam alaikum.'*

Alex stood up. *'Alaikum salaam.'*

Tehran was a partial success for Alex.

Alex's meeting with his old friend the Shahanshah was both extremely brief and almost as satisfactory. The Shah had learned, though he did not say from whom, about Alex's commission from the Japanese.

The dark, sensual eyes turned to Alex. 'And so you want me to release my country's assets to these men of Tokyo.'

'That was the agreement, I understand.' Alex sipped more whisky. 'It's only an oil refinery, admittedly very modern.'

An ironic eyebrow. 'You have an agreement with Japan, also.'

Alex put his glass down. This was Asian cunning; he was impressed. 'Over Arigata, the fast-breeder reactor, you mean?'

'A very interesting use of science.'

'Indeed it is.'

The Shah sighed. 'I told the Hideki men I would be pleased to have the benefit of the Arigata technology, and perhaps . . .'

It all became blindingly clear. 'They suggested an extortionate price?'

The dark eyes met his. 'A price in oil. Long-term contracts, the oil to be refined in their own refinery; a commitment from my government worth hundreds of millions of dollars, just to learn a little about Arigata!'

'I think,' Alex said steadily, 'I could pass on what my own staff have learned at Arigata. As a gift to you, majesty. In return, I would merely be obliged if I could tell Tokyo that Stanton Industries will handle the transfer of their refinery.'

'That seems reasonable.'

'I'll be very grateful.' Now he had power over Hideki. 'I was wondering also, about Iran's armaments programme.'

'You are supplying us with your new generation of Mark VIII tanks. The contract runs till the end of the year.'

'It does indeed, but with a new efficient factory, and a new light tank we call the Mark IX available—'

There was a chopping gesture. 'Alex, no more. Now, what do you think of this foolishness of President Carter's, trying to stop America's friends buying weapons?'

'Go through me, through Hacker Stanton International. I guarantee it. Whatever you want, we'll find ways to supply.' It was clear to Alex no huge arms sale would be arranged today: the Saudi Arabian had been right. But there would be other days, the current contracts were going well, and now he had the refinery to pass over to Japan, if the price was right. 'There won't be any problems.'

The Shah looked at him, lips curling. 'I have problems enough, already. My people are bemused by charlatans making use of the Koran. Did you know that? My revolution is in danger.'

'If there is anything I can do—'

'There was.' The Shah's nostrils flared. He stood up. 'That man Alan Hoyle, your enemy, my enemy. He has been in Iraq, acting under Saddam Hussein's orders.'

Alex was stunned. Hoyle, still working against the West, and on such a scale! 'Hoyle is involved with the so-called men of the Left who are trying to overthrow you?'

The King of Kings inclined his head, his mouth twisted sourly. He still wore the splendid full-dress uniform of the Imperial Guard. 'You should have killed him when you had the chance. Now, leave me, Alex Stanton.'

Early the next day Alex flew out of Tehran, heading south to Saudi Arabia. It was Sunday, and he was beginning to feel desperate.

We have to make *this* sale, Alex Stanton thought, as the Stanton jet landed outside Riyadh. The new factory is turning out tanks and so far there've been hardly any takers, and soon it'll be the official opening day.

The new manager of the Stantons' Riyadh office was from California; a former employee of Hacker-Stanton, a quarter of which still belonged to Alex. They shook hands.

'Must be a change from Saigon, Ross,' Alex said.

Ross started the car; he was driving to the prince's house. 'Pretty damn different, yes sir.'

'Like it, here in Saudi?'

'I've only been living here three, four weeks. I'll be spending a lot of my time on the Dharhan base, it looks like. But Riyadh seems a strange place, Alex.'

Alex glanced at the palms as they drove: a roadside oasis. For Britain, the arms trade meant over seven hundred million a year in sterling; and tens of thousands of jobs. 'Yes. But think of all that money, gushing out of the earth.'

'How long have these al-Saud guys been running things? Some of them seem kinda nervous.'

'How long . . . ?' Alex smiled at the younger man. 'There's an old mud fort here in Riyadh, with a rusting sword in it. I'll show you, sometime. They say it was left there in 1901 when Ibn Saud took this town. He was twenty-one at the time.'

'Seized Riyadh so young? A *big* battle, huh?'

'He took this place with just forty men – that's how all this began.'

'God in heaven. Forty men!'

'I hope it'd take a few more to take Riyadh, these days.'

'Thanks to guys like us?'

'Exactly.'

They were allowed into the low, white-walled house. When the young prince's aides arrived, there was a quick, efficient security check, then the royal strode in briskly.

Alex stood up, politely, but the prince gestured him down again, equally polite. They had known each other since youth and they had each other's measure and the respect that came with it.

The prince clapped his hands. 'Coffee for my guests!' He spoke with a distinct American accent: the Harvard Business School, as it happened.

They talked. America's lost war in Vietnam, the economic problems of the Shah of Iran, and the latest Israeli settlements on the West Bank. Then everybody else left: Alex and the prince were alone together.

Alex did not have much hope of a successful sale as he sipped Arabic coffee. The United States, very wrongly in his opinion, had continued to exert itself to prevent even its allies in the Middle East arming themselves.

It began.

'Last year Prince Sultan bought two and a half billion dollars worth of American arms, Alex.'

'I know.' Alex nibbled a piece of Turkish delight.

'And yet see how they treat us now!'

Alex was sympathetic. 'I understand. Of course I do. But the new men in the White House do *not* understand.'

They sipped more coffee, but for some reason the prince came to the point more rapidly than usual. He said resentfully, 'My government is oil rich; we are a free people, under Allah. Yet we're supposed to listen to your President Carter and automatically obey.'

Alex felt excitement begin to build up in him. He knew from Maggie that the President in person was a good, straightforward man: but the modern world was not like that at all. Was there a chance of selling something to the Saudis, even if only token amounts of arms to demonstrate their independence?

'So, you'll buy a little, to—'

The prince's face was fierce. 'Not at all. Alex Stanton, the world has changed.'

Alex swallowed. So the Saudis thought they had to follow the new White House line. 'Well, perhaps you may recall the specifications of our new Mark IX tank, and the demonstration film which we—'

'Yes.' The Saudi prince raised his hand.

This was the moment of truth. Alex sensed a great deal of tension concealed in the other man. Is he going to turn us down flat? he questioned himself. That'll prove to the White House he'll follow their orders, though he'll expect, and get, something in return.

'You were impressed, but you're going to turn us down?' I hope to God he doesn't. He must not. Maybe he knows I'm desperate to sell and wants to negotiate a low price . . .

'I was impressed. Sure I was.'

Alex looked at the Saudi prince, his instincts warming. The deal was on the table; any deal the prince could pay for. If he does say yes immediately, how far do I have to go along with it? Alex, as usual in the Middle East, was roundabout in terms of money. 'We can arrange payment to suit, should you decide to buy.'

The prince arched his brow. 'Has payment ever been a problem when the house of al-Saud is involved?'

'Never,' Alex said. 'So, if you should decide to buy . . .'

'I have already decided.'

'Yes,' Alex said stolidly, seeing that he had.

Alex regarded the hawk-featured man in black desert robes with a hint of uncertainty.

'You seem troubled. Is there something wrong, Prince Abdullah?'

'In our country there are the holy places of Islam; they must be protected from the infidel, and all the evil forces in the world.'

Alex sat back. 'Your Highness? What is it you foresee?'

'Alex Stanton, you remember that warning my father gave you?'

'About the Shah? Most certainly. I saw him before I came here.'

'A worried man,' the prince said curtly.

Alex could not deny that.

'You know Tehran calls the Gulf the Persian Gulf; but we know it is the Arab Gulf.'

Alex changed the subject quickly. 'I'd like to thank you for your information about Iran. And, believe me, no one knows or ever will know where that information came from.'

'That is good. For my family would think my father and me traitors, and I would compromise our secret, secret sources. See, in Iran, the heretic Shi'ites are disturbed; their exiled leader, Khomeini, the Grand Ayatollah, is still in Iraq. But he is the coming man.'

Alex felt his heart beginning to pound. Was the final crisis coming so soon? What about the other thing David had told him about: the Russian contingency plans to invade Afghanistan? He spoke rapidly, fighting for calm. 'But Khomeini was thrown out in 1963. Asadollah

Alam told me that himself, when he was the Shah's first minister. Listen, Khomeini is an old man, without a political party or any kind of armed force. There has been rioting, but apart from me nobody in the West believes the Shah to be in danger.'

'Insh'Allah,' the Prince said curtly. If God wills it. 'I am beginning to agree with my father. You in the West are weak. You do not understand the power of faith – even the faith of an heretic Muslim can move mountains. And remember, now there is a treaty, opening the border between Iran and Iraq. We have information that thousands of the Ayatollah's followers have crossed over. The Shah's men tortured to death Ayatollah Ghafari of Tehran. But against Khomeini the Shah will have no reply.'

'Because of the will of God?'

'No, because of the Shah's own excesses and the lack of will of President Carter.'

'It is certain?'

The Prince waved a hand. 'I say it now. The Shah of Iran will fall.'

'Jesus Christ,' Alex said. Alex touched his damp brow. Strange that the air here had turned ice cold. In the last five years the Shah's purchases from the US alone ran to $18,000 million; and in spite of his own efforts, Alex knew the Shah still owed over a hundred million pounds to Stanton Industries. If the Iranian régime collapsed, who could say what effect it would have? For the West – and for Stanton Industries.

The Prince hesitated, his eyes hooding. 'The armaments that you deal in—'

'I give you my word. Everything could be delivered here, before 1978 has ended, at the prices we will have agreed. If you choose to buy.'

The prince nodded. 'We want very much in the way of weapons, and the very, very best you have. Two hundred of your new Mark IX tanks, and a hundred more Mark VIII – if you can deliver within two years. Agreed?'

Alex thought his heart would stop. A hundred and fifty million dollars . . . He had got his project off the ground. He knew that if the Japanese could somehow be persuaded to go for his tank too, he would have a triumph.

'And there is more,' the prince said, opening one of Stanton Industries' glossy catalogues.

'More?'

'Much more!'

Alex, amazed, noted down the prince's additional requirements: arms and more arms, including fast missile hydrofoils for patrolling the Gulf, and two dozen more armoured helicopters he would use his Hacker Stanton links to obtain, indirectly, from the United States, as President Carter was still opposed to arms-sales in the Middle East, even to friendly states like the Saudi kingdom.

It was money beyond a fortune, and it meant he no longer had to worry about selling arms to Japan.

Chapter Twenty

A day and a half later, Alex was in Tokyo again.

The Hideki empire needed that source of refined oil in Iran: also, oil meant money. As far as Hideki knew, the Shah's government was not inclined to honour its contracts. A powerful middleman was needed, and Alex presented himself as the necessary intermediary. He spoke Farsi and had been a regular visitor to Tehran since childhood: the Shah knew him well.

'I'll make that deal happen for you,' Alex said at last. Takahashi's face was entirely blank. 'For no fee.'

A touch of scorn. 'No fee?'

Alex sipped single malt. 'Except this. The right in writing to vote your stock in Stanton Industries and the British bank Beauford Cleves until September 31st. Agreed?' No answer. Alex said it plainly. 'If you want your property made yours officially in Iran, you *have* to go along with me in this.'

Takahashi looked sour. He licked his lips. 'This matter of the Beauford Cleves bank is almost one of loyalty.'

Alex relaxed, looking at his most dangerous. 'Loyalty? To whom? To Beauford the traitor, who is loyal only to the money coming out of Tokyo? Or to *me* – the man who is giving you Arigata?'

'I'll need to think before I can choose!'

'Of course.' Alex was alone. Takahashi had two advisers in another room, and no doubt Saigo Hideki sitting near a phone.

In Takahashi's absence, Alex reflected again on how much difference the huge arms sales to Saudi Arabia would make to Stanton Industries. It was a very potent secret to keep.

Hideki's aide came back. 'Very well,' he said. 'As long as you do not fail us in Tehran.'

'Trust me, Takahashi. As they say, I know where all the bodies are buried.' He stuck out his hand. 'Done?'

'Done.'

Maggie Langton was doing the driving through the easy, late-night traffic of midweek London. Her Volkswagen GTi handled pleasurably, with plenty of power in reserve. Kiko was supposed to be coming to London soon. Maggie thought that over, driving through the light rain.

Terry Katz sat in the front passenger seat as they followed a black

Rolls-Royce from EC1 towards a company flat in Kensington.

'Interesting,' said Terry. He used a telephoto lens, snapped a couple of pictures. 'So, we already have your friend Battersby covered?'

'Yes,' she said absently. 'Franklin snapped him going in. He's there all right, waiting.'

'Oh-oh.' Terry slid his camera down out of sight as the car between their own and the Rolls up ahead turned left off Old Brompton Road. They stopped at the traffic lights. He murmured to her without turning his head, enjoying the chase but not really interested in any of this, 'Fortunately, even if the driver looks into the rearview mirror . . .'

'Beauford's chauffeur doesn't know me from Adam, let alone from Eve.'

They went further, turning off on to Queen's Gate, then unobtrusively passing the Rolls as it found a parking space. The passenger, a portly man, emerged.

Maggie hurried back, making sure the uniformed driver of the Rolls did not see her. She tapped on the rear door of a Transit van. Franklin slid the door open from inside. They all crammed on to a small wooden bench.

'Not very comfortable,' the black photographer said, smiling. He twiddled a dial on the display board in front of him.

'It sure isn't,' Terry said, squeezing in between them, yawning.

'Less of that.' Maggie said excitedly, 'Who's inside? Just Battersby, still?' Franklin nodded. 'Let's take a listen. The peer should be there in a minute.'

The radio-broadcast voice of Lord Beauford said, 'As I told you, James, I've had a few financial reverses. Even had to sell some of the shares in my own bank. God, these bloody recessions seem to cut deeper and deeper!'

'You'll be down to your last million or two,' Battersby said. There was a chink of glasses. 'I say, I'm really touched that you trust me in these things.'

A pause. 'Because I know you hate that man almost as much as I do.'

'Oh, I'm quite close to Alex Stanton's heart in some ways,' James Battersby said modestly. 'Anyway, things are going very well indeed. With you still on the Stanton Board we know everything about them, strengths and weaknesses and future plans. When you told me about their intention to dawn-raid that Dassault-controlled company—'

'Buy shares only through Switzerland!' Beauford said. There was another chink of glasses. Faint traffic noise came through the double glazed windows – the same cars that passed Maggie's van. 'That way we can't be traced and there's no proof.'

'No, thank God!' Battersby said. 'Although you must be in a difficult position,' he continued, goadingly, 'officially on the Stanton Board of Directors to represent your own shares, but effectively representing

Hideki – informing on and weakening the Stantons. Then there are these ever so slightly illegal deals on your own account . . .'

'Don't even think about it,' Beauford said menacingly. 'I can't abide a traitor. I prize loyalty above all things.'

'Of course! Trust me. Honestly, you can!'

For a moment rain drummed on the roof of their van as they eavesdropped, caught up in the conversation.

Beauford laughed. 'Anyway, this is what I want you to do now. And remember, not a whisper to anybody, and I'll put fifty thousand pounds into your pocket – all tax evaded, naturally.'

'I have him,' Maggie said excitedly. 'This time I have him.'

'What are you going to do?' Terry asked, idly curious. 'Get another scoop into one of the big Sunday papers? Or sell the tapes to Alex Stanton?'

She pursed her lips, still undecided.

A few days later Alex flew back from Tehran in a scheduled Air France 747, immediately after the Hideki Corporation was given title to its oil refinery.

In his absence, things had happened in London, as he had arranged. He read with pleasure an article headed BEAUFORD SCANDAL: BATTERSBY GIVES EVIDENCE.

More importantly, the Bank of England and, above it, the British government itself, had concluded that Lord Beauford was no longer a fit and proper person to run a British-registered bank. The Bank of England supervised and regulated the banking system of the United Kingdom, colonies and dependencies, and exercised similar supervisory rights over foreign banks domiciled or operating in British territory. Yesterday, it had acted. The Governor of the Bank of England had acknowledged that the odour of scandal around Beauford Cleves had become impossible to ignore. New blood was urgently sought, because the old blood had proved to be tainted.

In other words, Alex thought cynically, Beauford's been found out.

At Heathrow, he rang Kintyre.

'Last night,' said the soft Scots voice, excited, 'his fellow directors acted.'

'All legal and above board – and he doesn't know?'

'It went just as you wanted it,' Kintyre said primly. 'Beauford knows nothing.'

'I'll meet you there in an hour.'

A silence. 'Very well.'

Alex's red E-type was waiting in the long-stay car park. He jammed a cassette of Wagner into the player and drove straight into the city, his jaw set. Summer had come. London was hot, sweaty, crowded; exhaust fumes swirled over sticky asphalt. It was riot weather, except that you did not have riots in Britain – yet. He suddenly felt an overpowering rage. It was time to hit back at the traitors who wanted to make things worse.

Near St Paul's he turned into a side-street and entered the tall Victorian block by the back way; he had learned that storming the castles of the enemy is not always the best way to gain your objectives.

Kintyre was waiting in a small office, and he came out and shook Alex's hand. In the offices of Beauford Cleves the atmosphere was heavy and threatening: a thunderstorm, about to happen.

Alex led Kintyre to a closed door, then paused.

From behind the door a complacent voice boomed out. 'I understand perfectly, Mr Takahashi. Tokyo wanted to keep its hand hidden, so you worked through Switzerland. The banks there have an admirable sense of confidentiality; I've used them myself. As long as I meet your principals soon, the new owners, I'm entirely satisfied. After all, they have control of my company! Of course, I see that my *own* position is quite secure—'

Alex felt a wave of hatred so powerful that he kicked the door open. In the comfortably upholstered room, a Glenfiddich bottle near him, sat Lord Beauford. Takahashi sat smiling beside him. But Peter Cowan stood by the wall, muscular arms folded.

'Kintyre is the new chairman here,' Alex said. 'This bank is under his control, now – with the approval of the Bank of England. And you, Lord Beauford, are a trespasser.'

'What?' The older man stood up, flushing. 'Who the hell do you think— ?'

Alex outroared him, forefinger stabbing. 'I want to tell you, you are a fat, complacent traitor. You may think that the scandals you have been involved in will be treated in the traditional British way: that is, hushed up.' He gave a grim smile. 'But I am going to have the records of Beauford Cleves checked thoroughly. It may take some time, but I am certain I'll find enough dirt to ruin you, utterly and completely – if you dare to oppose my actions now or at any time in the future.'

Beauford had turned white. His breath wheezed in as he turned to Alex. His face was working frantically. 'But it's my bank! It's my life!'

Alex took a step forward, towering over him. 'Then you've lost your life as well as your bank – you traitor. You had the choice of looking after your own or taking that money from Tokyo. What do you think a Japanese like Mr Takahashi here would have done? Chosen loyalty! Why are they so great? Because they choose loyalty to their own – *every time.* But in you, greed triumphed over loyalty, and now you will pay.'

Lord Beauford's eyes were glazed. He turned to Takahashi, but his face showed only amusement. 'But it was such an opportunity! They are so strong, strong. They told me they were coming to Europe in force—'

'Oh, they will be,' Alex said. He was breathing hard. 'But too late for you.'

Beauford stammered, 'Why are you here?'

'To enjoy myself.' He turned to Cowan. 'Throw this thing out into the street.'

Alex turned his back so as not to see Lord Beauford's undignified squirming.

Takahashi pushed three cut-glass decanters forward. 'A drink?'

Alex chose the dry sherry. 'A small celebration.'

Afterwards, he left the offices himself. He had disposed of one enemy, but revenge was not as sweet as he had anticipated.

It all costs so much. Effort, strain, threats and violence . . . and for what? Loyalty to the firm, to my friends? To my country? What about me? Who gives that loyalty to me? Maggie, once? Kiko, sometimes? Caroline, my wife? What is this all *for*?

He had no answer.

He felt exhausted and dizzy, and very alone. He was trembling as he climbed into his sports car, and he felt strangely remote from everything as he drove through the beginnings of the rush hour back to the long, curving avenue in St John's Wood where he lived.

On his own doorstep he turned, wondering what Caroline would say. It was still now, and the summer trees were all in full green leaf, but he felt ugly. His mood darkened even more.

He sighed, and opened the door, calling out for Caro.

Nobody there. In the hallway lined with handpainted Satsuma plates he found he was trembling again and his vision suddenly blurred. There had been so much tension, and no one here to listen and soothe as he released it. Kiko had been right. Lord Ross's daughter was irrelevant to him, and his marriage was a sham.

He collapsed into a chair by the telephone. He felt cold, and he was shivering. For a moment felt an impulse to call Maggie, or David. But they had their own problems, and he had no certainty they would approve of what he had done. He put his tired head in his hands for a moment.

Then he saw the rest of the mail, neatly piled up on the floor. He squatted down to sort through it and then found the blue airmail letter with Japanese stamps on. He lifted the letter up, scenting a faint, familiar fragrance. Kiko?

Kiko . . . She had replied.

He was smiling even before he opened it. Things were coming together at last.

David Bryant was obliged to go to the House of Commons early in the afternoon for an emergency debate on industrial policy. He listened to the opposition begin, arms folded and legs crossed, an expression of polite interest on his face.

The chamber was not exactly crowded, he had to admit; but under his cool exterior worry had turned into aggression. He listened to the opposition's clichés politely, but when he rose to speak he tore into his opponent with gusto.

'As for my honourable and gallant friend's dislike of "lame duck" industries, I agree: but this government intends to turn them into profitable and attractive swans! I suggest that if he wishes to shoot some lame ducks, he should get himself back to his 12,000 acres of grouse moor near Jedburgh, and leave the reconstruction of British industry to those who understand it!'

There was a chorus of approval. David left the chamber soon afterwards, satisfied. He walked to the river in a thoughtful mood, crossing Westminster Bridge. He proceeded along the Albert Embankment slowly, giving himself some thinking time.

Arigata.

The Japanese thought he was helpless, did they?

David was hardly aware of his police guard walking behind him, eyes alert. The Minister, whom he had come to both like and respect greatly, was thinking so hard about something he seemed lost to the world.

David crossed the Thames again at Vauxhall, and entered the huge, coffin-plan Stanton Industries building.

Alex met him inside, in the private directors' club overlooking the river. He leaned one elbow on the bar and he was smiling.

'A fine performance, David. Scotch?'

'Thanks. You were there?'

'I came back early to bear witness to Lord Beauford's disgrace. He should make the Old Bailey!' Alex gave a big appreciative laugh.

'Congratulations on getting him off your back – and off your board.'

'His reputation is shot, now, even if he buys a not guilty verdict from the law . . .'

'How is Japan?'

'Still a problem or two, David, though I did them a service in Iran. Kiko's been in touch again, and she really does believe her grandfather and some of the others are – well, like conspirators from the age of dictators. Apparently this man Hakagawa has hinted a few times that the Russians ought to be made to give up the Japanese territory they occupied in '45 – *by force*, if necessary.'

'Armed force?' David gulped down his Scotch. This had to be confirmation for his fears. 'Then should we be dealing with such people at all?'

Alex looked at him before beckoning over the barman. 'Something bothering you? You look a bit grim.'

Worried that he was revealing so much, David forced himself to grin and relax, one foot rocking on the brass bar-rail. 'Must be the cut and thrust of debate. You're never quite certain who will win the duel, you know.' David finished his second Scotch and then followed Alex to the private elevator.

As Alex hit the button to call for the elevator, their eyes met. 'Do you have any more news about our friends east of the sun?'

David nodded. He knew he was about to break a confidence, but it seemed important. 'Yes. I can give some confirmation to Kiko's notions. A high-level delegation was sent over from Tokyo to lean on us – and I've been doing some official checking. This Hakagawa is genuinely a rightist, and both he and Hideki are pushing Japan hard towards nuclear power – and the possession of plutonium.'

Alex jerked back. 'I've always been afraid of this business erupting. Over the years we've had enough bad publicity over our involvements in Vietnam and Iran, but this could be a hundred times worse.'

Things became clear to David. 'I see. So that's why you've always made sure Hideki isn't directly represented on your board of directors?'

'Exactly. You see, David, Kiko might just be right . . .'

'And so – we have to try to stop them?'

Alex gave a grim smile. 'You say that as a question.'

'And I'll repeat it as a question,' David said with quiet force. 'If Hideki is involved in a conspiracy, and the conspiracy desires to rearm Japan, perhaps with nuclear weapons, we must try to stop it: yes or no?'

'Even if a "yes" costs me that break-through in Japan, David?'

'I asked a straight question first.' He moved closer to Alex. 'Now, what is more important: stopping them, or supporting Stanton Industries?'

Alex met his gaze. 'You mean you're asking me if we have to stop them taking power and getting nuclear technology, *whatever the cost?*'

'Yes, I am.'

Alex did not reply. They walked out of the main, guarded doors. David feared Alex would be no ally now. Could he really want his firm to flourish, even at the expense of letting Hideki win? Feeling very alone, David felt obliged to change the subject.

They walked by the river, going past the Tate and then Parliament, then along Whitehall: at the low barrier closing off Downing Street, a police sergeant saluted David and then stood back to allow them in.

David saw the door to Number 10 was still the familiar black, with the ancient lantern over the doorstep. They were escorted straight through to the garden party. The Cabinet Minister, and his guest.

It was a wonderful summer's day, and David breathed in quickly. In this greenery, you would hardly believe you were in the heart of London. People sipped Pimms and champagne and the shadows of the trees grew imperceptibly longer in the afternoon light. He turned to Alex, who was glancing around at the other guests. 'Maggie's right about the magic of flowers, isn't she? She used to flood her offices with them.'

Alex merely laughed. 'Thanks again. See you.'

David glanced around once more. It still pleased him to be here; the outsider had come inside, and been made welcome. He glimpsed politicians, diplomats speaking English, French, Russian, and half a dozen other languages. Artists of different kinds. Media faces. An entertaining mixture, in these pleasant and historic surroundings, though his mood was really too serious to appreciate the social pleasantries. There was no longer any choice, not if Kiko could really confirm the dangers of Japan rearming from the inside. He had to act.

First he saw the political officer from the US Embassy Alex had identified as a CIA agent. He drifted over, caught the man's eye. 'I wonder if I could have a word.'

'Huh?' The man had been hitting the whisky hard. 'Sure.'

David put it obliquely. 'I was wondering what you think of Japan.'

'Damn strange place.' He peered at David. 'Went there on R-and-R from Vietnam a couple of times. Me, don't like the way they get a free ride on our arms budget.'

'Is that official policy?'

'Who knows, with *this* president?'

David grimaced. Perhaps he should have done this through channels, after all. He looked up at Lord Nelson's statue on the huge column again as more guests arrived at Number 10. There was a hero: he wondered if Britain could make men like that any longer.

Nothing important is ever said . . . ever done . . . He saw the man he wanted.

It was Kerensky, the tall roving correspondent of *Pravda*. In other words, or so David had been told in Tokyo, a KGB agent. He was speaking in clipped Russian to one of his embassy's senior military attachés.

David came up to them hesitantly. Then, as the correspondent strolled away from the embassy's military man, David made his decision. Better push this through semi-official channels. Try to think of it as a private briefing to a genuine journalist. His stomach suddenly felt queasy, but he had to act. It was his duty.

'Oleg Kerensky.' His voice was determined. 'It's been a while since the Tokyo conference.'

The man smiled down, taller than David. 'Mr Bryant. Belated congratulations on your promotion; I'm sure it was well-deserved.'

His face was smooth and seemed comparatively guileless, though there was a concealed strength there which David recognized immediately. Then their glances met. Kerensky's eyes flashed at the contact.

They stood close together but facing away, and talked out of the sides of their mouths. 'I am listening, Mr Bryant.'

'I have something you may wish to take back to your government.'

The man's eyes momentarily flared with interest, then were hooded again: he quickly glanced around. 'Not here.'

'No, of course not.' David's heart was pounding. Then he committed himself. 'In an hour. Kensington Gardens.'

A whisper. 'Where?'

'Beside Peter Pan.'

'Who is he?'

'The boy who wouldn't grow up,' David said. 'It's a bronze statue, west side of the Long Water.'

'I see. Very well. An hour.' The Russian half turned away, then turned back. 'Either you are very foolish, or very brave.'

'Or both,' David said grimly. He watched Kerensky disappear.

David joined in with the political gossip for another half hour, then left.

He strolled through Downing Street. Once in Whitehall, he walked quickly to Trafalgar Square and then flagged down a black cab. He sat in the back, not relaxed, throwing quick glances around in case he was being followed. The Mall; then Buckingham Palace.

He got out south of Hyde Park, and walked quickly through the gate towards the trees. He checked his watch and slowed his pace. The trees in the park flourished masses of green. He reached the gleaming water of the Serpentine, and walked on between the green-striped hired deckchairs. He pressed both hands on to his heart to try to slow it, and he thought now of simply turning his back on the crisis and going home.

That's the easy, safe, cowardly thing. Never take a risk. See a problem and ignore it . . .

He could not do that. He had to go on, walking west, seeing the boathouse opposite flying its flags and the Post Office tower tall and grey in the distance. A few grey squirrels darted about among the grey pigeons; people threw pieces of bread to the swans. It was so peaceful he could not believe in the reality of what he was doing.

Then, to his left, he saw age-darkened bronze: Peter Pan. The boy's arms were spread wide and he was blowing a horn.

David stared at the boy who had refused to grow up. He came closer, touched the cold bronze.

He turned his back and sat down on one of the park benches facing the water. Wooden posts linked with chains crossed the lake. Green willows, swaying in the wind, hid the far shore.

He closed his eyes for a moment. It was a hot day and perspiration prickled. Then a hand touched his shoulder. He jerked awake, wondering if this was finally it. The discovery.

'We are not being overheard.' It was an accented voice.

David looked round casually. 'No.'

'But somewhere else would be better; back to back, maybe.'

David blinked, licked his lips. 'I suddenly find myself unwilling to confide in you, or in the people behind you.'

The Slavic gaze was level, concerned. 'You have already made that decision, Mr Bryant.'

David's lips twitched, but he still said nothing.

'Let's walk,' Kerensky said. They headed away into the trees. 'Maybe there is some favour I can do for you.'

'I will not be suborned and I will not be threatened,' David answered heatedly. 'That was tried in East Berlin – and in Tokyo. Didn't Alan Hoyle or your East German friends tell you?'

'Hoyle, tell *me*? He is English, your once-upon-time friend. Nothing to do with me.' He led David to another bench, this one concealed among the trees. 'Sit down, keep looking round. Do everything slowly.'

There was agony in David's voice. Hands folded into fists, he beat them together. 'How can I trust your country to do right?'

A grey squirrel scampered towards them, then sat up on its hind legs and regarded them, nose twitching. Kerensky touched his forehead. 'Pain and suffering and betrayal and disappointment; that's in the soul of Russia.'

'How could you use people like Alan Hoyle?'

'I don't. Even the mad old men in power don't any longer. Hoyle is a renegade, David Bryant. Surely you realize that? And he is a British traitor, you know. From *your* society, not ours. We wish to compete with you, that is true, but there is still our Communism, Socialism, still a belief in equality, liberty, and brotherhood – some of the time.'

Somehow he made the slogans seem right, and the humour was a very human touch. David gave a wan smile. 'Have you ever seen *Ivan the Terrible*?'

'Yes, and I cannot deny there has been that darkness. But Ivan is dead, Dzerzhinsky is dead, Stalin is dead, Beria is dead. We have emerged from the shadows. Now, what help is it which you wish to give me?'

David saw a girl who looked the same age as his elder daughter come running along the path, laughing, chasing a squirrel. He spoke with sudden frankness. 'What does the Soviet government feel about Japanese rearmament with nuclear weapons?'

The man's long, bony face froze. Then he hissed from between his teeth. 'Mr Bryant, is this a serious— ?'

'Deadly serious,' David said crisply, now that he had committed himself: he had to convince this man. 'I am speaking to you as a member of the British government and as a private citizen. In Tokyo there is a faction in the government, led by Hakagawa the Interior Minister.'

The Russian lips stiffened. 'Hakagawa. The warmonger from Manchuria.'

David knew the truth would be convincing enough, especially with a specific detail added. 'He has given secret speeches about the Pacific war: he regrets nothing. You know of the Japanese islands which Stalin occupied—'

The long face twisted. 'Those islands are no longer Japanese.' He patted his gleaming forehead. 'Believe me, Mr Bryant, the old men in the Kremlin will say this: "The soil of Mother Russia is sacred". But why are you telling this to me?'

'Why do you think? They want plutonium, in Japan. That's why Arigata exists! I am giving you a warning because I want this terrible thing stopped.'

The Slavic eyes narrowed, then widened. 'Oh, you suspect I have a direct line to the Politburo? Who do you think I am?'

David's eyes measured him: a poised, fit body, and a hint of ruthlessness in the blue and intelligent eyes. 'General Glykov's man. KGB.'

'Nonsense,' Kerensky said, a curt and automatic denial.

'But Glykov must take it to the Politburo. Listen, Hakagawa and Saigo Hideki want to build up the Japanese armaments industry, then rearm; and import plutonium, enough for bombs.'

Kerensky's face was outraged. 'Do they never learn? Very well. I will tell this to—' He made a visible effort to calm himself. 'Thank you. You are a man of peace, are you?'

'I am a friend of democracy and of peace, yes. That's all I want in the world! They are rearming in Japan and in the first instance it is aimed at you, just as their industrial might is being used against us in the West. What will you do now?'

The Russian was buttoning up his jacket. 'Make other checks. Then the Politburo will decide on some action, I presume. But we will make them know what we think, in Japan. We are the power in Asia, now.' His eyes looked somewhere else. 'I must go.'

'I have to tell you,' David said, sweat flowing under his arms, 'there may not be much time left.'

Chapter Twenty-one

There was a tap on the door and his secretary poked her head round. 'Your visitor, Minister.'

Alex bustled into the big room overlooking Victoria Street, tanned and grinning, right hand outstretched. 'Industry and government, hand in hand?'

'Literally as well as metaphorically?'

'Of course! A new beginning. Never give up, David.'

'Never.' David sat down, sat back. He steepled his fingers. 'So. What about your arms deals with the Shah and the Saudis?'

Alex was immediately cautious. 'It's an old-fashioned design, but it looks like the Shah is sticking with the Challenger tank rather than coming to Stanton Industries. And I've heard some things from Saudi.' Alex grunted. 'Carter's people are leaning on them not to uprate their defenses, although the Russians of course are still building up their friends in Iraq and other places.'

'Oh, those OPEC countries can afford your tanks, Alex.'

'Even the Shah? He might be in trouble, David.'

David was shocked.

Alex looked at him. 'A quick sale of the Mark VIII to our own country would be the best advertisement of all – apart from the money.'

'Apart from the money.' David sighed. 'We're still in the hands of the International Monetary Fund surgeons, and their motto is cut, cut, and cut again. Maybe by the end of the year there might be something I can do . . . Where does that leave your Mark IX?'

'In limbo – maybe. Don't tell my board!'

'Your secrets are safe with me, Alex.'

Alex's tone became serious. 'Hope so.'

David stood up, turned to the window to look down on the street. At this time in the evening it was busy with SW1's grindingly slow commuter traffic. Friday; the weekend starts here, David remembered from another life. 'You must be pleased to have seen Beauford off. You always distrusted him.'

'I most certainly did.' Alex put his black attaché case on the huge desk. 'He was the lesser of two evils. Effectively, he stood for Hideki's shares: that's still about thirty percent of the company. And our articles of association say a large holding like that has to be represented.'

'And you preferred to have him rather than an open Hideki man?'

'A hell of a choice!' Then Alex's voice turned threatening. 'Let's just say the Hideki business might be best kept at arm's length.'

David sighed, and his eyes strayed to the family photograph by his elbow. Megan and his two girls, one sunny morning on Caernarvon Castle. He wanted his family, not business. There were books and bound government reports and legislation behind glass in this brown study, along with dictionaries and grammars for the languages David spoke.

Alex had clicked both locks, and the spring-loaded case opened up. 'Now, to show my appreciation, presents.'

David smiled. Arabian jewellery, cheap from the bazaar, suitable for his two girls; and some posters of the exotic countries Alex visited. 'The girls will like this.'

'They're still being raised on Welsh leeks and Welsh rhetoric in Fishguard, are they? I bet you miss them.'

'Yes. You can imagine—' Abruptly, he changed the subject. 'Alex, if you'd married Maggie and had children, how old would—?'

Alex stepped back, his mouth clamping shut. His hands were still full of jewels. These were real, and his present for Megan. 'I don't live in a world of make-believe. And as for children, well, I'm hardly ideal father material – or husband material – am I?'

'I suppose not . . .' David felt oddly embarrassed.

'But I do have my moments.' Alex grinned lasciviously.

David Bryant sat down again and picked up a gold Parker. He swivelled about in his chair. 'So what's the latest?'

Instantly, Alex too was all business. 'As for our friends in Tokyo, will they choose my Mark VIII and IX, when they re-equip their ground forces? I hope so. But thanks to your pressures at the Tokyo Trade Normalization Conference they'll certainly buy the uranium we mine in Australia, and with that and our involvement with Arigata we should make a great deal of money.'

The leather chair creaked as David shifted about uncomfortably. 'It's a pity it had to be nuclear power and nuclear reprocessing. I don't want this country turned into the nuclear dustbin of the world. I mean, you've read Maggie's pieces?'

'Bloody strong stuff,' Alex admitted. 'She's almost scared *me*. Leukaemia clusters, cancers. Twenty thousand years of pollution – or more.'

'Right. Already we're getting complaints about the Irish Sea from our opposite numbers in Dublin – and they don't know the half of it.'

An eighteenth-century Dutch seascape made a watery-blue, colourful blur on one wall. Alex went up to look at it, admiring the texture of the brush strokes. There was corkboard alongside it, with telegrams and postcards. One showed a da Vinci painting. He reached for it. 'All being well, David, uranium and plutonium will be unpleasant hangovers from the past, come the twenty-first century. There'll be nuclear fusion instead, clean and cheap, and without harmful by-products.'

David went to the drinks cabinet. 'What do you think Hideki wants, long term?'

Alex tensed, but luckily David had turned his back. 'Kiko seems to think he has some serious plans for his country.'

David turned around with a silver tray, single malt Scotch and tumblers rattling on it. 'You make him sound both mysterious and threatening.'

Alex sat on one corner of the desk. 'Hideki? Maybe Kiko has just dragged me into a family argument. After all, in your circles there must be enough prejudiced and unfavourable rumours about me.'

'In which you take considerable pride. I sometimes wonder why you don't enter politics yourself.'

They clinked glasses. 'I need to straighten out the family firm, first.'

'And you're still trying to diversify out of armaments?'

'Of course. There's been the good luck of the North Sea oil boom, and now we're switching more resources into civil projects.'

'How's the new tank factory coming along?'

'A miracle, a dream come true. Far ahead of schedule.'

David regarded him. 'The factory . . . you really think you can compete on equal terms with Japan?'

'I'd better be able to,' Alex replied.

'Any news from Tokyo, then?'

'Naturally, anything referred to here is in confidence.' Alex said. 'But this is the situation. We've cast our bread on to the waters; it must return.'

'Arigata will be formally opened soon. They'll probably set the date around September 1st. You'll get a big completion bonus, won't you?'

Alex rubbed at his eyes. 'Supposedly. But it's beginning to look as if the odds are against us, David. We only have a minority interest in Arigata, and whatever good deals we come up with, I can't make Tokyo accept them. I've got the terrible feeling that Hideki and Hakagawa will win – unless you in the government can do something.'

David pushed his chair back. 'We're running things as a coalition; effectively, we're an unpopular minority government. There's little interest in abroad. Our priority is survival. There'll have to be an election in '78 or '79. The government that emerges then will be in a strong position, but for now, in the cabinet we're just living from day to day.'

Alex stood up, stretching his arms. He looked exhausted, but David already knew he was at his most dangerous when backed into a corner. 'So we're both waiting for the returns?'

'So it seems.'

David had them driven to St John's Wood.

The government Rover drove away, leaving them on the quiet, tree-lined street near the park.

'Sir Hugh Stanton,' Alex said, flatly. David had just broken the news to him. 'It has a very respectable ring, doesn't it? Almost as good as Lord Stanton. Lord Stanton of Craigburn, no doubt.'

David clapped him on the shoulder. 'Respectability isn't everything.'

'In this country? I think it is.'

'Then something is wrong with this country. Achievement should be what counts; and achievement against the odds should count more than anything.'

Inside the house, Alex described the firm's situation in more detail. The huge amount of debt they had taken on could become a crippling burden, especially as some was from Beauford's bank and some was from the Hideki Corporation's Nagasaki Bank, and might be withdrawn. But it had been a necessary risk.

'Things could be looking up soon, though?'

'They'd better be, David,' Alex replied as he mixed the drinks.

'Is the Japanese reactor at Arigata still on schedule?'

'Very nearly. Very nearly.'

David stared at him. It was not like Alex to equivocate – not to a friend and ally, anyway. 'Is Arigata up to schedule?'

'No.' Alex turned around suddenly. His face bore a worried expression. 'Look, I have somebody coming here later I'd like you to meet. I have to do it right in Japan. Otherwise things could get desperate.'

'Oh?' David threw his overcoat across a chair. 'McCourt, is it?'

'A woman.'

'A woman! Christ! Where's Caroline tonight?'

Alex put the drinks down and gestured towards the front hall.

David glanced around. The house, as always, was as quiet and perfectly groomed as a corpse fresh from an expensive undertaker; Caroline's orders had seen to that. But there was no life here, no warmth. He looked at Alex's turned back and suddenly felt sorry for him.

'What's that you're tidying away, Alex?'

'Sportsgear.'

'Oh? You've started to do something with Caroline?'

'God, no,' Alex said, startled. 'It's my kendo kit.'

'You're really getting into things Japanese, aren't you?'

'Maybe I just like hitting people, David.'

They sat down in the huge kitchen. Every surface was gleaming, David noted. The sterility was painful. Alex put down some blue Wedgwood plates, plugged in an electric kettle, then opened one of the tall fridges. David enjoyed the snack; chilled mange-tout soup, smoked haddock pâté, a spicy lentil salad that tasted Indian, and an exotic Chinese tea to follow.

'Anyway, hurry up and finish. I'd like to get going.'

'Who,' David asked before following Alex downstairs, 'are we shooting dead tonight?'

'You'll find out.'

He did.

They were shooting money.

The target boards, set fifty feet away in the cellar, today held crosses of reproduction banknotes – a green thousand-dollar bill in the centre, then hundred dollar notes, then single greenbacks. The rules were simple. One bullet per note.

David laughed, the noise sounding flat and dead in the corklined, underground gunroom.

Alex unlocked one of the reinforced steel lockers and then pulled out a wooden case. He flipped it open to reveal two massive, gleaming revolvers, and then selected a box of cartridges. He rolled up his sleeves and held one of the shiny brass casings up to the light. 'In 1878 Colt brought out another model of pistol, a 44 pistol calibred to match the Winchester 1873 rifle.'

'So what do we have here?'

'Straight from a Dallas saleroom – here we have examples of the earlier model, the single-action Army issue Peacemaker which was the real cowboy's gun, the Wild West gun. A pair of genuine 45s,' Alex said. 'Frontier Colts. They beat anything any Stanton ever did for longevity. Did you know they were in production continuously from 1873 till 1941, and they restarted the production line in the fifties? Let's do some shooting with them.'

He began loading, whistling quietly.

David picked up the other gun. The ironmongery weighed enough to make it an effort to lift, let alone aim properly. He pivoted to the right, arm extended, and closed his left eye to take aim. He had death in his hand, cold iron death, and to his own shock he suddenly felt excitement: this was power. 'How many men have these guns killed, do you think?'

'A few, maybe. They came from Texas, and – hell, you've met Ray and heard his stories. The Colt 45 is good for four hundred yards range – if your shooting is good enough.' Alex spun about on one heel and fired the first shot. 'Excellent! In a dead President's eye, almost. That's a thousand dollars I've scored!'

'And bloody noisily,' David said as the smoke curled away into the airconditioning vents, 'if I may say so.'

He fired two shots quickly himself, coming within a foot of the target's centre in both cases.

The recoil was tremendous, and you had to fight to keep the gun under control, but that was part of the excitement.

'Let's make a proper start. Twenty pounds to the winner.'

'Done!' Alex said.

The cork panelling muffled the gunfire sounds, but they both put on earmuffs when firing; the rounds made a deafening noise in this confined space, and David found the black-powder smoke quite choking, in spite of the powerful suction from the air conditioning system.

Alex now used the two-handed stance first popularized by the FBI, and shot quickly and accurately. 'Four thousand, two hundred dollars!'

David replied more slowly, not really liking guns.

'Three thousand.'

After both six-shooters had been emptied Alex leaned against the wall. He looked very tired now, and haunted.

'David,' he said, 'I'm in trouble.'

David put the gun down. 'Right. We'd better talk about it.'

They went to the conservatory examining some rare hothouse flowers. The heated air in the glassed-in space was heavy and perfumed. David stroked pretty, pale flowers; Madagascar periwinkle, *Catharanthus roseus*. Alex would read from the little cards Caroline had printed with Latin, botanical names; there were flowering plants from Burma, Ceylon, Chaco Boreal, and the Molucca Sea, with a little note on latitude and longitude.

'I didn't know Caroline had such green fingers,' David said to his old friend.

'She can make some things flourish,' Alex replied, rather sharply.

David glanced at him. 'You really won't get back together?'

'Bloody women! I don't even know if she's actually left me.' Alex still had his Colt pistol in his hands. It dangled between his knees when he sat down. 'She comes back here quite often, quarrels, sometimes cries, sleeps with me always, quarrels again, goes. Can you believe that?'

David remainded standing. 'So what is the problem you mentioned, exactly?'

Alex looked straight at him. 'I believe Arigata is behind schedule to teach me a lesson, and remind me that I need that money from Japan. Hideki and his people have control of the schedule. They can let me finish the contract and pick up the money for it – or they can postpone till my firm is financially desperate.'

'I see,' David said thoughtfully. 'How do they know that much about your financial – ah. Lord Beauford.'

'The bastard. No doubt he was selling Tokyo information.'

'Then it seems to me you'll probably have to go along with what they want.'

Alex twisted his lips. 'David . . . I have reason to believe that Saigo Hideki is involved in a kind of conspiracy within Japanese politics.'

David swallowed. Then a buzzer sounded. 'A right-wing conspiracy, obviously?'

Alex was looking at him curiously. 'Exactly. Something like a secret society. And more to the point, I believe we have been tricked. Both of us, tricked and pressurized. Arigata is not for peaceful industrial uses;

nor is the plutonium and U235 my company has agreed to send, given your official authorization.'

'Jesus Christ,' David said. This could be the end of much more than their two careers. But then he remembered the other things he and his predecessors had always signed, allowing contracts for chemical warfare and other, worse things, to stand. Then, 'But you don't know any of this for certain?'

'Not for certain.'

'Nor does Kiko, who I presume is your source?'

'Not proof, David,' Alex said bitterly. 'Not proof. And Maggie has been digging around for facts, too.'

David shook his head. There was a pause. 'I'm rather scared. Hideki scares me.'

'Yes. This could be the biggest conspiracy of all time.'

'If, you say! Could be! Then how can we possibly back out – if all we have is suspicion?'

'We can't back out, David.'

'If we found proof, what then?'

Alex closed his eyes for a moment. His voice was grim. 'The multi-million dollar question, eh? I suppose I would have to try and stop him. But as it is . . .' He spread his hands. The buzzer called them again, a flat, abrasive sound. 'Like I told you, I'm in trouble. It's semi-public trouble, too. The Japanese ventures have been delayed, I suspect deliberately, so I will have to attend Arigata in person to collect the final payment. And I need that money, David. I'm committed.'

'I see,' David said, shocked. 'I see. And so you'd like me to do something, if I can?'

'Exactly.' Alex shook his head as the buzzer sounded again. 'Excuse me. I'm expecting a visitor, who'll tell you more.'

At the front door, Alex looked at the video monitor. It was dark outside and, beyond the tall metal railings, it had been raining; wetness gleamed everywhere. He recognized his visitor, and hit a concealed switch. The steel reinforced door clicked open.

Kiko Hideki was here, alone. Two cases were beside her knee. After the black cab roared away down the street she stepped inside, blinking, and lowered her umbrella. It dripped. 'Alex?' She peered around myopically. He put the hallway light on.

She wore a thick white fur coat and her blue-black hair trailed, wetly, into her eyes. She saw David and turned immediately back to Alex. 'Your friend in the government. So this is business?'

Alex embraced her, towering over her. 'It always begins in business, Kiko. I don't know how it ends. Haven't read the script. Come inside. It's warm.'

She smiled crookedly. 'If only that was so.'

They sat around the large, polished table in the dining room. The atmosphere was strangely businesslike in spite of everything. In the middle were decanters and mineral water and ice.

'I've asked you here, Kiko, because our Japanese ventures are in trouble. Therefore, I'm in trouble.'

Kiko only looked at him: her eyes were wide, and her lips were quivering.

'What has been happening?' David asked.

'The government in Tokyo are slow over the paperwork for our people and the things we must import. Arigata is behind schedule and we are getting the blame. Further, I don't like the atmosphere that's being generated there. We've even been hit by riots.'

Kiko had sat patiently, saying nothing. Her eyes gleamed at Alex, the sparkle of anger in them. 'You have disappointed me. I told you not to deal with my grandfather, and yet you dealt with him. Tanks and guns, then – the worst thing of all.'

David jerked away from that last comment. She had to mean atomic weapons. It occurred to him then that Alex was opening up like this, which was so unlike him, in the hope that David could get HMG to do something.

'I didn't see any alternative,' Alex said, still not seeming to take her quite seriously.

She closed her eyes and looked weary and alone. 'Why am I here, Alex Stanton?'

'Because,' Alex told her gently, 'we need to know about Japan. And you are our best source.' Alex tugged at his chin. 'Why is Stanton Industries having so many problems inside Japan?'

She sighed, tracing shapes on the polished wood. 'My grandfather wishes to make use of you, and has made use of you. You see, in our newspapers the reactor is now seen as part of foreign schemes, foreign pollution; *you* will be hated. Even in the eyes of the Left . . .'

'Bastard!' Alex's eyes blazed. 'But Hideki isn't the only one with deep pockets and access to the media in Japan!'

'No. I and my friends have used your money well; you will see. But Arigata will not be completed on schedule, no matter what grandfather has told you. Foreigners, you, will take all the blame. Other reactors will be entirely Japanese. Then, we will have enriched uranium, plutonium. The bomb.'

David threw up his hands. 'How can you know that for certain?'

Her face was like stone, her integrity was impressive. 'Do not doubt me.'

Alex said, 'So it's confirmed? Hideki does not intend us to complete Arigata ahead of schedule.'

'So you lose your reputation in Japan, and all those bonus payments.' David knew how serious that was. 'But how do you know they don't intend to pay you in full?'

'Because,' Alex said in a steady voice, 'and this must stay a secret, Kiko has seen a copy of the Hideki conglomerate's estimates for 77/78.'

'God! How did you manage that, Kiko?'

Alex barked a laugh. 'Kiko, do you want to tell us?'

'I have a good friend, in the head office in Tokyo. He is twenty-four; a young man with ideals. His name is – much more than you need to know.' Her eyes were bright with anger and remembrance. 'I had another friend, hacked to death in front of me because grandfather found out . . .'

David felt sick. 'Your grandfather has people killed?'

'Of course. So I tell you, my man with ideals is risking far more than you know.'

'I see,' Alex said, brightening. It was always good to have inside information. 'But what about the tanks we—'

'Do you not understand?' she asked them both, fiercely. 'You are playing straight into grandfather's hands! If you continue to follow the path he has made for you, you will be hated. Some of your tanks and guns will be bought, perhaps; but only a few. We do not buy foreign products! To our government and to our people that would be no more than foreigners seeking to invade our divine land with their goods. All you will do is make legitimate my grandfather's plans – plutonium, tanks, guns, bombs!'

'This is his plan?'

'Yes,' she told them, bright-eyed. 'That was all laid down in the Manifesto of the Unsheathed Sword Society, which I believe he signed sometime before 1947 and has promoted to this day! He hates you all, but he will never admit it.'

'Kiko,' David said awkwardly, 'you must be cautious, investigating all this. Think of it! What if your grandfather finds out what you've been doing?'

She turned to Alex. 'I told you before that I have inherited his courage. What can he do to me? Kill his own flesh and blood? Even in pain and shame you can only die once!'

There was no whisky left in Alex's glass. He refilled it again, to the brim. The tension in the room was painful, but looking at this woman as she talked of pain and shame he realized he was in the presence of heroism. 'Why is all this happening, Kiko?'

'Do you understand what defeat in the war meant to us? The culture of the *haiku* and the *samisen* collapsed; and as for the divinity of the Emperor, suddenly he was no more than a voice on the radio, telling us to endure the unendurable, endure defeat . . .'

Alex crossed over to the French windows, limping slightly, and parted the heavy drapes. Endure defeat, so that victory can come later.

His garden was dark; he had turned off the floodlights. He was reminded, suddenly, of the very beginning of his career – coming back from Greece with nothing, nothing at all except desperately wounded pride and the desire to achieve revenge through greatness. Saigo Hideki suddenly made complete sense to him.

'So his business is really just a front . . . He lives a lie, doesn't he?'

'No,' she answered, curtly. 'You insult him.'

'I'm sorry,' Alex said hastily, turning around. 'So how does he live?'

'He lives duty. Samurai, Japanese duty.'

'If we could only get him to admit what you have told us . . .'

'He will never tell you. Unless perhaps on his deathbed, if his plan would still succeed. Otherwise, a samurai would lie and lie, always with honour, till the end.'

'Till the end . . .' Alex murmured. Kiko excused herself and left the room.

'I really must be getting back,' David said. 'It's late, and I intend to be in the office by eight tomorrow. But I could perhaps give Kiko a lift to her hotel.'

Alex caught his eye. 'Just on the off chance of Caro coming back here tonight – is there a bed going spare in your place, by any chance?'

David was shocked. 'Bring you and Kiko back to the flat for *adultery*?'

Alex smiled. David was very much a married man. 'No, Megan wouldn't approve, would she?'

David said tightly, 'No.'

'I suppose I might try the Dorchester, then.'

They took a room overlooking Hyde Park. She sat at the enclosed balcony as room service delivered the champagne. Kiko was, luminously, herself. He came up to her quickly, and kissed the nape of her neck.

'It's been so long,' he murmured.

Little was said as he undressed her quickly. Her eyes were shining, and he saw that she had more dignity naked than most women clothed. Words meant nothing now, and only actions counted as he led her to the bed.

After they made love she squirmed under the sheet to whisper in his ear. 'Grandfather's conspiracy is a sword society. Those people called Bloom were investigating it.'

'They were? Then if we found their notes . . .' His eyes opened again after that moment of thought. Perhaps he could unleash Maggie and her investigative skills. 'Thank you, Kiko. You give me so many weapons – I only hope I can be a real champion, and win.'

'You must not lose, Alex Stanton. I had so much faith in you. You must not disappoint me.'

He stroked her black hair, sighing. 'What more is there to do?'

'Everything. You have changed your Stanton Industries, you and your friend can change your country here. Now you must help me change mine.'

He half rolled away. 'What can *I* do in Japan? Realistically?'

'Earn my respect by opposing him. You can give me money, and I will make use of my connections in the political parties and the media. Not everybody will look up to, or vote for, Hakagawa and his puppet-master, my grandfather. Not if they know the truth!'

'Now I suppose by "him"—'

'You must defeat my grandfather and what he represents. He has inherited the past . . . You see, we have to change in my country. We have to be helped to change. Or there will be more war, without end, until the world is laid waste or is under one rule.'

'War?' He held her tightly. 'You mean your grandfather is conspiring to go to *war*? Surely not!'

'I am fighting for the soul of Japan, for the soul of my ancestors. In the past that soul was deceit, cruelty, aggression – and hatred and contempt for the *gaijin*, the foreigner. We have brought pain to all Asia. We might bring pain to all the world. You must help me stop him!'

He heard the agony and the fierce integrity in her voice. 'Is he really so dangerous?'

'My country is,' she said. 'My country.'

He heard a muffled sob. 'We're on the same side, Kiko.'

'It all endures, under the surface, but Japan has to change. We must take foreign values, liberty, democracy, into our hearts. If there was even one man who could come to us from abroad, and be so great that we could not help but respect him – that would mean so much, Alex Stanton. At last we would be open to a new world.'

It was then he realized who that one man was supposed to be. He drew breath.

'Is that really possible?'

'What do you think I was telling you in Japan!' She hit out at him. 'It is possible to stop Saigo Hideki. Just possible.'

Chapter Twenty-two

As soon as he had returned from 10 Downing Street, Kerensky sent his message straight to the Moscow Centre. After extensive cross-checking, he was summoned home.

In its own right, the Union of Soviet Socialist Republics was the third most populous state on earth, and the KGB men at 2 Dzerzhinsky Square controlled a sixth of the world's land directly, and all of Eastern Europe, too. Their power spread throughout the world, far outweighing the influence of such as the Pope, or the government of Great Britain. The State Security apparatus answered only to the Kremlin, and in Russia's turbulent history it had sometimes been the other way round. Now, there were rumours in the highest Moscow circles that the present head of the KGB, Andropov, had ambitions for supreme power.

It was summer in the city when Kerensky returned. Moscow was still a city of churches, though many had been given irreligious, modern uses by the State. But the onion domes of the Kremlin go back to the days when Russia was openly religious, and Czar and Patriarch pursued the same policy: expand Holy Mother Russia, and thus bring the world under the control of Orthodox religion. Of course, since Lenin and his revolutionaries took power in 1917, Kerensky mused, it has all seemed very different.

The First Chief Directorate of the State Security Committee divides up the world, with the Far East department's head usually holding a major-general's rank. Anatoly Glykov was that man. He reported directly and very privately to the chairman of the State Security Committee. There, at the level of the Politburo, information was bartered for influence: for Yuri Andropov, as the Far East chief knew, truly nursed ambitions for the highest office.

Glykov was wearing his KGB uniform, with his ribbons and decorations. There was a knock on his office door, which hesitantly opened.

'Here.' He rose, beckoned the young man in, and embraced Oleg Kerensky. 'Sit at the table with me, share a vodka. I am sorry to have recalled you from being schooled in Farsi, but there has been a change of plan.'

'I imagine there has been,' Kerensky said, drily, 'if there really is a conspiracy in Tokyo for rearmament.' He sat down before the old man.

'For rearmament? For the nuclear bomb. And revenge on us,' the old man said, brooding. 'They are like the Germans. Secretly, they feel their loss in the great patriotic war was a mistake. They want a second round, on their terms.' He shook himself. 'What do you feel about this British minister, this man Bryant?'

Kerensky was much, much younger: he still wore a trim herringbone suit from London, and his hair was slicked down. He had used journalistic cover so long it felt only too natural.

'My report? I think David Bryant was speaking the truth. In so far,' he added carefully, 'as he knows it.'

'We must be careful,' the old man said. 'The British are weaklings, but sometimes still clever. Our man Philby was a master of duplicity beyond anything a Russian could ever be.'

'I do not think it is a British lie.'

'A lie to set the might of the Soviet Union against the yellow man? No. Most probably it is true. So, we face conspiracy in Japan; their own arms-making industry, plutonium, satellites and rockets, of course for "peaceful purposes" only – then the nuclear bomb. We have had hints of this before.'

'But who is behind it?'

'The elements you would expect. International industrialists control the democratic process in Japan. They have their friends in the ministries, and in the armed forces. It's a conspiracy, whether organized or not.'

'Is it really possible so be so secret, in a bourgeois-democratic country like Japan?'

'Oh, yes. How few outsiders even know the Japanese language! They can be the most secretive people on earth.'

Kerensky breathed it, in his imagination seeing World War III begin, frightened. 'So there is conspiracy there.'

The other man stood up. His heavy fists were clenched, his shoulders hunched. 'It is almost the Japanese way. I was in Tokyo when one secret society moved. The twenty-sixth of February, 1936. You know, I once heard Hideki's name mentioned as a supporter of that conspiracy . . .'

'*Did* you?' Kerensky considered. Not impossible at all: Hideki had been powerful for a long time. 'What happened?'

'There was snow in the streets, quarrelsome soldiers manning barricades. And fear, fear everywhere. Two cabinet ministers were dead in Tokyo, and the prime minister was on the same death-list. And do you know what the conspirators wanted?' He gave a harsh laugh. 'A government more in favour of the military, and more likely to declare war!'

Kerensky, trying to remain calm, sat back from the table. So this old Asia hand believed it was probably true. He found himself strangely alienated by all this: it seemed bloody and barbaric. 'What do our agents in Japan say?'

'I have gone through the files, these last few days. Nothing there is as bold as this, nothing so brutally simple – but there have been hints and whispers. Tokyo wants back the soil we claimed after the war, those islands, because there is precedent.'

'There is?'

'Yes. The Americans were weak enough to do it. They gave back Iwo Jima in '68 and Okinawa in '72. Can you imagine a Japanese government, victorious, doing the same to a defeated enemy? But the yellow man will arrogantly expect the same from us. It is all reverting, in Japan. I have myself seen their schoolbooks which call their rape of China "so-called atrocities" for which Japan "was unjustly blamed" – and soon theories of Japanese superiority will be in the textbooks as facts. I have heard recordings of Hakagawa, and Hideki's executives. Their war is still on! Even a cabinet minister has said publicly that Japan "committed no crimes" in the great patriotic war, and now "needs strategic greatness as well as economic greatness".

'Yes, I believe this David Bryant. He must have heard things from British diplomatic and intelligence sources, and from the Stanton Industries men. He is on our files too, you know. A friend of those Stantons, the arms-makers, but not a man of the right. At one time our associates in the DDR tried to recruit him.' He grimaced. 'Bryant defied them. I suppose we can admire courage like that. No, he has pointed us in the right direction. I believe it is true and there are powerful people in Japan who intend to rearm.'

'We will not be on the side of Tokyo in this,' Kerensky said softly.

'Most certainly not,' Glykov said, missing the importance Kerensky had given to the sentence. 'So we must be firm, ruthless: as Chairman Andropov is. He knows what Japan represents – something worse than the Germans. And I know, too. Did I ever tell you how I helped the great heretic Mao? We fought the Japanese in Manchuria and elsewhere, when their puppet emperor the last Manchu was on the false throne. So I know what the yellow men are! I saw their army occupy Peking. And now, to think they have ambitions to get the atomic bomb! I would sooner see Germany reunited and rearmed!'

'Indeed, Comrade General Glykov. So, we must stop this?'

'We must try.'

'Good. Last time I was in Tokyo I sensed something in the atmosphere: even the crowds at the Yasukuni Shrine seemed . . .' Kerensky sought for words, then shrugged. 'They are a dangerous people. Very violent behind their politeness – and they have always been too ambitious.'

Glykov sat down and said irritably, 'I must recommend something serious to Chairman Andropov.'

Kerensky made it a very polite leading question. 'Will he decide on the party's policy himself?'

There was a silence. Old Glykov scratched one ear. 'No. It will be a Politburo matter; General Secretary Brezhnev himself will speak, no doubt. But my voice will be heard, too. So, how can we stop this Hideki and this Hakagawa?'

The young man spread manicured hands. 'Ordinarily, our agents of influence might have been strong enough, working for "peace" and against this conspiracy and the rearmanent that would be necessary before the Japanese could engage in more imperialist wars.'

Glykov was openly scornful, but there was a fountain pen in his hand and a file was open in front of him. 'So that's what you recommend? Propaganda only, and in disguise?'

You did not rise high in Soviet society without knowing when not to give an opinion. Instantly, and very smoothly, the younger man added, 'Of course, in view of the internal situation, perhaps Comrade Chairman Andropov will advocate strong action in defence of the struggle for peace.'

'Very likely.' Glykov rubbed his hands together, thoughtfully. 'Comrade Brezhnev, our beloved leader, is ailing. Everybody knows that. Our own chairman stands aside while Brezhnev's protégé Kirilenko intrigues against the Central Committee Secretary for Industry.'

Kerensky looked up. 'But surely Konstantyn Chernenko is likely to win? He is an engineer, untainted by – the rumours.' Their eyes met. It was no secret among the Moscow élite that Brezhnev's son Yuri was an alcoholic, and that his daughter Galina, along with her lover Boris the Gypsy, were secretly under KGB investigation for corruption.

Glykov grinned, a squat, powerful peasant. 'If our beloved Comrade Brezhnev has failing health, as some say, it will be time for a new man to take power.'

Kerensky was excited. This was as close as he had ever come to the real intrigues for power. 'Grandfather, I—'

The old man's face was thunderstruck.

Instantly, he corrected the error. His voice was calmly thoughtful. 'Comrade Chairman Andropov could hardly hope to succeed, could he? As he is the head of the KGB the foreign repercussions could be very bad.'

'I think you have spent too much time in the West.' Glykov laughed, as the younger man flinched back from this supreme insult. 'We will have Chairman Andropov dressed up for the western press. A chess-playing intellectual, lover of Mozart and Beethoven, a secret liberal . . . You can imagine it.'

'Will that be believed?' the younger man said dubiously.

'Of course. The secret of *dezinformatsia* is to tell the fellow-travellers what they want to hear. And they will believe anything, won't they? Their minds have been rotted by years of exposure to slick, lying advertisements.'

'And besides,' Glykov added, 'I know that Mikhail Suslov is an Andropov supporter.'

'Ah, yes,' Kerensky said, his eyes lighting up. 'That is different.'

Suslov was the grey eminence of the Kremlin, the ideologue in chief. He promoted the dogma of world revolution and party infallibility, and had been a power in the Politbureau since the days of Stalin. Mikhail Suslov could effectively be the kingmaker. If he threw all his weight behind Andropov, anything was possible; even supreme power in the Union of Soviet Socialist Republics.

And if that happened, both men knew the supporters of Andropov would rise with him.

Glykov sat down again: old, ugly, a gargoyle of Bolshevism from the days of the dictators. But Kerensky knew the old man would never think of himself as obsolete. 'I must think this through. Chairman Andropov himself will decide on what to say to the Politburo. I am inclined to advise a very strict measure. More than propaganda, more than anything the friends of Marxism-Leninism inside Japan can do.'

Then tension in the office was frightening. 'What do you mean by a very strict measure?'

Glykov reached for another file, mouth looking sour. 'I remember when we gave those madmen in the north permission to take the southern part of Korea.'

Kerensky could not believe it. 'Are we thinking of war? But who would fight Japan? Unless we ourselves—'

'Fight? I think nothing and say nothing – as far as *you* are concerned. My advice will go to the highest in the land.' He flapped the thick file at the young man. 'Do you see that Mr Hugh Stanton has finally gotten his knighthood from the Queen? It is lucky he lives such a private life.' He sat brooding for a minute.

'Excuse me, Comrade General,' Kerensky began, waiting for his orders.

'Go, now, back to the KGB school for languages. I will see Chairman Andropov tomorrow and make recommendations. But the Politburo will decide.'

The meeting was over. Kerensky was obliged to stand up and go, though his heart and soul cried out to know what would be decided.

The First Chief Directorate of the KGB had a headquarters outside the Moscow ring-road, south-west of the city. If you followed the main highway towards Zvenigorod, you would find a numbered turn-off which has no name. This road passes beneath surveillance cameras, then reaches two rings of metal fencing, the inner ring carrying 950 volts. Uniformed and heavily armed sentries from the KGB Guards Division with blue flashes at their lapels and blue stripes in their trousers wait at both gates.

The black Chaika saloon was saluted, but only after the identification papers had been carefully checked.

Today, Kerensky was being schooled in the other KGB arts – unarmed combat, sabotage, gunnery. He took the chance to practise with an Uzi submachine gun one of their Palestinian agents had captured.

He laid down the weapon he had emptied into the wooden target, in a glow of aggression. The painted outline of a man had been chewed away savagely. Then somebody tapped him on the shoulder. 'Major Kerensky? One of the high-ups is outside, wants to see you.'

He saw Glykov, in his brand new Chaika. He was beckoned inside as the driver was curtly ordered to go away and come back in quarter of an hour.

Kerensky accepted a foreign cigarette, bought in a hard-currency shop where ordinary Russians cannot go. 'So, Comrade General, you have been to Andropov, and he has been to the Politburo. Are you able to tell me the plan?'

'The plan?'

He recognized what was on Glykov's face: awe. It shook him very badly. 'Is it something very serious?'

The old man hissed, 'It is absolute courage. We must use our might openly.'

Kerensky licked his lips, deeply uneasy. This was not the patient, subtle cunning of a legendary Chekist. This was more like the blatant risk-taking for which Khrushchev had been dispossessed of power.

'But for the record: David Bryant never approached you, and you know nothing of what is happening inside Japan, and we have no plan.'

'But we *are* taking action?'

'I went to the Chairman personally.' Glykov hesitated. His face was haggard, but triumphant. 'He agrees with me. We saw the Americans turn tail in Vietnam. Cambodia has gone, too, and soon the Horn of Africa, and even more of the Middle East. Since 1945 the West has never been more weak. We are to use our great strength directly, if all else fails, to stop the capitalist-militarist plot over there . . . and I am responsible!'

Kerensky stared at him. The old man was profoundly, dangerously elated. There was a plan to take action, then. Ideas spun through his mind like cards, cards picturing assassinations, or more bombings using their terrorist fronts. Anything.

'I am dispatching you back to Tokyo again: with the same journalistic cover.' Glykov tapped a knuckle on the car's window. 'A plutonium agreement has apparently already been signed, probably with more to come. So our Japanese sources say. In early September, Arigata is officially opened. We must pressure the Japanese government to withdraw.'

'Pressure a government directly?' He stared at the KGB general, his superior, wondering in fear exactly what the plan was. 'How? Is this wise?'

The old man's dark gaze turned to him. Those smouldering eyes had seen Berlin in ruins, and the victorious Japanese armies occupying

Peking. 'It is the order of the Chairman of the State Security apparatus. We are to use any means. Any means at all.' He shrugged. 'We will make the stakes frighteningly high. And Carter had better be weak, here.'

'Otherwise?'

'Or at least know his own self-interest.'

Kerensky was still breathing heavily. *'Otherwise?'*

The general pantomimed an explosion.

They were all here to celebrate. Flags thrashed in the high wind, where thousands of people had gathered in front of a high-tech factory.

Alex Stanton had delivered the necessary hardware for production. David Bryant had provided firm government support. Will Langton had delivered the new working practices.

'Now here there's concrete proof,' Alex said quietly, very proud, 'that we really can make it work – together.'

'More like plastic and stainless steel proof,' answered David. 'Mind you, the landscaping is very pretty. Shrubs, flowers. It hardly looks like a factory at all.'

'That's because of our idea of factory is outmoded – dark Satanic mills and such.'

Long and low, made of red plastic with a partly transparent sloped roof, the new tank factory had been built by the Tyne's side. David followed Alex on to the platform, to applause.

Earlier that morning, David's official black Rover had arrived at the new, futuristic-looking factory, and the two Stanton cousins had conducted their special guest around. David had toured the factory with great interest, followed by the press.

Inside, the huge building was well lit, and the workforce in new Stanton overalls had looked up cheerfully from the machines. The visitors had passed through an almost spotlessly clean open space, with the latest machinery around the assembly line. Here, a hundred-ton press worked noisily, controlled by computer. Further along, outfitting men from the various trades swarmed over each tank as it moved down the line. Automatic welding units sprayed arc-bright light, but the fumes were sucked away by the air conditioning. The factory was finally ready. Arigata had paid for it. Over twelve million pounds' worth of machine tools and computers had been installed. David looked round, still exhilarated. Would the country's turnaround start here?

The two Stantons were to his left. Maggie's father was beside the works manager, on the platform. David glanced surreptitiously at his watch. It was not quite one o'clock.

To the surprise of all of them except Alex, Maggie had turned up, with a film crew. She was tanned and full of continental style, but there was a certain tired grimness about her. David had overhead Alex mentioning a name: Bloom.

David threw a smile at her for a moment as the Labour Lord

Mayor of Newcastle-upon-Tyne finished his speech with a rhetorical flourish.

David moved to the microphones, thanked Alex, and then began to speak in his familiar style. 'I won't keep you busy men waiting too long,' he addressed the workforce directly. 'I understand you have a couple of hundred tanks to make before this time next year.'

There was a ripple of amused laughter.

'All I want to say is this. The government has backed this project, and your management believes in it. The entire nation must make sure we succeed here. There were great days, once, when what we built here was sent to all the corners of the world, to Japan, and India, and to America. I remember the old Scotswood Road works; I remember the old pubs that used to line the road – the Hydraulic Crane, the Forge. Those days are gone, those pubs are gone. *But all of that was built by men who believed in greatness.* Lord Armstrong, the Stantons, others. If we are to do anything like that today, we must not only believe in greatness, but we must *work* for it, every hour of every day! That is the only way we will have anything left to hand on to our children.

'But it seems to me that there's cause for optimism. This factory was built in less than a year, and finished ahead of schedule and under budget. The government has given grants for the kind of ultra-modern machinery you'll see is installed here, which will make this factory the very best of its kind in the world.'

He looked up for a moment. There were thousands of people standing patiently in front of him, and TV cameras too. There would be time for the pictures to make the early evening news; and tomorrow, though there might not be banner headlines, the opening would be celebrated on the front pages, as it deserved.

'It has been a hard year for the region – hard times for many years, now. But this factory is proof that if we keep our faith in our own ability those hard times will not continue for ever. A change will come. We will share it together.

'In that spirit, I declare the Bryant Works open.'

The applause continued for a long time.

The next morning Sir Hugh Stanton himself flew to Japan to meet McCourt, hoping to finalize three more contracts for their proposed civil projects division.

When the chauffered Silver Cloud brought him back from Heathrow airport, Hugh immediately called Alex to the boardroom. Though it was only summer dusk outside, the chandelier from St Petersburg was glittering diamonds of light over their heads.

Alex sat down. 'How was Japan?'

Hugh's head was bowed. Wearily, he rubbed at his eyes. 'I need another holiday, Alex. God.'

'Take a holiday – after September. Now, what happened?'

'All the contract bids were lost, though only by suspiciously slender margins. It soon became damned clear that Stanton Industries had been haemorrhaging information at board level. You were right: in spite of our company rules I should never have taken those bid proposals to the board, not with Beauford present. One hundred and twenty million pounds worth of work was bid for, you know. And . . .' He looked out of the huge window for a moment, at the grey Thames. 'In our politely rancorous negotiations in Tokyo, with some MITI officials and others, the ultimatum was at last clearly spelled out.'

'Off the record, of course?'

'Of course. No more civil engineering work was offered, nor in my opinion will be offered. But they seemed keen to entice us into armaments work, though we would have to—'

'Sell arms to the Tokyo government through a Japanese corporation like Hideki's, you mean?' That did not sound too bad. 'Bump up the price to pay for the middleman's commission. It's standard practice.'

Hugh laughed, stretching his arms out. He looked as tired as Alex had ever seen him. 'It certainly is. But that wasn't their idea. They proposed that we agent here what they build – I think they have a notion that, ultimately, we might be prevailed upon to sell their products for them.'

'God in heaven,' Alex said slowly. 'Talk about effrontery. They see Britain as a Trojan Horse for them, inside NATO and the EEC?'

Hugh raised his head. Regained strength was in his long features. 'I didn't get to see Mr Hideki, you know; and that lost me face, of course.'

'By God,' Alex said, 'I hope Hideki does lose and that Kiko inherits!'

Hugh glanced at him. 'That's hardly likely, is it?'

'Faith can move mountains, Hugh.'

'So they say, though I've never seen it.'

'I have some other cards up my sleeve.'

Hugh grunted. 'Before we move on, there is one small thing you can explain to me. A personnel matter.'

Alex knew what it would be. 'Oh yes?'

'As part of a rolling programme of transfers, last month thirty-six of our people were withdrawn from Arigata.'

'I don't have the figures.'

'Eighteen were sent out. As welders, electricians, clerks, whatever.'

Alex relaxed himself. 'Is that a problem?'

'Ten of them have assumed identities.'

'Assumed?' Alex asked, innocently.

'False identities, false names – because they are all from our central security office.'

'They can pass as electricians, or whatever other trade they own to. I can assure you of that, Hugh. I designed the training programme myself.'

Hugh said tiredly, 'I just don't know why you've sent some of our finest people, ex-SAS and similar, off to a project where we are winding down our involvement.'

'Insurance,' Alex said pleasantly. 'Also, I take full responsibility.'

There was a long silence.

'The buck stops here, Hugh,' Alex said gently. 'On my desk. Anything else from Japan—?'

'They raised the issue of the reprocessing contract for nuclear fuel, too. They want the deliveries of high-grade metals expedited.'

Alex sat back from the table. 'To speed up the supply of plutonium, in other words. That is a matter solely for the government.'

'They seem to think you can apply pressure, there,' Hugh said delicately.

'On David, you mean?' Alex threw up his hands. 'They really want everything, don't they? As well as our hearts and souls, our balls.'

Hugh drummed his fingers on the long, glossy table, which reflected the myriad lights of the chandelier. 'I'll tell you what I think. They know we're overstretched, and they'll do nothing for us till we've helped them complete Arigata . . . and then, I fear, there'll still be this nuclear question to be resolved.'

'They want plutonium,' Alex said harshly, 'even more weapons-purity plutonium – and only if we help provide that will they reward us with more work.'

'If something goes wrong and puts us in a cash-flow crisis, I fear they'll try us with an offer we can't refuse. An "agreed merger", they'll probably call it.'

Alex felt ice-cold. Their shares had been sliding noticeably over the last months. 'You mean, a takeover bid?'

'Exactly.'

'Well,' answered Alex, 'I think I know how to respond to that.'

Alex paused, leaning on the table. The Board of Directors, with Beauford now removed, stared at him expectantly.

'Stanton Industries still intends to put its bid in place before 1978. A bid to sell hundreds of millions of dollars of military hardware to Japan. But our Tokyo office has made it clear we cannot take it for granted that we will do well, though there are increasingly frequent rumours in the Tokyo press that the government will announce a changed emphasis on Article IX of their 1947 Constitution. In other words, remilitarization.

'Where does that leave Stanton Industries? Perhaps it leaves us nowhere at all.

'State Department policy specialists have calculated that as soon as the trade deficit between Japan and the United States becomes insupportable there will be pressure in Congress not only for a fairer trade system, but for what might seem a simpler and more easy option: persuading Tokyo to use its great wealth to rearm . . . So quite probably the Japanese government will start rebuilding the

Japanese arms industry – and start rearming the Land of the Rising Sun itself.'

He stepped back from the table for a moment, wondering what the Russians would say, when all those divisions stood poised off the shores of the Russian-held Kurile Islands – and what the White House would or could do if those divisions were ever used in anger.

'We could think of selling to Great Britain,' Hugh said regretfully, 'but the country still has bad financial problems. I daresay two Stanton Industries divisions will eventually be involved in the complicated, expensive process of updating our defences, but it'll be a long time before there is a bonanza here.'

MacKenzie asked, 'But look at the state of our defences! Supposing the Kremlin does lean on us!'

Hugh turned to Alex, brightened. The knighthood had certainly made him more comfortable, Alex reflected. 'What's the government's view? You've heard they have plans to modernize our armed forces?'

Alex looked around the table. Nine of the most intelligent and tough-minded men he had ever worked with. He told them straight, 'No. They have no plans to do that whatsoever.'

'I see you are certain.' Hugh's eyes held decision. 'That's information from cabinet level, is it?'

He meant David, of course. Alex gave only a thin smile. 'More to the point, it's accurate information.'

'No sales bonanza from this country . . . What about Iran and the Middle East?'

Alex shrugged. 'Iran, like Britain, is beginning to suffer guerrilla strikes in the major public industries. It seems clear there will be no more major orders from Iran.'

'Then what, exactly, are you proposing? More Arigata reactors?' one of the non-executive directors said. 'I really don't think we can approve that.'

'No,' Alex said. 'But I'd like your authority to consider something else to do with Japan.'

'And that is?'

'A partial merger with the Hideki Corporation.' The room erupted. Alex had fought against this for years. He stood up, raised his hands. 'No, listen to me. Saigo Hideki is eighty years of age. His heir might have different ideas.' He touched a buzzer.

'Oh?' MacKenzie of Shipbuilding said. 'You sure?'

Kiko Hideki walked in, shyly smiling.

'The lady will tell you herself,' Alex said.

Chapter Twenty-three

The lights in the little room came on. Maggie Langton blinked. Her film had ended. It was still in rough cut, but soon the music would be edited on to the soundtrack – and her story of Stanton Industries would be complete.

'Like it?' the American woman asked them. She was a film editor Maggie had imported from Los Angeles, who had worked with D. A. Pennebaker and Coppola.

'I love it, Stephanie,' she said firmly, kicking the black curls of discarded film across the floor. David Bryant shifted about beside her. She crossed her long legs, remembering images: Concorde, a shipyard launch, Stanton faces fading into the past. 'You gave my ideas real wide-screen style. I'm sure Alex Stanton will like it, too.'

'Thanks.' Stephanie Bloom sipped coffee from a plastic cup. 'You surprised me, Maggie.'

'Nothing wrong with that.'

'I was expecting something much more cutting.'

'Because I've had some fallings out with Alex? I don't want to spend my entire life belittling. The world is too rich for that. Look, maybe we can keep you longer. I have a project I just have to have you working on for me, Steph. Something on Japan – Japan from the inside out. What happened in the thirties, the war, and what they've been doing since – and what they intend to do in the future.'

The woman's long fingers stroked her dark eyebrows smooth. 'Hollywood is the place.'

'I know that,' Maggie said, 'and some day I want do business there.'

David laughed. 'So you're going to be seeing stars?'

She took it as a straight question. 'I'm thinking of a major project. Terry knows lots of these Hollywood people: I know people who can write. That's a start. Christ, even *Easy Rider* was just a brilliant idea cheaply filmed, a sixties road movie done with style . . . But now I've actually interviewed the likes of Al Pacino and Warren Beatty. They'll remember me. So I'm thinking of producing a movie. Famous faces, that's where Terry could help.'

David touched his tie and looked at her curiously. 'What did you have in mind?'

'I want to do a kind of thriller, mostly set in Japan. But it'll be based on truth. I'll get this country *right*, and I'll do the same for other countries!'

There was a pause. Then David said, 'You expect Terry's help?'

'As long as I can trust him to work with me diligently, why not?'

'Well, I suppose so,' he responded. 'I saw that Sylvester Stallone film recently, with the girls. The one about boxing, what was it, *Rocky*, and he seems to have made good money.'

'Fairytales,' she said sharply, 'are for kids.'

David shook his head. 'Film is very expensive.'

'A treatment or even a full script isn't much to commission,' she said tartly, annoyed another man was failing to take her seriously. 'Christ, sooner or later somebody is going to do a bare-knuckle version of the truth about Japan! I'd just like it to be me. I mean, I can make documentaries: *Capital Reports* has the prizes to prove that. If I want, I could get inside the White House, and show people what a good man is trying to do to change things.'

'You're moving in exalted circles, these days.'

'Look, I'll come clean. I have reason to believe their ambitions amount to a conspiracy, and that Saigo Hideki is behind it. Documentary cinema isn't enough. I want the biggest audience I can get, and the biggest debate.'

Stephanie Bloom's nose wrinkled. 'Me and my husband started work on a programme about the same thing . . .' She looked away, and her voice changed completely: it became hollow and distant. 'Then the Tower of London blew up.'

Maggie and David both looked at her compassionately. Maggie said softly, 'I remember, Stephanie.'

'And so do I.' It was a deep and resonant voice, and Maggie immediately turned towards it. 'That's why we invited you here to work with us.'

Alex Stanton had arrived. He stood tall in the doorway. From the other editing suites came bursts of speeded-up dialogue and music. 'In fact, I was hoping – we were hoping – you could help us continue your husband's work. He had material we'd like access to.'

Maggie felt his presence, but kept her voice level and businesslike when she spoke up to support him. 'Japan is wonderful and terrible, doing what this country did two hundred years ago, and the States a little later. But along with the industrial ferment is a desire for mastery.'

Stephanie nodded, looking from man to man. 'Saigo Hideki was one of the people Irv was targeting in his own documentary. But I suppose you know that already.'

'That was our presumption,' Maggie said. As she swirled her red hair, patchouli oil filled the room with musky sexuality. She looked directly at Alex. 'Find the facts and give them to the public – that has to be the way to do it.'

'Maybe. But don't forget, the old man could be dangerous.'

'Hide the truth, just because you do business with him? Or are you afraid?'

'Maggie,' he said slowly, emphatically, 'when it comes to Hideki, *be* afraid.'

Maggie turned to Stephanie. 'Look, I don't know how much more time you want to spend here, but I would like to work with you some more. You've done preproduction, research, and front-of-camera presentation, haven't you?'

'Yes.'

'Then why— ?'

'Why did I get into film-editing?' She turned her head away. 'I really thought with Irv that we had it made. Work, family, everything. I just loved him so much. And then after . . . after . . . I didn't know what to do. I just wanted to be private.' She sighed, turned her head back. 'I suppose that working alone in the cutting room was just a convenient thing to do, for a while.'

'You could do a lot more than that,' Maggie insisted. 'Look, let's all go for a drink. You can see historic Southwark, right, and imagine Shakespeare and Kit Marlowe helling around, or Henry VIII's wife stepping ashore in England for the very first time.'

They left Maggie's building at dusk. It was in a dingy brick alley, which they followed into Copperfield Street and along Marshalsea Road. In front of a redbrick church called St George the Martyr they turned left. It was a summer's evening, and hot. Here, across a busy road and through a narrow entrance, was an old galleried coaching inn from the seventeenth century. They sat down at one of the tables in the cobbled yard and had cool beer. The tables were crowded with girls in summer dresses and men in open-necked shirts. Looking round, Maggie had a terrifying flash of thought: death, in an instant of white light. Unless they stopped Arigata and the other places like it, death . . .

Alex saw her face as he poured out the champagne he had ordered. To Maggie he had seemed a little distant, but now he was unexpectedly charming, and he also paid solicitous attention to Stephanie. He was the centre of the group, but Maggie sat right there with him. I've known this man since I was twenty, she thought, and David longer than that. It was a comforting sense of continuity.

'All right,' Stephanie said, after they had talked about Hideki. 'You've persuaded me. I'll fly back home and send all of the material Irv and me had assembled.'

'What do you have?'

'Film interviews, magazines, bootleg tapes . . . a few bits of propaganda film from World War II. All kinds of stuff.'

'You send it,' Maggie said. She glanced at Alex, who raised his glass without speaking. There was something about being with him: a sense of trust and security and intensity. Maggie felt happy about their plans, and the champagne that bubbled inside her.

'What about Arigata?' David asked, curiously. 'Was there any mention of that in your material?'

'Far as I remember,' Stephanie drawled, 'not a word.'

Maggie bit her lip. 'Still, maybe that would have made it too easy. I'll be going to the opening ceremony, and there'll be other film crews there – the world stage, right. We'll say something to friend Hideki, and then *about* friend Hideki.'

'I'm sure that must terrify him,' Alex said.

'Yes,' she responded sharply, 'I bet the truth does! But you have a better idea? If so, what is it?'

Alex laughed harshly.

'You see!' she chuckled, exhilarated by the champagne, and spoke directly to Alex. 'Maybe you could help me with my movie. I'd run to a co-production credit. Come on, you'd enjoy it, and I'm sure you must have a million or two to spare.'

'A million or two – but not to spare,' he answered. 'I like to take my own risks, in my own way.'

'You think I'd lose your money?' Looking at Alex, self-confidence and defiance flooded her. 'But I know exactly what I'm doing. Stephanie, tell the man! I've done it before, remember.'

When somebody suggested a stroll, Alex led the way out of the pub. She followed him, then walked side by side. In the darkness a window was slammed shut. They left the inn yard, turned into a wide street, where traffic went past in both directions, making them stop. The buildings here were all smoke-stained; then as she crossed with Alex at the pedestrian lights she realized they would soon be on London Bridge itself.

There, on the bridge, Alex stopped them with a gesture.

Maggie looked over his shoulder. Far down the river she could see lights, signs that ships and boats still made the Thames their pathway. Through the sweet haze of the alcohol everything seemed warm and alive to Maggie, and she smiled dreamily to herself as Alex turned her with a hand on her shoulder.

A flight of steps, then a darkened, old building, under the moon.

'Southwark Cathedral, Stephanie,' Alex said with satisfaction. 'I don't know if this particular building was here in Shakespeare's day, but it's part of a thousand years of history.'

This piece of London, dark under the moon, seemed magical and ancient. Maggie loved it, and when Alex linked arms with her she did not resist. They climbed over a locked gate and through some kind of covered market, where she could smell overripe fruit and vegetables, and she kicked away a carboard box marked Oranges du Maroc. They passed another pub, where the doors were open on this hot night and people were singing along to the jukebox records. Terry seemed a million miles away, and their time together before the fall of Saigon was an empty episode from someone else's life.

She felt joy. She turned to Alex, and she was smiling.

* * *

David stared into Maggie's eyes for a moment. They were large and liquidly green, and very beautiful. Her breath was sweet with champagne as she kissed both men. The women were sharing a black cab back to Flood Street where Stephanie was staying.

Alex waved, then turned to David. 'Lift home?'

'Thanks.' David pulled open the red E-type's passenger door.

Alex said nothing during the drive, and David did not press him. He sensed his friend's preoccupation, and presumed it was to do with Hideki and Japan. Alex drove fast and well, as ever, but there was an edge to his expression David had not seen before, and it made him uncomfortable. Alex had the Stanton inheritance: he was a dangerous man.

In Kennington, a little before midnight, David got out of the car. 'Like a walk, Alex?'

Alex's face was hard. 'I'd mainly like to talk.'

David headed away from his flat. They walked leisurely on this warm summer's night, not speaking. Finally, David broke the silence, curious about Alex and his intentions. 'Still want me to come to Arigata?'

'You're still supposed to take those papers to sign, aren't you?'

They passed the spice-importers, where the air itself tasted peppery and exotic.

'Yes, the Hideki Corporation still want those reprocessing contracts . . . So we both have to go to Arigata? Me, for my duty to the government. You, to collect that last instalment of the contract money. I suppose that's necessary.'

He saw Alex grimace. 'I have another line of credit set up, with the new chairman of Beauford Cleves. However, Hideki could dump all his Stanton stock. Costly for him, but that would damage us badly. And we need that final £65 million payment on 1 September.'

'Maybe Ray over in the States would help support your share price, and you're not entirely without admirers here in the City. Also, I've heard you've made big recent sales, or hope to. What about your plans for India and Hong Kong?'

Alex snorted. They passed a parked Rolls-Royce, and then a few estate agents with photographs of housefronts lit up in their windows. 'If only it was that easy! Christ, to have Maggie's beliefs – the truth, and it will make you free.'

'But that must be better than lies.' David finally said it. 'Hideki wins, you're saying?'

'He's a problem, you tell me? So what do you suggest? Assassination? Denounce him in the press? What do people want me to *do*?'

'Something final. I still think it could be easy. Lean on the Prime Minister of Japan, and he dismisses the Hideki Corporation from the Japanese atomic programme. But whatever happens, Arigata has to be stopped.'

'Has to be!' Alex suddenly turned on him, fists clenched. 'You're a bloody government minister! Stop it yourself!'

David hurried to catch up with him as he stalked off. 'Of course I've tried. Governmental channels.' He thought of Kerensky. 'More than you'll ever know.'

Alex grunted.

'Why don't we try telling somebody like Akira Nanwara what Hideki is up to? He's a decent, honest and very successful businessman. I'm sure he wouldn't want Hideki rocking the boat.'

A streetlight was reflected in Alex's eyes as he stood considering. 'But would he believe us?'

'If we approached him correctly.'

'If . . .' Alex took a breath. 'Listen, sorry if I've been a bit abrasive. I think it was meeting Stephanie Bloom.'

'Why did that bother you?'

'It brought back memories. The Tower bombing, David. You see, according to Kiko, it was Saigo Hideki who arranged that bombing – using Alan Hoyle as his agent.'

'Jesus Christ,' David said, stunned. 'So Hideki and Hoyle . . .'

'Now you can see how serious all this is.'

Once home, David climbed the stairs and sat down in front of his briefing papers. He worked for three quarters of an hour. Then the phone rang. He reached for it automatically, knocking aside an empty coffee-cup.

It was probably Alex, with some new ideas about confronting Hideki.

'Mr Bryant,' said a smooth, accented voice. 'It is a friend of yours from journalism. I am speaking from outside Moscow.'

'Outside Moscow—' He jerked upright in his chair. Immediately he thought of Alan Hoyle. 'Is this some sort of hoax?'

There was a harsh laugh. 'I am sincere. You said so yourself.'

Then David realized. It was Oleg Kerensky, the KGB officer.

'I will be in Tokyo soon, about the important matters we have discussed. I beg you to contact me there, before the opening of Arigata, because I hope two men of goodwill such as ourselves can come together to help resolve this crisis peaceably.'

He held the phone against his face, painfully hard. 'What "crisis"? What do you mean, "peaceably"?'

'You will find out in Tokyo,' Oleg Kerensky said harshly. 'Be there.'

On Saturday morning Maggie went down the steep stairs to her white-washed basement. The crates of material Stephanie had airfreighted from Los Angeles had arrived the day before yesterday, and it was time to make a start on sifting through them. Arigata, Maggie remembered, was due to open in little more than a week. Kiko had said there was the beginning of a furious reaction in Japan.

After some persuasion Terry helped her carry the crates upstairs. Inside each one was a mass of folders, box-files, tapes, and bundles of yellowing newspapers and magazines. Much, not all, of the Japanese material had translations appended. Many of the photographs and spools of ancient film were carefully annotated; but many were not. Irving Bloom had died too early to make complete sense of this. When she spread samples on the floor she sat back on her heels, depressed at the chaos.

Some of what was there was shocking. There was a twenty minute tape of Hakagawa as an ordinary member of the Diet, giving a speech introduced by somebody called Iwata, at a closed meeting of a far-right cultural organization back in 1963. Maggie listened to it, sitting with Terry in her stripped-pine kitchen, while trying to follow a rough English transcription. She frowned. Though she could not understand the spoken words, the raw aggression in the voice had come across clearly.

As the spools spun freely she spoke. 'What did you think of that?'

He did not seem very interested as he put down his magazine. 'Not very good quality, technically.'

'What he actually says—' Maggie looked up. 'It's frightening, if this translation is correct.'

'You ought to sell it to Alex Stanton, then.'

His voice had an unexpected harshness, but she said scornfully, 'This isn't a money matter. This is history!'

Terry raised his hands, palms out, and gave her the old charming smile. A gold bracelet shook around one wrist. 'Is there anything there about this Hideki guy?'

She lifted up a pile of old newspapers from Japan, and found a time-browned document in Japanese, with a symbolic unsheathed sword on the cover. Then she looked up. 'This is ridiculous! I don't speak Japanese, let alone read it.'

He was looking away. 'So what are you going to do?'

'Ask Kiko for help.'

The schedule for the next few days was hectic. Two days in Delhi, then Hong Kong, then Tokyo. The Stanton Industries sales team were in the specially appointed Stanton Boeing 727 on their way to India. There was leather upholstery everywhere, gold fittings in all the bathrooms, even a sauna. In the middle of the plane was a conference suite with computer equipment, and all-frequency radio units that allowed you to talk – either by satellite relay or crackly, Marconi-age longwave – to the other side of the world.

In New Delhi, Alex met an old friend again, a newly-promoted Indian general Stanton Industries had once entertained at the Edinburgh military tattoo. Though India jealously guarded its neutrality and independence, and relied mainly on Soviet weapons, Alex's salesmanship was supreme, and Hugh flew in to support him. The

Mark IX tank, like the Mark VIII, was a world-beater, and he proved it.

The Indian general staff persuaded their government to listen. Alex walked away with the promise of contracts for over a hundred and fifty million dollars.

Alex spoke with satisfaction to his cousin. 'It's going well. MacKenzie'll have that new shipyard yet.'

'I hope so, Alex.'

Next, the Stanton 727 flew east, to Hong Kong.

As they approached Kai Tak airport, Hugh watched the tall buildings their descending plane closely passed by and said to Alex, 'I hope the captain is in good form, or it'll be more than our paintwork that gets scratched today.'

The cousins disembarked together into this territory of sweltering skyscrapers and slums. An official car driven by a uniformed constable was there for their use, and a quiet man called Burke who was on His Excellency's staff accompanied them, as Hugh had arranged to stay the first night in the governor's historic mansion, though the governor himself was absent in London.

They travelled without speaking. Traffic was heavy, before they went through the Cross-Harbour Tunnel, worse in the tunnel, and almost as bad afterwards on the Victoria side.

In the governor's mansion they were taken to a small office, and Burke sat down so they could all drink tea. After this comfortable ritual he said quietly, 'MI6 in London has requested our cooperation. We have some cables for you, passed on by London station.'

'That's good of them,' Hugh said with hearty innocence that fooled nobody, and added, 'and I suppose you're in secret intelligence yourself?'

Burke smiled, handed over some papers. 'Irish Guards, originally. Anyway, you have use of our secure communications while you're here, if needed. Oh, and congratulations about New Delhi. Was posted there myself, '63 to '68.'

'Thanks,' Alex said, speed-reading what his London office had passed on.

Information had come in, in code, from friends in the intelligence community and from his Tokyo office. From Kiko Hideki came a redirected cable again imploring Alex to help her and not go to Arigata. Instead, he should denounce the whole project. She added that she was going to London to be with Maggie. He crumpled her message in his fist. He had to do this his own way.

'What else was involved with the Indian generals?'

Alex did not bother to disguise anything. 'The Indians exploded their own bomb in '74, but they're still paranoid about Pakistan and the rumours of an Islamic bomb. The request was about Arigata, keeping them informed, and maybe some similar favours one day . . .'

'Any particular plans we can help you with?' Burke asked.

'Actually, there is,' Alex answered, scribbling on a slip of paper. 'I'd like to be notified of this man's arrival.'

'I see.' Burke eyed the paper. A famous name. 'He usually stays at the Mandarin Hotel.'

Alex stood up. 'Thanks.'

Later that night, Hugh was sitting with him, pouch-eyed and weary through jet lag. Alex was finishing the bottle of expensive single malt. 'What's the plan now, Alex? Go early to Japan?'

'No,' Alex said shortly.

Hugh sipped the Scotch. He looked grim. 'This is it, Alex. We need that next, final instalment of the money, but we only get that if Arigata opens on schedule. And as you say, too much has leaked out: this is likely to be a scandal.'

'Expect more controversy in Japan, Hugh. Not less.'

'The publicity is going to be very bad for us.' Hugh sighed. 'And I did so want to be a lord, and continue to sell to NATO governments . . .'

Alex was wondering if Kiko and Maggie would hate him, if he appeared to celebrate Arigata. 'You're right. But Arigata has to open. We are, or I am, so publicly and openly committed to that happening that no purpose would be served by trying to back out now.'

Arigata and its official opening was the next major item on the itinerary.

The phone in their sitting room rang. Alex reached for it. It was Ray Hacker. 'Listen, Alex, I may as well take that earlier flight with the Senator and Tom, and meet you in Hong Kong 'stead of Tokyo.'

'What about the naval meeting at the Pentagon?'

'It got postponed and I think it'll stay postponed for a while.' Ray's voice became heavy with caution: this was an international line to an important British outpost, and so an obvious target for espionage. 'There's some kind of problem, distracting the high brass. The National Security Agency people in Fort Meade over in Maryland are involved, too.'

'It's serious?'

There was a pause before Hacker spoke again. 'Might as well say – it'll be obvious, headline stuff, very soon. I heard mention of a Soviet push; something about their fleet in Vladivostok.'

'There might be a Soviet naval action?' Alex said, not bothering to disguise his shock. 'Where?'

'Western Pacific, judging by signals intelligence. So the C-in-C Pacific will have to do some muscle-flexing in response, and I guess all the paperwork and meetings and stuff is getting backed up in the Pentagon.'

'Well, come with the others, then.'

Maggie did not come down the stairs quickly enough, so the one who greeted Kiko at Flood Street's front door was Terry.

He tried to be very charming, embracing Kiko, taking her coat, and complimenting her on her perfume. He said he would cook proper spaghetti for them all, and he dropped many of the magical big names from the sixties.

Nevertheless, Maggie could tell Kiko did not like him much. Not sincere enough, no doubt. Kiko, immaculate in loose white trousers and cashmere sweater, hardly even wanted to sit down. She said, small, exquisitely mannered, 'Maggie, dear, can I suggest checking the material immediately? We should get busy. Otherwise, my grandfather is on schedule to win.'

'I have to work late at the studio,' Terry said, smiling. He was wearing a designer suit of mustard-yellow linen and he looked darkly handsome. 'Maybe very late.'

Maggie was annoyed. 'Can't you stay? It's important.'

'I have this glamour stuff to do,' he told both women, shuffling his feet like a little boy.

Maggie had the notion that this glamour was no more than a polite name for pornography, but there did not seem to be any point in objecting. She followed Terry to the front door and allowed him to peck at her cheek.

Kiko was still in the tiled kitchen, sitting on a high stool. She sipped sweet English tea. 'Didn't you tell him what we have been doing? Yet I don't think he is interested.'

'No. He isn't.' Maggie swallowed tea and years of regret. 'But Terry used to—' She remembered Saigon, the drugs, the sadness, the people and the memories left behind. That betrayal had been the end of something for Terry. Maybe the end for her and Terry, too. When was the last time they had had a meaningful conversation?

All of Stephanie Bloom's crates had been brought up from the cellar now. Papers and tapes already lay scattered about, mostly unmarked and in no particular order.

'Well,' Kiko said, after the first, rapid investigation, 'this may take some time. But there are things here I never dreamed I'd see.'

Maggie was still preoccupied, thinking about Terry. 'Anything about this conspiracy?'

'Some things. Enough, perhaps, to damage it.' Kiko's dark eyes flashed. 'Let me see what else I can find. Make your calls and don't worry about me.'

Maggie went to the living room, threw herself into the new leather sofa and dialled. She wanted family, she wanted anything except worry about Terry and horror about Japan, so she was soon cradling the telephone and speaking warmly to her father.

It was about half an hour later, and a Steely Dan record was playing, when she heard the door open. Kiko was in the doorway, looking down at some age-browned papers she held. Her hands were trembling. Maggie felt the tension rise in the room.

'Maggie,' Kiko whispered, 'I think this might be it.'

Maggie stood up. 'What have you found?'

Kiko's face was strained. 'This is a signed copy of the Society of the Unsheathed Sword's manifesto of 1945. There are some of the most famous names in Japan on this. But first is my grandfather's!'

Maggie asked, 'What do we need to do?'

'Go to Japan,' Kiko said fiercely, 'just as soon as we can. Tomorrow! There are things about Arigata . . . We must stop it all.'

'Right.' Maggie knew how to take charge. 'This'll show up Alex, won't it?'

'Maggie,' Kiko said wearily, her lovely face pale, 'he gave me money, much money, to make sure the Japanese people knew about the scandal of Arigata. Even though some of that scandal was certain to rub off on him.'

It rocked Maggie. Was this another side of Alex, revealed to Kiko but not to her? 'He's really trying to stop Arigata?'

'I think he's taking this risk: get the contract paid for, then see Arigata decommissioned, or at least out of the hands of my grandfather.'

'Look, I'll try and get hold of Terry now. Let's book a flight for tomorrow – then maybe we can even stop Arigata before the official opening! I mean, I met a lot of the new White House people in the campaign, you know. I can pull strings.'

'Pull them.'

Even after hanging on for minutes, there was no reply from her south bank studio complex.

By now the security guards would have gone home. There must have been nobody free to pick up Terry's private phone on the top floor, either; if they were really busy up there they would ignore its ring, and he had told her that he would be working very hard and very late tonight. Maggie decided to go over there and bring him back.

'Can you hang on for an hour or so?' she asked Kiko. 'I'll go and pick Terry up and we can decide what to do together.'

A raised eyebrow. 'Together?'

Maggie winced even at such polite irony. 'Look, I know we're not married or anything . . . Oh, he'll do what I say.'

'Is he necessary?'

'Necessary?' Maggie spread her hands, helplessly. 'I just feel committed.'

'Of course. Look, take your time. I'll make a photocopy of this document, then start an English translation. There are probably other things to find, also.'

Outside, Maggie walked south, away from the King's Road, then climbed into her fire-engine-red Ferrari for the drive through town. She went straight over the river to Battersea, enjoying the roar of the car and its excellent handling on this hot summer night. She went by the unlit park, glancing out to see dark trees behind the spiked iron railings. It was a quiet night, with a few spatterings of warm rain to keep people indoors.

When she reached the five floors of her converted warehouse in Southwark, there were few lights on. She let herself in and took the slow old lift to the top floor. There, she looked out left, through the huge curving glass windows.

The view across the Thames here between two London bridges was spectacular. Tonight there were discotheque boats on the river. Floating over the dark roofs of the City was the lit-up dome of St. Paul's – Wren's cathedral, raised out of the ashes after the great fire that tore through London in 1666. Her mood lifted.

Her heels sank into the carpet, which had black and white yin-yang designs Terry had specially commissioned. Only Terry had liked the results. 'Terry! *Terry*!'

There was no answer. She pushed open the double doors and walked into the big studio.

The lights were on here, dimly; they were special lights that could be set to imitate any kind of sunlight, from a watery Parisian March to the harsh glare of the south of Spain in August. She turned them up briskly and then poured herself a whisky from his drinks cabinet.

Here, a coffee-table book was open.

Naked women had their thighs spread wide, around red-lipped sexuality and bushes of pubic hair. Their smiles were come-ons: crude masculine fantasies. Maggie's lips pursed. Was this what the freedom-seeking sixties had come to? Lurid magazines from Soho, done for profit? Maggie brushed back her hair, suddenly tired. The bright lights made her squint as she looked around. Now that he had switched away from the news, was Terry's working life only here? Sadness descended on her.

The luxury props were all fake. Glittery costume jewellery, empty bottles of champagne and French perfume, gold coins that were not gold. So this, she thought in pain, is the Terry Katz of today. The man I love.

She walked on, hands outstretched, touching the props. There were tripods set up for Terry's cameras, which looked like stilt-legged creatures from low-budget science fiction. There were battered aluminium cases stencilled with his name, which contained light meters, precision lenses, and the expensive cameras themselves. Her mind flashed back to Vietnam and the other places she had seen those cameras used. Terry had been a hero to her back then: the ex-Marine turned hippy, the wonder boy out of San Francisco, the idealist out there in the big, hard world. The man who would be strong for her whenever she needed that, but would also let her be strong for herself, too.

So long ago, she thought. her eyes filled with tears. So many mistakes . . .

She touched the big studio spotlights, but they were stone cold; they had not been used for hours. Her mouth twisted. Wherever he was now,

Terry wasn't working tonight. She looked at the background screens, and the gold, silver and white umbrellas for the smaller flash units. Everywhere she saw cables snaking, black and intertwined, plugged into multi-socket blocks and heavy-duty wall-sockets.

Behind a screen of tropical greenery in one corner of the main studio, she discovered a pile of cushions, and a 16 millimetre German cine-camera pointed down at a leather saddle on a knee-high frame. A jewelled G-string was laid across it, and on the floor somebody had discarded thigh-length black leather boots.

She found herself blushing as she stood over the saddle, hands on her hips. Apple-smelling perfume hung in the air, but could not disguise a salty odour. She bent down, picked up a tiny black curl and held it up to the light. A pubic hair. So a woman had been here . . . Under the camera, twisting in passion, a woman had been here.

But the worst thing of all was that she had been here, too. Many times. Memories flooded back; her, stretching a leg out in front of Terry, his hands freeing a black stocking from her suspender belt, rolling it down and smiling all the time. Then getting down, with her, in this same comfortable corner under the poster one of his Tina Turner photographs had been turned into.

Maggie remembered her bare buttocks writhing on the cushions and Terry telling her that he loved her as he pumped into her. Had that just been a rehearsal for *this*?

Maggie felt weak, suddenly, and squatted down. There were even the unmistakeable stains on the leather of the saddle – sex, right here in her building, on her time, and probably with some beautiful, long-legged Latin model she had paid for. She knew Terry's tastes by now.

Maggie stood up and flung her glass at the wall, tears in her eyes.

'Why do you do this to me? Why?' There was no answer. This building, like her life, was quite empty. Her voice rose into a self-pitying wail. 'Terry Katz, you're a bastard.'

Then she went home the same way she would go to Japan. Without Terry.

Chapter Twenty-four

When the Stanton cousins moved into a suite in the Mandarin Hotel on Connaught Road, they took rooms high enough to have a spectacular view of Victoria Harbour. They had business meetings most of the next day, did some sightseeing, then went to the Admiralty building in the late afternoon. It was dark by the time they returned from a meal in a recommended restaurant in Causeway Bay. Incredible buildings surrounded them as they rode in the taxi: the illuminated signs flashed on and off, making the night gaudy.

Later, Alex stood at the window of their suite, sipping his tonic water. He thought of Hideki, thought of Arigata, brooding on his own involvement: was this guilt he felt? Hugh eventually asked Alex what they were waiting for, but he refused to answer directly. 'Asia, dear cousin.'

'We're waiting for Asia?'

'For the Pacific century to start.'

'Are we? Myself, think I'll go to bed,' Hugh responded sleepily.

David Bryant flew in by British Airways, early the next morning, straight from an EEC meeting in Paris. After the respectful immigration and customs officials, Alex welcomed him at the bar in the VIP waiting room. He told Alex, blinking, that he had slept a little on the plane. He looked around. Here there was a view of the runways and, beyond the crowded bay, Hong Kong island itself.

'Incredible sight,' David said, shaking his head.

'It is,' Alex answered soberly. 'Erected out of a barren and waterless wilderness by the power of money – and individuals' self-belief.'

They sipped straight Scotch. David looked tired. So did Alex. 'I hope I'm doing the right thing, Alex. You realize, I'm legitimizing Arigata and everything it represents just by my presence.'

'I appreciate what you're doing, believe me.'

They went to the governor's mansion in another official car. As a minister of the crown, David was received with respect. Alex left him to it, but before he could head back to the hotel he was met by Burke.

'Thought you'd want this. It came in overnight.'

'Thanks.'

The message said simply: ARRIVES 5 P.M. TOMORROW, VIA JAL TOKYO. STAYING MANDARIN HOTEL AS EXPECTED.

'What you wanted?' Burke said.

Alex adopted the other man's terse style. 'Yes.'

Burke opened a door. 'Could I have a word? In private.'

Alex sat down as the SIS man closed the heavy door behind him.

'Something from Germany,' Burke said. There seemed to be a hint of accusation on the inexpressive face. 'A con man their intelligence service let run. Faintly embarrassing, therefore: the meeting took place in Zurich.'

'The Swiss wouldn't like it, if they heard the West Germans were operating on their territory . . . Who did he meet?'

'A man purporting to represent the Iraqi government. A Dr Sidqi. Subject of discussion, calutrons and uranium enrichment. Mean anything?'

Alex folded his hands together. 'Tell me more.'

Burke blinked, astute, judging. 'Sidqi was fishing for technology to help with an Iraqi atomic bomb. Point is, he claimed he already had support from a big British firm and its Japanese counterpart.'

'I see,' Alex said.

'The British firm was Stanton Industries. The Japanese firm was the Hideki Corporation.' A pause. 'Well?'

'Hugh doesn't know anything about this,' Alex said. He considered. 'Would it be best if I was debriefed when I return to London?'

Burke nodded, slowly. Then he opened the door.

Back in the hotel, Alex put his feet up and thought. Hideki had all the cards, so far. And if there really was something in this atomic story . . . He sighed, got some sheets of writing paper, put the date at the top of the first and began to write.

As Alex was sipping fresh-squeezed orange juice, Hugh came in from his meeting at the Hongkong and Shanghai Bank. He flourished a newspaper excitedly. 'There's something in the FT. Take a look.'

The headline said STANTON: TWIN TRIUMPHS IN SAUDI ARABIA AND INDIA?

'It all had to leak out sooner or later.' Alex looked at his cousin. 'Well, it gives us money, which is power, and that means a bit of freedom from Hideki.'

Hugh sat down and said seriously, 'Might annoy the Carter White House, Alex.'

'But it will please our own employees, shareholders, and bankers.' Alex wiped his lips. 'I have something I'd like you to take back to England today. Don't open it yet.'

Hugh picked up the large, sealed envelope. 'Something secret?'

'For consideration later. If I say so from Tokyo. Or from Arigata.'

Hugh looked thoughtful. 'What are you expecting there? Trouble?'

'Just being prepared.' Alex stood up.

'You don't want to tell me exactly what you're doing?' Hugh was hurt. 'What about the military types you've smuggled into the Arigata workforce?'

'Hold the fort in London, Hugh. Just give us a secure base. Please.'

Alex saw his cousin take off on a scheduled 747 for London. He felt a strange mixture of emotions. Sir Hugh was going on, one day to be Lord Stanton, and perhaps Alex Stanton was not. But he knew that the company would be in safe hands now, family hands, whatever happened at Arigata.

Alex checked his watch as a Japan Air Lines flight came in, and he considered staying, then decided not to meet his target at the airport. That might attract attention. So he went back to the Mandarin. He left a message at reception, showered again and put on a clean shirt, then settled down to drink in one of the private bars, pleased by the comfortable leather chairs and oak tables and nineteenth century paintings on the walls. He sat pretending to read a *Wall Street Journal* and in reality thought over his situation, inwardly on edge, outwardly tanned, calm and relaxed.

It's one more thing to try, he thought as he considered his plan. Nanwara is powerful in Japan. I *need* him.

After half an hour someone sat down beside him, and he put the paper down and looked up. A grey-haired Japanese, kindly-looking, wearing spectacles.

'Well, this is great,' Alex said, pretending to be surprised, pretending that this was a coincidence. 'Akira Nanwara!'

They shook hands. Alex ordered drinks.

'You here for long?'

'Fly out late tomorrow afternoon,' the man said, straightening his tie. 'I have morning meetings about two new factories here. Low-cost production.'

A fine euphemism for cheap labour, Alex reflected.

Nanwara added, proudly, 'Tomorrow night, I will be in Moscow.' He pronounced it the American way.

'And the day after?'

'Tokyo again,' Nanwara replied, sipping Perrier water, giving nothing away.

Alex looked around, noting there were no women at all in the bar. 'If you're free tonight, perhaps you can eat out at Aberdeen with us.'

It was very polite and very non-commital. 'Us?'

'Myself, a British Secretary of State – I'm sure you remember David Bryant – and some American visitors.'

Nanwara blinked, slowly. 'I feel rather tired, and of course my staff here had plans.'

'I'd consider it a very great favour,' Alex said. 'I have one or two things you might care to look over. Things of considerable importance to Japan. Of course, I'll be in Tokyo soon myself.'

It was said lightly. 'For the Arigata opening?'

'Exactly!' Alex sat back. 'Eight o'clock suit you?'

'I'll be here,' the Japanese billionaire said. 'But I can't stay late. Moscow is far away, remember.'

'I do remember,' Alex told him, 'though some people tell me it's getting closer all the time . . .'

Alex walked out of the huge hotel, excited and pleased by the arrangement with Nanwara. In spite of his modest bearing, he was an extremely powerful man in Tokyo, not to mention rich. More powerful than Hideki, Alex judged, if not so personally wealthy – but imagine buying stock in, or founding, companies like NE and Sony and the many arms of the Mitsubishi combine at 1945 prices . . . He strolled on through the busy streets that led to the waterfront, glancing around, automatically observant. Chinese faces, cars and bicycles, signs in other scripts as well as English. In these side streets small children raced about; he passed open-fronted shops and walked under lines of flapping washing.

Hong Kong. Millions of people; one of the largest ports in the world. He saw water again soon after smelling it. Here he joined the jostling line running through the turnstiles, and boarded the crowded Star Ferry that would take him over to Kowloon side. He wanted to kill a little time and give himself some extra thinking space.

It was a hot and cloudy afternoon. Eighty-one Fahrenheit and high humidity made Hong Kong a sweatbath. He spread his feet apart as the ferry moved off, and he looked back and up at Victoria Peak, smelling the salt and stink of this historic ship-crowded harbor. Soon Hugh would be safe in London. He thought of Maggie as he leaned on the rail, and then he thought of Arigata. To her, it would be a story; maybe the story of a lifetime, if Hideki went far enough. He sighed, watching the waves and the gulls circling above them, knowing that going to Arigata might be dangerous and that Maggie was not responsible for Arigata at all, and also a woman, and a woman that some part of him still admired above all others.

Sorry, my dear, he decided, as the small boats quickly made way for this big, powered ferry. I will not invite you, and I hope you'll stay at home. I'll just have to see this through myself, one way or another. The responsibility and the risks – mine, all mine.

I love you, he found himself thinking. We should have stayed together. Caroline Ross was a big mistake, and a worse marriage.

He took a cab, Kowloon side. Back at Kai Tak Alex welcomed more visitors. Ray had come over from LAX, the international airport at Los Angeles, bringing the other US guests with him.

The Senator for Colorado was an old friend of Alex's. Michael Perry was a tall, slender and donnish Republican, a former Rhodes scholar and an intelligence officer veteran of Korea; his interest in Asia was longstanding. Tom Kalbach was a friendly East Coast lawyer Hacker Stanton International did business with, and he had been the American representative at the '76 trade conference at Tokyo. Both men were members of the standing White House special commission on trade.

They would be good witnesses, Alex decided as he shook hands.

David appeared, with a Chinese man in a police uniform with HKP shoulderflashes.

Alex felt good to have his friends around him. 'Okay,' he told them. 'I'll see Nanwara tonight, before he gets to Moscow, and I'll find some way to denounce Hideki.'

'Make it a very convincing way,' David said with tired cynicism.

Alex merely winked.

Hacker murmured, 'No chance of Nanwara cancelling this Moscow trip and going back to Tokyo to pull strings?'

'Cancelling a prestige trip like that? No. But I have hopes, when he gets back. But by then, we'll be in Japan ourselves.' He turned to David. 'Any chance of putting a diplomatic spoke in Hideki's wheel?'

David patted his forehead with a handkerchief and then shook his head. He had heard the latest. 'The Foreign Office seems to have its hands full at the moment. The junta in Argentina are kicking up a stink about the Falkland Islands again: the crazy so-and-sos have fired on a British vessel there *and* arrested a bunch of Soviet trawlers.'

'Christ,' Alex said, 'maybe we should just nuke Buenos Aires and have done with it!'

'That's a terrible thing to say,' David said testily, 'especially under these circumstances. Where's your sensitive side?'

'I'm sitting on it,' Alex said coarsely. He sighed. 'Okay, take your point. Anything else?'

'The FO mandarins also pointed out,' David said, 'that Arigata is signed, sealed, and delivered – all by means of legal contracts.'

'Ray, anything from the States?'

Hacker shrugged. 'The CIA is in chaos, man. State Department, don't know. If there is a policy it's probably that Japan oughta boost its defences anyway.'

'That's the feeling in Congress.' Senator Perry spoke frankly. 'Don't know if I'd disagree with the sentiment myself, actually. At least they should damn well pay for it.'

Alex said, very softly, 'The nuclear issue?'

David steepled his fingers. 'Very complicated and delicate, I was told. Apparently the Nonproliferation Treaty should be enough; there are international inspectors who check.'

Alex snapped, 'So it's down to us. Let's hope the Soviets start putting some pressure on, too. They can start with Akira Nanwara, maybe.'

'Lean on Nippon Electronic and Nanwara?' Tom Kalbach said dubiously. 'I don't see how they can do that.'

'There are ways,' Alex said dangerously. 'Anyway, let's get you guys settled in. Tonight, we dine in style.'

At eight, they found Akira Nanwara in the Chinnery bar again, surrounded by a half-dozen pushy Hong Kong businessmen. He seemed glad that Alex and the others rescued him.

They all drove in two cars along the coast-hugging road through

Sheung Wan and Kennedy Town, and then on towards Aberdeen harbour, on the south side of Hong Kong island.

Nanwara sat with Alex in the Rolls, quite relaxed and at ease. 'Where will we eat?'

Alex held a thin document case under one arm. He felt oddly nervous. 'Surprises are easily spoiled.'

Nanwara gave a strange smile, but his eyes were supremely intelligent. 'I do not care for surprises. Fortunate that I am rarely surprised, therefore.'

'Life is full of surprises,' Alex contradicted, politely.

Aberdeen harbour was crowded with lit-up boats and sampans and junks. They got out at one of the wharves. Here were the towering, gaudy and famous floating restaurants, coloured electric bulbs strung everywhere, sampans sailing further out, full of tourists or trying to attract tourists.

They were sculled across by Hoklo boatswomen. Further out, the dimly-lit junks of the boat people. The heavens had cleared, and they would be able to eat and drink under the stars and take advantage of the light sea breezes. They chose still-living fish from the tanks and then went to the large table they had been given, which overlooked the water. The boat was crowded with chattering diners and decked out in scarlet and gold, the dragons representing China everywhere in the decoration.

Ray threw back a cold beer, wiped his lips. Food smells, quite delicious, wafted around. 'This is great.'

Alex agreed. He glanced around, seeing the rich Chinese crowding the other tables, the waiters scurrying about, agile, always smiling, hearing the Cantonese and other dialects he did not understand. 'Shall we start, Mr Nanwara?'

There were twelve courses, tea all the time, any beer or wine you wanted.

'Five million Chinese,' Nanwara said softly. 'Yet, when the British seized these islands in, let me see . . .'

'In 1841,' David supplied. 'They were almost entirely barren and uninhabited when the British China traders forced their government to annex Hong Kong island. In fact, though the harbourage was always superb, the Queen's Foreign Secretary called this place, not inaccurately, "a barren rock with nary a house upon it".'

'Yet think of what has been built,' Nanwara said, openly admiring.

'A little British know-how, Chinese labour, universal free trade,' Alex said. 'A recipe for success.'

Nanwara said quietly, 'As opposed to other recipes for success, you mean?'

'Christ,' Hacker threw in, 'we're all businessmen these days, right? Whatever works, works?'

Nanwara and Alex both used ivory chopsticks.

They all sampled shark's fin soup and spiced chicken and stir-fried beanshoots and green peapods. Everything was delicious. Little bowls held oyster, soya and ginger sauces. They drank wine and jasmine-scented Chinese tea, still surrounded by the press of rich Chinese businessmen and their wives on the other tables.

Alex said quietly, 'Not long ago, almost a third of the world was coloured red on British maps. The British empire: our co-prosperity sphere, if you like.'

Nanwara stopped eating. 'All that is gone,' he said, politely.

'Peaceably,' Alex said to him, very quietly, hoping Nanwara would understand. 'As all things should change, now. Peaceably, and through the changing patterns of trade. And if Hong Kong has become great, though it is only a group of barren rocky islands, how much greater has Japan become – and how much greater could it be, in a peaceable world that changes through trade?'

'It is perhaps *karma*,' Nanwara said. He sampled pure white rice. 'Or perhaps *joss*. Luck, as they say it here.'

'Whether it is destiny or luck, as we both know, all things change.' It had to be done very delicately, now, and he hoped that nobody except his friends could overhear. 'I'd like you to read something.'

'Something?'

'A few little-known facts about a certain Hideki.'

Nanwara's smile was avuncular. Hideki was his enemy, though in the Japanese code this was never publicly admitted. 'Of course. Back in the hotel? I am always willing to learn.'

Alex toasted Nanwara, and began to talk lightly of lesser things. In the folder he carried was a thin dossier about Hideki, his private army, his political attitudes, and his off the record boasts about Arigata. 'You plan much business in Moscow?'

'This is exploratory meeting, really. I must watch rivals, Sony, Matsushita.'

'Of course.' So you won't tell me about your Moscow meeting, and who could blame you? But I hope you think carefully about Hideki, though.

Hacker was talking about the rumours of naval actions. 'It's the usual push-pull. They go out of Vladivostok, we go out of Hawaii and Subic Bay.'

'And what happens when both sides meet?' David asked harshly.

Hacker shrugged his broad shoulders.

They went back to the Mandarin in the same cars, Alex relaxed now, and a little drunk. As they passed the China Ferry Pier off Connaught Road Alex turned to Nanwara and gave him the folder. 'Pleasant reading.'

'Really?'

'No, I'm lying. It's unpleasant reading, I'm afraid.'

The older man weighed the thin folder, sighed.

Alex said nothing. Both cars drew up in front of the huge hotel among the other cabs and cars, Rolls-Royces and Mercedes among them; motorcycles roared by on the road. There were still many people about.

David did not wait for his own door to be opened. He strolled about, beaming. 'Fancy another, in the hotel?'

Alex sniffed the air, stepped back for Nanwara.

Then two Chinese youths rushed them, faces masks of aggression. Alex dropped into a fighting crouch but he was not the target. One howled, threw some kickboxing moves and attracted everyone's attention: a mugging. But the other pushed Nanwara over and simultaneously grabbed the cardboard file Alex had given him.

They ran away across the still-busy road, dodging the traffic, stopping and sidestepping, slipping away in the confusion as brakes were squealing and horns honking.

Alex sprinted after them immediately, ignoring the pain from his damaged leg. Cars braked, went left and right: there was a sound of smashing glass.

One following another the youths mounted a Honda motorcycle and started it. As soon as the motor was blaring the passenger glared back at Alex and mouthed obscenities, folder tucked inside his sweater. The bike went swinging out quickly into the stalled traffic.

Alex stood there, shaking his fist. As he had hoped, the youths drove straight for him, jeering, the motor screaming.

At the last moment he sidestepped and hit out with his left fist, the blow superbly timed, much of his weight behind it. The handlebars ripped a hip-height pocket, but the driver screamed as his jaw was broken. The bike crashed down on the road, spraying sparks. There was a crunch of metal as a taxi went over the Honda. Somebody was shouting.

Alex bent down, grabbed for the folder which had flapped free, but the passenger rolled on to his feet again and came forward with a knife in his right hand. Maybe he was covering his broken-jawed and stunned companion, maybe he wanted the folder back, maybe he would kill.

'Alex, leave it!' David shouted, as a police whistle shrilled somewhere.

Alex stepped back quickly, as his opponent feinted, left, right, intending to drive Alex onto his back foot and then stab him. In the melée the document folder was hacked twice and one of the slashes cut Alex's right wrist.

But other people were coming, from both sides of the road, and the other thief had already fled. This one looked around as Hacker came rushing up, huge and enraged. He spat, ducked under Hacker's roundhouse right and sprinted off with impressive acceleration.

Alex was breathing hard, and he held the two sides of the cut on his wrist together, though blood had leaked out and stained his linen shirt red. 'He's gone, Ray. But thanks for the back-up.'

Ray glanced at his cut wrist, then continued checking their surroundings. 'I see you still keep in shape. That was good. Bastards!'

It was over. Traffic had begun moving again, and he and Hacker threaded back through it carefully. Here, parked, the two drivers who had collided were arguing with a bored-looking Chinese police constable.

Nanwara was still huddled against a car, open-mouthed and shocked.

'I'm sorry about that,' Alex said. He handed the folder over unobtrusively. 'You're flying out tomorrow, destination Moscow? I'll have somebody have a word with the police commissioner and get you some protection till then.'

Nanwara swallowed. 'Thank you.' He lowered his voice. 'I'll read your document with interest. In fact, please, can we talk?'

Alex escorted the older man into the Mandarin, made his excuses to his friends, and followed Nanwara into his suite. A doctor, summoned by the staff, swabbed the slash on Alex's wrist with antiseptic, then put five small stitches into it. As he bandaged Alex's wrist, Alex watched Nanwara check the Japanese and the English of the Hideki dossier.

Alex thanked the doctor, wondering if a tip was appropriate and deciding it was not. He turned to Nanwara. 'Well?'

'Sit by me, please.' Alex did so. 'Let me see your hands.' Nanwara turned them over: they were very tough. 'Hard hands. Martial arts?'

Alex took his hands back, shrugged. Nanwara was surprising him.

'And you shoot.'

'Shoot birds, like grouse on our moors? Not me. First, they don't shoot back, so where's the challenge and risk in that? Second, the rules don't let me use a machinegun.'

Eyes opened wide, Nanwara asked, 'What are you? What they say?'

'I've made some rough deals, Akira Nanwara. That's true. But I got out alive – every time. Anyway, what do you think of the Hideki papers?'

'All so terrible, Alex!'

'I agree. Question is, what are we going to do about Hideki now?'

Nanwara sat there, sagging bonelessly. Alex was glad he had told this man.

The Japanese said, 'I had a quiet war, as a technician. I never believed it was right, nor that we would win. I felt shame, over the Pacific war . . . And though I believe in hard work, and hope that Japan will be made rich and strong by our hard work, this . . .' He gestured helplessly at the document. 'But this secret society you allege, you do not have more details, such as the names of the members?'

'A manifesto was signed in 1945, Nanwara-*san*,' Alex said, 'along the lines described in those papers. But the key points are these. To achieve technological superiority and then to rearm Japan. To make use of nuclear power and then get a government into power in Tokyo prepared to – ah, hell, you've read it, and you obviously find it credible.'

'Credible – and dangerous! What will the Russians say, or our American friends!' He spread his hands, looked around his suite.

Alex pressed the point home. 'And now I have to apologize to you.'

'To me?' Puzzlement was plain.

'Hideki knows me. He'll know what I know, more or less – that I would appreciate Japanese allies such as yourself. Perhaps the mugging tonight was no coincidence.'

'You mean that Saigo Hideki sent those men with knives!'

Alex shrugged. 'Maybe they were just muggers. But if Hideki is tracking me to Arigata, if he sees me meeting you like this . . . Hideki is paranoid, I think. He might put us both on his enemies list.'

This time the expression seemed only thoughtful. 'So you're really telling me I should stop him, yes, otherwise he might one day come after me?'

'You must draw your own conclusions.'

Just then the phone rang. He glanced at Alex, picked it up. There was rapidfire Japanese Alex could not follow, though he tried hard. Then Nanwara said, 'My staff in Tokyo have heard from their Honolulu office. Advance elements of the huge US Pacific Fleet, the Third Fleet, have sailed out of Hawaii, to reinforce the Seventh Fleet – and the Seventh Fleet has been put on high alert and is supposed to be heading for the Chinese coast!'

Alex said quietly, 'Let's not overreact – unless you imagine Jimmy Carter and Cyrus Vance have decided to invade China?'

'Or Japan?'

Invade Japan? Alex could only answer with something even more outrageous. 'Or restart the war in Vietnam?'

From Hong Kong, later that night, Alex could not contact Maggie at home. Her business said she was heading for Tokyo.

'I see,' Alex said. 'Thanks, Kai.' He turned to Hacker, rubbing at his wrist. 'Straight to Japan, that's what I say. The Senator finishes his fact-finding mission here tomorrow.'

'Then we go. How's the wrist?'

'A minor cut.' He laughed. 'It certainly got Nanwara's attention, though.'

'You mean—' Hacker's amazed expression turned to one of admiration.

Alex nodded. 'Oh yes, a set-up. If you want to get attention, shock tactics will do it. Now, we have the Russians involved, the United States, the press and the opposition parties in Japan, and also Akira Nanwara. That's some coalition stacked up against Saigo Hideki.'

'Is it enough, though?'

Alex could not say that for certain.

Chapter Twenty-five

Satellite photographs had been the first proof.

One of the standard targets of US intelligence is the home base of the USSR's Pacific Fleet, Vladivostok, which is a warm-water port on the Amur River. East and south-east of the spit of land curling across its mouth, over the Sea of Japan and not very far away, you will find the many islands of the Land of Nippon itself – and a turn north will take you to Hokkaido and the islands off it, territory still sacred to the rulers of Japan, though it was occupied by Stalin at the close of World War II.

The analysts at the Defense Intelligence Agency recognized what they saw immediately.

Vladivostok port was empty.

The Soviet Pacific Fleet had sailed. All of it.

Interpreting motives was a more difficult matter, and here naval intelligence as well as the CIA were called in. The White House was given outline opinions an hour later.

The real question, of course, was why this had happened at all. Polite interrogations of the usual diplomatic sources said this was no more than a large-scale exercise. The Pentagon analysts were more dubious. There was an unconfirmed report that the Politburo had taken action on the advice of State Security Commission Chairman Andropov. Also, the staff at the Soviet Embassy in Tokyo had been increased the previous week, and signals traffic from there had gone up by sixty percent.

From Washington the word had gone out to CINCPAC – Commander-in-Chief, Pacific. The US Seventh fleet, which had once pounded Vietnam, was mainly scattered off the Philippines. The order was received to take formation and head for Japan.

The even larger US Pacific Fleet, based in Pearl Harbor, Hawaii, was also ordered out to sea – to sea, and then west towards Japan and the Soviet Union.

The Russian Ambassador had asked for an appointment with the Foreign Minister of Japan. It was granted for one o'clock in the afternoon that same day. The ambassador followed strict protocol, as members of the USSR's Foreign Service usually do. He gave a verbal ultimatum from his government in Moscow. The Tokyo government would have to agree to allow unlimited international inspection of its nuclear programme. There would be no importation of weapons-grade plutonium under any circumstances.

Through his translator, the Foreign Minister of Japan replied with excruciating politeness, smiling all the while. The matter of the Japanese reactor-building programme was open for all the world to see, and the nonproliferation treaties would be adhered to. However, they could not allow individual parts to be inspected except by prior arrangement with the International Atomic Energy Authority. That was the law. There was no question of Japanese imports of fissionable material being illicit.

As soon as the ambassador returned there was a crisis meeting in the embassy.

Glykov chaired it: he outranked everybody here, by far. 'Will they submit?'

'No,' the ambassador said, tersely, disliking being put in an inferior position by this brutal man. 'The Moscow ultimatum has not been rejected. Neither has it been accepted. In other words, they will go ahead and do exactly what they want, with regrets, apologies and promises of further discussion and change as necessary – as usual.'

General Glykov shook his head pityingly. 'Do they not realize what forces we have? All our ships and carriers, now heading out from Vladivostok – enough to defeat Japan in a few days, as they should know!'

'They know, Comrade General, but they do not believe, perhaps, that we would dare use force,' the ambassador said.

'So they think that the good Christian President Jimmy Carter will protect them, do they? That he is so foolish that he will be strong for the first time, the *only* time, when it would be right for him to be weak?'

'I do not know,' the ambassador answered, stolidly.

Glykov looked at his watch. 'Then we are agreed that there is no alternative. I must recommend we take active measures to enforce the will of the Politburo.' He snapped his fingers. 'Take this down, send it in a secure cable to Moscow Centre under my authority—'

'Comrade General.' In his stylish grey suit Kerensky seemed out of place here, but he spoke up strongly though his face was shiny with perspiration. 'It seems clear that Hakagawa and Hideki are the leading figures in this conspiracy. The prime minister is not in a strong position, merely a compromise between the Tanaka, Fukuda and Hakagawa factions . . .'

'Then he can't stop Arigata, can he?'

'Perhaps not. But I would like to be given a few hours to approach other leaders here, other ministers and people who have influence over the Liberal Democratic Party government.'

The craggy-faced general gave a thin smile, and sipped at a glass of cold water. The stenographer, a middle-aged woman with heavy framed glasses and hair tied up in a bun, sat waiting beside him, head bowed deferentially.

'To Moscow Centre,' Glykov said. 'Top-security codes, my personal designation. Foreign Minister refuses to accept our ultimatum stop Embassy staff do not believe he will even take it to the cabinet stop Friends of the Hakagawa faction are becoming increasingly influential stop I see no alternative except to take the prearranged strong and direct measures stop.'

There was silence in the long room with shuttered windows. More cigarette smoke swirled towards the air vents.

'I will give Comrade Kerensky till ten o'clock tonight. Otherwise that message will be sent.' He looked around the table: the eyes of eight men failed to meet his. 'But there will be no idleness here, no drinking of export vodka, no reading the decadent Western press. No. Instead we will use all of our agents here, both covert and open, to influence the actions of the Tokyo government. That is all.'

The others recognized the harsh voice of mastery. They stood up.

From his borrowed office Kerensky immediately rang to make an appointment with one of the paymasters of the ruling political party. Then he looked at some of the newspapers. There was coverage of Arigata, and the consensus was breaking down. Some commentators advocated rearmament and a Japan free to say no to the outside world of foreigners: and others presented Arigata as an expensive scandal. Organizations like Friends of the Earth were becoming involved, and so was the Socialist Party.

First, Kerensky met one of the USSR agents of influence, and briefed him. Then he checked that the other man he wished to see had now returned from abroad.

Kerensky dressed carefully, took a cab, took the subway, then another cab. He was sure he had not been followed, though tension prickled along his skin. Face it, he said to himself, if this really is a Hideki conspiracy, there will be no hesitation about assassinating me.

He met his contact in a Korean restaurant in the Shinjuku area. It was not at all the place to take a man as important as Akira Nanwara, but Kerensky explained the reasons why quite openly, deliberately sacrificing his cover. They both spoke English, the only language they had in common.

'I am tired,' Nanwara said. 'Just back from Moscow. There I met some very important people, young man.'

'Mr Nanwara, you have met me four times now, and you have seen me in high-powered company. I am more than I seem. I have the rank of major in the KGB, First Chief Directorate – you can check me out later if you wish. My rôle will have been suspected, I think.'

Nanwara ate in solemn silence, bamboo chopsticks clicking, then paused to wipe his lips with a napkin. He said with astringent distaste, 'I suppose no Russian would make such a boast falsely.'

'Then we accept that much. Accept what I say as truth. You know a little of me. You, a public figure, are more known to me. So, you give money to the political factions here; you follow the faction-fighting in the government, as you must.'

The multi-millionaire chairman and owner of Nippon Electronic looked at the athletic young Russian with distaste. 'Do I? I am close, close friend of Toshiwo Doko, the head of our industrialists' organization *Keidanren*. Like my friend, I do not bribe politicians.'

'Because they must court you anyway, money or not – since you are so important?'

Nanwara seemed offended by this bluntness. He flung the soiled napkin down. 'What is your point?'

Oleg Kerensky lowered his voice. 'You know there is a faction in the government here which has Hakagawa at its head.'

The smile was bland and Japanese and meaningless. 'That is Japanese affair.'

'He must not be allowed to take power here.'

A pause. 'I might agree with that. As a private citizen, you understand. Old-style militarism profits us nothing.'

Kerensky gave a grim smile. 'Further, the secret plan for buying tons of weapons-grade plutonium from the impoverished British – it cannot be allowed to go ahead.'

Nanwara's eyebrows had risen. 'This is an official protest, about an official agreement?'

'Of course this is not official; supposedly I am a journalist, and deniable. That is the entire point. The official protest was made this morning to your Foreign Minister. As far as we know he has refused to take it further.'

'He will not tell the cabinet, you mean?' The old man sat back from the table, his tired face stern. 'You are talking all this up into a crisis, aren't you?'

'This *is* a crisis! Don't you understand, ships are sailing, planes are flying!'

'They should leave us alone. We are neutral.'

'Are you on the side of Minister Hakagawa?'

The Japanese face was shuttered and tight. Perhaps there was rage there; but with Nanwara's control it was impossible for Kerensky to know for certain. 'Are you trying to bring down our government?'

His lips peeled back. 'I am trying to stop a disaster!'

'So you tell me.'

They sat back from the private table in the restaurant, annoyed with each other. There were other people in the place; the air was steamy and filled with the spicy smells of cooking and the sound of voices – filled with life. Kerensky blinked, considered, then said slowly, 'Mr Nanwara, I know you are a well-respected man, and that you contribute heavily to the governing party here.'

He slurped at his tea, put it down heavily. 'Everybody in business contributes to the Liberal Democratic Party. It is the expected thing, to make sure you can be heard in Tokyo.'

Kerensky realized he was still not being taken seriously enough. In his despair and anger, he stood up and pushed back from the table. 'Look at my watch.' He tapped its Swiss, glass face. 'For hours our forces have been taking up position. Understand: military forces. The Kremlin has decided. Please, let our old men win in this. Your country is so rich, and I know what you plan.'

'Do you, now?'

'Let it be done slowly, and with peace. It is madness to make atomic weapons here! What if people find out? You anger Russia, all South-East Asia, your enemies China, even the Americans!'

The air conditioning rattled. Nanwara said nothing for more than a minute. Then he spoke carefully. 'I do not like Hakagawa. Not like Hideki. That is known. But this . . . Listen, you should tell your superiors, or let me tell them. Leave us alone. Don't rock the boat. Remember, we are in a sense fighting your battle: we are directly in competition with America.'

'But you have to pull back from Arigata, change that policy!'

Behind spectacles the eyes blinked, suddenly hard. 'Have a little patience, young man.'

Kerensky stood up, deciding that his grandfather the old general was right. 'Something will have to be done to teach you that we are serious. And it will be done.'

Glykov's coded radiogram was sent to Moscow Centre.

This meeting was very private, in a penthouse apartment owned by Iwata Hiso. Hiso was Hideki's near-equal in industrial power, and the paymaster of another faction in the Tokyo government. Five men, therefore. Hideki, the eldest at eighty, had been alive when the Manchus were on the dragon throne of China, and Victoria R was Queen-Empress of Britain and India.

Hideki led Hakagawa and the other leaders of the Society of the Unsheathed Sword to a low table, but first they all kneeled and bowed deeply to the portrait hanging on the wall. In this picture, taken when he was wearing Imperial Army uniform in December, 1941, the Showa Emperor Hirohito was not aged and ill.

Hakagawa sipped tea, belched. 'If his imperial majesty should pass on, what must we do?'

Hideki spoke precisely. 'The Crown Prince is a good man, they say. A weak, modern man, I think. He will be our cover as we take all necessary steps to expunge all this pretended shame about our past.' He remembered the hours he had walked through wrecked and burning Hiroshima.

'Shame!' Hakagawa's shoulders shook. 'I will send some more people with guns and swords to frighten those traitors in the teachers' union.'

Iwata's eyes glittered. 'I must point out, they have not been frightened so far, and the publicity is very bad for our cause. My contacts in the National Police Agency are predicting riots over Arigata.'

'No bad thing,' said Hideki coldly. 'Disorder always gives authority the right to suppress it – and the worse the disorder, the stronger our oppression can be. I hope the Leftists *all* take to the streets and insult our Emperor. Then they can be identified and smashed.'

'Ah, perhaps you are right,' Iwata said.

'So, let us settle our plans,' Hideki said quietly. 'All we need is a slight change at the top. We do not even need to formally renounce Sato's three non-nuclear principles, do we? *Tatamae*, we will not possess nuclear weapons, we will not manufacture them, we will not allow them into the country. *Honne*, we already have the means, we will merely be experimenting with nuclear power, and as for Japan being non-nuclear, we can point out that the Americans have always had nuclear weapons here – and if they can do it, so can we.'

A telephone rang. Iwata picked it up, barked an interrogative into it, then some other questions. Hideki remained impassive, but the others stirred. Then Iawata stood up suddenly, a huge, stooped billionaire, almost with the build of a sumo wrestler. He stared out of the window at the moated Imperial Palace. 'The godless Russians are moving. By sea and by air, in great power.'

'That is not a problem,' Hideki said quickly. 'We will get our friends in Washington to defend us. I will speak to the Ambassador immediately.' He bowed low to the Emperor's image. 'For the sake of Japan, we must humble ourselves a little to the Americans. Ah, but they are fools! Though we take their industries and their wealth, *still* they pay to defend us.'

'But it is demeaning to go to America for help,' Iwata said, his belly shaking. He turned around abruptly. 'And our enemy Nanwara, the "good man" of Japan, is to have questions asked in the Diet about Arigata!'

Hideki spoke soothingly, before Hakagawa's anger achieved expression. 'We must resist the Russian pressures for a little time only, then the secret agreements will be signed – and we will have our reactor programme, and unlimited uranium fuel, and plutonium, by the ton. And then, *tatamae*, we tell the Russians and the world that nothing is happening, that we are innocent. How can they prove what is real?'

'True, true,' Iwata said. He sighed. 'But I am tired of all this dissembling, polite half-truths – these people are only *gaijin*. When will we sign the Society's manifesto in public?'

'The ceremony will be at the Arigata reactor, after the official opening there.'

'When we are in charge?'

Hideki smiled. 'When the spirit of this Society is the spirit, again, of Japanese society.'

* * *

The Stanton private plane left for Japan a little after dawn.

They cruised at 12,000 feet, at the conventional speed. The course was obvious, their flightplan on the record at Hong Kong. Across the South China Sea, to Taiwan. Then they would overfly the East China Sea, and the Japanese island chain where Okinawa is. Then, crossing the coast of Kyushu near Nagasaki, on to Tokyo.

That was the filed plan. It was an hour before noon, Tokyo time, when the plan was abruptly changed.

Alex sprawled in the Boeing's main lounge, reading yesterday's papers. In the other sofas and chairs sat Hacker, hunched up by himself in an armchair, and a little group of talkers made up of David Bryant, Tom Kalbach, and the US Senator for Colorado, Michael Perry. There was the smell of fresh-baked French rolls, buttered hot, and strong coffee. Alex had an opened bottle of Jim Beam by his elbow. Occasionally he would pour a little into a tumbler, or Ray Hacker would.

Alex put down his newspaper. 'I just wonder what the Russians are up to in South-East Asia now. Straight into Taiwan, maybe, or South Korea. Reports say that some Russian vessels are already off Pusan and Nagasaki.' He stood up, as the floor slid away momentarily – he grabbed for the back of the swivel chair, which was bolted down. Clear air turbulence, he thought; this was not the proper season for the *taifun*, the great wrecking storms that sometimes hit China and Japan.

He went over to the wall behind the computer display screens. Here, a large map had been hung. Idly, he traced their projected course from Hong Kong over the sea to Kyushu and Honshu, the main Japanese islands. They were not far from Nagasaki, now. He remembered visiting the shipyards and the colossal Hideki dry dock. Then he noticed a moving dot on the radar repeater screen. It meant that some other large plane was coming from the west to intersect their course. He frowned, watching it. Was it somebody who knew what this Stanton plane was? He grabbed for the white telephone that connected him to the flightdeck.

'Captain Carter, I see we have another aircraft heading for us. Do you have an ID on it?'

'Let me see.'

He saw the faint white blip alter course. As far as he could see, it was now following the Stanton Industries jet, on exactly the same heading. Was it gaining? Maybe not. Maybe they were just biding their time . . .

He looked over his shoulder. Everybody was relaxed. He felt a moment of uneasiness, as if some sixth sense was warning him. 'Anything?'

There was a moment's pause: then the familiar Arkansas twang answered, 'I'll try and interrogate by radio, Mr Stanton. I'd say it's a long haul flight, probably civilian though. And big.'

Probably civilian. 'From where? Japan?'

'Korea, maybe. Or the Philippines or maybe Singapore.'

Alex wondered if he had enemies in the Kremlin, or in the Forbidden City in Peking. He stiffened. They might not act themselves, but through intermediaries who could afford to ignore the West. Like Kim Il Sung with his nuclear ambitions . . . 'Make sure it's not from the China mainland or north Korea – or Vladivostok.'

'I'll try.'

Alex sat down, looking at the radar display.

I had so many promises from Tokyo, he thought; so much enthusiasm for our history and the quality of our products. And I'll still have to sell them all that raw uranium, just as David will have to sell them reprocessed plutonium. It's humiliating, but beggars can't be choosers.

No. I can't let Hideki get away with this. I can't . . .

He glanced up. The blip was still there on their tail, pursuing them. And there seemed to be some other, fainter signals up ahead. He raised the handset again. 'Any luck?'

'Apparently, Mr Stanton, it's a Korean Airlines 747, en route to Osaka.'

Alex chuckled. He was taking this too seriously. 'Maybe I'm getting a little nervous. What about up front?'

Just then there a squawk of radio static, live in the cockpit. Alex listened in.

'—civilian flight – zone of the – United States military advise you – suggest ceiling of 3,000 feet—'

Ray Hacker had come over to him. 'Now what in hell is that?'

Alex glanced at him. 'Let's go up to the flightdeck.'

They passed the little bedrooms, the galley, a library. Then Alex opened the door marked STRICTLY NO PASSENGERS. He was not a passenger, and there were no closed doors in his world.

The pilot and co-pilot were at the controls, the flight engineer a little behind them in the incredibly crowded cockpit. Alex automatically glanced at the dial displays both below and above the heated windscreen: he checked airspeed indicators, rev counters for all engines, weather radar display, fuel reserve. Everything seemed normal. Then he felt Ray stiffen alongside him.

'Now what,' Ray said, gesturing with a thick thumb, 'is that?'

Alex whistled.

Above their altitude, lazily circling and intertwining, were the con-trails of upwards of a dozen fast aircraft – a white scrawl on the dark blue sky that spelled crisis.

'I acknowledge,' their pilot answered sharply. 'I repeat, this is a civil flight, a private flight. But, yes, it's agreed. We'll stay out of your way.'

Alex saw something on the horizon, a faint, steel-grey smudge. He squinted, his eyesight excellent. Their plane began to lose height. It was a big grey warship, may be a carrier. Other vessels screened it.

Then with shock he recognized what he was seeing: the nuclear powered carrier USS *Enterprise*, all 89,000 tons of it – and he realized Captain Carter was heading them almost straight for it. He stared at the angled flightdeck and the creamy wake trailing behind. Warplanes were on deck, ready to go.

Carter turned his head back momentarily, hands tight on the controls. The airframe vibrated faintly.

'It's the Seventh Fleet, Alex – they've scrambled their planes!'

'They've made contact with the Soviets,' Ray said heavily. 'And till the Hawaii force gets here you can bet our guys will be outnumbered and outgunned.'

Alex looked up again, uneasy. You could not actually see the supersonic planes that were playing tag high in the sky, but you could see the trails they left – and he wondered if any of the Soviet or American planes was armed with nuclear missiles.

Carter spoke into his throat radio mike again. His voice showed nervousness. 'I hear you. I will level off and hold to this present course. I will be available for in-air inspection.'

The note of the engines dropped, and with more slight shuddering their airspeed decreased again. Then a shadow momentarily fell across the cockpit.

Hacker turned his head quickly, excitement working in his rugged face. 'Well glory be, Alex, take a look at that.'

Flying parallel with them, no more than two hundred yards away, was an F-14 Tomcat in US Navy colours. Sidewinder missiles were slung below it.

Alex reached for the radio microphone. 'Is that the Tomcat flying with civil flight Sierra Tango Alpha 2?'

The answer crackled out of the loudspeakers. A deep, drawling voice. 'It is.'

'As you can see we are a British-registered plane on a civil flight to Japan. What do you advise? Over.'

'Keepin' out of this,' the laconic reply came back. 'Us and the USSR are playin' macho games up above 10,000 feet. Stick t'your present course, because if you drift left you'll be overflying the Soviets, part of their Pacific Fleet, and they might be feelin' trigger-happy – and if you go right, you'll be above our surface support ships, and they might just happen to feel itchy to shoot, too.'

'Message understood,' Alex said tersely. 'Over and out.'

The altimeter read 1,500 feet. That should be safe enough.

Then there was more radio noise. Alex, with a cold thrill, recognized it as an angry Russian voice.

The Korean pilot responded shrilly. Alex pursed his lips, listening to the argument.

Hacker glanced at him, gripping a handhold coming out of

the roof. 'I love the way those guys try to talk our language, Alex.'

'Regulations: English is compulsory for international air traffic.'

There was much background shouting on various frequencies: Alex recognized a Russian obscenity. The Koreans, notoriously touchy, argued for minutes, until their captain finally agreed to lose height and change course slightly, under protest.

'I am a civilian flight, and this is international airspace – the Russian navy has no right to—'

'I am ordering you to obey my instructions,' the Slavonic voice said, 'and to keep clear by a full mile of all peaceful Soviet ships, also in international space.'

They lost height again. In the sky above the combat planes were flicking towards each other, flicking away. The adrenalin was beginning to flow; the voices, both Russian and American, were charged with excitement.

Alex felt nervous. The sky was much too full for his liking – and he knew much better than the general public how often such manoeuvring led to accidents or even actual combat, and deaths both sides would conspire to cover up as accidents.

Kiko was beside the porthole window, holding her borrowed Nikon in both hands; the long snout of the telephoto lens was fixed to it. The dawn had come about an hour ago, from the direction of Japan.

'Look down there,' she said, snapping another long-distance photograph. 'Look at that flightdeck. An American aircraft carrier, isn't it?'

Maggie leaned over her, squinted at the 65 painted on the deck. 'I think that's the *Enterprise*, a nuclear carrier that used to sail off Nam.'

Maggie was peering out of the window too. The carrier was steaming north, with a picket line of other US vessels north, west and south of it, as if even the huge 89,000 ton bulk with its planes and tactical atomic weapons needed protection. Then she saw what the problem was, and she gasped.

As far as she could see, from horizon to horizon, more than a dozen Russian vessels were ranged out in a huge arc. This fleet was also steaming north – perhaps even on a course meant to intercept the Americans. Two of the grey ships had a swarm of antisubmarine helicopters around them.

She suddenly felt frightened.

The Soviet Pacific Fleet out of Vladivostok, and advance elements of the American Seventh Fleet, had come together on the open sea.

Maggie took a deep breath and tried to be calm. In the row behind her a child began crying. The floor trembled, then again. They changed course and she saw that the no smoking and seatbelt signs had come on. One of the pretty stewardesses began to push back the trolley serving cold drinks and alcohol; Maggie saw that she looked concerned. The Boeing suddenly twisted to port. The lurch was sickening, and then they headed down, so quickly that Maggie's stomach contracted.

There was a faint booming that shook the plane, and a Russian jet pulled away at super-Mach speed.

The child next to her stirred. Its American mother was still away, so Maggie put a hand on the girl's forehead and murmured a pleasantry. The note the 747's huge engines made deepened. Kiko looked around; other passengers had noticed, too. Then the loudspeakers crackled, and there was a human cough. A short speech in Korean. Then, 'This is the captain speaking,' said the voice in English, with a faint incongruous Australian accent. 'Afraid we have strayed into an area of – military concern. It's somewhere the Russian and American navies are holding, ah, manoeuvres . . . I'm therefore having to take, as a routine precaution, a slightly different course to the one arranged. I must ask everybody to refrain from smoking and to remain in your seats, with seatbelts on, at all times. Thank you.'

The little girl sat up, blinked her eyes. The few people who had been standing began to come back to their seats. The American mother was in the aisle and looking in the direction of the toilets; then the deck shifted underfoot and she scampered back to her row of seats.

Kiko had already strapped herself in. 'What's happening, Maggie? A Russian fleet! Do you think it could have anything to do with—'

Maggie bit her lip. Her stomach stirred uneasily and her ears hurt for a moment. 'I dread to think.'

Alex and Ray had strapped down behind the crew. Alex listened to the tersely excited radio chatter. He flinched as more sparring planes swooped by above, two F-14s thundering past at almost Mach 2. They had to dip down again, and go left. Then two Russians were shouting at them on the same channel.

Carter turned back, perspiration on his face. 'We have to go down more.'

Then, suddenly, they were less than eight hundred feet up, wheeling hard to the right to get away from a Soviet carrier: a 36,000 ton *Kiev* class boat. Alex saw a couple of Yak-36 fighters rise up from it and come straight towards them.

'—Korean plane, the Soviet navy *orders* you to head east immediately—'

'—civilian airplane Sierra Tango Alpha 2 is under the protection of the United States navy. I repeat, Sierra Tango Alpha 2 is under the—'

Then a louder voice came from the carrier: 'I am speaking for Vice-Admiral Korshov, and he tells American plane code STA2, the Boeing 727, to leave our area now, *or we will shoot you down.*'

Alex found his hands gripping the arms of the chair. 'My God! Listen, tell them we're not an American plane but we've got the Senator from Colorado on board – are they going to kill a US Senator!'

Then he heard another, angry Russian voice, this time shouting at the Korean airliner, and on the same frequency a New England voice was giving the Russian fighters instructions to stay back. There was tension that was turning into panic.

The Stanton plane was flying between two converging, armed fleets. The Korean 747 was following them. American and Russian fighters continued to spin about in the sky.

Alex saw the 30mm guns of an Osa II missile boat turn to track them, although the Russian carrier was several miles behind them now. Then he heard Ray Hacker yell and looked up in time to see gunflashes from the missile boat – just as the floor fell away.

'They've opened up on us!'

He heard them screaming in the lounge as their plane canted over, pulling towards the US fleet and turning its belly to the Russians. Carter took emergency evasive action, swearing quietly. Engines screamed; the gee-force was pushing Alex hard into his padded seat as he strained to see. With a supreme effort he turned his head and leaned to the left.

The shells arced up quickly, going above them, hundreds of feet above.

Perhaps there had been a trigger-happy sailor in charge of the guns, or simply a terrible, terrible mistake. And the Korean 747 had not reacted quickly enough.

Much of the long, long burst caught the Jumbo cleanly, raking it. Alex glanced up as they headed due east and saw the explosions, flashes of light on the hull and wings followed by trails of smoke. His own plane was barely two hundred feet above the wave-crests and, he hoped, safe.

At first the Korean jet did not appear to have been really hurt. It dipped down for a time, then the nose lifted, and it flew on more slowly. He took a breath, wondering how many people were on board. 'Do you think they'll make it?'

The co-pilot wiped away sweat. 'I think it's still losing height.'

Alex turned his head, to keep watching as long as possible. The big Boeing continued to fall. Then Carter said it had vanished from the radar screen, and there was another Babel of radio conversation. Was the 747 downed?

Explosions ripped into the plane, through the fuselage and into people. The concussions were slaps.

Maggie screamed along with everybody else. The floor dropped away, and as the main lights failed the plane became a terrible, down-tilting dark tunnel.

Her nose began to bleed and there were painful, spiky pains stabbing into her lungs. No air! The noise of the engines was a faint howl, now. They leaned forward, heading down and down in a crash dive. She could smell smoke and she began to scream as the terrible alternatives came to mind: die by fire in mid-air, or crash into the sea and, strapped into the seat, drown.

The cannon shells had hit fuel lines, power lines, and pierced the pressure cabin in half a dozen places. The air was still shrieking out. Maggie's hands clenched on the arms of her chair as she began to black out from lack of oxygen and panic.

Kiko's face was tight-drawn with terror, but Maggie saw that she had clutched her little leather case with the documents in it to her chest.

'We're dead, Maggie!' Tears had formed in her eyes. 'And now my grandfather will—'

'What?' Maggie said. This was obviously the complete story at last. '*What?*'

Kiko coughed and started again in desperation. 'He has this crazy kamikaze scheme – you see, Arigata is really about—' Her mouth worked soundlessly. 'Explodes!'

The low pressure meant the air was suddenly thin and icy-cold and full of condensation. Children and other women were still screaming. Then the plastic masks did come dangling down.

Against a stiffening panic Maggie grabbed for her own oxygen supply with one hand, pressed the mask over her mouth and sucked gratefully on the new, lifegiving air, turning her head to Kiko. Where were the emergency doors? If they were going to come down into the sea, she had to know where the emergency exits were. Red lights had come on. She blinked her tear-blinded eyes, and the smoke became thicker and blacker.

But then, a hundred feet from the whitecaps, the 747 managed to level out. The sound of the slipstream blasting past and through the holes in the fuselage was a roar rising to a scream.

Maggie heard the loudspeakers begin to speak again as it occurred to her this might not be death.

'—in case we crash-land into the sea you must remove your shoes and spectacles and brace yourselves—'

Level flight. Breathable air. In spite of the terrifying noise and the smell of burning and vomit Maggie turned to Kiko again. 'I think we might make it.'

Then the fuel failed completely. The engines died. Maggie saw them turn nose-down. She opened her mouth. Emptiness blew up in her stomach.

Then they smashed into the sea at over a hundred and fifty miles an hour.

Maggie yelled again and tried to cover her face; the impact had been stunning. She felt the plane bounce back from the sea, and it partly rolled over, so that people hung screaming from their safety harnesses, a few falling across the cabin.

Then the water began to rush in, in a tepid, killing flood.

The Korean 747 had crashed into the sea twelve miles away from the

Russian ship that had shot them down, at one-fifteen in the afternoon Tokyo time.

Every hour or so, a Russian long-range aircraft would invade Japanese airspace. The Soviet Pacific fleet was a long, menacing picket line, west and south of Japan. Elements of it were heading east, for the great Japanese ports of Osaka, Nagoya, and Yokohama–Tokyo. Another flotilla was heading for the coast off Arigata.

The Diet was about to be called into emergency session: the plutonium programme had already received a massive jolt of unwelcome publicity, and only the serious illness of the Emperor threatened that story's status on the front pages.

After the Korean 747 had been shot down, there were different headlines. Everybody had become even more tense. Abruptly, both the Japanese people and the West in general realized that this was not a negotiation but an evolving crisis – and that the problem was the desire of elements in the Japanese government to obtain the means to make nuclear weapons.

The US Ambassador was acting on the direct orders of Jimmy Carter's White House; he was advising caution, and was echoed by most of the European states.

In contrast, the Russian diplomatic force was making ominous noises. Their agents in Japan were already screaming for a reduction in tension, but they were almost drowned in the mass of ordinary people demanding the same thing.

The government seemed paralysed. Before he left for Arigata, Hakagawa used the Interior Ministry to issue a statement explaining, in ambiguous but understandable terms, that a strong and modern Japan should fear no other nation on earth.

It was beginning to look as if war and peace were in the balance.

Chapter Twenty-six

Both fleets sent out helicopters and boats, quartering the area where the Boeing had gone down. They found mainly wreckage.

By dusk, there were only twenty-three survivors reported, and one hundred and fourteen drowned corpses. Eventually, there were excuses from Moscow. Errors had been made; but the plane's death had been the fault of American interference and American pressures. Before the day's end, headlines all over the world were blaring RUSSIANS SHOOT DOWN KOREAN AIRLINER.

Among governing circles in Japan, the Russian ultimatum soon became well-known. Arigata had to be decommissioned as a fast breeder, no atomic weapons were to be held by the Japanese, and Article IX of the 1947 Constitution had to remain inviolate. Otherwise, as President Kennedy had done to Cuba in 1962, first the sea and then the air forces of the USSR would interdict Japan.

Without compromise.

All day there had been protests in Tokyo's streets and in the Diet. This time, with the ground carefully prepared by Kiko and her allies, the Hideki and Hakagawa faction found publicity was directed against them. Many of the citizens of Japan did not want nuclear weapons either. Without plan or organization, people began to head for the Arigata site.

The black Bentley David Bryant rode in had diplomatic licence plates, and a Union flag was flying above one wheel arch, so that red, white and blue fluttered as he rubbed at his tired eyes. The car journey from Haneda Airport into the city had already been fearfully difficult, with many diversions. He had seen armed police, but for some reason they were staying on the sidelines.

As the sun began to set red and gold above the city, you could still see black whirlwinds of smoke standing over the capital of Japan. Roads were blocked off, and he thought more demonstrators were on the streets than commuters. Rail and subway employees were mostly on strike, and many ordinary people had stayed home today. Tokyo was in chaos.

A 747 plane, and something over two hundred casualties, might only be the beginning.

David's car rounded a corner and the brakes were jammed on. His limousine screamed to a stop on burning rubber. Here in front of him, a barricade of smashed-up cars had blocked off the street. Students wearing crash-helmets or with red scarves tied around their heads stood in front of the road block, carrying clubs and home-made spears.

Bryant flinched. This looked bad.

Three of the demonstrators started to run towards them.

Wondering if he was about to be lynched, David forced calm into his voice as he instructed the frightened embassy driver. 'If you know another route, use it. And quickly – *hayaku, kudasai.*'

The first demonstrator was already upon them, his lips drawn back savagely to expose the young man's teeth. He screamed in broken English, stabbing with a finger, '*Gai-jin*! You help them make bombs!'

It was a true indictment, David silently confessed, as others now raced to surround the vehicle. They were rattling the doorhandles. Fists began to beat on the roof and windows, then someone ran up with a baseball bat.

Bryant sank down into his seat, looking around desperately. Was this how it would end?

Suddenly the Bentley reversed. The demonstrators continued shrieking as it went into a three-point turn, and a brick bounced off the near window, cracking the laminated glass. David stayed well down as the car accelerated away from the growing throng of demonstrators running from the barricade.

Only a street or two away, everything was different. High office buildings, shops open for business: things were quiet and normal here, David saw in surprise. Even a white-gloved policeman stood calmly directing traffic.

In the embassy grounds, when they reached them at dusk, was a contingent of riot police. David also saw four dark-windowed police vans, parked in a line on the eerily still street. When David got out of the car he found he was stumbling slightly through stress and tiredness. Am I here? Am I *safe*? Now Hong Kong and the floating restaurants in Aberdeen harbour seemed a world away, London and Parliament a different life entirely, Megan and the children in Wales the merest dream. He looked around at *this*, the modern world. Tokyo itself, Soviet fleets, atomic power and atomic proliferation. All ugly and all dangerous.

Inside, a harassed official took him straight from the lobby to see Sir Oliver, who was still HMG's Ambassador.

'Ah,' the diplomat said wearily, in the busy office. Annigoni's portrait of the robed Queen was still smiling regally over his shoulder, the only unworried face in the room. 'You managed to get here from the airport, I see.'

'Not without difficulties, Sir Oliver.' He sat down, his dark suit crumpled, and his face greasy and grey with tiredness. 'What's the position now?'

Another official tore off a page from a news agency teleprinter, read it, and looked up. 'More telephone lines have been cut, apparently. Some power lines down, too. Riots in several districts of Tokyo, and equivalent trouble in Osaka and other big cities. Rumours of some kind of people's march on Arigata.'

David reached gratefully for the cup of Earl Grey tea a secretary passed him.

The man at the teleprinter continued, 'It looks like the Soviets have put pressure on their union friends here. Public transport has been hit in all the big cities. Media, too.'

The Ambassador was looking grave. 'Minister, you can't possibly leave for Arigata now. It isn't just pacifists and Left-inclined people demonstrating against the West. The rightists are out on the streets with the yakuza gangsters, shouting for Hakagawa. Several people are already dead.'

David's face was tired but determined. 'I'm going anyway.'

There was a pause, after the voice of authority. 'As you wish.' Sir Oliver tapped his fingertips together, then said gently, 'Your query.'

David's heart sank. He had telephoned from the airport as soon as he arrived. 'Yes?'

'I'm afraid you were right. It's been confirmed from the Heathrow end.'

David took a deep breath.

'Both Akiko Hideki and Maggie Langton were on that Korean flight.'

'And neither are on any list of survivors?'

As the Ambassador merely shook his head, David slumped in his chair. 'I see,' he said miserably. Then he looked up. He had to do something for Maggie and Kiko, something for what they believed in. His hoarse voice said with passion, 'Anyway, I've made a decision. I suggest you secure-cable it back to Whitehall, because it's rather important, at least to me.'

'Minister?' Sir Oliver asked.

'Tell the Prime Minister I'll not be signing the Osaka accords about supplying plutonium and uranium 235 to Japan. And if Jim Callaghan wants my resignation he can have it.' He stood up. 'I think you're right, that it might be dangerous to go to Arigata. So I'll attend the opening ceremony on my own. If my luggage is still in the embassy car, can you transfer it to some less conspicuous vehicle, and find me a driver?'

'You're leaving *immediately*?' Sir Oliver was shocked. 'Where do you intend to go now?'

David was in the doorway when he turned around. Fatigue and worry made him speak harshly. 'Where do you think?'

David watched as Alex threw away his silk tie and rolled his shirtsleeves up. They were in the Stantons' new Tokyo building, in a small top floor office. 'So you see, Colonel Itoshi, it would be a matter of public security, public safety. Minister?'

'I completely agree.' David said firmly. 'Your official guardians should be in Arigata.'

'Don't leave it to Hideki and Hakagawa's security people. I've seen them, they're highly effective – and loyal only to Hideki.'

The Self-Defence Forces officer smiled, in plain clothes and seeming quite relaxed. 'Hakagawa? Is VIP and Minister. Hideki is big-corporation VIP. I have not orders for Arigata.'

Alex stood up, his patience slipping. 'Hideki has invited the Prime Minister and other members of the government to Arigata for the opening ceremony tomorrow. Ideally, your Prime Minister should go – and give an *order*, not a request, to Hideki. An order to stand down the atomic programme. And if you take my advice, you'll make sure your SDF force is there to back up his commands!'

'Ah, so difficult,' the man replied, gazing out of the window. 'No orders, no nothing.'

'Try the JDA again,' Alex said, referring to the Japan Defence Agency which was Tokyo's Ministry of Defence. 'They might have decided something by now.'

It was Japanese politeness. 'Even if so, even if orders or permission came, how can I get into Arigata except by bloody fighting? Is a secure area, guarded as you say by armed men. Good men and loyal to Hideki.'

Alex said quietly, 'How can you get inside, since Arigata is guarded? It's not impossible.'

The Asian face revealed nothing more than friendly interest.

Alex gave a grim, considering smile. 'What if you were handed plans and blueprints detailing everything about Arigata, including alarms and the surveillance systems, a table of organization of the security detail – and where their arms are stored?'

'That might be different,' Itoshi said calmly. 'If I had such things, that is.'

'Here. Study all of this at your earliest convenience.' Alex gave him the folder, shook his hand, then buzzed for Fujiko, his personal assistant. 'I'll have you escorted out of here, unseen. I hope to meet you again soon.'

'Some time,' Itoshi said, grinning as he bowed. 'Soon or maybe not.'

The door closed behind him and Fujiko. David said in desperation, 'Did you see his face? I think he's laughing at us! Jesus!'

'He won't make a move without specific orders from the highest authority,' Alex said, 'and who can blame him?' He picked up the telephone again, dialled, and hung on for five minutes till it was answered. Then he banged the handset down, furious.

'The Prime Minister's private office, David – and they won't let me talk to him, even! They say he's too busy over this "international crisis". I told them that's exactly what I wanted to talk about, but . . .' His voice trailed off. He looked tired and his face creased. Then his usual ironic look returned. 'I suppose I'll have a chance to get to him at the Arigata opening tomorrow.'

'Maybe, but don't count on it.' Another phone shrilled above the chanting of the demonstrators outside. 'The whole country's suddenly gone mad! Or gone sane,' David said, reaching for the phone. 'Yes? I'll see.' He turned to Alex, still holding the phone to his ear, and something in his own face changed, as if a glow had come into it. 'Yes. You can send her up.'

A minute later the door opened and a woman walked in. Everybody turned.

She stood there, tall and proud but also weary-faced and pale, her red hair piled up on her head.

'Maggie!' Alex stood up, and went over quickly. So she was *alive*. Out of the sea, and alive. 'This is a miracle!'

She stepped back. 'Don't touch me!'

He jerked away. 'I'm sorry.'

She looked around, blinked a bruised eye. Then she said, 'Not that I'd object to being hugged. It's just that after I was pulled out of the sea by the Americans they found . . . I've got a couple of cracked ribs.'

David's eyes were wide with delight. 'Thank God you're safe, Maggie.'

She was holding herself together with difficulty, but with great courage also. 'Now, gentlemen, aren't you going to offer me a seat, and maybe a cup of decent English tea?'

Alex led her ceremoniously to his own leather chair, settled her into it. Then he said, his face bitterly sad, 'No Kiko?'

Maggie shook her head, and then, at last, she began to cry. 'It was horrible, horrible. The plane going down, people drowning all around me . . . Kiko . . .'

The others sat there, moved. Finally Alex reached out to touch her shoulder.

'We *have* to stop this,' she said, without looking up.

Alex looked outside. Night had come to Tokyo.

Osaka, on the Kizu River. It was the unlit commercial waterfront.

In between the Minami Pier and the Hideki Corporation private quay a Mazda two-seater sports car stopped, in front of the oil storage depot's mass of tanks and pipes. The 12,000 tons of refined North Sea oil stored here had been drilled for and transported by Stanton Industries.

Takahashi glanced around, dark glasses his only disguise. It was quiet here by the river, at least after dark. Lit-up ships rode out to sea, or stayed moored near the deep-water channel. He waited, listening to the radio, which reported rumours that Russian bombers were already on their way. A surprise attack, he thought. A Pearl Harbor in reverse . . .

A figure detached itself from a shadowy wall, and Takahashi leaned over to open the passenger door, ducking so that nobody could see him. He was certain now that Japan would not emerge from this crisis unchanged; he intended to get through this as Hideki's heir.

A man in a seaman's jacket sat down in the other seat and pulled the car door closed. He turned, and grinned at Takahashi. 'We meet again.'

The Mazda drove away quickly, up the narrow dockside street. 'You are a merchant seaman, this time? How was your trip from Singapore?'

'So-so,' Hoyle said indifferently. 'Arrived dead on time, though.'

'Of course. It was a Japanese ship. And how about our – results?'

'The prototypes? All safely shipped from Iraq – in the ship's freight in packing cases. It stands off Osaka now.'

'That's good.'

'Another two or three years and you'll have your atomic weapons – as long as you continue your support. And you get a guarantee of Iraqi oil in part payment, too.'

Takahashi was pleased. 'My suggestion, you know, to do some of our nuclear research there. On your advice, of course.'

'It's a very *secure* country. Saddam Hussein controls the Jihaz Haneen personally, and they torture spies to death. I've seen it.'

'And joined in?'

Hoyle gave his big laugh, and even Takahashi felt momentarily intimidated. He drove on carefully, under the yellow streetlights. 'You are still prepared to help us at Arigata?'

'I did what you wanted in other places,' Alan Hoyle reminded his paymaster. 'Like the Tower of London – just to get that man Bloom.'

'And in Saigon?'

Hoyle smiled. 'A good lesson, I think.' He remembered it well. Questioning Van Tien Trung persistently, the man tied up and screaming as Hoyle used the sawblades on his flesh. Then he had beheaded Hacker Stanton's employee and left his bones burning in a trash can. 'One mother of a slow killing. There was blood everywhere.'

Takahashi continued on towards the corporation's Osaka headquarters. 'That meant nobody ever got to prove we'd been recruiting outside people to work on military avionics and armaments.'

Hoyle's raised eyebrow mocked him. 'You had someone killed just to avoid embarrassment?'

'That's the Japanese way, man! Now, in secret, we can develop the missiles and bombs which we will need in the future. Arigata is a fast-breeder, and your friend David Bryant has been forced to agree to reprocessing. Therefore we get enriched uranium and plutonium. Therefore, the possibility of the bomb – if we can get our military technology up to scratch quickly enough.'

Hoyle nodded, as the car slowed down behind a big truck. He

rocked his broad shoulders and scratched the tip of his nose. 'Your Prime Minister is still scheduled to come?'

'To Arigata? Certainly. Though he will not, of course, leave it.' Takahashi chuckled. 'Not as Prime Minister, anyway. The Cabinet will soon be my master's – either hostages, or resigned, or willingly obedient.'

'Or dead?'

'Or dead. Anyway, you yourself are ready?'

'For Arigata?' Alan Hoyle relaxed into the bucket seat, hugging his duffle bag. 'Of course.'

'I will go with you. First to headquarters on Midosuji Boulevard, where another car will take us to a Hideki helicopter pad. Then, Arigata. I don't know how it'll go there. Might be sweet and peaceful, might be – well, you know. But I have another order.'

Hoyle was yawning. 'Tell me.'

'I just wish it had happened when you took care of our problem Irving Bloom . . .' He accelerated, not speaking.

Hoyle murmured, 'More convenient, you mean, if both Alex Stanton and Ray Hacker had died there in the Tower of London, with the others.'

'Yes.' Then Takahashi said it. 'Kill Alex Stanton, just as soon as you can. I don't care when, or how.'

Hoyle answered truthfully. 'It'll be a pleasure.'

Maggie borrowed some more clothes and then slept. At first, her dreams were nuclear-age nightmares. Then, gradually, calm came.

Early the next day, the Stanton Industries helicopter came down from the north side of the snow-tipped Kanto mountains, the backbone of Japan's Honshu island. Tokyo was perhaps a hundred miles behind them.

Down through the foothills they dipped, following a plunging river valley towards the Sea of Japan which gleamed up ahead. McCourt was piloting the copter, with Alex seated beside him and three passengers behind.

Alex was flicking through the maps. 'Vladivostok . . . do you know that means "Ruler of the East" in Russian? They don't mince words, do they?'

'Is it far?' Maggie asked.

'Let's see.' His finger traced a wavy line. 'Noto Peninsula, left. Sado Island, right. Straight on over five hundred miles of empty sea and you're in Vladivostok, saying "Hi" to the Russian fleet.'

'I don't imagine it'll be empty sea now,' McCourt said tensely, after checking in with the Arigata area's ground control. 'And if the Soviet Air Force are prepared to shoot down a 747 passenger plane in international airspace, what's to stop them taking potshots at a helicopter obviously heading for Arigata?'

They had passed over the first green paddyfields on the plain before

Alex replied. 'I don't think it's reached that stage. Not quite. And, besides, we already know some of the US 7th Fleet is out there, a protective screen.'

'Russians're out there, too,' said Hacker from beside Maggie. 'US Navy says there's Russian carriers and missile boats offshore, and nuclear subs undersea.'

Still, it seemed a very peaceful morning.

Then they saw it, clear across the glittering water of a small bay.

It was almost beautiful, set beside another river – the soaring white dome of the reactor containment shell, and the fat curved cooling tower issuing steam, which rose above the silver-spangled sea.

As they approached the site, Alex remembered the blueprints in McCourt's briefcase. He was able to identify other, lesser buildings, half submerged in the earth. David and Maggie leaned forward to follow his pointing finger as he explained. Maggie was snapping pictures with one of Terry's Nikons, even through the glass of the hull.

'That dome is around seven hundred feet high. Inside it is a sodium-cooled reactor core producing enough megawatts for a small city – not to mention all the plutonium it breeds.'

David was curious. 'What are those other structures?'

'Steam heat-exchanger, there, leaching power out of the molten sodium indirectly heated by the reactor. Also, big turbine generators and transformers. All highly automated, though. Only six hundred and fifty people staff it; less than two hundred are on the site at any one time, with another hundred back-up people on call.'

David had to cup his hands and yell over the noise of the engine as McCourt began to speak into his throat-mike again. 'Think of the profit.'

Alex laughed, bitterly. 'I often used to.'

Maggie snorted, then threw a searching glance at Alex. There was something ahead that really worried him, and she wondered what it might be. The fear of no arms sales to the Tokyo government – and the consequent heavy blow to his own armaments division profits? Something much more serious and immediate than that, an instinct told her.

Then the chopper stopped in mid-air, and tilted to the right.

'Look at that!' she said, just before they began their final descent.

All the landward side of the Arigata site was surrounded: there was a black tide of people, perhaps fifty or a hundred thousand strong, pressing up against the perimeter fence.

In the passenger helicopter they all exchanged glances. This was serious politics. It seemed that many people here in Japan shared Maggie's opinion of importing weapons-grade plutonium and uranium – the radio news said that two of them had died on the way.

'A hell of an achievement,' Alex said hollowly. Nobody was sure if he meant Arigata or the demonstration.

'Yes, it is hell,' Maggie retorted.

'I just hope the Japanese PM can sort this out!' David yelled.

The helicopter dipped even lower, turning east. The whole site was high-security, with two razor wire fences enclosing the complex. They could see the domed reactor still rearing above them like a concrete mountain, the other concrete-housed equipment, the two uncrowded car parks, and the ancillary offices.

Alex looked down at the helipad: a big white H inside double rings of yellow. There were already some people waiting for them on the outer edge.

The engine noise in the all-glass cabin increased to slow the rate of descent, but not enough to drown Maggie's voice. 'It's a terrible sight, and you were wrong to be involved with it, Alex! A fast-breeder reactor is even more full of toxic and radioactive substances than a standard PWR.'

The copter settled down in a swirl of dust.

McCourt killed the engines, sat back from the controls and wiped his hands. Alex gazed out past the compound, in the direction of the demonstrators. Rumours, reported by the surprisingly hysterical media, had suggested that armed radical students intended to invade the Arigata site – and either hold it for ransom, or blow it up.

'Do me a favour, Maggie,' Alex said to her quietly. 'Don't rock the boat too much. Hideki just might be more vulnerable than you think. You already know David will postpone signing the agreements. The only fissionable materials they will get are the ones supplied already. Besides, what kind of problem has nuclear power ever caused you or anybody you know?'

'The atom *isn't* safe,' she answered almost desperately, talking to the back of his restlessly turning head. 'Do you know just how dangerous plutonium is? Breathe or swallow a millionth of a gram of plutonium dust – an amount so small you could barely see it with a high-powered microscope – and that's your death-sentence from cancer!'

Alex said only, 'There are triple, autonomous shut-down systems here. Nuclear power is safe.'

'No. Take 1957, when there was a huge nuclear waste disaster in the Soviet Union near Kyshtym—'

'Was there?' Alex's response was abrupt and harsh. 'How come *I've* never heard of it?'

Maggie stood up. 'Evidence *was* gathered by the CIA, if you want to know. But it was never released.'

'No?' It sounded more patronizing than he had intended. 'Now why was that?'

'Because "it might have undermined the faith of the public in atomic power"!' She felt her heart pounding. This place already scared her. 'And let's not forget our own Windscale fire back in the same year. Not far from where we were both living then, Alex. Burning graphite and uranium! Tons of it! Exactly what might happen here!' But then she stopped, sounding shrill even to herself. Would Arigata join that long list of infamous names one day? Still another reactor accident, this one perhaps what everybody dreaded, the China syndrome of complete meltdown?

Efficient Japanese in blue uniforms or dark business suits were coming towards them, led by a smiling, youngish man.

Alex stepped down, ducking the windmilling rotor blades as Takahashi bowed.

'Mr Stanton!'

It was obviously introductions time, and Alex responded smoothly. 'Allow me to present to you first my colleague from the British government, the Right Honourable David Bryant MP. Mr McCourt, another old friend, you already know well.'

'Indeed I do,' Takahashi said brightly. He seemed strangely excited. 'And Mr Hacker of Texas.'

Ray merely nodded, squinting with his good eye and picking at his teeth with a fingernail.

'And here, Miss Magdalen Langton.'

Maggie came forward quickly, holding her hand out like a man and giving him her best disarming smile. 'The name is Maggie, please.'

None of them liked the way Takahashi was grinning.

One of the Japanese pinned a numbered radiation tab to Alex's collar first, then did the same for the others. They were told to hand them in when they left. More Hideki followers crowded around, showing lots of teeth in those disconcertingly wide smiles.

'Maggie,' Takahashi said, 'these other guys've already seen the great work we have accomplished here, but I'd like to show you around myself, personally.'

'The normal tour will do,' she said, her nose wrinkling in suspicion, camera dangling.

He was still smiling. 'No photographs without permission! Though I persuade easily . . .'

She was looking around. 'I thought this was partly a British venture. Where are your Western engineers?'

'Earning their pay,' Takahashi said. He took her by the elbow and ushered her away, so that the others had to follow.

David, too, wore a fixed smile, and lowered his voice to speak to Alex. 'Our Suntory-drinking friend is very happy and very much in charge. I don't think they're going to do much more for you.'

'No.' Alex spoke very quietly indeed. 'I don't like his look at all, so I'll get our contract money just as soon as I can. I have the feeling something serious is going to happen.'

As they walked along, he heard the crowd chanting something beyond the wire, but he could not understand it.

The main road led through double gates into the site itself, by-passing the huge dome and leading to the quayside. A few smaller offices and storage buildings lined it.

At the head of this small procession, Takahashi waved his arms towards one of the windowless white buildings near the rim of the gigantic containment dome.

'The main circuit starts in the reactor. Molten sodium circulates through the core. That's extremely radioactive, getting more so as the operation continues for months and years, therefore extremely dangerous. So it heats more molten sodium, in a separate circuit inside the big dome. Only clean, if extremely hot, liquid metal comes through the walls of the dome. In that building, there, it turns water into steam in the sealed heat exchanger.'

'Isn't that a dangerous process?' Maggie said. 'I understand that sodium encountering water can be explosive.'

'Just an engineering problem.' Takahashi shrugged. 'Technique. Then, the steam goes straight under our feet, well protected, into that other building where it powers the generators, and then it is piped back again to be heated up once more. Think of it as a vein of pressurized water, like an artery running with hot blood.' His foot tapped down on the reinforced concrete. 'Naturally, the proctective lining is very strong, therefore very safe.'

'What's inside that end building?'

'Two huge generators. Arigata works like this. We take heat, power, out of all that hot and radioactive metal inside the reactor by using liquid sodium. Then we make steam with it, with which we power the generators and make electricity. It's very straightforward.'

A helicopter flew by, too far off for them to make out any markings. It hovered, but did not land.

Takahashi frowned up at it, then turned to point a finger elsewhere. 'On that side of the reactor, inside the containment dome, spent fuel will be removed with remote-handling devices. It's highly radioactive, of course, and therefore highly dangerous – you find isotopes like caesium-137, cobalt-60, or gold-198, and other impurities which must be extracted before you have useful plutonium-238 and fissionable uranium.'

Maggie took a photograph. 'Who does the extracting for you?'

'You, our British friends. Didn't you know? You have agreed to take all these dangerous waste products back to your own land and do the dirty work there, then give us back, after reprocessing, only the valuable fissionable materials. You keep the radioactive waste.' Takahashi strode on. His excitement was contagious, and they found themselves walking ever faster to keep up.

As they approached the first of the low and windowless buildings, the sun was obscured behind the huge humpback of the reactor containment building; and now it seemed suddenly cold.

'After you've eaten, I will show you the plant control room,' Takahashi said. 'Please accept my apologies for those demonstrators outside. Un-Japanese! Everything here is authorized and permitted.' He gave a quick smile, but he seemed overexcited, Maggie told herself he was too excited and nervous even for a billion-dollar occasion like this.

There was something going on.

The Stanton Industries contingent ate with the other foreigners in a clammy private room in the restaurant building, with a French chef on hand. Alex guessed that the Japanese would be dining more spartanly in the main hall, on things like rice and pickled seaweed and raw fish.

The people at the next table included a CBS film crew and a dour man from Agence France Presse. There were journalists, radio people, film and television crews from eleven countries on the Arigata site; almost a hundred in total. From Australia to Zaire, there were links set up and the Interior Ministry seemed very happy with the publicity.

Though the Arigata reactor had first gone critical several weeks ago, Hideki's official party would not arrive until an hour before it came officially 'on stream'. The ceremonial switch-on was timed for well after sunset, and as part of the publicity programme there were banks of coloured floodlights and lasers, set up ready for the Prime Minister of Japan to switch on.

Hacker was eating slowly, but with good appetite, as he described what had happened at the Tower of London bombing back before Christmas 1973.

'We headed down to see the jewels and regalia. Rich history, boy. Alex and his wife Caro. My friends Irving and Stephanie Bloom, over from the States. A bunch of schoolkids from Italy. And me, and my wife . . .' He stopped speaking for a moment. 'We had just got married. Married by a preacher in a place called Valentine, Texas. We went to Vegas for our honeymoon. Then on to London.'

'What happened, exactly?' asked Tom Kalbach.

Hacker said stolidly, 'I don't remember much. Except waking up in hospital, with one eye gone – and a widower.'

Alex stopped eating and pushed his plate of cooked white flesh away as the sickening memories returned. 'There was a terrific flash and bang. I came to lying on the floor, my leg ripped open. There was a stench of burning, and people were screaming. I saw one of the children, headless, beside me . . .'

'Oh God,' Maggie said, touching his hand.

Hacker continued softly, 'Angie, my bride, was just about blown apart. And so was Irv Bloom. Whoever made that bomb packed six-inch nails around the plastic explosive.' He touched the black eye-patch. 'So I lost my eye. And my wife.'

'And you never found out who did it?' This time Senator Perry had spoken.

Hacker did not reply. Alex only said, shrugging, 'Even after all these years, only a few rumours along the way.'

Maggie sipped her Perrier water, then looked at him curiously. 'Can we speak freely here?'

Alex gave a cold smile. It had been the first thing he had contacted Reid about. 'That's the only thing in Japan I can vouch for. No eavesdroppers here, guaranteed.'

'Then I may as well say it straight out.' She took a breath, looking around the table. Only Tom Kalbach and Senator Perry were comparative strangers to her. 'I inherited some documentation from the Blooms, which Kiko Hideki translated. From that I learned her grandfather Saigo Hideki has always been a conspirator: and I believe he really does want atomic weapons and to see Japan remilitarized – as do all the other members of the Society of the Unsheathed Sword.' She gave a bitter smile. 'That's probably my biggest scoop, ever. Now, if you'll excuse me a moment, I think I'll go phone in some first impressions.'

'It occurs to me,' Alex said, 'that we should have tried to warn off the Prime Minister and his cabinet from coming here today. Just in case a different Prime Minister goes back . . .'

'Jesus, like a coup d'état, you mean?' David wiped his lips. 'Surely not.'

Alex shrugged.

'Any news on whether the Japanese Prime Minister is going to come? And what about Hideki and your defence-equipment deal?'

'Hideki is still playing games with me. Before I left Tokyo I asked for a meeting with him, face to face. I need commitments, I need the money he promised.'

'And?'

'And his underlings didn't respond, David.' Anger flared up in his face, then died. 'Except with meaningless bits of politeness, of course.'

'But he'll be coming here?'

'Oh, yes. And so will Hakagawa. And one way or another, we'll all meet again.'

That said, Alex added little else to the conversation, but toyed with his food, his appetite almost gone. The tension could almost be felt, and for once he felt no great optimism. Things were out of his hands completely. It was merely a few hours to switch-on, and he wondered what the Russians would be doing now. Though the press here mostly made light of it, it was not impossible that Soviet bombers were already on their way.

'But Japan can't be allowed to move into arms-making – for all our sakes,' David was saying. 'That can't happen! Nor can we give people like Hakagawa access to the nuclear bomb.'

'How do we stop them? Or Iraq, or India, or Pakistan?'

'Nuclear proliferation is the worst thing in the world, just about.' David hesitated, moving his chair sideways as Maggie came back. 'But we can't tear up the old contracts we've already signed, can we? I mean, they are enforceable international law.'

Alex's answer was grim. 'Even a treaty is just a scrap of paper, David.'

'Yes, but the last time that phrase was used the Germans had just invaded Belgium to start World War I!'

The two men were staring at each other when somebody tall and lean came over from one of the other tables.

'Maggie Langton! Thought I recognized you!'

It was Ellis, wearing a press badge.

She stood up and slapped palms with him. 'Saigon seems like a long way away, now.'

'It isn't,' he said, looking her up and down. He snapped his fingers. 'You filed that story! The Korean 747 – you were actually inside the plane the Russians shot out of the sky!'

She sat down again, motioning him to take a chair. 'Yes. But, believe me, I'd rather cover the news than make it that way. Lots of people died, there.'

'I know,' he said sympathetically, 'and you're upset.'

She opened her mouth to deny it, but then a rush of disconcerting emotion came. 'You're right. I am.'

Ellis was smiling at her gently. The press pass on his lapel said he was working for the East Asian News Agency, out of Hong Kong. 'Where's your guy Terry?'

'Back home,' she said, then added something not quite a lie. 'Sorting through some more Vietnam pictures, for a book, I think. Actually, we're not getting on too well.'

Ellis asked it. 'What'd Terry do about his Saigon women and his kids?'

'What?' She blinked. Alex looked over. 'Terry's wife and children—?'

Hacker put the spoon down, regarded her. 'I wondered if you knew. It was no secret in Saigon. I heard he had at least four kids by two different Vietnamese women, and that he married one of them round about '72 – I knew a few people who'd met her, in fact. Which one did he pick to bring out of Saigon?'

'None of them.' Her voice became a harsh whisper. 'As far as I know, he didn't even try.' She blinked back quick tears, and pushed her chair away from the table. 'Excuse me.'

Alex followed her out to the balcony. Her back was turned; her hands were tight on the rail. He touched her shoulder lightly, allowing his hand to stay there.

'That's it,' she said tightly. 'That's the end. Even if he'd told me . . .'

'He didn't even mention his marriage – or his children?'

'Never said a bloody word, the bastard – not to me.' Her voice was harsh. Terry had let her down once too often. If he wanted an independent life, well he could have it. 'But that's only a breach of trust between him and me. What's worse is to think he didn't even try to get his women and his children out of Saigon!'

'Too many complications, I suppose.'

She showed him her tear-stained face as a warm wind from the sea licked against them. 'Including me, you mean? Something else I should feel guilty about?'

He did not dare hug her because of the broken ribs around her heart. In spite of her tears, she was beautiful, and suddenly he wanted to do something about this sadness of hers. Maggie was a strong and vital person: she deserved better than the pain her lover Terry had caused her.

He found himself kissing her. They pressed their mouths together, hungry for comfort and love in this time of danger.

'Right.' She pushed him away. 'Let's not have too much emotion. Not in my present delicate state.'

'No? But I enjoyed it,' he said. He found he was smiling and he felt a great surge of joy and self-confidence.

She gave him her old familiar direct look, considering him. 'You still like me, don't you?'

'In spite of everything?' he asked wickedly.

'Not in spite of everything, Alex – only in spite of you and me.'

He laughed, then was suddenly serious, looking towards the mountainous reactor looming over everything. Now, he was inclined to think the demonstrators out there were right. 'Maggie, I think this might be dangerous. That's why I wanted to withdraw my invitation to you. Do some quick interviews and take pictures, by all means. But then I'd like you to go, before it's too late.'

'Alex, I've covered *wars*!' She was suddenly furious, her courage and her professionalism challenged.

He raised his hands placatingly. 'A suggestion.'

After a moment she laughed, tossing her head. 'All right. I'm sorry.' She touched his cheek. 'You meant well.'

'You won't leave?'

Flatly, 'No. I'm staying at Arigata, and I'm seeing it through. I've had a good career in the media, Alex. I've been places, met people I wanted to meet, enjoyed myself. And I ran out of Saigon when other people didn't – or couldn't. I *ran* – away from the story! Now it's time to pay back for all that. I've suspected what Hideki might be up to for ages – Kiko told me. And I didn't do enough to stop it.'

'Now, you will?'

'Now, I'll try. Just like you!'

He traced a finger down her face, lightly. 'I've never forgotten you, Maggie. Oxford. The Greek islands. They were some of the best times of my life. Now . . .'

'Now?'

He shrugged, deciding to put an end to it. 'As you may have heard, my own dear wife has been seeing too much of an old and not so dear friend of ours. Battersby, James P.'

'Oh, no!' She hugged him instinctively, then caught his eye and they both started to laugh. 'Him!'

He mussed her red hair, thinking now of those times long before.

Lazy evenings in warm pubs in wintry Oxford, and excited student conversations putting the world to rights. Then, bright mornings in 1965, among the sun-kissed Greek islands. He focused on her again. Warmth spread through him suddenly. 'You want to start again, Maggie? You want to tell me that everything between us hasn't been lost?'

The green eyes regarded him. 'It hasn't been lost. No. It hasn't.'

'Terry? That's over, too?'

'For years.' She shrugged. 'It's truth-telling time.' A pause, as her green eyes blinked. 'But I want to get everything clear. What about Kiko and you?'

'How could I live up to everything she represents? I want warmth and common humanity, Maggie. A home to share. I don't need to live with a saint.'

She gave a slow-burning smile. 'Then you can live with me.'

He imagined a future with her, if they managed to get through the next couple of days without the world ending. Everything part of him had always wanted Maggie would provide. He saw the rich, full life that would be shared with her, and the family he hoped would come. He had plans now, he always had plans, and he was a lot closer to making them real than anyone else could suspect.

There was one more thing, however . . .

He turned back to her. 'I'd better tell you something, though I suspect you'll be the only one who approves.'

'Yes?'

'I left something behind me in London.'

'Your wife?' She laughed. 'Well, I've left Terry. For good, this time!'

He shook his head. 'Something much more important than my sham of a family-arranged marriage. I've handed in my resignation. I've quit Stanton Industries. I'm on my own.'

Chapter Twenty-seven

After the meal, Maggie insisted on seeing the reactor first hand. As she pointed out it was, inside its huge concrete shell, the hot living heart of Arigata.

They dressed in yellow overalls to go, and wore filter masks. Disturbed, Maggie looked around: her fellows looked like long-snouted creatures from a science fiction movie.

Up close, the containment dome was even more monumental than it had seemed from a distance. It was made of a rough, chipped, reinforced concrete. Ugly and thick, Maggie thought, touching it. Is it genuinely warm, or is that just an illusion produced by fear? A pockmarked skin around... Her words dried up, left unrecorded in her notebook, and unspoken.

A shallow ramp descended into the concrete-roofed tunnel to the main entrance. Takahashi led them forward, jauntily.

Then a cluster of men with radiation masks stopped them. They were polite, but they were all uniformed and armed. McCourt looked on without expression as there ensued a rapid exchange of Japanese.

Takahashi turned, spread his hands. In his yellow overalls he managed to look appealing and boyish. 'It isn't necessarily very spectacular, the reactor.'

'I think I can speak for everybody,' Maggie said politely. 'Senator? Tom? Alex?'

'We'd like to go inside,' Senator Perry confirmed, flashing a practised grin.

'As you wish.' Takahashi made a chopping gesture.

Quietly, smoothly, an airtight steel door thirty feet tall and one foot thick slid open. In front of them lay twenty yards of empty, echoing space. They walked on, the big door closing behind them.

Only then did the door in front of them open up.

Maggie looked in, inside the containment dome, at the Arigata reactor.

It sat there in the middle of vast, flat floorspace. It was huge and chunky, metal partly encased in concrete – the biological shield, as Takahashi explained. Its mass loomed above them, humming, clicking. The air around it was warm and humid, and a musical note constantly ticked away, a heart-beat meaning the radiation levels were standard.

Maggie swallowed, unable to tear her gaze away. There it was, on the other side of the shield: uranium and other metals, white-hot, in a flood of liquid metal that exploded on contact with water. 'What do all those huge pipes connect to?'

Takahashi answered very soberly. 'They conduct the hot liquid sodium out of the reactor to the first heat exchanger, over there. The reason they're so thick is because the sodium is hot in every sense. We must be protected from it.'

Perry seemed fascinated. 'It's "hot" now?'

'Extremely so, Senator.' Takahashi turned back to Maggie. 'In the exchanger, there, heat is transferred to clean sodium, which is piped outside. That heats the water, as I explained before.'

She looked around. This space was huge, and floodlit to about a hundred feet up, just above the reactor.

Above that, darkness.

All around, remote handling equipment hung from overhead rails; a crane, and gigantic claws. Nothing moved now except a very few men in full NBC protection, who were checking instruments and performing routine maintenance.

Alex pointed. 'Inside the concrete shield is a stainless steel pressure vessel, yes?'

'Yes.'

'And inside that, at white heat, is the reactor core itself – all that uranium and other metal together, causing a controlled nuclear chain reaction?'

'That's right,' Takahashi said proudly. 'Many tons of it. A level of energy that is incredible . . . but safely confined, of course.' He checked his watch. He now seemed strangely sobered. 'Please, follow me outside again.'

The sound went on, mournful, slow.

'I'll be glad to get out,' Tom Kalbach said, a little shakily. 'I just don't feel safe here, somehow.'

Takahashi conducted them quickly up the ramp, and out through the doors again.

It felt good to be outside under a clear blue sky, and to feel the warm salt-tanged wind coming off the sea. They stood for a while, savouring the feeling.

'Let's go.'

They walked. In the middle of the Arigata site, near the restaurant building, a pair of armed men guarded another door.

'We can go inside,' said Takahashi. There was a ramp leading down in front of the concrete blockhouse.

Off an underground corridor lined with other rooms was the control room.

Takahashi stopped them. 'Into the control room?'

Another massive door, made of inches-thick steel, suddenly opened. They crowded in.

It was an oval shaped chamber partitioned by armoured glass. There were a dozen incredibly complex control panels, all fully manned now.

Needles flickered, lines were scrolled on paper: the concentration was intense. A shift operations manager sat at a raised chair which allowed him to see all the panels by turning his head.

Alex recognized the man sitting there as the nuclear engineer Ito Katayama. He came down to greet them, unlocking a door in the thick glass wall that separated the visitors' viewing gallery from the theatre of operations. A small and bespectacled, usually benign man, he was now so clearly nervous that Alex was made to wonder if there was some safety problem with the plant.

Then he noticed the two uniformed men sitting down in opposite corners of the control room. One had his hand dangling over his holstered pistol. So, Alex thought, Hideki's private army is already in occupation. Nevertheless, he performed introductions with rapid ease as McCourt translated.

Katayama raised a hand to prevent Maggie taking any photographs. 'Please, not allowed. For danger of terrorism, you understand.'

'I understand,' Alex said grimly. He was suddenly very aware of Takahashi's presence.

The small man's fearful eyes seemed to bore into Alex. 'Now, I explain, if you ask questions, yes?'

The visitors stared through the armoured glass, watching flickering needles on dials, and coloured lamps going on and off.

There was tension there also, faint but perceptible. If this beast ever escaped, it would be disastrous. Alex studied the instrument displays he had first seen as artists' impressions over three years before. There were graphs displayed on video screens, and hard copy was inked on to the scrolling paper. A row of video monitors showed the inside of the containment dome, and other interior and exterior views of Arigata.

Maggie stared for a long time, like the others. She understood virtually nothing: but the rituals here seemed as incomprehensible and death-obsessed as those in an Egyptian tomb, and she felt frightened.

'Fuelling took place several weeks ago,' McCourt explained. 'For the next month or so we'll be slowly powering up to maximum, checking all the while the status of the core and the circulation of the coolant – liquid sodium, in this case.'

Katayama said nothing, hanging his head. Alex was disturbed by this. The man ought to be celebrating and proud.

'Note the temperature dials again,' McCourt continued. 'In the core, three hundred and eighty degrees. Eventually, come full power, there'll be over five hundred degrees Celsius. In the turbines the steam is at half that. Then you can go down the scale to the room-temperature air conditioning here in the manned offices of the plant.'

The air circulating here was set to blow low and cold, so you could hear a murmur and feel a chill breath around your ankles, a cold Maggie could not help associating with the grave.

'Can we get out of here now?' she asked.

Takahashi sighed. 'Indeed. But I'm afraid I'll have to take you back to the press centre, to join the others. Other duties, calling.'

There is something terrifying here in Arigata, David Bryant thought. They were in a room off the press hall. This technology takes modern science right up to its limits, and engineering past those limits, and the undiscovered territory beyond is made up of disasters we can barely imagine . . . He frowned as he sipped his tea.

The uniformed man by the door lifted up a ringing telephone, and shouted out. 'Another helicopter arrive. Visitors! For Mr Bryant! A Mr Bryant here? Very important, he say, the visitor outside.'

He had to excuse himself and go.

The stairs outside led down, in the grey, warm twilight. The sea was glittering.

Somebody tapped David's shoulder. He turned around and felt himself blench. 'You . . .'

'I've been waiting for you,' the tall Russian said ominously. A crowd of people went by, journalists, mostly round-faced Japanese, all laughing together. 'I want to speak to you in private,' Kerensky continued. 'I have a room laid on.'

David held on to the handrail. 'How did you manage that?'

'Russians,' Kerensky said harshly, 'may not be loved, here, but we are feared.'

David followed the KGB agent down the stairs. On the ground they turned right. A smiling man in hardhat and yellow overalls stepped aside from a doorway, and David followed the Russian into a prefabricated storage hut. There was an overhead light above a wooden table and chairs; shelves full of pipe sections and coils of cable were all around.

Kerensky wasted no time. 'You see how it will be? The Korean airliner . . . then attacks on other civilian ships and planes, to show how serious we are . . . If necessary, perhaps even attacks on American military craft.'

'Your people will hit out at America!' David shut the door firmly behind him. He was suddenly scared. 'Tell me what you want.'

Kerensky sat down, a lit cigarette in his hand. Others had already been crushed in a saucer on the table. His glazed eyes showed he was under massive and prolonged stress: he looked as if he had not slept for days. 'I only want to tell you this: that the old men in the Kremlin are absolutely determined.'

David remained standing. 'To do what?'

'To halt this conspiracy in Japan. We know it exists, you know it.'

'*Suspect* it. I've talked to Alex and to Hideki's granddaughter. Seems to me there's a great deal of suspicion and a very small amount, if any, of hard proof.'

'And so it seemed to me.' A mirthless smile, another crushed cigarette. 'But now I have seen and heard that proof.'

'What?' But the man was sincere: all David's insight confirmed that.

'Now I know about their conspiracy: the Unsheathed Sword of Japan. They intend to use that sword.'

Although this sounded very close to what Kiko had described, David knew he had to be cautious. Anybody in the press corps could have seen him disappear with a presumed KGB officer. 'So, in response, Russia is threatening Japan.'

'Threatening—' Kerensky laughed wildly, pushed fingers through dark hair already disarranged. 'We are talking about the peace of the whole world! Yes, we will threaten, and the old men must be allowed to win. Tell your government that – and the Americans.'

David folded his arms. Never negotiate from a position of weakness. 'Why should I?'

Kerensky raised shaking hands again, to rub at his face. David felt his tension. 'Do you want us to be bombed here, David Bryant, to be left as shadows on the wall or swirls of radioactive dust?'

'No,' David said, at last. 'Is that possible?'

'*Possible?* Japan was atom-bombed before! And not by us! I know what the Hakagawa conspiracy is all about, David Bryant. War. And I think you know that, too – even if it may implicate your friend Alex Stanton.'

David took a step away. His back hit the closed door, but he was grateful for that support.

Kerensky was staring at him. 'I thought you were a man of peace, a socialist. You even told me about the Hideki conspiracy! But what about your rich friend Mr Alexander Stanton!'

'What about him?'

'He is a warmonger. Selling these people tanks and guns – and now uranium!'

'But you supply the Saddam Husseins of the world!' David found himself defending his old friend. 'Alex is desperate to do business, don't you understand? Otherwise he'd—'

'Would do what?' Kerensky was looking distraught. He paused to light another cigarette.

David stared back, wondering what to say. Finally, he gave a very English answer. 'Nobody's perfect.'

Exhaling smoke, Kerensky shook his head. 'Do you know what the right-wing Tokyo people are planning? With, so my superiors think, secret American assistance? They want to *win*, David Bryant. But let them win now, and for five years, or ten, there might be a little peace, as Hakagawa builds up the army and navy and air force and re-equips with the bomb – all, needless to say, so *very* profitable to Hideki and the other big capitalists. Then, what happens?'

David stared. The KGB knew everything. 'Tell me,' he rasped.

'Within twenty years, the neo-right will move to make their national base entirely secure. I would imagine some kind of military or political coup. Even the present sham of democracy they have in Japan will be stripped away. If there are any political parties left at all, they will be the merest masks, run by men who take orders from above.'

David listened to this prediction with frigid respect. 'Unless we stop them now, you mean?'

'Unless we stop them right here, the Hideki conspiracy will win. Andropov himself knows what will happen, I tell you! Once they have become the richest power on earth, the Japanese will start staking out their claims in the rest of the East – squeezing Korea, raising economic blockades throughout South-East Asia, watching the Soviet Union carefully with their nuclear missiles primed. They'll want their islands back, then Manchuria, and then they'll move into Australia, either by military means or unequal diplomatic treaties, or—'

'Or simply by buying up Australian land and companies till they control virtually everything,' David finished. It was not quite what Kiko had predicted, but it made terribly clear sense. He looked at Oleg Kerensky. One Russian missile would do it. One low-yield missile on top of the concrete containment dome over the reactor . . . 'The Politburo have decided, have they? They are serious: no possible compromise?'

'No compromise, Mr Bryant! Arigata *must* be closed down.

'Marshal Ogarkov, Chief of the General Staff, is giving the orders personally. He will be in full-dress uniform, wearing his orders and decorations. Him, the others, they are the ones who ran Stalin's camps. They fought Adolf Hitler's legions to a bloody standstill, then rolled them back into Europe.

'I fear those old men! They are a million miles away from your comfortable democratic politicians. They are men of war. Don't you understand that? Japan will change its policy for them or they will make Japan pay – in blood.'

The Russian fleet was already standing off the Japanese coast. It had nuclear arms. David's voice was dry. 'I understand.'

'Good! Telephone your embassy, tell London and Washington! Then perhaps we can stop this, even now.'

'All right,' David said. 'Is there any hard evidence I could give my friends, to show this is not just more Soviet bullying?'

Kerensky's eyes were wide, and bloodshot. He opened his black case, and extracted a photographic copy of a faded document with a sword on the cover. It was in handwritten Japanese characters, with a typed English translation stapled to it. 'This is the manifesto of the Society of the Unsheathed Sword – Hideki's organization, Hideki's plan.'

'Jesus Christ.' David took it with trembling fingers.

'Hideki is condemned by his own words.'

David flicked through the English version. The plan originated in 1945. Its aim was to dominate the industries of the world. Foreigners were to be prevented from investing in Japanese companies, forbidden even to settle in Japan. Imperial Japan yet again, using the yen as a replacement for the sword. A fully rearmed Japan by 1990.

He saw the name typed at the end of the translation and his blood froze. Kiko Hideki. What did this mean? Had Kiko despaired of Alex and started passing secrets to the Russians?

'You have phones here, radio links. There are well-connected journalists from all over the world, and diplomats, even a United States Senator. You must all work together to get the Americans to take their ships elsewhere. Otherwise the old men in the Kremlin will think you and all the others in the West want the Japanese to arm against us. And if they believe that . . .' He threw up his arms.

Outside roared the sound of amplified voices. The hundred-thousand-strong demonstration was preparing to welcome Hideki and his Minister with hate and violence – in spite of all his electric fences and armed guards.

In the restaurant building, when David Bryant went back, the bar was crowded and noisy, with shouted jokes and drunken laughter. He finally found his friends in the big press hall, silently watching a television. As David approached, McCourt began to translate.

'The Hideki chopper is just taking off now, on live TV – and the crowd outside will know what's happening!'

Alex immediately turned to the others, 'Maybe it's time for us to get out of here.'

David felt sick with tension.

'I must have a word, everybody. In private.'

McCourt found them an empty office. As soon as David got his party inside he slammed the door shut, savagely. He believed Kerensky: he believed this was already a worse crisis than the blockade of Berlin, or the missile crisis over Cuba back in 1962, or the fall of Saigon. He told them so, Alex, the Senator from Colorado, Hacker, Tom Kalbach, McCourt, and Maggie Langton. 'I have a copy of Hideki's manifesto. It's already started, and it will take extreme force to stop it!'

Maggie tossed her head in exasperation. 'But this is becoming a thing between Russia and America, David. What can *we* do?'

His pale face was nervous. 'Maggie, the only reason the people in Tokyo can defy the Soviets like this is because of America – American money, and American sons out there on the high seas and in the skies, Americans risking everything to let the men who caused Pearl Harbor win.' He glanced at the Senator. 'Now, does that make any sense to you? Senator, Tom, maybe you can have a look at this.' He flourished the Sword Society manifesto. 'It's pure Hideki from 1945, translated by his own granddaughter. If either of you have any remaining doubts I suggest you take a look at this.'

'Well, I don't have any doubts, now,' Maggie said helplessly.

David turned from Alex to her. 'What else did Kiko say about her grandfather?'

'On the plane?' Maggie thought a moment. 'Once she said something about "the old Japanese tradition of government" and "the League of Blood".'

'Christ,' Alex said suddenly. 'The Prime Minister . . . Now it all makes sense. David?'

'The old ways here meant assassination. You want a list of those murdered? Hara Takahashi, a Prime Minister. The prewar officers' plot to murder the entire Tokyo Cabinet . . . The League of Blood killed an ex-minister of finance and targeted the Prime Minister, too. In 1932 another prime minister was assassinated, and in the attempted military coup of 1936 two former prime ministers were killed.

'If the Prime Minister of Japan turns up here, he will not go back.'

'So what can we do?'

David grabbed one telephone and held it out to Maggie. 'You met a lot of the people who helped President Carter, didn't you? And some are in the White House right now?'

'You know that.'

'Then ring them up. We have four telephones here. Tell them we have to go along with what the Russians are up to here. The US fleets have to pull back – that's the only thing that will break Hideki's will, now. And, believe me, Japan must not be allowed to rearm.'

'But . . .' She looked totally dismayed.

He waved the telephone at her again. Every face was turned to her now. 'This is your moment, Maggie. You didn't stop Vietnam, you didn't abolish the bomb. But you *can* help stop this.'

She stared into his eyes for a long moment, then picked up the phone and began to dial.

Alex was already in action. It took three minutes to get through to Nanwara. 'Nanwara-*san*, I understand the Prime Minister listens to your advice.'

'I hope so,' the understanding voice said.

'If he's on his way to Arigata, you'd better tell him to change his mind!'

There was a silence. Then, 'I have already given that advice. But he may still go.'

'I see.'

'You are at Arigata now?'

'I am. Right. And I want to tell you that Hideki isn't going to surrender peacefully.'

'Perhaps not. But you are there, aren't you?'

'You,' Alex said, 'should use your influence.'

'And you must use yours.'

Alex gave a cold grin. 'I'll do everything I can.'

All the phone lines out were busy now. No doubt the press were reporting to their headquarters in the media capitals. Arigata was, at this moment, perhaps the most famous place on earth.

David dialled 03 for Tokyo, then the British Embassy number. Soon he was speaking to the top man. 'That's the situation, Sir Oliver. Tokyo *must* disown Hakagawa and Hideki; so must the world. Please apply all the diplomatic pressure you can. I'll try to get hold of 10 Downing Street myself, then the Foreign Secretary.'

Hacker was telephoning, too: his broad Texas accent loud in the room, as he leaned hard on a Detroit industrialist he knew. 'We ought to back off. Let the Japs be pressured. Why should we be defending them? Anyway, hope you agree, Charlie, and you can let your Senator and Congressman friends know what you think as straightforward as you can tell 'em . . . Me? I'll say it to Carter's own face, if necessary. Think of me as a pay toilet, boy. I don't give a shit for nothing!'

Alex tried to find his wife, but four international phone calls failed to locate her. He turned away from the table, back and shoulders already aching, and grabbed for his half-empty cup of coffee. What happens now? The Russian missiles hit us? The Tokyo government capitulates? He rubbed his eyes, heard a knock on the door. Tom Kalbach got up to answer it, coming back with a tall and gloomy-looking man. Alex's memory supplied a name. It was that Russian from the trade liberalization conference of '76.

'Mr Kerensky.'

'I wanted to see how you were doing,' the Russian said, his face perspiring and tired.

Alex banged his cup back on to the saucer as the KGB man sat down. 'We're trying to fix things so the Japanese back down. Don't worry, you'll get your promotion out of this!'

Kerensky sat there, so tired he seemed almost indifferent. He closed his eyes. 'If you really believe anything except a desire for survival motivates me now, survival for us and the world, then you are wrong and a fool.'

Alex looked at him, assessing him. 'Maybe,' he said at last.

Senator Perry was still reading through the Sword Society document, frowning, Tom Kalbach looking over his shoulder.

'What'll be happening in Washington, Ray? Anything we can influence?'

The big Texan spoke slowly. 'There'll be a White House crisis management team in permanent session. It'll come down to this: either risk a war by keeping our boys in place here, or see that the Soviets are making sense – for once.' He grimaced. 'Unless what we say has some effect, I don't know which it'll be.'

'Senator?'

Perry at last put the manifesto down. 'I think David is right, Alex. The people around Hideki and Hakagawa . . . they have to be stopped.'

'Very well. Let's keep at it.' Alex pulled a slim diary out of his pocket and began to look up some more private numbers. Kissinger: he would try him, though he was no great friend to the

Carter administration. 'Let's make calls to all the influential types we can.'

The Senator murmured, 'I know Cyrus Vance pretty well.'

'The State Department? That's great news,' Maggie said, waiting for her third call to be answered. 'All branches of the executive, and the media besides. All we need now is a Justice of the Supreme Court.'

'Or a few more guys with guns here at Arigata,' Hacker growled.

McCourt checked his watch. 'I'd say we have about another half an hour till they get here, Hideki and Hakagawa. And don't forget, they have plenty of armed help here. They aren't going to back down. Not just because of sweet reason.'

Alex looked up from his dialling. 'Maybe not, but let's give reason its chance, sweet or sour.'

For the next twenty minutes they continued making crucial calls, piling on the pressure through government, diplomacy and industry, though they knew that only the White House and the Pentagon could act with decision.

Maggie could not help thinking about Saigon as she dialled. Was it cowardice, to have run from that story? She could not be sure, but she knew this: from Arigata, she would not run.

Her third call struck gold. 'Please, just tell the President it's Maggie Langton . . . Of course he knows me, and I'm right here in the *middle* of the Arigata crisis. You can . . .' She frowned. A minute or more went by. Then, 'Mr President! It's Maggie Langton. Yes, I'm here on site. Listen . . .' And she explained, A long pause. Then, 'I think the Russians are dead right! Arigata has to be stood down, but even worse, Hideki has politicians in his pocket and I think he's aiming to set up a far-right government here. Can't you make it plain in Tokyo you don't want to see that?' Another pause, longer. Her face was screwed up, as if she was about to cry. 'Thank you for listening, Mr President. And goodbye.'

David tried ringing his family in Wales. He could not work out the time difference. Was it mid-morning there, on a school day? He hung on for a while but there was no answer. Maybe that was for the best, he thought. What do I say? Megan, I love you, and the kids. And I'm a dead man . . . Remember Maggie's articles on the dangers of nuclear power? Then you know how it will be when the concrete dome cracks and that nuclear demon escapes to shower us with hot poison. Radiation sickness. Vomiting, nausea, diarrhoea. Fever, increasing exhaustion, the white cell count plummeting. Delirium. Open wounds everywhere, ulcers that will not heal. Death.

Without even the chance to say a last goodbye to you . . .

Alex said curiously, 'Are you all right, David?'

'I'm fine,' David said, putting the phone down, trying to master the fear and the loneliness.'

Suddenly the news came. Hideki's black helicopter was touching down at Arigata.

The sky began to flash with colour. Outside the window, searchlight beams criss-crossed, green, red and gold. A monitor screen showed the main gates to the plant as thousands of people poured forward.

Maggie looked around in despair. 'What are we going to do?'

Alex was first to stand. He stretched, wearily. 'Let it be. What more can we do?'

Ray Hacker gestured at the now cradled phones. 'Will that have been enough?'

'It better. Now, let's go greet Mr Hideki.'

By the time they were out in the open again, and heading for the assembly point where the outside broadcast cameras had been set up, an inflated red sun was sinking over the Sea of Japan.

Around the giant H of the helicopter landing area were gathered numerous security guards, all Japanese and most of them armed. They stood in a wide circle around the sleek black machine as its rotorblades stopped threshing. Then the door opened.

Faces and cameras were all turned there; microphones pointed.

Hideki paused in the doorway: a short man with cropped grey hair framing a harsh face. He raised his hands. Silence fell. Hakagawa, large and frowning, stepped out to join him.

Hideki made a short speech, which produced a magic effect on the Japanese. They threw up their arms and cried out, 'Banzai!'

McCourt was looking concerned. Maggie moved close to him as Hideki's guards fell in beside their leader.

'What did he say?' she asked. 'What did he *say*?'

'He warned that terrorists, foreign terrorists, or perhaps even actual secret agents of the USSR, have been spotted on this site. He instructs us to report that Japan seeks only a peaceful solution to this crisis, and reminds us that there are many foreign workers and journalists here – here, and vulnerable. Therefore, for security reasons, Minister Hakagawa has ordered this site be sealed off. Everything is placed under armed guard. No telephoning without permission. No one in, no one out, under any circumstances . . .'

'Christ,' Hacker said. 'They've finally pulled the plug!'

Chapter Twenty-eight

This windowless corridor was deep underground, but was it safe?
Safe enough, Saigo Hideki decided. At the far end, he could see the closed door to the reactor control area. But he turned left, towards the administrative offices. As Hideki and his big-bellied ally strode into the room Takahashi rose immediately and bowed low.
Here were telephones, internal and external, and a bank of television screens. The large communications office next door housed a teleprinter and telex, yet more telephones, and message clerks and other officials. The two older men sat down at the oval table. Saigo Hideki reached for some green tea. He sipped, smacking his lips appreciatively, then asked curtly, 'What is happening at Arigata, Takahashi?'
'We have all the hostages contained on site – hostages from our own country, America, Britain and other nations. Just about every important power there is, even Russia!'
'Excellent,' Hideki said. 'No trouble so far?'
Takahashi considered, fingertips tapping on the table. 'They are expat engineers, experienced journalists. I don't think they'll panic and cause us problems. Besides, what could they do? There's no escape from Arigata! So, no risk to our plan. When alarm begins to spread we'll have our liaison staff suggest that the Russians are planning an attack, therefore the hostages should get on to their governments, especially of course the Americans, to keep up that high-profile defence.'
'Superb!' Hakagawa clapped his shoulder. 'What else?'
'Well, I have been monitoring all the screens, and we're surrounded. Look!' Takahashi wiped his mouth, nervousness showing on his face.
Hideki, knowing how this younger generation was corrupted and spineless, looked upon him with a concealed disdain. Fortunate that he had as yet done nothing final about declaring an heir to his billions of yen and his power. 'Be calm,' he admonished.
'There must be a hundred thousand people out there, all come to protest! But what they're doing is protecting us.'
'The reactor will also protect us,' Hideki said curtly. 'Who in our weak government would dare order an attack? Tokyo cannot risk our nuclear power programme, and we have our own armed and loyal men here to defend us.'
Hakagawa looked satisfied. 'That should cover all possibilities.'

He settled into the black leather chair. As it creaked, he glanced curiously at the colour screens over in the corner. 'No army or police helicopters?'

Takahashi responded quickly, 'Helicopters have been spotted occasionally, yes. But unmarked – so for news coverage, I think. Nothing military. And since we have air-traffic control radar, we cannot be taken by surprise. Our people observing the perimeter have seen nothing either, except for all those unarmed demonstrators blocking both approach roads.'

Hakagawa rocked back, his mouth opening in a wide grin. 'Then we have a human shield of one hundred thousand soft bodies. What could be better for us than that?'

'All the Cabinet, right here, right now,' Hideki said tersely.

'Yes.' Hakagawa sighed. 'If they were here with our guns at their heads, then soon *we* would be the government of Japan.'

Takahashi said softly, 'The Soviets, and other governments, are putting pressure on our cowardly leaders not to come here.'

Hideki gave a slow nod. 'Who told you that?'

'Our Tokyo headquarters have a source in the cabinet office.'

'They will not come?' Hakagawa looked shocked. 'But our government cannot turn its back on atomic power, no matter what some journalists or the troublemaking filth outside may say – let alone the Russians!'

'No, they cannot,' Hideki agreed, with a grimace. Ever since the oil shock of 1973 the Japanese plans for atomic power had been an open secret. 'But I think the Prime Minister may not come now. Suppose he has suspected we would demand his resignation if he came here to Arigata? So I think it is now time for more direct action.' He glanced towards Takahashi. 'Is Hoyle here? Has he been seen by our witnesses?'

'One more *gaijin* – yes, he has been seen, and so he will be identified afterwards, if that's necessary.'

'Then we have a perfect excuse for sealing off Arigata. Takahashi, please get me the Prime Minister's private office.' Hideki sat meditatively watching the various screens, till Takahashi reported back.

'Apparently the Prime Minister and the rest of the Cabinet are unavailable due to the political crisis in Tokyo.'

'Insist!'

Another five minutes passed. Takahashi was standing up, perspiring, his voice threatening and cajoling by turns. He knew what was set to happen if the government did not come here to Arigata.

But no one in authority would respond.

'So,' Hideki said icily, 'the cowards do not even dare to speak to me!'

'There is this debate in the Diet,' Takahashi said weakly, sweat visible under his arms.

'Then it is Minister Hakagawa who will have the honour of

officially opening Arigata. At eight o'clock, I think. Announce it.'

Takahashi licked his lips. Had Hoyle seen Alex Stanton? When would he act? A telephone rang and he picked it up. 'I understand.' He turned to the others. 'Another official from the Defence Agency. A high-level request that, please, we should allow a Ground SDF unit in here, to increase security.'

Hideki's answer was harsh. 'Tell them we have heard terrorists have infiltrated the crowd outside, and have SDF and police uniforms. For its own safety Arigata must be defended against *all* those outside – by force. Tell them! Tell the press that, also.'

Takahashi gabbled it out.

Hideki added thoughtfully, 'Emphasize that we have the situation under control for the moment, but that there are explosives out there and the number of terrorists is not known. The reactor itself might be under threat. So tell them to keep well away from Arigata – well away. Anything might happen, otherwise. And remind Tokyo that disaster here would spread radioactive poison for a hundred miles or more, to Niigata certainly and maybe to Nagoya or Tokyo. And that would certainly mean the end of our civilian nuclear power programme. Tell the Cabinet all that.'

Takahashi passed this message on, too.

Hideki was now looking almost relaxed. 'I do not think they will dare to interfere. Arigata is ours for as long as is necessary to complete this battle of wills.'

'But if they do interfere, *oyabun*?' Takahashi asked, covering the mouthpiece.

'Then we fight. And if we lose that fight, we blow up the world. You must make that clear to them in Tokyo!'

Takahashi finished speaking. He still held the phone in his hand and he looked uneasy. Hideki turned back to him, frowning. 'Get me the operations manager – Katayama. Then order our hostages assembled in the press hall before eight o'clock, for the official switch-on. Meanwhile, find Alex Stanton, pay him what is his due. At eight, take up your own post.'

Katayama was escorted into the room by a uniformed guard.

'Ito Katayama, how are things?'

The round-faced man was pale but keen to please: 'Early days, Hideki-*san*, but no major problems as yet.'

Hideki remained sitting while the other man stood. 'Everything is functioning? Excellent. Now I want you to bring the reactor up to full power. A thousand degrees, yes?'

'Six hundred degrees . . .' The man in spectacles began wringing his hands; his forehead gleamed with perspiration. 'But, sir, I regret so much the great difficulty of doing that. The impossibility, I mean. The operating manual advises . . . We need to check the installation carefully. To go straight to full power is against all accepted safety procedures. I cannot do it.'

Hideki stood up abruptly from the table, eyeing Katayama as if he was something unwholesome. Then he walked up to the engineer and slapped him hard across the face. The glasses went flying and Katayama yelped. 'You have my orders. Do what I tell you! Don't you understand, yet? I *want* the reactor to be dangerous.'

Sirens had begun wailing, to signal the security alert Hideki had ordered.

'Let's go down to the main gate and check the situation first-hand,' Alex said.

From the chopper landing pad you could see the tall main gates, which were still closed. Full darkness had settled outside them, grey above, black below. In the shadows beside the gates were armed men, some lying prone to cover the approaches. Alex already knew they had Uzi machine-guns and rocket-propelled grenade throwers; they could stop everything short of armoured assault.

His face tightened. Even two Mark IXs would have done it, though he was not optimistic about help arriving. He turned to Maggie. 'I think we could probably get at least one of the hired press 'copters out of here safely. You should be on it.'

'Leave?' She looked angry, her red hair swirling. 'That's very protective of you, but what about everybody else concerned in this!'

He bit his lip. 'I'd rather you were safe.'

'I just hope you're satisfied now. How much bigger and more profitable will all this make your armaments division, might I ask?'

'How much bigger—?' He laughed, but his gaze was coldly determined. 'I don't think you understand. Whatever happens here at Arigata, Stanton Industries can't avoid controversy. Certainly we can't avoid violence; and since we have a fast-breeder reactor, maybe we can't avoid disaster with a capital 'D'. That's why I gave Hugh my resignation, post-dated.'

She beat her clenched fists together. 'Why didn't you stop this before?'

He stared at her. 'Perhaps I could have stopped some of it before.'

'Then why didn't you?'

'Because after this is over, one way or another, we'll be able to stop a whole lot more. But all that's my responsibility, not yours.'

'Remember, I'm press. It is my responsibility, in part!'

His voice became appealing, as he touched her shoulder, the red hair tickling his fingertips. 'Maggie, please go. Just leave this place! You've already warned me what might happen if that reactor blows.'

She looked at him with a face sad and proud. 'I wanted to expose injustice, to bring it home to people. Don't you remember, that's what I once told you at Oxford, Alex? And can I look at myself in the mirror and say I've always done that? No, I can't. So now I'm staying. I have to follow this story through to the end. Can't you respect that, at least?'

There was so much intensity between them it seemed as if they were now the only two real people here. Their eyes met, his hard blue against her Irish green. 'I do respect you, Maggie. Always have, always will.'

'Then why don't *you* get out, now! You're damaging your reputation by being associated with this, damaging Hugh's reputation, and the firm's!'

He shook his head, liking her, knowing they were similar in so many ways, dissimilar in many others. 'I accept what you say, but I can't leave – especially if this turns out to be dangerous. Obviously, yes, I could have stayed home, and been safe. Maybe other people could have taken on the responsibility of trying to stop Hideki. But that wouldn't be right, Maggie. It was by my authority that Hideki was given help. Therefore it has to be my responsibility, my risk, to stop him. That's all. Now, please, won't you go home?'

Her eyes were shining. 'And let you exclude me from the biggest story I've ever covered? No way!'

'You really understand what you're risking? Remember, you don't have to prove anything to me.'

She took a breath. 'Maybe I have some things to prove to myself. Understand?' She tried to smile. 'Wait till I see Hideki. I have a speech already planned that'll bring tears to his eyes.'

Alex looked around quickly, and made his decision. 'Then let's get going.'

Arigata had one main street leading down to the reactor and the quayside with its huddled cranes. Yellow sodium streetlights, set high above, were glaringly bright. He walked quickly, limping slightly as always. Engineers, Western as well as Japanese, were standing around in yellow overalls, arguing in groups. Alex spotted John Reid from the Stanton security office, and gave him a beckoning nod.

Reid moved towards him, a filter mask hanging over his chin, which partially disguised him. 'Mr Stanton.'

Alex moved away from his friends and spoke quietly. 'Have you got the weapons?'

'Assault rifles, Browning automatics, and a box of grenades – phosphorus, high explosive and smoke.'

Alex thought for a moment. 'All right. I'll be upstairs with the press for the official opening. Wait for my orders afterwards. Here will do.'

Reid nodded. 'I suppose there's not much chance of this ending peaceably?'

'None.' His eyes flashed. 'Hideki mustn't live to be the victor here. No matter what happens to me . . . Any other information?'

The broad-shouldered man scratched his nose. 'There's a rumour the Japs have chased everybody out of the reactor containment dome.'

'Yes?'

'Rumour also says, they've wired it up to explode.'

'Christ,' Alex said. 'So the reactor might go up!' He thought a moment, hoping the story was untrue, then slapped Reid's shoulder and turned back across the street. Maggie's eyes looked large and ghostly. The others now grouped around Alex as he addressed them grimly. 'It seems Hideki is winning everything, so far. He has a hundred thousand hostages here – and the reactor itself. The US Seventh Fleet is out to sea as his protection. I don't think even the Russians will dare to act, now. Not in the full glare of publicity. Hell, there must be a hundred journalists here.'

David murmured, 'But I still tend to believe Kerensky. What if the Russians do strike?'

'Then we're all dead,' Alex said bluntly. 'But so is Hideki.'

'I don't think so,' David said harshly. 'Not if he's underground with stored oxygen and air filters and everything. He might win, even then. I can see him coming out of this as the strong man, standing up for Japan against the evil Russians. The strong man whose survival was itself a miracle, decrying a weak and cowardly America which failed to honour its promise to protect Japanese citizens – after the same weak and cowardly America had forcibly disarmed them through Article IX of the '47 Constitution!'

Alex glanced back at Reid, but he had vanished. 'You paint a terrible picture, David.'

'Terribly convincing?'

'That, too.'

The formalities, though delayed, were still due to take place in the glass-walled press hall on the top floor of the Arigata restaurant building. In they went, passing the NHK outside-broadcast truck parked outside. The NHK – the local equivalent of the BBC – would be carrying the opening ceremony, and Hideki's message, live.

'Mr Stanton!'

Alex turned around, one foot on the first of the outside stairs. It was Takahashi, grinning, accompanied by two uniformed men with holstered pistols, their peaked caps pulled low over their faces.

'What do you want?'

'I want you to know that the money due to your company has been paid. We telexed it through from Tokyo headquarters five minutes ago, at Mr Hideki's personal order. So, we have fulfilled our promise. You get your £65 million completion payment.'

Alex stared at him and his armed protection. Sirens still wailed. 'You expect thanks?'

'I expect nothing and do nothing, only my duty!'

Alex watched him stalk away, then turned back to his friends. 'Any suggestions? Nobody? Well, I think this. We now do what we can, whatever we can, to stop Hideki. Because if he ends up as the new government, he will win everything.'

David banged clenched fists together. 'You don't have some kind of plan?'

'I always have plans. And I don't believe, after all this, that the Cabinet will tamely turn up from Tokyo to put itself, and so all the authority of government, into Hideki's hands.' He turned from David to Maggie. 'That means the only real problem is here in Arigata. Solve that, and everything is solved. Come on, now.'

They climbed the outside stairs to the top. From the balcony, they could see for miles. Alex's gaze focused on the flashing lights of a police car in the dark landscape beyond. It had been trapped in the crowd as it vainly tried to hold the road open. He then looked upwards. Stars had come out.

He heard a gasp beside him as, amid the huge crowd spreading out to landwards under the star-spangled sky, countless people lit matches and cigarette lighters, and raised them. Countless anonymous people, but they produced a hundred thousand tiny flames stretching for what seemed miles. The lights were small and guttering, but there were so many of them.

Suddenly aware of all the people Arigata had helped put at risk, Alex wondered just what he and McCourt had been striving for for so long. He grimaced, feeling a personal responsibility, only hoping now to keep everyone safe as best he could.

'Alex!' Maggie sounded desperate. 'We're hostages, and we're helpless. What are we going to *do*?'

'Attend the switch-on ceremony with good grace.' He turned to McCourt. 'Try the phone again. Get somebody military in Tokyo. We need help here!'

From the press hall, it was clear the crisis was deepening. Arigata's electric fence had been charged. The guards were at every gate. Nothing short of armed assault could enter the plant. Nobody, short of violence and surprise, could hope to leave. The Japanese government had so far done nothing.

Maggie turned her head from the transistor radio held to one ear. 'Hey, radio news – BBC World Service.'

Apparently the White House had just issued a statement deploring both the Russian blockade and the Japanese plutonium programme. In the interests of peace, the US naval forces would remain in the sea-lanes around Japan, but would not interfere – at present – with the Soviet dispositions.

'Will that reduce tension much?'

'No,' Alex said tensely. 'Because Hideki still holds this place, and all the explosive potential of the reactor.' He turned to point at a television screen showing a crowd of seated Japanese men. 'Let's see what comes of the special debate in the Diet, about the nuclear agreements and Hakagawa.'

They watched and tried to follow. All through McCourt's spasms of translation, Alex concentrated on the expressions. Then he turned to her. 'I don't think the government is going to crack over this. Not quite yet. Not if they're calling on the people holding Arigata to let SDF troops inside.'

'No way will Hideki allow that,' she said steadily.

'Then they might fight it out over our heads. Either the Russians or the Japanese might hit Arigata.' He glanced over at Kerensky as he barked Russian into another phone and crushed out another half-smoked cigarette. 'And if anything goes wrong, if the reactor blows . . . tens of thousands of people are dead.'

David Bryant opened a door and ushered a man inside. It was the plant manager. The round-faced Japanese waited till the door behind him was closed. His wire-framed spectacles were askew, and swelling made his face lopsided.

'Mr Stanton, are we safe here?'

'Just tell us,' Alex said tersely.

Ito Katayama bowed to them. 'Mr Hideki has given a very dangerous order. He has brought the reactor up to full power.'

Alex frowned. 'What exactly does that mean?'

'That any accident might turn quickly into disaster.' The manager of the Arigata site was now looking frantic. 'Worse, I have seen people inside, with forklift trucks . . . seen them on the closed-circuit television that monitors the interior of the containment dome. They've been taking in gasoline drums and reactor fuel. All the fissionable material has been collected from storage and shifted inside the dome. It looks like they've been wiring up explosives, too.'

'Inside the reactor building!' David looked ill.

Alex wanted it stated plainly: 'Exactly what might happen?'

'Start up the reactor, bring it up to full power and heat, cause a big enough explosion – then the pressure vessel round the core cracks, and the molten sodium spurts out and starts to burn. Then the whole core will burn, thousands of degrees, so the dome is ruptured . . . Fire. Fire, don't you understand? And meanwhile the white-hot core of the reactor has melted down completely!'

'Jesus,' said Hacker. 'Somebody inside that dome is prepared to start that?'

'Or maybe it will be done remotely.'

'So somebody needs to get inside the reactor dome itself,' Alex asked curtly, 'to stop all this?'

The Japanese stared at him. 'You have seen. What can I do? Hideki, Hakagawa the Minister, they have men in my control room and they have threatened to shoot anybody who scrams the reactor – shuts it down, that is. Even I!'

'But maybe we could go into the containment vessel and close it down from there?'

Katayama replied softly, 'There is an emergency button. I could show you where. Even help you get through the armoured doors.'

'I see,' Alex said, rapidly making plans.

'They say there are only two men being allowed inside, now: Hideki's own man, and some Englishman I do not know.'

'Just the two of them?' That sounded ominous. 'Any descriptions?'

'Tall and dark, fit-looking, in his thirties, the English. The Japanese man is I think Hideki's chief aide.'

Alex nodded. Takahashi.

He delved in McCourt's case, and opened up a roll of blueprints of the reactor itself, inside its huge concrete dome. 'What ways can we get in?'

Katayama pondered. 'Only two entrances. The main one is impossible. Armed men outside. However, there is a second entrance, and maybe I can open that remotely. Or somebody could trick their way in, perhaps.'

'And once inside?'

'Inside, it is just as you see on these plans. And if I can be free in my control room, I could help – operate equipment remotely, open hatchways.'

'You could open hatches and doors from *outside*?' Alex homed in. 'What else can you do from there?'

'Operate some of the lights, the sprinkler fire system.'

Alex nodded. 'How much can you see on the TV monitors?'

'Enough. Inside there are still armoured firehoses. All high pressure. If hoses are turned on, we could perhaps flood the chamber completely.'

'Flood the chamber . . .' Alex sighed, studying the blueprints.

'Yes, indeed. But, please, I must regain authority in my control room. Otherwise, disaster.'

Alex Stanton made his decision.

Inside the large press hall, the front seats were already crowded. Television cameras, as yet unmanned, pointed at the stage, where the British and American flags were draped on either side of the blood-red Rising Sun.

The audience included representatives of the world's press, some diplomats and politicians, and men from all the companies involved in this thousand-million-dollar project. Alex stood quietly to one side, leaning against the wall near the door out to this floor's balcony.

There was already disorder and much shouting.

'I repeat, you are not hostages!' A dishevelled Takahashi had come on to the stage and seized the microphone. Two armed guards appeared to back him up. 'You are guests here in the cause of peace. Russians and other powers should note this! Now, please, to your places. We begin the official opening.'

As the nearby door opened, Alex glanced over and was stunned by what he saw.

Here was the final witness.

'Kiko Hideki came here with the last helicopter – my helicopter,'

Kerensky told them. The stern-faced Russian went to hold the door for her.

She entered like a queen. Heads turned and stayed turned. She had a solemn loveliness in her face, and wore a high-cut golden blouse and loose white trousers. Her hair gleamed black as she strode towards Alex.

'Kiko,' he said, opening his arms a little.

She stopped, hissed, 'Why are you still here helping my grandfather? I told you not to come!' She struck him hard across the face. 'Only you were strong enough to defy him – but instead you helped! Alex Stanton, I *believed* in you! And here you are, giving my grandfather everything his heart desires!'

His jaw stung; he rubbed it. But the only tears were in her eyes. He stared at Kiko grimly. 'This is the real world, Kiko. If you want to judge me, you can judge me – *but wait till all the evidence is in.*'

'I have seen enough.' She was white with rage, not caring that other people were staring openly at them.

Alex suppressed his anger, but did not turn away. A fierce heat was building up between them.

Kerensky came closer, his face grey and tired. 'I have news from the USSR Embassy here. An ultimatum. Either this situation is cleared up by dawn,' the Russian said softly, 'or the Soviet fleet will wipe this installation from the face of the earth.'

'They mean it?' Alex said.

'We will now watch Hideki all together, and then the whole world will blow up.'

Alex straightened up. His friends huddled round, listening. 'Then we have no alternative except to step up the pressures.'

Kerensky said only, 'Act. There is nothing more to be said.'

Alex hesitated, then said simply, 'We can try things ourselves, right here. Seize stocks of fissionable material. Close down the reactor. Take hostages of our own.' Alex glanced around the vast room, lowered his voice. 'I have a special weapons and tactics team from my central security office, with smuggled weapons; hand-picked men.'

'Outnumbered.' Hacker fiddled with his eye-patch. 'But Christ we're going to need 'em.'

At that point more people walked out on to the main platform. Hideki, old and small but with a fierce face, led them. He gazed down at the audience, forcing a smile as there was a scattering of applause from the Japanese.

I stand here, Hideki thought, *and I am destiny. The destiny of Japan*! Takahashi had prepared the reactor. If it must be a fate like that of the kamikaze pilots, self-sacrifice for the good of Japan, then so it must be. He threw up his arms, and suddenly there was loud cheering.

Hideki began his speech, pausing often to give the translator a chance.

'We are all here to celebrate another great Japanese achievement.

We have in Arigata a marvel of the atomic age. From a few handfuls of heavy metal, we take heat and power – almost a thousand million watts of power. For us, this reactor is something which will open many once-forbidden doors, and it will lead us along many once-forbidden roads – *roads which we now intend to walk!*'

Hideki stared at his audience, eyes bright in triumph. He was a charismatic figure, and his spirit filled the hall. The interpreter, sweating, eyed his master with fascination, on edge to turn Hideki's words into sonorous English.

'But this would never have been possible without support from all quarters here in Japan. From one people, with one philosophy of life, one supreme future!'

Alex listened, fascinated. NHK television cameras were broadcasting this to all Japan.

'In the absence of our Prime Minister, Minister Hakagawa will have the honour of putting Arigata's power to work.'

As Hakagawa strutted forward to the microphone, a silence fell. He stared around him, and nodded, an expression almost of distaste on his face. Hideki was behind him in the crowd of dignitaries, his own face now without expression.

Hakagawa spoke slowly and plainly. 'There has been much indecision in our country over nuclear power. That is nonsensical. The atom has been split; we have suffered from that, so we are entitled to accept all the benefits, too. Today, we make official the agreements that will guarantee us uranium fuel. Then later—' He paused, significantly. Alex wondered how brutally he would put it. He spotted Kiko, on the far left of the audience; her face was fiercely blank. 'Later we will have other plans for nuclear power. That is our right.'

He spoke softly, not ranting at all. Then, except for the glare of TV lamps at the front, all the lights in the glass-roofed hall were turned off one by one. The harsh voice continued in Japanese; a translator made it sound more civilized. 'Does anyone in this room, in the world, deny us our rights?' There was a long pause. Tension gathered. 'No? Then I declare the Arigata project successfully begun.'

He pulled down the big switch.

Instantly, the dark sky outside exploded with light and colour. People gasped.

It was a stunning light-show. Laser beams in vivid colours crisscrossed. Light and colours danced off the low cloudbase in surreal shapes.

People were now standing and mighty applause filled the room. Alex realized, appalled, that Hideki had carried it off.

Kiko, her expression rigid, suddenly pushed up to the stage and pulled the translator's microphone towards her.

'I will say something for the ears of the world. You all see here, today, the benefits of nuclear power. We'll see now what Hiroshima and Nagasaki did – what the nuclear bomb has already done to the Japanese people.'

She ripped off her silk blouse. Other than the bra restraining her small breasts, she was naked from the waist up, and the dark scars the Hiroshima bomb had left on her were terribly visible under the bright television lights.

There was a sustained gasp.

'We must not allow this,' she shouted in English, turning around to make her appeal to the cameras, and so to the world. 'We must not have these weapons! See the results. Remember how many died!'

Hakagawa glared at her with murder in his eyes, and he spat out one word: 'Traitor.'

Kiko had never looked more proud to Alex. He heard her call out again, 'I am the soul of Japan, I am the bleeding mouth of Japan *and I will not be gagged*! We must not do this!'

Then Hakagawa, in front of all the cameras, jumped down from the platform and struck her across the face. He was screaming abuse as he shook Kiko and drew back a massive hand to slap her again.

Alex vaulted over a row of chairs and pushed people out of his way. Others had moved to restrain Hakagawa, but Alex got there first. He grabbed Hakagawa's wrist, and with a twist of his shoulders wrestled the heavy man to the ground. Kiko had already been beaten half-unconscious, and there was blood over her face.

'Get a doctor, somebody!' Alex said, kneeling beside her on the floor as she moaned. He clenched a fist at Hakagawa, knowing it would give him great pleasure to hammer this man.

But the armed guards were at hand, guns drawn. Hakagawa rose shakily to his feet, sneering as if to say, 'Now you see the new Japan, Alex Stanton! Now you see your new masters!'

There was a murmur of disquiet in the hall. Most people were standing.

Tom Kalbach was one of them. His voice quavered a little. 'And why are we here now?'

Hideki, on the stage, gave a gap-toothed smile as he watched Kiko come round. 'If all of us here, all of us safe.'

One of the American journalists, a beefy, red-faced man, began yelling. 'I don't want to stay here. You let us go, man!'

It was an Australian engineer next, who had obviously been doing some off-duty drinking. We are bloody hostages!' He turned around: some of his workmates were with him. 'Let's take some hostages ourselves!'

Five or six men stood up. Tom Kalbach turned around and, waving his arms, tried to hold them back, but it was too late. The Australians started a rush towards the stage.

Hideki snapped orders. Guns were pulled and one of the guards fired twice. The Australian fell down, moaning; blood began to leak from around his shoulder. Other people screamed, and tried to hide behind the chairs and each other.

Alex stood up, supporting Kiko. He turned to Hacker. 'Christ.' He pointed.

Tom Kalbach lay sprawled on his back, mouth wide open and quivering, his limbs twitching. On the floor spread a widening red stain.

In the control room, cradling an Uzi machine-gun, the senior guard Masuhara sat on a tall stool. His colleague had a holstered pistol. Masuhara tried not to yawn, though he had been on duty for twelve hours. He remembered Hideki's words from a Bushido session at his estate: In Japan, we do not complain, we obey.

Noticing the red lights on the panels, he picked out one of the younger engineers. 'You! Come here! What is the situation now!'

The young man bowed politely and explained. Overheating, but not yet critical; a leak of pressure from the steam heat exchanger.

Three times Katayama had respectfully asked for permission to lower the power of the reactor. Three times Masuhara had curtly refused him.

Masuhara picked up an internal telephone and rang through to the main gate. Nothing outside, except darkness and strangely quiet demonstrators.

He listened with only half his mind to the NHK channel carrying the opening ceremonies for Arigata. Hideki's speech was a fine, uplifting one. But Masuhara whirled around to gape when he heard the fired shots. Was somebody hurt, or dead? The gasping, alarmed commentator did not make it clear.

Masuhara tightened his grip on the Uzi and turned his scowl on the others like a weapon.

Alex had to see.

A gaping wound, in the left temple. Tom Kalbach had been shot through the head. People were still screaming; some battered on the doors to try to escape.

Maggie stood up from the blood on the floor and called out clearly, 'Isn't this the truth, Mr Hideki, at last? All along, you and the faction you have in the ruling party here would do *anything* to get atomic power and weapons?'

Hideki said, 'I want a free, unafraid Japan. That is all.' He gave her the terrible smile of a man afraid of nothing.

Chapter Twenty-nine

Alex made a hurried call to his cousin Hugh Stanton. It was not much of a last will and testament, but the best he could do.

'Hugh,' he said into the phone, 'it's happened. The nightmare scenario.'

'What?'

'Hideki *has* been running a conspiracy. And now Arigata is completely in his hands.'

'There must be something the Tokyo government can do!'

'McCourt's been trying to persuade them and so have I, but this place is armed and guarded. And apparently if there's any interference from outside Hideki has threatened to blow up the Arigata reactor.'

'Oh my God.' Hugh spoke very quietly. 'You know, Dr Sidqi came over from Baghdad, and he seems to know something about Arigata . . .'

'Listen, before it all hits the fan, publicize my resignation, and give honest reasons why I did it. Start a debate. We can't have more Arigatas, more secret nuclear weapons plots – we just *can't*.'

'I regret all this,' Hugh said miserably, half a world away. 'I regret it so much.'

'My risk, now,' Alex said sharply, as Ray Hacker came back into the room. 'Now, wish me luck – all of us luck. I have to go.'

Hacker was making sure his Browning pistol was loaded.

Though the armed men guarding the doors to the reactor chamber recognized Takahashi, they formally checked his identity anyway. He waited patiently, sick with a tense excitement he did not wish to regard as fear.

A steel door opened, he advanced alone, and it closed behind him. Another door opened, and warm air swirled around.

Takahashi entered the chamber cautiously. 'Everything okay?'

Hoyle, indifferent, turned his back.

Takahashi tapped his holstered pistol and frowned, as he glanced around this vast, domed space. A cathedral, where atomic energy was sacred. From the thousand-ton reactor assembly emanated a rumbling vibration, and a much stronger heat than usual. The deep thunder of the sodium pumps had been loud for a long time, and heat was building up inside the containment dome. A fast-breeder reactor, he thought. Full of heat and energy and deadly fission products. Full of death. My death, also?

In the middle stood the pressure container. Inside that huge layered and armoured bulk, the four-ton core was a minutely-engineered framework of incandescent metal. He knew it held a full ton of plutonium oxide and other heavy metals, almost but not quite on the point of melting, through which flooded molten sodium. Emerging at the top, huge armoured pipes led across to the prime heat exchanger beside the core. Here radioactive sodium heated other sodium, so that none of the radioactive molten metal went beyond the pressure dome.

Unless disaster happened . . . The thought made Takahashi queasy.

He glanced at the biological shield which concealed the lower part of the central pressure vessel. Even at low levels, radioactivity was a danger. Arigata frightened him.

Fork-lift transporters had been used to pile up steel drums of lubricating oil and high-octane gasoline around the concrete biological shield. These drums now entirely surrounded the hot-running reactor. Wired up to them was plastic explosive. And among the fuel drums were the tall, sealed, cans of fissionables – U235 or plutonium oxide. Enough for nuclear bombs a dozen times over.

'Check everything again,' Hoyle said. 'I want to be sure.'

Takahashi looked at his electronic detonator, and traced the long wires towards the core as Hoyle probed at the Semtex explosive which Hoyle himself had placed around the rim of the reactor. There was three hundred pounds of it. It would provide enough of a blast to crack the reactor wide open. That should start a real fire: burning sodium and burning heavy metal would churn up into a thousand degrees of firestorm, hot enough to crack the containment dome like an eggshell . . .

'No problem. Are you satisfied now, Alan Hoyle?'

Hoyle turned, gave a death's-head grimace. 'I am. It'll burn like a furnace, when the time comes.' He wiped his hands together.

'If the time comes!' Takahashi said sharply. 'If!' He took a breath.

But Hoyle could foresee it. In the impending blowtorch of a fire, the burning reactor core would be a nuclear volcano, spraying contamination everywhere – the most serious nuclear accident ever. It would render the Arigata plant unusable, and kill tens of thousands of people downwind. He grunted. 'What happened to the famous *kamikaze* courage of the Japanese? You should be ready to die. I am, if it's spectacular enough.'

It was said blandly: 'Of course you are ready to die. If that is necessary.' Takahashi shrugged. 'But Tokyo has been warned. Invade the Arigata site, and the reactor will burn.'

Hoyle's eyes glittered. 'A disaster at Arigata would make a man's name live forever.' Tokyo was hardly more than a hundred miles away, so with a good strong breeze from the north . . . How many people lived in greater Tokyo? Ten million? Twelve million? It was a thought to sober some, but it excited him.

Hoyle studied the detonation box set on a table beside them. A flipped-up LED screen showed 5:00. Five minutes and no seconds. Hit the red button, and there was a five minute delay till the explosion. In theory, that was enough time for them to get safely out of the dome and escape. Then a helicopter could take you miles away. Hoyle thought it over, then he laughed. 'Why run?' He stood up, and stretched. 'This is Armageddon, and we have grandstand seats.'

Hakagawa rubbed at his nose: a summer cold, making him cough and sneeze. 'Are you sure Takahashi will know his duty?'

Hideki put down the phone. 'He will obey me,' Hideki said quietly. He turned back to watch the live TV broadcast of the Diet debate.

Hakagawa peered over his shoulder. 'The situation is not developing to our advantage?'

'I think not.' Hideki sighed, uneasy and distressed, and flapped a hand at the screen. 'Is this truly the country's spirit? I had expected a vigorous defence of our position. It has been on the unadmitted agenda for years!'

'It's all talk-talk, and those politicians are professional liars and whores! They sell themselves to faction chiefs, who sell themselves to big businesses. Where is the loyalty?'

'Or practicality,' Hideki added quietly. 'Because, if it comes to it, the Arigata reactor will burn, and that will be the end of this country's nuclear power programme – and the government *cannot* allow that to happen. One way or another, they will have to surrender to us.'

'May I,' Hakagawa said, 'give advice? Reinforce the guards on the gates. Block off the helipads with parked vehicles. Keep all lights on. We must not be taken by surprise.'

'Very sensible.' Hideki gave the orders, then spoke by telephone to the guard detail outside the containment dome. 'Nobody is to get past you – into the reactor. Understand? If necessary, I want you to shoot – to kill.'

'I understand,' a voice said obediently. Bushido was alive.

Then Hideki glanced at the red telephone, which was a special direct line to Hoyle and Takahashi inside the containment dome. His hand moved towards it. One order given, and it would happen: a nuclear-age open hearth . . . He pursed his lips, wondering when it would be time.

In the control room Katayama sat watching the readings, fascinated. Was this going to be the big one, which everyone involved in nuclear engineering had always dreaded? Melt-down? He looked over at the operator who had once managed the safety circuits – the circuits Hideki had ordered to be torn out. The man sat stooped and tired in his chair.

There were even more red lights on the instrument panels, now, and more dials had gone into the danger zone.

Katayama glanced at the uniformed intruders who had taken over his control room.

Masuhara was sitting bolt upright, an Uzi in his hands. Suddenly he bawled to a junior engineer, 'You, what are you doing?'

'I am only checking the pressure in the turbines.' The young man stood back from the control panel, frightened.

'Don't you touch anything till ordered!'

Katayama, small and middle-aged, studied the two uniformed men who could ruin everything. Though they carry guns, I *should* defy them, he told himself. If only I had courage . . .

I am a coward, he told himself miserably. A telephone rang. The door security. He picked it up. 'Katayama.'

'Two men with a delivery.'

Excitement stirred in the middle of his fear. 'Let them through.'

He glanced behind him and saw two large Western men in yellow overalls approaching down the long corridor, carrying a box between them.

Katayama moved over to the armoured glass partition. Both guards watched him as he unlocked the door to the control room. He said curtly, 'Bring the box in here.'

Hacker and Reid came in slowly.

Masuhara spoke to the younger guard. 'Search that box.'

It happened in a second.

Hacker went for Masuhara bare-handed. Reid pulled out an automatic pistol and turned on the other guard. Masuhara leapt off his stool and started to raise his Uzi machine-gun, but Hacker's big fist was already connecting with his face. There was a brief burst of fire: everybody jumped back. The Browning fired twice. Hacker's second blow smashed into the back of Masuhara's neck, killing him instantly.

'Oh, no.' Katayama stared in horror. One of the operators had slumped forward in his high chair. In front of him, the bullet-riddled panel sparked and smoked with short circuits. 'That's the board for the control rods!'

Hacker loomed over him, intimidating in every respect, and now the Texan had a gun in his hand. 'What?'

Katayama turned to Hacker, almost sobbing. 'The board is damaged! We can no longer shut down the reactor from here!'

'Get busy fixing that panel!' Hacker snapped, 'Lock Hideki into his office! Then somebody can tell Tokyo that we've got the control room!'

'That won't matter now.' Katayama stared at the red lights and the explosive-rigged reactor, and knew that it was already too late. 'That area of the panel was the safety zone, Mr Hacker. The shut-down systems are controlled from there.'

Even Hacker felt scared. 'You mean you can no longer control the reactor?'

'Nearly all of the safety systems were deliberately disabled.' Katayama looked at a temperature gauge. The technicians were at work again. 'Core temperature has just gone up another four degrees. Main pumps to maximum,' Katayama said. Sweat was running down his face, making his eyes sting.

From his control desk Katayama flicked the switches which secured the other office doors along this corridor, then he turned to lock himself in with a key. This control room had armoured doors: they might stand up to attack.

Hacker knew something about nuclear engineering. 'How far from meltdown are we?'

'Perhaps eighty degrees. An hour. Or less.'

It was deep night outside as Hacker and Alex trotted with two more of their security people towards the huge humped back of the containment dome. Each man had an assault rifle in his arms. McCourt followed them, unarmed.

They stopped where a broad concrete ramp tilted down to the tunnel entrance. Armed guards had been posted down there, at main doors which were thirty feet high and made of foot-thick high-grade steel. Inside, at the reactor end of the tunnel, were other armoured doors. Sodium-yellow floodlights glared overhead.

Alex risked a quick glance down the ramp, then he turned to McCourt, talking in a whisper. 'I can see three of them. And there's maybe a couple more, under cover of that stupid little sentry-box.'

Hacker waved a broad thumb at the door. 'They could be dead men, as soon as you say the word.'

A silence. Alex said, finally, 'How will we get through those doors, even if we win outside? And reinforcements would come from the perimeter, as soon as we started shooting.'

McCourt followed his thinking. 'So we can't storm this castle by frontal assault, eh?'

As Alex backed away, the others followed him into the shadows. 'Where's the other entrance? Is it manned?'

'Over there. Two guards, should be.'

'How'll you get in?'

'By asking, maybe.'

Hacker stared.

Alex glanced at his watch. 'The phone lines to the reactor chamber all go through the control room. And Katayama is now monitoring them. He thinks we might have half an hour, if we're lucky.'

'I see,' Hacker said harshly. 'That might give us at most fifteen, twenty minutes to get you inside. And what happens then? How do we get you out, afterwards?'

If there was any afterwards.

'At least I'll be inside,' Alex said. 'Armed and dangerous – and with all that armour keeping Hideki out.'

'And when you're inside, Alex?'

'I'll use the arts of persuasion,' Alex murmured. He stared up at the vast curve of the dome. It was a concrete mountain, imprisoning the nuclear age demon. Maggie was right. No prison could contain that demon, if it was allowed to escape.

He turned to the others. 'We've no alternative. Let's go.'

McCourt came up, holding his walkie-talkie to his ear. 'Listen,' he said. 'They've finally shown up.'

'Make a deal.' Holding a Stanton assault rifle, Alex crept forward a step at a time, very quietly. Thirty yards. Twenty yards.

This was the second entrance to the reactor.

When one of the guards turned around and said something urgent in Japanese, both guards raised their guns, and Alex reacted automatically, yelling as he pulled the trigger. 'McCourt, get down!'

The automatic rifle bucked as McCourt threw himself flat. Both guards fired at once. Alex's burst of shots caught the guards high in the chest, and they fell back. He realized this burst of firing would have been heard all over the Arigata site, and beyond.

They met at the doors. Hacker was breathing heavily. It could not be long till other guards arrived.

'Now what? Use plastic explosive to get in?'

'Just tell McCourt to stay where he is. Ask him to give me half an hour. After that, do whatever you think best.' He picked up the phone and pressed the call button. When Takahashi answered, he said, 'Tell Alan Hoyle that Alex Stanton is here, and that I'd like to talk to him in person.'

In the Diet the long debate was continuing. The government had been appealing for full authority to accept the Soviet ultimatum, to close down Arigata, and renege on its reprocessing contracts.

Hideki had been listening carefully. He turned to Hakagawa, enraged. 'The government are traitors!'

The big man shrugged. 'What can they do? What would they dare to do? Arigata is completely under our control.'

A clerk handed Hakagawa a note. 'A report from one of our agents in the crowd outside.'

Hideki sipped more green tea. Considering the circumstances, he felt remarkably calm. 'Yes?'

Hakagawa's voice was leaden. 'There's been a rumour. Armoured vehicles out there in the foothills.'

'So.' Hideki closed his eyes for a moment. 'The SDF may be here.' Images of Hiroshima and Nagasaki came back to him. The walking dead. Some charred black, he recalled vividly; others swollen and red. Weeping and wailing in the destroyed streets. Smoking rubble everywhere. But his country had survived all that horror and suffering, survived the napalm raids on Tokyo – and gone on to further greatness. That suffering had justified and purified Japan. When he opened his eyes, his face was coldly determined. 'I do not think that the government or any SDF officers will dare take direct action against us. And if they do, the reactor burns.'

A telephone rang on Hideki's desk, and he picked it up, glancing at the minister. 'I see.' He touched his lower lip. 'There has been shooting, inside the site. Our men have gone to investigate.'

'Shooting!'

Hideki cradled the handset, then lifted it again. It occurred to him to speak to Takahashi, even to order the final destruction.

Is it time? he asked himself. Time for this country to burn again for its failures? He considered, weighing the odds carefully.

No. I might still win.

Chapter Thirty

The massive door closed behind Alex, and then he heard the electric rim-bolts crash home. He blinked; the light at floor level inside the containment vessel seemed blinding, though the roof of this artificial cavern was lost in shadows up above.

'Alex Stanton!'

He swallowed the brassy taste of fear as his gaze flashed around. He was trapped in a roughly-welded security cage. Fifteen feet away were steel bars set about a foot apart. Takahashi stood with Alan Hoyle, and a table with tools and litter on it was next to the bars.

'That's me.' He took a breath. He walked towards the locked gate, limping steadily, feeling the pain of old wounds. He remembered the Tower of London bombing, which Kiko had put down to Hoyle. So this was the man Hoyle himself, at last, tall, dark, smiling. Alex did not underrate him. 'It's been a long time, Alan Hoyle.'

'It has,' Hoyle said quietly, his grin charming, coming forward himself with a gun in his right hand. He stopped beside the table. 'Keep your hands in sight.'

'Of course! Would I stand here with my hands in my pockets? That's not the way they taught us to do things at my school, y'know,' he drawled, hoping to annoy Hoyle and put him off-balance. Every second of delay and distraction was valuable.

'No.' Hoyle scowled, pursed his lips. 'Here for the show?'

'Be serious, Hoyle.' The pistol was pointed at him immediately. 'I came to confront you. I have a good idea what could happen.'

Contempt. 'Just to you?'

'To everybody between here and Tokyo Bay.'

Losing today meant death, Alex reflected: certainly for himself, probably for Maggie and his other friends here, and perhaps for hundreds of thousands of others downwind.

'That bothers you? Yet you helped build this place, Stanton . . .'

'You going to thank me for it?' He glanced at the massive machinery in the middle of the cave. The fast-breeder reactor, full of deadly isotopes and molten sodium. It hummed and clicked to itself, and an oven heat wafted over in waves.

Takahashi laughed.

For a while Hoyle did not speak. He stood unmoving, head cocked, as if listening to a music nobody else could hear. 'Have you ever touched plutonium?'

'I've done many things,' Alex said quietly. He was aware of the gun, and tension had changed the quality of the light, slowed down time, tilted the world.

'I liked the feel of it. It's eerie and warm; it actually feels dangerous.'

'Do you really want another Hiroshima, another Nagasaki – or worse?' His gaze drilled into Hoyle as each man tried to dominate the other. 'Don't you know what the Russians have threatened to do?'

Hoyle was a power in his own right and his eyes glittered back. 'Russians?' He laughed. He glanced at the steel security cage, smiled. 'Your sort would like to put me away, wouldn't you? But who is behind bars now?'

Alex glanced around, hands still high, and observed the hoses by the door in their heavy fireproof jackets, and on the table wirecutters and lengths of electric cable. He saw heavy, sharp-pointed scissors, and turned his gaze away immediately. 'I suppose I am.'

Hoyle's rage showed. 'It would be all right if it was me behind bars for life, though?'

'Nobody made you do the things you've done.'

'I'm a free man, Stanton. Isn't that what our freedom is all about? The power of the individual to say "no".'

'I hope it's something more than that,' Alex said.

'To say "no". That's me! The Japanese obey each other; in the West we compete.' He pointed the gun. 'Do you like my way of competing, Alex Stanton?'

Alex said scornfully, 'Would you want me to like it?' A light-emitting diode display on a table in front of the reactor showed 5:00. Five minutes, Alex guessed. 'What's that?' he asked.

This time Takahashi spoke. 'My work. The detonation circuit, right? To blow this place!'

Alex could sense the fear barely concealed behind the bravado. He imagined it happening: the sharp crack of the explosive, the roar as the doomed reactor split open and spilled incandescent radioactive sodium everywhere . . . He wondered what was happening outside the reactor. Had Kiko managed to do something? What about the Tokyo authorities?

Hoyle, eyes unblinking, was still pointing the pistol. He threw a quick glance at Takahashi. 'Leave your gun here. Then go into the cage and body-search him.'

Takahashi hesitated, then walked forward slowly. A security camera followed him.

'Five minutes?' Alex asked. 'Is that really long enough for you, if you hit Takahashi's switch?'

'If, always if!' Hoyle laughed, as Takahashi fumbled to unlock the cage door.

Alex pressed the point. 'You want to miss the end of the world?'

Takahashi licked his lips, unlocked the cage door.

'Fire,' Hoyle said quietly. 'I like it. Remember the fire in your Tyneside headquarters? That was me. The Tower bombing . . .'

'You again.' Now Alex eyed Takahashi. A terrible violence was going to happen, he could tell.

'Turn around,' Hoyle said, and when Alex hesitated, he levelled the gun. 'Step backwards, come up to the bars slowly. Keep your hands high and your back turned. Takahashi, search him.'

'I know how it goes,' Alex said quietly, hands high, back turned to the gun.

'Of course you do,' Hoyle replied. 'So you won't lower your hands or make any sudden movements, because if you do, I'll shoot you down like a dog.'

Alex made his reply ambiguous. 'You can rely on me.'

Takahashi's fingers fumbled at his ankles, crotch, armpits, chest, fished inside his jacket and pulled out the 9mm Browning. Alex turned around without being told to. Now, he stared at Alan Hoyle. He saw death in the fiery grey eyes, and braced himself. Takahashi patted down his back this time. Alex used the delay to check out the table again. Heavy scissors. Wire.

'Just this gun, Alan Hoyle.'

Takahashi held up the military-issue Browning between finger and thumb, then tossed it through the bars. It clattered on the table, landing just out of reach.

'Now, Stanton, turn around again. Walk.'

He walked towards the concrete wall, stilling the trembling in his legs with an effort.

Hoyle laughed. 'Push your face into the wall. Push it hard.'

Takahashi moved towards the locked gate. Alex's face was on the rough concrete. He was breathing heavily, because his every instinct told him that Hoyle was ready to kill.

There were two shots.

Maggie sat listening in the press room as Kiko translated the Diet debate for them.

Some speeches had been shocking displays of racism and aggression, but there were fine sentiments, too. Kiko, caring and a pacifist, was as genuine a product of Japan as her grandfather was; and Kiko was contemporary.

Maggie passed judgement. 'It sounds as if Saigo Hideki and his gang are losing!'

'No. Because here they might win.' Face still twisted in pain, Kiko turned around. McCourt had appeared, face grey and drawn, no hopeful sparkle in his eyes. 'Where've you been? We heard shooting.'

He nodded. 'Alex got inside the reactor. They're watching what happens in the control room.'

'But?'

He shuddered. 'We had to shoot to get in. Then more guards appeared – Hideki's people. There was a fight, Ray was hurt, we killed two of theirs, but they've got the doors into the reactor again.'

Maggie blurted out, 'What's happened to Alex?'

'I don't know! He's still inside. And if the reactor blows up—'

Kiko was pale, but poised and calm. 'I think we must try to do something, Maggie.'

Maggie straightened up. Her heart was beating, her palms moist. 'What did you have in mind?'

'Supposing Tokyo does move in? We must try to make sure the reactor is safe. Otherwise . . .'

Maggie nodded.

'We have heard nothing from Alex.' Kiko looked determined. 'Let's go.'

The two of them led some of the press out of the hall, and down the outside stairs. Maggie hoped nobody would dare to kill them all.

Alex jerked back, feeling sudden nausea, the concrete wall before his face seeming to swirl. Then he realized he had not been harmed.

There was a gurgling sound, which diminished gradually.

'You can turn around, now.'

He turned very slowly, to see Takahashi writhing on the floor, his mouth opening and closing like a fish's. There were two wounds in his chest, one a sucking wound over a lung. He was clearly dying.

'And how will you do it to me?' Alex's voice was throaty. He took a step forward, then another, wondering if Katayama was monitoring all this, as arranged.

Hoyle scratched his chin with the pistol's muzzle. 'I thought one in the kneecap first, so you can't run around too much. Then one in the groin. I'd enjoy that, hearing you scream, seeing you squirm around in your own piss and shit.'

Alex felt sick, but took another step forward. 'And to finish it?'

'I'd get up close, make you turn your head and look at me.' Hoyle glared. 'Yes, our eyes would meet. Then . . . well, come closer. If you dare.'

'It really has to be this way?'

'Yes, because of you, Stanton! Even though you're no different to me and not my moral superior.'

'No?'

'There's a man dying right beside you, and that means as little to you as it does to me!'

'It depends just who is dying, doesn't it? And, besides, you're the one responsible. You shot him; not me.'

Hoyle was enraged. 'Think of it; you can dine with the best, be honoured and rich and respectable, but me . . .'

'We are all responsible for what we do.'

'What have I ever done that's so different, except they call what I do "terrorism"?'

'There is a difference.' Alex had almost reached the bars. His legs felt heavy as lead, but he took another step forward. 'I might enable a man to buy a gun. I certainly don't put it in his hand. Above all, I don't make him shoot.'

'But I have the gun, now.'

'Yes.' Alex swallowed, his eyes aware of everything. 'So how will it end?'

'When I give you the last one right in the face.'

Takahashi whimpered something. Automatically Hoyle glanced in his direction.

In one blurred motion Alex reached through the bars, grabbed the heavy scissors by their points, and hurled them like a throwing knife. A lifetime of training, skill and luck powered one smooth and powerful movement.

Hoyle screamed, and his gun dropped as he put both hands to his face. The red handles of the scissors stood out from one eye-socket. He howled again. Alex snatched one of the fire hoses out of its housing, and turned on the high-pressure spray. He was already yelling to the listening microphones, 'Get the hatches open!'

The first blast of water knocked Hoyle off his feet. Alex saw the remote-controlled hatches begin to open up as he held the bucking nozzle in his hands. He hosed Hoyle away towards the nearest hatchway – a twenty-foot drop.

Water foamed everywhere. Hoyle was now on hands and knees, head lowered, trying to force himself forward against the flood. He inched forward, towards his gun. Then another cold surge knocked him backwards.

Alex continued to direct the spray. Then Hoyle managed to roll on to his knees and slap a hand on the detonator, before the next blast of water finally swept him away. He hung on to the edge of the hatch for a moment, only his head visible. Then he lost his grip and slip on down. The hatch closed, and Hoyle was gone.

Only five minutes. Five minutes till doom.

Takahashi mumbled, 'Key . . . Key . . .'

Alex ran over to the dying man, searched him for the key. Finding no key, he stood up, frantic. The count-down now read 3:49. He grabbed a length of stiff wire, twisted it in his hands. Reaching through the bars, be tried to fish for the Browning automatic Takahashi had tossed away. It took three attempts to snag it, but then the gun slipped off his makeshift hook. He snagged it again, pulled it close, grabbed it. Two and a half minutes left.

All he could think of now was to shoot at the cable leading from the electronic timer. The Browning holds nine shots. He squeezed off two quickly – but missed. Then a third and a fourth. The down-counting figures taunted him.

'Oh, Christ.' He glanced up at the monitoring camera and called out, 'Katayama, start the evacuation!'

Then he fired four more times, slowly, The timer said 0:11. Eleven seconds. He stared up at the vast bulk of the reactor, which would kill him, the first of many.

McCourt lowered the walkie-talkie, looking desperate. He was standing outside now, with Maggie and Kiko Hideki, and some of the press. In front of them Reid and two more of Alex's security people were still shooting; uniformed men with guns exchanged bursts of fire.

'I don't think we're going to do this! Alex is still in there, and the guards've closed the main doors. The rest of the guards can just come and kill us.'

Kiko turned her face to Maggie. 'I must try to persuade them. The reactor must be closed down.' She started to move away.

'No.' McCourt reached out one arm, stopping her. 'They'll kill you for sure.'

'That is my risk. But I must try.'

She stared up into McCourt's face, and then he stepped back and dropped his arm. Yellow sodium glare transfigured her as she began to walk. The path to the containment dome was long and already littered with bodies. All around her was the sweetish odour of blood.

Hacker hung back against the wall, his upper arm bandaged, holding the machine-pistol in one hand.

Kiko continued along the path to the downwards ramp, moving slowly but with great determination. In Japanese, she called out, 'I am Akiko Hideki. I am the heir of Saigo Hideki. You must let me approach.'

'I have been told to kill anybody approaching,' yelled the leader of the surviving guards. 'Those are my orders.'

She started to descend the ramp. Maggie and McCourt began to follow – and others followed them. Kiko was twenty-five yards from the great doors. 'I tell you that you must not fire upon me.'

She counted three gun barrels pointed unwaveringly towards her.

Twenty yards, now.

'Stop immediately or I will fire!'

She paused for a moment, threw her head back. 'I cannot stop now. It is my duty to go on.'

Maggie could not tear her gaze from the scene. McCourt whispered, 'Is she really going to do it?'

'This is the bravest thing I've ever seen,' Maggie replied. 'Kiko really is the soul of Japan – a true heroine.'

Kiko continued, more loudly, 'I order you, *order you*, in the name of Hideki, to stand aside and let me go on.'

Suddenly the guns were turned aside, the first steel door was opened, and she went on into the reactor chamber. Maggie hurried forward to join her, gesturing for the others to follow, and they did.

In front of them the reactor loomed, humming to itself, warm and gigantic, a hundred feet tall in the bright yellow light.

Alex heard the noise as the huge door opened, but he could not turn his attention from the timer as he shot again and the connecting wire was parted.

Now it said 0:00. Zero. The end of the world.

Nothing happened.

Hearing Takahashi scratching faintly, he realized suddenly what had happened. He kneeled down by Hideki's man. Amidst little rivulets of red blood, Takahashi was turning blue-grey. He looked up at Alex.

'You didn't want the explosive going off!'

'Fake circuitry,' the man wheezed. 'Do you think . . . I *wanted* to die?' Then he choked on his own blood, and died.

There were quiet footsteps, and Kiko appeared. Alex stood up, but said nothing.

Kiko stumbled on towards the reactor emergency control panel. She gazed up at the heart of Arigata, the fast-breeder, as a guard came over to Alex with a key instead of a gun.

The Arigata reactor seemed alive, and baleful, and aware of her. She sensed this with hallucinatory vividness. Inside that cylindrical mountain of metal and ceramics was the core: a burning radioactive heart, a burning mind that longed to be free. Fuel rods, control rods; molten sodium circulating through a twelve-foot-thick pipe and going outside to the huge heat exchangers. In that core was enough fissionable material for a hundred Hiroshima explosions, and enough radioisotopes to pollute ten thousand square miles for centuries.

Kiko was aware that people from both sides of the conflict had followed her inside. They were no longer fighting.

But she was mainly aware of the reactor.

It was full of death.

Outside, McCourt saw the helicopters approach from the sea. He spoke rapid Japanese into the walkie-talkie, saying that people had gone into the reactor chamber to shut it down. Then he paused to listen.

The colonel in command gave his instructions over the secure radio. 'You go in hard, and go in immediately. Don't wait for further orders.'

Itoshi knew his troops were well trained, but he gritted his teeth, realizing that any delay could prove fatal. What if this Sword Society really had set explosive mines around the fast-breeder core?

The Mitsubishi type-73 mechanized infantry combat vehicles now approached the Arigata site from two directions, their sirens wailing hysterically. Police had to clear the roads quickly. In the new Japan, military vehicles were not common: so two high-speed columns of armoured personnel carriers provided a double shock, to the massed onlookers.

Itoshi crouched down low in the hatchway as people scattered away from the road. He saw the tall gates of Arigata's main entrance and ducked. Then, at top speed, they impacted. Shards of metal flew everywhere, tortured out of shape, but now they were through. More onrushing vehicles raced into the site.

Men spilled out, all wearing masks and some in full NBC gear. Ahead the dome of the reactor loomed against the dark night sky. They were nearly there.

Four heavy helicopters came sliding out of the sky, disgorging yet more armed men. Amplified voices began to order the defenders to surrender; but this was met by the sound of machine-gun fire.

Simultaneously, navy patrol boats were coming into the shore, searchlights as well as guns turned on to the dockside, to prevent any escape.

'This is it,' Itoshi yelled excitedly over the radio network. 'Finish it!'

In the reactor dome Maggie hugged Alex tightly, her red hair swirling around both of them. There were tears in her eyes. 'The Diet has voted. The plutonium agreements are null and void. Hideki has been renounced. Whatever happens here, he's lost! He has lost!'

But he could not tear his attention from Kiko Hideki, as she lifted up the first barrier with her thumb. Then, the next.

Here, with two safety catches protecting it, was the emergency button which could shut down the reactor and make it safe. Once this was touched, the rods would be powered into the reactor core to 'scram' it.

She pressed the button, and the emergency systems gave a huge, long, dwindling wail, the sound of an animal dying. There was a faint, rapid vibration.

The Arigata reactor was finally made safe.

Armed Japanese troops took control of the Arigata site with professional swiftness. After Kiko's display there was not much resistance.

As things became quieter, Maggie, Alex and Kiko joined McCourt and went in search of Hideki.

They found him sitting in a private room, under guard, staring out at the moonlit glimmer of the sea – the Sea of Japan, with Korea and the USSR lying beyond. Itoshi, smiling, let them in to confront the old man alone.

Alex waited till they were all inside, then shut the door. 'It's time for a reckoning, Saigo Hideki.'

'We Japanese are great and strong,' Hideki said tonelessly. He folded his thin arms across his chest, not looking at Alex at all – almost as if he could negate reality by ignoring it. But suddenly he was a small, crumpled, tired man, and for the first time he looked really old. 'In spite of everything, the spirit of Japan remains strong and pure and unpolluted.'

'You make it sound like vodka,' Alex said scornfully.

Kiko was more gentle with him. She knelt down and, for the first time in years, took the old man's hand. 'Grandfather.'

But the calm tide of fanaticism rolled on. 'We are greater than mongrel America, far greater than Bolshevik Russia. China and Britain are degenerate—'

'Grandfather,' Kiko said again, exquisitely polite, 'you have lost your war. Finally, it is finished for you. You have lost.'

He blinked, then looked at her, looked away. 'Our spirits are pure, I tell you!'

'So what?' Alex sat down, as McCourt switched on a tape recorder. 'You must resign your position immediately, and make way for another – for your blood relation Akiko Hideki. You are finished now, and the plutonium agreements are negated. You must surrender.'

The ancient face was parchment-white and dead.

Alex's voice grew harsh. 'Now, sign this!'

The aged face screwed up in sudden rage; then grim triumph flashed in the black eyes. 'It must also be the finish of you, Alex Stanton.'

Alex was as calm as Hideki himself. 'I've already resigned. So, we've both been brought down. All we can do now is salvage what we can, for the sake of others. For me, that's my cousin Hugh Stanton; for you it is your son's daughter. Now, *sign*.'

Hideki closed his eyes. He imagined the headlines in the honest newspapers, still hardly believing he had been defeated. The closed, controlled Japanese society, that tool fashioned so carefully to promote high production and strict discipline, that society which would conquer the world, had failed again. Failed as it had in 1945.

Hideki's face was thunderous. His fists clenched and his body hunched up, distorted with hatred. He was being asked to betray Hakagawa and his own nature, and his dead son's soul – and yet it seemed he had to endure the unendurable, because there was no alternative.

He opened his eyes, which looked dazed. 'It is 1945 again. All that shame!'

'Change,' Alex said. 'All that change. And change is necessary. Now, even if it lets you save some of your reputation, sign these papers.'

'I must be false to everything I believe in?'

'Better that than the shame of utter failure and jail. Hakagawa is finished. You're finished. It's up to you how you end it all.'

There was nothing at all in the black eyes now. 'Then my granddaughter Kiko will be *the* Hideki of my company.'

'Exactly.' Alex took a breath, then said it loud and clear before McCourt and his other witnesses. 'So you, Mr Hideki, do now acknowledge that you have been mistaken in supporting the Hakagawa clique. You hereby renounce them, and you also renounce the Society of the Unsheathed Sword.' McCourt translated, tonelessly.

'Lastly, Mr Hideki, you will agree to sell to me, at one dollar a share, all the shares you and your agents have in Stanton Industries.'

'I must agree,' the old man said at last. He still seemed dazed.

'Take this gold pen. You may remember it. Now, sign.'

With a brief flourish, Hideki abrogated his authority, gave Alex complete control of Stanton Industries, and made Kiko his inheritor. Tears glistened in his eyes.

Alex stood up. Excitement had surged up in him; his heart was pounding. He had won back Stanton Industries, fair and square, and also freed it. With his help and advice, the new Hideki empire would be quite unlike the old, and instead become a great force for good.

'An excellent day's business.' He looked at Hideki meaningfully. 'But I won't shake hands.'

Epilogue

Tokyo, and now it was high noon.

Somewhere above, Russian missiles arced down. Alex twisted about. An alarm began to shrill.

He reached out automatically, grabbing the bedside phone. 'Hello?'

'Alex?'

It took a moment for Alex to clear his head of memories and nightmares. Then he was back in the big luxurious bedroom and daylight was filtering through the blinds. 'Right.'

'I just wanted to thank you properly.' Kiko's voice was a little unsure, but soft and happy. 'Now I understand. In the end, you risked it all. You stood between Hakagawa and me, and you went to the reactor.'

'I did that.' He made his voice warm, lying there with an elbow on the pillow. Maggie, naked, rolled over sleepily. 'But thank *you*, Kiko Hideki. I know who the real hero of this story is.' He let that sink in. 'How are you now, Kiko?'

'A few loosened teeth. In fine spirits otherwise. I'm in Tokyo, at company headquarters. You have made me the chief person in the Hideki Corporation,' she said, with wonder. 'One of the great people of Japan!'

Alex laughed, trying to reach out to her through the wires and give her what she needed: friendship, support, the necessary self-confidence. 'Now you must earn that position. The risks and responsibilities are all yours, and you can bet the system here will not be on your side.'

'No,' she said. 'It won't.' A pause. 'And since you have resigned from Stanton Industries, I thought perhaps you could spend time here in Japan, as my adviser.'

'Of course, Kiko,' he assured her. 'I'll give help any way I can – to both companies, both countries.'

'Thank you,' she said simply. 'I hope you'll be in touch soon. Is Maggie with you?'

'She's somewhere close,' he said, grinning, slapping Maggie's buttocks.

'Then thank her, too.' Maggie was sitting up now, breasts bare beside him, yawning. 'I will never forget either of you.'

Outside, they found a watery sun had come out over Tokyo: a red-streaked September morning. Eight floors up, they relaxed on the hotel-room balcony. Only a bottle of Laphroaig and a bowl of icecubes stood on the table between them.

'Do you think there'll be much of an official inquisition?' he asked Maggie, sipping whisky.

'This can't be hushed up, with twenty-odd casualties! Or can it?'

He stroked his chin, looking down at the traffic-choked street. 'Investigative journalism isn't a Japanese thing, or so you told me, while consensus is. I think they'll play it something like this: a *foreign* terrorist threat to the Arigata reactor – so the authorities had to step in . . .' Alex shrugged, sipped more Scotch. 'Political adjustments followed.'

'Maybe I'll be the inquisition: a book or TV documentary about Arigata and its creators!'

He put down his drink down and unloosened his tie. Without looking at her he asked, 'And will I be hero, or villain?'

She hesitated for a moment, thinking of what had been averted. Hiroshima and Nagasaki all over again, or worse. 'I don't know. Not a hero, quite. Not a villain. Somebody big and vital, and ultimately on the side of life.'

'That isn't much of an endorsement.'

'But I've always admired you,' she told him ruefully. 'Even when I hated you. I often used to think back to when we split up in Greece, but I was never sure . . .'

His voice was quiet but very firm. 'Never sure you should have stayed with me? Or never sure you did right by leaving?'

'I never could decide.' She touched his hand, held it. 'But now I know I'm doing the right thing, the true thing!'

'That's very good of you, Maggie,' he told her soberly. 'But I'll need to finalize my divorce from Caroline. And that could be bloody and long-drawn-out – not to mention expensive.'

'I don't care. I'll wait a million years if I have to.' She suddenly hugged him, licked at his ear. 'I'm just so proud,' she said, 'of all the risks you took to stop Hideki.'

He opened his blue eyes wider, his gaze sardonic. 'I was partly responsible for empowering him, so it was my duty. Sometimes you have to turn against your inheritance,' he added cryptically. 'As Kiko, too, appreciates.'

'And now, after so many years of winning, you've finally lost.'

He gave a rough laugh and leaned back in the chair. 'What have I lost?'

'All the armaments contracts you tried for here. A little or a lot of your reputation – I haven't decided which. And, worst of all, your position on the board of directors, and so your power inside your family.'

He folded his hands together and said with cold satisfaction, 'Merging some of Stanton Industries with the Hideki Corporation will be a masterstroke. No more secret sponsorship of ugly right-wing causes here in Japan, but the reverse. Kiko will see to that. And thus Britain and Japan in some kind of industrial alliance – and hopefully in harmony.'

She touched his hand. 'But what about you?'

'What about me? Maggie, I'm still a Stanton shareholder – a very big one. McCourt will take my place on the Board and carry out the policies we have already agreed. I'm still the London partner of Hacker Stanton International, a player in the Middle East, and now a heavy investor in Japan.'

'It's business as usual!' She was surprised. 'So you're not sad about resigning?'

He shrugged. 'Never regret what is necessary. In the Japanese fashion, to retain face someone has to take the blame. Me. In my personal capacity, as well as Head of Division for Stanton Industries, I helped Hideki become a threat. That can't be denied.'

'But you gave up the firm. It was your life!'

'I resigned for honour's sake; to save my family and the firm from as much controversy as I can. But don't forget, I'd already brought down Hideki's agent Beauford, *and* I kept the Hideki people off our Board. So, apart from myself, our reputation remains clean.'

She looked at him wide-eyed. 'Did you plan all this?'

He did not answer directly. 'Besides, I'd taken Stanton Industries as far as I could.'

She was impressed and even a little awed. Stanton Industries meant billion-dollar business. 'More to come?'

'Maybe I hope for a larger stage.' He gave his old devil's grin, and sipped his single malt. 'There'll be great work to do. For both of us.'

He had always been sure of himself, for good reason. So she believed him now.

He glanced at his wristwatch as he finished his drink. Then he stood up. 'God, but you look beautiful.'

'And you're a liar still, but I love you.'

'Then prove it.'

'In bed?'

He grinned. 'Unless this table is stronger than it looks.'

They had one more appointment next day, needing one more answer before they flew out.

Akira Nanwara, a widower, had his home in Tokyo in a penthouse with windows overlooking the Imperial Palace. The anteroom they were ushered into was full of *Nihonga* art. Nanwara had displayed sets of folding screens, vertical hanging scrolls, horizontal hand-scrolls. Washes of colour on paper, or ink and gold on silk, pictured flower-gardens, seascapes, landscapes.

'So lovely,' Maggie said.

Nanwara welcomed them, led them into a big comfortable office where he served them personally. Alex took English tea, Maggie black coffee.

'I'm glad you could see us,' Alex said. 'I suspect you have a story to tell.'

The tycoon looked at them for a moment. 'Let me show you my company's story. Look at the photographs on the wall.'

They stood up, followed him. The story began in 1945, at about the same time as Sony, in a half-burnt warehouse in the Shitamachi district. In the years since, stupendous expansion. The most recent photographs showed factories in Singapore, California, and Wales. Nanwara was obviously proud of what his company had achieved: something not far from the electronic leadership of the world. It was certainly different from the heavy industry of the Hideki Corporation and, as Alex recalled, it was expanding even faster.

'Very impressive,' Maggie said, examining the company brochures and posters. 'I've seen your televisions and your computers everywhere, from Manhattan to Milan.'

Nanwara, white-haired, smiled sadly before sitting down. 'Yet, what do those televisions show, or those computer screens? Not my culture.'

'Excuse me?'

A surprising harshness entered his voice. 'We began at the end of the war, when Japan was in ruins. America occupied us; suddenly the culture we had believed in for so many centuries was no more. We had to replace it with something. But sometimes . . .'

'You doubt America and Western values and culture?' Alex still felt buoyant. He laughed. 'Then you must thank God for the Japanese language. It insulates you from abroad.'

'It does.'

'And yet I have to agree with Kiko.'

Nanwara's face revealed nothing except bland politeness. 'Really?'

'Yes. The Japanese people need more influence on the powers who govern them, because they deserve more.'

'You wish to change us, do you?' The usually kindly round face was stern. 'Alex Stanton, you uncovered the shame of my country.'

Alex had never heard him talk like this. Looking more closely, he felt a small shock. While this gentlemanly man's mouth was smiling, his expression friendly and sincere – the eyes behind the steel-framed spectacles were as cold as ice. Alex gazed at him in surprise. Then he shook his head. 'The Hideki business? No. I uncovered *a* shame – of the world.'

The unlined Japanese face bowed towards him. 'That is a noble thought. I thank you for it. It will be appreciated here.'

'When I do business, you mean?' Alex rattled his teacup, wondering how much irony there was in this conversation. 'There are still two things I'm curious about.' He stood up, and looked over the Imperial Palace grounds. Inside that building, somewhere, was Hirohito, the Showa Emperor since 1926 – Showa meaning Enlightened Peace. 'Could Hideki have done it?'

'Please?'

Alex said heavily, 'Hideki almost took over my own firm, the largest defence company outside America. He is a billionaire with a private army. He could reach out to Saigon and have murder done, he has influence and agents all over the West – and he is so much of a giant in modern Japan that we're agreeing now that his misdeeds will remain secret. So could he get the Sword Society or an equivalent into power? Could he have turned Japan back into a militarist state?'

Nanwara sighed. 'He was an old man in a hurry.'

'He built Arigata, he had agents inside your government and probably others. Couldn't he have won?'

Nanwara said with distaste, 'Hideki – don't think we approved of him. Embarrassing links. Even his business practices, like mounting a hostile take-over bid in a NATO country, for your *armaments* firm!'

So Nanwara did not care to answer that question directly. Alex probed him again. 'And another thing. The Russians put pressure on, but did not act. Rather than stretching out their power to crush Hideki and his conspiracy once and for all, and probably killing off the Japanese nuclear programme, they withdrew.'

'They chose not to act. Wisely.'

'And *you* were there in Moscow while they were making up their minds.'

Nanwara folded his hands, glanced at Maggie. 'I suppose the Carter White House, Miss Langton's friends, finally put enough pressure on Brezhnev's Moscow. Fortunate, *neh*?'

'I don't think it was like that,' Maggie said suddenly.

Nanwara pursed his lips, sipped more tea. 'Is this conversation confidential?'

'If not, at least deniable,' Alex pointed out.

Maggie asked, 'Please tell us the real story.'

'As you wish.' A small, polite laugh. 'Somebody assured leading elements in the Soviet Union that we here would take care of Arigata and the Hideki conspiracy – by force if necessary.'

'So I was right,' Alex murmured. 'Was it always your plan, to use Itoshi?'

'Itoshi's military action might be considered a useful precedent – in a disarmed and defeated country which now has a pathological fear of its own military power.'

'A useful precedent?' Maggie longed for her tape-recorder, or at least her notebook.

Alex said, 'A man like yourself, it seems to me, might be happy to let the USSR and the USA slug it out, very expensively, for military mastery of the world, draining their economic lifeblood . . . while Japan achieves a much more permanent economic mastery.'

'Yes. A man, like myself, might be happy with that.'

'And you really told the Kremlin all this?' Alex asked, awed. And sometimes he thought of himself as ruthless, with careful, long-term aims. No doubt Nanwara realized that an economically predominant Japan would be a military superpower again, just as soon as it chose to be.

'In Moscow, the man I met is called Andropov. Have you heard of him? He is head of their State Security Committee.'

'I've met him,' Alex said quietly. 'Long ago. 1956.'

Nanwara's eyes were distant. 'Impressive, in his way. Languages, cultured, very hard and determined.'

This time Maggie asked it. 'And yet?'

'And yet, he is as obsolete as a vacuum tube or a steam engine. Those senior Russians know nothing about science, real economics, nothing about R&D, marketing, growing a company . . . But I explained my thoughts to him. And he accepted them.' A shrug. 'For those Russians, it is not to their disadvantage to allow Japan to flourish. Japan cannot compete with the Soviet Union, as Andropov sees it, because we have no military power. But we can, by trading, help hollow out the great colossus of America. And that is the only way that the colossus of the United States will ever be defeated, and fall. I think Andropov knows that.

'As for me, regarding all of Hideki's notions about regaining our islands, about a strong and rearmed Japan – if that comes, it will come. But destiny cannot be hurried, *must not* be hurried. We learned that in 1945.'

'I hope so,' Alex said soberly.

Maggie stirred. 'Why are you telling us all this?'

He was looking at Alex, his eyes bold and laughing. 'You have worked it out, I think.'

'You are telling us what is inevitable. You hope I will recognize it.'

'Exactly.' Nanwara smiled. 'Recognize the inevitable. Relax to it. We in Japan have proved our goodwill and good faith, have we not?'

Alex felt ice-cold. 'You've proved something.' They had, too.

Nanwara put it plainly: 'You cannot win. You must realize that. Join us – in second place.'

'No. Never.' He paused. 'But as far you're concerned, now the militarists are out of the government, it's business as usual?'

'Understand me, Alex Stanton.' The old man's tone was ominous. 'It *will* be business as usual.'

Suddenly, he knew what Nanwara meant. 'You mean that Japan's destiny is set? Your companies and methods must prevail? That is business as usual?'

'I give you my word that the competition will be adequately fair, and it will be peaceful. But it is the only competition that counts – as you have already realized, Alex Stanton.'

Alex gave a strange grin. 'Have I, indeed?'

'Let us look ahead and let's be frank. Because when America does turn up the heat, as it inevitably will after Carter, the Soviet Union will melt down. And what can the Americans do with all their military might, then? I will tell you: nothing. Nothing. They will look around the world, mighty as they are, able to crush any other military power, whirling their big fists till they exhaust themselves – and still there will be no alternative except to wind down also. That is what their victory in the Cold War will bring them. But you have become aware, I think, of what a victory in the war Japan is now fighting will bring us.'

Alex felt cold again. 'It will bring you economic mastery of this planet – and maybe beyond.' Then he realized with a shock that this had been and always would be the way of the world: you take a risk, you hope to win, to build up that fortune which allows you freedom and gives you the future. Britain had long since had its day; America was now beginning to fail. Perhaps there would be a Japanese future, therefore. 'But the competition will nevertheless be fair and civilized and open?'

'What else?' Nanwara came forward.

'That is all we ask.' Alex stood up, and beckoned to Maggie. 'We're flying back to London now. I hope we can still meet as friends.'

'I have read of you Stantons. If you fight to a finish and still lose, you do so without complaint.' Nanwara extended his hand. 'True?'

'I'm still fighting, this isn't finished, and I'm not complaining.'

They shook hands again.

Waiting at the airport, they followed the Arigata story as it faded away.

When their flight began he opened a *Times*. 'All quiet on the Eastern front. This must be the official version, for export.' He showed her. Page two. The story was headlined JAPANESE GOVERNMENT RESHUFFLE. He read it, frowning. So much of the truth was not on the record, and unless Maggie revealed it, it never would be . . .

'News management,' Maggie breathed. She shook her head. 'How could Arigata and its consequences become a non-story!'

'But enough has changed, I hope.' Alex glanced at her. 'Even the Tokyo government is different. And the people, as much as anything else, stopped Hideki and turned what could have been a disaster right around.'

'Alex,' she said to him, 'what happens now?'

'Oh, there'll be other battles,' Alex said as their plane banked over ship-crowded Tokyo Bay. He seemed relaxed to her, but she knew that was always when he was at his most dangerous. 'Nanwara is right. He knows exactly which war to fight.'

She sighed. 'Does it have to be that way?'

'In ten years, or twenty, there'll be a tidal wave: capital, coming out of Tokyo. They'll use the almighty yen instead of the Imperial Army, but they will definitely come, and they will still want the world.'

Feeling disturbed, she touched his hand as a stewardess swept down the aisle towards them, bright, smiling, efficient, and Japanese. 'Is that so bad?'

'How can we tell, so early in the game?' he said. 'It's only one more risk in world history – as long as we're ready for them.'

They sat quietly together, thinking, often holding hands, all the long flight home.

Author's Note

What is the source of a book like *Risk*?

It has more beginnings than I can conveniently mention here. The characters and incidents are of course products of my imagination: their truth is metaphoric, not literal. Also, like many books, this one is partly inspired by questions.

One beginning, one set of questions – standing on Masada in Israel, in the August of 1990, with a little of this book written and much of its predecessor *Winning* already complete. From that high, destroyed fortress you can see the Jordanian shore of the Dead Sea, and you cannot help but think about the past. The destruction of the Temple of Solomon, the Zealots' last stand at Masada, the end (for two thousand years) of Israel. The end. It was impossible not to be moved by that thought.

But when I came down, the television in the open-air bar was frantic with news. Not understanding Hebrew, I only understood this: that Saddam Hussein had invaded Kuwait, he was threatening to do more, and the people of Israel did not know what was going to happen next. Would he use chemical weapons? Or even nuclear weapons? How many countries had nuclear weapons – *and who had helped*? (Israel, of course, had atomic weapons already, as anyone who has seen the Dimona reactor could have guessed.) I still think of such questions, as you will see from this book. They may even be the crucial questions of our age.

Finally, this. The second set of questions.

I grew up on Tyneside, in England. Its great men made the first industrial revolution. Steam, ships, coal, iron, steel. The Japanese ships which sunk the Russian Baltic fleet early this century were mostly made on Tyneside. Swan, not America's Edison, first demonstrated workable electric light. Even when I was growing up, in the nineteen-fifties, the river was lined with shipyards and factories, full of ships that hooted through the fog on the Tyne, and the railway by my door thundered as it transported the coal that made industry live.

When I wrote my first book, *Fortune*, I went home to do publicity for it, and I had my picture taken, smiling and windswept, back turned to the river of my childhood. Then I turned around, no longer a boy but a man. It had all gone. Industry no longer lived here. How has this happened? In the story of the world, a much bigger story than any I could hope to write, industrial might has gone to Asia. The Japanese achievement has been a great one, though it is not without a dark side, as this book hopes to show – a dark side even now, perhaps. But one thing is clear to me. In the United States, in Europe, there has been a long complacent sleep: a process of decline that, until recently, has been managed in a civilized way. But without industry, without heart, energy, self-confidence and optimism about the future, what sort of future will there be in the theme-park societies of the West?

You will draw your own conclusions. I have drawn mine.

RS/1992